MW00613403

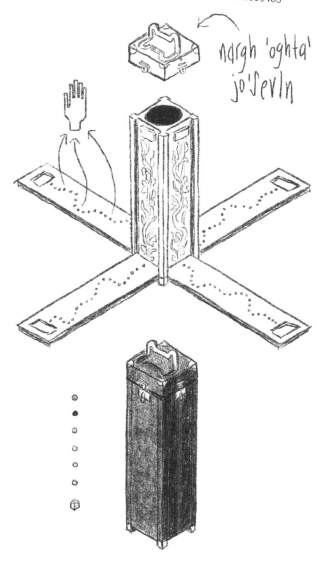

nargh 'oghta'
jo'SevIn

Josephine's GAME

CLAYTON TUNE

To Otto and Titus.

For allowing me to push my love of scary shows and movies onto you so early, even if it meant always having to leave the hallway light on so you could sleep.

This one's for you guys.

Just don't leave the lights on all night this time.

Murray, KY

Earlier This Morning
Part 1

*S*he was alone in the water.

Her skin prickled from the icy waves lapping onto her chest. Heat from the sun warmed her neck and shoulders. The hum of a boat engine moved past her, though there were no boats around. The sky was orange and a deep purple—*was it already sunset?*

Her reflection on the water's surface dissipated to reveal a girl floating vertically just beneath her, eyes open. Iylah sucked in a breath of surprise and shoved her arm into the water. "Jo!" She called. "Jo, I'm right here!" She reached down farther, feeling the cold rip between her fingers, but there was nothing to grab hold of. The girl, still clearly in view, remained expressionless with one arm now extended upward. Iylah tried to grab it and noticed the girl's arm moved erratically with hers. Iylah stopped, studying the face.

She reached, slowly, back into the water. The girl mirrored her movement. Iylah tilted her head to the right; the girl did the same. Then she raised her hands and waved them in the air, the reflection copied. Iylah opened her mouth to say "weird"; the girl's mouth opened wider. The face stretched back as its jaw unhinged and produced a piercing scream unmuffled by the water. Once. Twice. Three times. The face becoming more decomposed with each horrifying cry—

Iylah gasped for air and frantically sat up in her bed, flailing her arms to untangle herself from the sheets. An earsplitting *clang* was coming from one of the rotary phones her parents still kept in the house, stationed in the hallway, just outside her bedroom. Iylah continued taking deep breaths, trying to catch up to her body's lack of oxygen. She scanned the room, struggling to remember where she was. Footsteps sounded in the hall before someone picked up the phone.

Memory was slowly coming back to her. She noticed her cell phone next to her and removed it from the charger. She fell back onto her pillow, turning to stare out the window as it booted up. She could feel her heart starting to slow as she reminded herself to breathe. *In for four, out for four.* Just like she'd been taught. The images of her nightmare were still flashing in her brain.

It was nearly ten in the morning. She'd been asleep for almost an hour. A combined total of maybe four for the whole night. An hour more than usual, and only *one* nightmare.

Progress.

1

NOW

The woman coming up the walkway was not the babysitter.

Cole Gibson would have been livid with the idea of his parents hiring a sitter to watch him overnight—which is why they never told him. A series of knocks rapped against the front door in a musical-like arrangement. *Dum-da-da-dum-dum. Dum-Dum.*

"Cole!" Renee Gibson yelled from her bedroom, nearly falling forward to slip on her heel.

"Yeah?"

"Can you get the door?"

"Yeah."

"Yes ma'am!" She corrected.

"Yes ma'am." Cole set his phone on the bed. He moved at a comfortable pace down the stairs and unlocked the door to open it. The woman standing in front of him was attractive enough to get his attention, but not so much to leave a lasting impression. She wore a pair of washed-out yellow shorts and a mostly faded black t-shirt with what looked like the word *Breathe* written across it. Her scruffy jet-black hair was pulled back into a ponytail. "Hey," Cole said. "Just one second." He spun around and yelled, "Mom, your voice student's here." He pointed with his thumb toward the stairs. "She'll be right down."

"How are you?" The woman asked.

"I'm fine."

"What's your name?"

"Cole."

The woman's mouth seemed to slowly melt back into a large, rather awkward smile. Cole felt his face betray a hint of recoil when she held it for longer than normal. He decided to break the uncomfortable silence. "You can come in. My mom will be right down."

"Okie dokie, Pokie," the woman said, cheerily.

Cole spun toward the stairs, raising his eyebrows and mouthing "weirdo" to himself as he went up to his room. He heard the door shut behind him.

"Did you get the door?" His mom asked, nearly running Cole over on her way down.

"Yeah, she's waiting for you," Cole replied.

"Couldn't be bothered to keep her company, huh?"

There was a double knock at the door.

"Cole! You left her outside?" His mom carefully began moving down the steps in her heels.

"No. I told her to come in," Cole replied. "I thought I did at least." He shrugged and went back into his room.

Earlier This Morning
Part II

A little before 10:30 am, Iylah got out of bed. She nearly tripped over one of the boxes in the hall on the way to the bathroom and slid it with her foot to the side against the others. It had been nearly six months and her parents were still "getting adjusted." Half-full moving boxes were stacked haphazardly against the hallway wall, waiting to be emptied. Iylah knew it wasn't for lack of trying. Three years ago, her dad's mental health took a slow downward turn. And then, after the accident last year, he became almost bedridden with depression. Unable to hold his job, they were forced to move. It didn't help that Iylah herself became unwilling to live on her own around the same time. Her mom's workload practically tripled.

On the upside, things were certainly improving, especially over the past few months: her dad was eating more regularly, able to leave the house on his own, and he'd taken an adjunct position at the College to try and get back in the swing of things. But when it came to getting the house in order, there was only so much they could do. On top of that, there was more stuff than space.

Iylah wrapped her hair up into a messy bun while she yawned and sat down to pee. Her parents were talking in the kitchen. The words were muffled but not because of distance—it was obvious they were trying to be quiet. Something about their tone suggested agitation. The walls might as well be cardboard.

Iylah still hadn't gotten used to this new house. She hated having to move back in with her parents—not that she had much of a choice—but she hated even more that it wasn't the home she knew. She heard her dad say her name, and froze, still sitting on the seat. It was hard not to eavesdrop.

She wiped, and stood up, not even bothering to flush so as not to alert them to her presence. She crept into the hall, still listening to their conversation. The tones were getting harsh but the voices more hushed.

"I don't see what the big deal is Silvia, just tell them no," her dad said sharply.

"It's not a big deal—that's what I'm trying to say. We should let her decide," her mother replied, pointedly.

Iylah stood in the dark, box-cluttered hallway, motionless. She strained to hear them, but now the conversation had become almost completely inaudible. *What am I doing?* She took a breath and moved into the living room. Her mother was sitting at the kitchen table; her dad was standing, leaning back against the stove with his arms crossed. He was the first one to notice her.

"Hey boo bear." He smiled, straightening up. "Good morning. You sleep okay?"

"Hey," Iylah replied, tilting her hand back and forth. "Eh. Better than usual, I guess."

Her mother gave her a welcoming smile before clicking the mouse on her laptop and speaking into her microphone. "Time is almost up. Please make sure to submit your outlines into my Dropbox and let me know if you have any other questions." She was in the middle of teaching her class.

"You want me to make you an omelet?" Her dad asked.

"I'm okay," Iylah replied. "Not too hungry right now." She noticed the pink bakery box on the counter. "Are these from

Mrs. Burgers' bakery?" She opened the lid and smelled the fresh, warm dough. "Mmm."

"Thought you weren't hungry," her dad said.

"I wasn't until I saw the blueberry donut."

"Who said it was for you?" He came over and put his arm around her, kissing her on the head.

"Everything okay?" She asked, hugging him back.

"As far as I know," he replied. "I saw you were—" Silvia snapped her fingers indicating that they were being too loud, never taking her eyes off the screen. "Sorry," her dad whispered. "I saw you were still at it when I went to bed last night. How's the thesis?"

"Still trying to flesh out the last of it. I keep going back and forth on how to end it."

"You want me to take a look? See if I can help?"

Iylah shrugged. "It's okay. I'll spare you, today."

"It's bound to be better than reading these *Dracula* essays but suit yourself. I'm here if you need me." He kissed her on the head and started into the hall.

Iylah went to the refrigerator to rummage but was too distracted by the events of the morning. She could interpret enough Spanish to know that her mom was about to sign off from her lesson. With a final "adios" Silvia got up to refill her coffee mug and hug her daughter.

"Did someone call this morning?" Her mom's sudden pause was all Iylah needed to know that the call had been about her. "Was it for me?"

Silvia sighed and came back to the table. There was hesitation on her mom's face; her lips tightened, curling under her teeth. "Yes. Someone did. Go ahead and have a seat." She glanced at her watch. "I've got a few minutes until my next class." She careened her head around toward the hall, as if someone might be listening.

"Is everything okay?"

Silvia studied her daughter's face, pulling her reading glasses down to hang around her neck. "It was for you. And I'm going to tell you about it, but I want you to hold all comments until I finish, okay?" Iylah nodded. "Renee Gibson called this morning. She has a son named Cole. Renee and her husband are going out of town for two days and they wanted to know—"

"Absolutely not," Iylah interrupted, standing up. "No."

"Iylah. Stop." Silvia didn't raise her voice, but the sternness was evident. Iylah stood still, staring at her mother. "You said you would hear me out."

"Well, there's no point."

"You can't keep avoiding work," Silvia replied.

"I'm not avoiding *work*. I *have* a job."

"And yet you're never scheduled," Silvia fired back in a carefree tone that came out rather snarky.

"Oh my gosh, Mom! I've told you I took time off to finish this paper."

Her dad appeared in the hallway and made eye contact with Silvia, not hiding the disappointment on his face.

"Is that what you both think? That I don't work? If you need money for rent, I said I would pay—"

"Whoa, whoa, hang on a minute," her dad interrupted, defensive. "This has nothing to do with needing money, Iylah." She regretted saying *money* as soon as it came out.

"Sam . . ." Her mother interrupted.

After a moment of tense silence, he took a breath. "Iylah, we don't *need* you to work, okay. This isn't about that."

"She said I didn't have a job," Iylah pointed toward her mother.

"I'm sorry. I don't mean that you're avoiding work—I know you have a job. What I'm trying to say is that you're avoiding *this*." She tapped the yellow pad next to her.

Iylah walked over to the paper and made out a telephone number with the name *Renee* circled.

"I told you she could hear us," Sam said, rubbing the bridge of his nose. He let out a frustrated chuckle to himself and muttered, "Never gonna get used to this house." Then, looking up, "I didn't want your mom showing you that message. To be frank, I think it's too soon."

"And I think that's for *you* to decide," her mother replied, nodding to Iylah.

"And you're right, she *should* decide, but . . ." He threw up his hands. "Iylah, I feel like you're in a really good spot. Therapy's been helping, you're excited about finishing your program. Why put yourself back in that same position?"

"Because it was an accident," Silvia said. "And there was nothing she could have done."

Iyah's eyes flicked between her parents before landing on her mother. "I'd rather not."

There was a pause. Iylah could tell her mom was fighting the agitation when a long breath escaped through her nose. "And why not? You don't think it'll be good for you to—" Silvia began.

"Look, why are we even having this discussion? You know as well as I do that as soon as I say I'm interested, she'll do a background check—if she hasn't already—and come up with some lie about how they're not going out of town, or how the kid got sick, and they won't need me anymore."

"She already knows about what happened," Silvia said calmly. "I went ahead and asked her myself."

"You asked her, what? If she knew about me?" Iylah snapped back.

"Yes, as a matter of fact," Silvia spoke confidently. "Asked if she'd heard what happened. And she said she had. I even went so far as to ask if she still wanted you to come and she laughed and said, 'I called didn't I?'"

Iylah stood still, chewing on the edge of her lip, bouncing her knee back and forth, unsure of what to say.

"I told her that you'd have to think about it—said you were swamped with school and finishing your thesis. She told me to assure you that both her and her husband believe that what happened was an accident, and that they have no reservations about having you watch their son. Okay? They're gone for two days, one night. She said they have a big house with plenty of rooms for you to work on your paper if that's an issue."

"Mom . . ."

"Iylah," Silvia waved her hand, as if brushing away dust in the air, "Your father's right, you've been doing so well these last several months, and if you don't feel like you're capable or up for it, it's okay. It wasn't my intention to press this on you. But I did want to press on you that I believe you're capable and I believe you're ready. You've hidden away from this for over a year, and I think this is the perfect opportunity to come out—"

"It's not hiding when everyone shuns you."

Silvia paused. "Point taken. And if you're really hiding away because you're no longer interested, or because you feel it's beneath you, then let's move on. But I don't think that's the reason." Iylah didn't respond; only stared back at her mom. "Shelby was an accident, honey. Had nothing to do with you. I think opening yourself back up may help to alleviate some of the stress you've been feeling. At least it would reassure you that you are more than capable of looking after someone again."

"Mom. It's not *babysitting* that scares me. There was so much that went on that night that I still just can't explain—"

Silvia's laptop flashed on and began letting out a jingle. "I'm sorry, sweetie." She tore off the top page from her yellow pad. "Here's Renee's number, and this is her husband's cell too. She said you may have to set it up with him since she'll be in meetings much of the afternoon."

Iylah took the paper but before she could say yes or no her mom cut in. "*Hola Señor* Cliff. *Un momento, por favor.*" She clicked mute and gently touched Iylah's arm. "Hey. Whatever you decide is fine with me. I just didn't want you to say *no* without really thinking about it. You should also know that despite what she's heard, *you* were her first pick." She kissed her daughter's hand and unmuted her mic. "*Señor* Cliff! *Buenos Dias! Como estas?*"

Iylah took the paper. Her father was still standing by the counter, watching her. "You really think it's too soon?" She asked.

Her father took a moment. "I know what you went through at that house is unimaginable for me. But having to *watch* your daughter go through that, I wouldn't wish on anyone." A gentle smile came over his face. "I was more so saying it was too soon for *me*. But you're a lot stronger than I am."

2

NOW

Renee Gibson opened the front door.

The young woman outside mouthed "hi" and smiled. She was on the phone and held up a polite finger as she stepped back, her damp ponytail flicking over her shoulder. "Okay, I'm here," the girl spoke into the phone. "I'll text you in thirty minutes. Just stay by your phone, okay?" The girl turned back to Renee, ending her call. "Sorry about that—"

"Oh, you're fine. I didn't mean to leave you standing out here. I was getting my shoes on. Come in," Renee said.

"I hope I'm not too late. I feel like I hit every stop light in town. I didn't keep you, did I?"

"Goodness, no. I just finished getting ready. Please, come in. I-Luh, right? Did I say that correctly?" Renee closed the door.

Iylah smiled. "Yes ma'am."

"Good. And thanks for coming on short notice; Ivan and Maddie spoke very highly of you. I'm Renee; you spoke with my husband." She extended her hand.

"Oh my gosh, I love the two of them. And it's no problem; happy to help." Iylah looked around the home. She could feel Renee looking at her as quiet settled between them.

"Look," Renee cut into the silence. "I don't really know how to say this. I'm sure my husband did a better job than I'm about to do, but um . . ." She paused.

"Listen, Mrs. Gibson," Iylah cut in. "I know you've probably heard a lot about me, and I'm going to assume that much of it was pretty troubling. Please know, as I told your husband, that I will be fully up front on what happened last year with Shelby Gray. If you have questions, please don't hesitate to ask. I don't know what others told you—though I've heard some crazy versions of that night myself by word of mouth—just know that I'll be honest about whatever you want to know. I want you to go out trusting that I won't let *anything* happen to your son—"

Renee held up a delicate hand: "Iylah," she said softly. Iylah tried to continue but Renee cut her off again. "It's okay." She spoke gently. "Keith and I are well aware of what happened last year. We've talked about it several times and neither of us has any reason to believe it was anything but an accident. Seems clear as day to us, at least. Maddie and Ivan are some of our closest friends and there was no end to stories of how remarkable of a person you were to *their* daughter. Said despite everything that happened with the Gray family, *they* would never doubt your integrity. So, please know, there was not a bit of hesitation in selecting you to watch our son." Renee studied Iylah's face for any sort of reaction but there was none. She kept her head tilted down, still with her eyes locked on Renee's; a face that expressed nothing but humiliation.

Finally, there was a head nod. "Thank you. That means a lot," she said softly. She hiked up her bag, readjusting it on her shoulder.

"Oh, my goodness! I'm so sorry. Feel free to set your stuff anywhere," Renee said. "Please make yourself at home." She nodded toward the stairs. "I think he thought you were my voice student. He's back up in his room; hang on, I'll get him." Iylah set her bag down onto the floor as Mrs. Gibson leaned in and lowered her voice, "We actually didn't tell him that you were coming." She grimaced, as if to indicate she made a mistake. "I don't know how much my husband shared with you about him."

Renee noticed a look of concern on Iylah's face. "He doesn't get into trouble or anything and he's pretty low maintenance. We just didn't feel comfortable leaving him overnight."

"I understand. I've watched plenty of kids his age—" She paused. Renee could sense a sudden discomfort as soon as those words came out. Shelby was Cole's age.

Renee abruptly continued, changing the subject. "Well, with your experience, I'm sure you won't be offended if he never looks up from his phone, or even comes out of his room." She forced a laugh.

"Definitely not," Iylah replied. After a moment: "Is there anything special I need to know? Allergies? Rules?"

"Nothing special. Eats anything—everything. He usually goes to bed around midnight. We all stay up late normally. But no, nothing out of the ordinary. Typical fifteen-year-old; on his phone a *lot*."

Iylah smirked. "That's pretty standard. I brought some games he might like, if he's up for it. We're a pretty big game family."

One side of Renee's mouth inched up. "If they're not on the Xbox you may be on your own. Make yourself at home. I'm sure there are some shows you need to catch up on."

"That's alright. I'll probably just work on my school stuff. That's pretty much been my only entertainment for the last several months."

"Oh, that's right! Your mom mentioned you were finishing that up. There are some wonderful writing spots in the house. The sunroom and the red couch in the living room are my favorite places to write. And nap."

Iylah smirked.

"How's it coming along?" Renee asked. "Your thesis."

"Just about done," Iylah replied. "Need to tighten up the

ending, but I'm almost there. Maybe I'll knock it out this week-end."

"Well, believe me, if I know Cole, you'll have plenty of peace and quiet if you want it."

"Are friends allowed to stop by? And is he allowed to leave? Go out to eat?"

"He can go out, but we don't want anyone here while we're away. He knows that, and he knows to be home by his curfew—ten p.m. He'll most likely stay in but if there's an issue, just call me. Or if you'd prefer he not go out, just tell him we said no. I'm happy to take the blame." Renee winked. "Really, he will most likely spend tonight and tomorrow playing Xbox. Don't over stress yourself. If you tell him no, he won't fight *you* on it—probably just shrug and call *me* something under his breath."

"Fair enough," Iylah replied.

"Gimme just one second, okay? I'll let him know what's going on—and, I apologize for any rudeness in advance." She stepped up onto the main stairs and yelled: "Cole!" There was no response. She tried again, then proceeded to walk up the steps to knock on Cole's bedroom door. There was a quick shuffle and he cracked open the door, trying to block any visual of the inside. "Hey," he said.

"What are you doing?" Renee asked.

"Cleaning," he said hesitantly. "Well, kind of. Just redecorating a little; I don't want you to see it yet. Trying something different."

"You're not painting in there are you?" Renee asked.

"Maybe . . ." Cole's eyebrows bounced.

"I need to either come in or you need to come out here," she replied.

"I'll come out there," Cole said. Renee scooted back and

Cole shoved himself through a slightly cracked open doorway. "What's up?" He looked down at his phone.

"Put your phone down." Cole did. "I'm going to meet your dad. We'll be gone all night."

Cole smiled. "Awesome," His phone chirped, and he lifted it back up to check. "Will you guys be out late?"

Renee sighed. "Cole. I just said, *we'll be gone. All. Night.* The lady out there is *not* a voice student. Her name is Iylah Maddox." Cole's eyes narrowed. "She's your babysitter."

"*What?* A babysitter? I'm fifteen!" Renee tried to interject but Cole continued. "I stay home by myself all the time!"

"You're right. Normally, it's not a big deal, but this is overnight, and your dad and I won't be back until late tomorrow. She'll only be here until early tomorrow evening—"

"Are you serious right now? That girl looks like she's my age." Cole said, running his hands through his hair and leaning back against his door.

"Well, I'm certain she'd appreciate hearing you say that. Be that as it may, you can't stay almost two nights by yourself. I'm sorry."

"Why not? Jared stays home by himself like every weekend. And Sherry's parents aren't even home during most weekends."

"Good for them. Now, listen." Cole let his head fall back with an audible breath. "I'm leaving her some money for food tonight, and tomorrow. You guys can order in or go to the store."

"Mrs. Gibson?" Iylah said from the bottom of the steps. "Sorry to butt in; I brought some stuff to make dinner if that's okay."

"Oh. Well how 'bout that," she said to Cole. Then, to Iylah as she began down the stairs: "Okay. I'll still leave you some money in case you wanna go out for dessert."

There was another dull sound from Cole. "This is bull-shit . . ."

Mrs. Gibson stopped midway down the steps and twisted sharply to her son. "What did you say?"

"Nothing," Cole mumbled, not wanting to look at her.

Renee stepped slowly up toward her son and spoke in a low voice when she was directly in front of him. Even in a whisper, Renee voice was authoritative—confident; almost terrifying. "Don't. You. Ever. Talk like that to me. Do you hear me?" Cole nodded. "Look at me." He did, hesitantly. "I asked if you heard me?"

"Y-yes. Yes ma'am. I heard you."

"Okay then." In an instant, her unforgiving expression gave way to a cheery smile. She stepped carefully down the steps and into the foyer to retrieve something from her purse. "You don't have to use it, but it's here if you need it." She walked through the adjacent room and past the French doors into the kitchen where she placed several bills on the counter. She filled up a water bottle at the sink, then began mumbling to herself as she walked back to the front door: "Keys, wallet, water, bag . . . oh! You have my husband's cell phone, right? From when he called you? Do you need mine? Here let me give it to you."

She began rummaging around in her purse for a card. Iylah watched her for a second and then finally said, "I think we'll be okay."

"Cole has my number if you need it. Is there anything else I can give you? Do you think you'll need more money—"

"Mrs. Gibson," Iylah said, walking over to her backpack and hoisting it onto her shoulder. "We'll be fine. You two go have fun, alright?"

"Okay." Renee leaned toward the stairs and yelled up: "Cole.

Be *good*. I don't want to get a call from her complaining. Thanks again, Iylah. I'll have Keith text you when we get there."

Cole appeared at the top of the steps and yelled back to his mom that he loved her. She replied with the same and closed the door. Before Iylah could get a word out to Cole, he went back into his room, unnecessarily slamming the door. Iylah shrugged her shoulders and peeked out the front door window to watch Mrs. Gibson's car pull out of the driveway and then vanish behind the line of shrubs at the edge of the road.

"Well, this is gonna be a blast," she said, with little interest. The house *was* charming, though. The foyer itself was inviting; a dark wood floor covered by a large, worn rug. Iylah set her bag on top of a nicely finished bench against the wall, next to a thick, wool blanket that likely no one ever used. Renee or Keith had an affinity for antique design: family photos were framed in what resembled old barn wood, a butter churner and washboard were neatly displayed in corners, along with hung shadow boxes of old tobacco tins. If the house wasn't in a neighborhood a couple miles from her parents' house, she could easily fool herself that she was staying in a bed and breakfast in the country.

Iylah wandered into a small adjacent room that she guessed might be for reading or just perhaps an extension of the foyer. Natural light filled the room perfectly, with a peaceful view of the front yard. An old couch sat in the corner behind a wooden coffee table, across from an antique hutch with stacks of opened mail. It looked similar to the one her parents had sold before the move. The French doors on the other side opened into a country-style kitchen of oak and stone. A far cry from the plywood-themed eating space her parents now called home.

She retrieved her bag and found the guestroom that Renee had directed her to, earlier. On the door was a wooden sign welcoming all guests and pets.

She set her bag down on the floor. The room was cozy with a small writing desk in the corner, a chair that she knew would be dangerous to try and get any work or reading done in, and a queen size bed she couldn't wait to sleep in. She smiled. "I can get used to this—" A shadow moved in her vision, startling her. She glanced around the room. "Cole?" There was a *thud* somewhere near the foyer. "Mrs. Gibson?" She stood frozen only for an instant before creeping to the bedroom window for a hesitant peak and sighed. A tall man dressed in a blue USPS uniform was making his way back toward the white mail truck on the street. Iylah let out a long breath. She could feel her heart picking up and let out a subtle laugh. "Get it together," she whispered, wiping the sweat from her palms on her shorts.

Earlier This Morning
Part III

Iylah's head fell onto her arms as an irritated moan escaped her mouth. She sat there motionless at her desk for a long moment. So long in fact that her friend, Erica Lang, present through FaceTime on Iylah's phone, began singing to herself while she drove.

"You're supposed to tell me what to do," Iylah said toward the floor, and peeked up when Erica didn't reply. She was still singing softly to herself, watching the road when she noticed Iylah staring at her helplessly.

"Did you say something?" Erica asked. Iylah repeated herself. "To be honest, I think you're making this harder than it has to be."

"Easy for you to say," Iylah said.

"You're right," Erica replied, still not making eye contact with the phone, "it is easy for me to say, that's why I think you're making this too hard. If it was me, I'd say no."

"Because you don't think it's safe?"

"No, because it's fucking *babysitting*. You're 22 years old. Get a real job!" Laughter came from both of them at exactly the same time, and Iylah could almost feel the tension in her body seep through her skin as she exhaled a deep breath. She needed that laugh. "I'm kidding," Erica continued, "but let's be real, it's babysitting. You only do it if you're broke or fourteen—" Erica cut herself off and looked down at the screen with a look of guilt. "I'm sorry. I didn't mean it like that—"

"It's fine," Iylah said, faintly. "To be fair, we *are* broke so . . ." She shrugged with a thin smile.

"You know what I mean. This isn't a job, you don't know these people, and it's not like the money is gonna go a long way to helping out your mom and dad so, really, why do it?"

Iylah sighed. "I know." She watched Erica maneuver in her seat to parallel park. The music in the background went out as Erica switched off the ignition. "You at school?" Iylah asked.

"Yeah, just got here, but I've got a few minutes." Iylah watched Erica rifle through her bag, holding an apple in her mouth. She took a bite of it and spoke, "There's obviously something pushing you to say yes, otherwise this would've been a much easier decision to help you make. So, what's up?"

"My therapist."

"Oh lord." Erica shook her head and with a voice of undeniable disinterest said, "Can't wait to hear how *Dr. Boyd* thinks you should handle this."

Iylah sat up and folded her arms. "You know, he's actually been really helpful for me so . . . can it."

"Yeah he *was* super helpful," Erica replied, "when he was our softball coach." She chuckled to herself. "So, what'd he say?" Iylah now protested against telling her, fearing that Erica would just laugh, but Erica relented and promised not to comment.

"He said that deep down I knew what I was capable of handling and could make the best decision."

"You're paying two hundred dollars an hour for that?"

"Yeah, basically," Iylah replied, playfully.

"Did he think you *shouldn't* do it?" Erica asked.

"He said whatever decision I made was fine and good for me."

Erica pursed her lips, then shifted them in suspicion. "Yeah. Real helpful."

"It was just nice to have reassurance, I guess. He said if I wanted to do it, he felt I was ready, and if I didn't, he thought that was a good decision too. Basically, I'm in a good place to make a rational decision. If I start having severe panic at the thought, then I should back out."

"Back out? You already called them?"

"No. Not yet," Iylah replied. "I'm leaning toward it, I think. Just nervous about saying yes."

"What're you nervous about?" Erica asked. Iylah looked at her. "You nervous about what happened to Shelby? Or what happened to you and me?"

Iylah contemplated this. "Both, I think." Erica nodded. "But more so, what happened to Shelby. Happening again."

"Yeah . . ." Erica muttered. "Did you tell Dr. Boyd about . . . us . . . about what happened?"

"No," she replied.

"Did you mention that thing being at Shelby's?"

Iylah shook her head.

"So, he just thinks you're traumatized from finding her?"

"Basically, yeah. And from the lake, still," Iylah replied. Erica nodded, understandingly. "He did give me the idea that I could have someone come in and check on me. Just to put my mind at ease." Iylah winked.

"I am not driving two hours to spend my Friday and Saturday babysitting." Iylah smiled, but only to hide the disappointment as Erica tapped the screen. "Oh shoot. I gotta go. You gonna be okay?"

"Yeah," Iylah replied, lightly. "I'll be fine. I'm fairly certain that what's making me nervous is the fact that I haven't gone out on my own in over a year, so, it's that thought of something going wrong and not being able to—"

"Wait. What? You haven't been out in over a year?!"

Iylah reclined back in her chair. "Nope." She'd known this in her mind but never spoken it out loud. She was slightly embarrassed but surprisingly, a little relieved to say it. "Not since . . ." She gave her friend a shameful look.

"Since Shelby?"

Iylah looked away.

"Since you and me? That night at your house!?" Iylah nodded. "Iylah! That was two years ago!"

"I know!" Iylah threw her hands over her face and slumped forward.

"Wha—how? How is that even possible?" Erica asked.

Iylah shook her head in bewilderment. "I don't know. I just . . . haven't. After that night, I was so scared to be by myself I spent the rest of the summer at home."

"What about school? You never went out?"

"Not really. I moved into the sorority house and never left." Iylah forced an emotionless chuckle. "Why do you think my grades were so good?"

"Hold on. You've gone out! You and I went out a ton that year."

"Let me rephrase, I haven't stayed on my own in two years. I've either been in the sorority house or my house. If I was the only one left in the House, I went home." Iylah paused to let this sink in with Erica. "We may've gone out but if we did, I promise you I wasn't having the best of times."

Erica was dumbfounded. "Gosh," she muttered. "Baby girl, I'm so sorry." Iylah shrugged. "Is that why you switched to online school at home? After Shelby?"

Iylah nodded. "I couldn't be alone."

"Wow," Erica said, stunned. "Has it gotten any better? What about work?"

Iylah peeked at the screen, humiliated. "Erica, they fired me months ago." Erica mumbled a curse of disbelief. "I couldn't go in anymore. I'd be there thirty minutes and start panicking. My last day there I was making copies and went to change out the toner and . . ." She paused, wondering whether or not to reveal it. "I saw it." Erica didn't have to say *what* because she knew. "It was sitting right there on the shelves of toner and paper. Clear as day."

"Oh my God."

"At least, I thought it was clear as day. By the time my mind unfogged I realized it was a used toner cartridge." She intertwined her fingers and rested her head against them. "After that, I just kept calling out, and after a few weeks they let me go. That's when I started back with Dr. Boyd."

"Iylah. Baby girl. How have you never told me any of this?" Erica asked.

Iylah turned up her palms, and let them fall, slapping her bare thighs. "Because it's embarrassing?"

"How?"

"Because, I'm a mess. I can't make it through a whole day without fighting off a panic attack. I haven't slept in months. If I do sleep, it's with a nightmare most times. I can't even function awake without seeing . . ." She trailed off. Erica apologized. Iylah fought back the urge to cry. "It sucks."

"Yeah, that's why you should tell me this stuff. Iylah, I was there with you. Not for Shelby, but I at least know what happens. If you can tell anyone, it's me."

"Erica, I don't know if you realize this or not, but up until a few weeks ago we didn't exactly talk as much as we used to. I mean, crap, you were in Spain the majority of last year. We texted, and chatted maybe once a month, but I hardly ever saw you."

Iylah could see the guilt on Erica's face. It wasn't her intention to make her friend feel bad—pity was the last thing she wanted—but it was the truth. Erica hadn't been there and deep down it frustrated Iylah to feel that in her darkest moments she had no one to confide in. "Look, we can talk later. I know you gotta go—"

"No. You know what? Screw it. I'm coming down."

"Erica, it's fine," Iylah cut in. Erica tried to cut her off, but Iylah continued. "Erica, seriously. I'll be okay. This was helpful; talking it out."

"You sure?"

"Positive. I definitely don't *want* to do it but let's be honest, after everything, I'd be pretty content not ever going out." Iylah looked out her window at the bright blue sky. "I think if I keep holding out for a better outlook, I'll never do anything." She picked up Renee's number, feeling her stomach instantly drop. "I need to do this. Or, at least, try to do it. And the money isn't bad."

"Anything I can do?"

"Not right now," Iylah replied. "But give me a couple hours and I'm sure I'll be asking you to come down."

3

NOW

Cole's mom was right: the sunroom *was* perfect for writing. If only Iylah was in a mood to write. By the time she got comfortable in the large, microfiber easy chair it was nearly dark outside, and her mind was not in the mood for thesis work. At first, she sat at attention, perusing her research to try and re-work some of the phrases, but the longer she sat in the quiet, the more unnerved she became.

Every movement—or what seemed like movement—from the corner of her eye pulled her out of concentration to examine the spot in question, and every sound made her cut the music from her laptop and listen intently. Before long, she had stretched out into a reclining position with her legs on the ottoman—computer balanced on her lap—and was staring out over the screen toward the windows at a darkened sky. The ripples in the clouds reminded her of the lake. She occasionally felt her mind wandering to places it shouldn't, and she would snap back to attention, refocus, type a word or two, then revert to her trance.

Her index fingers danced on the F and J keys until finally she groaned and slammed the laptop shut. "This is ridiculous!" She stood up, glancing at the clock on her phone. "Okay." She swatted at the air as if shooing gnats. "What to do, what to do, what to do, what to do." The photos on the wall in the dining room caught her attention. Mostly family photos, many of them candid: Cole laughing with a group of guys, Renee sitting with

Christmas wrapping paper on her head, a young child—Cole, perhaps?—wearing nothing but underwear and tall rain boots pushing a toy lawn mower across the yard. Iylah smiled at that one. Pictures were everywhere she turned. It reminded her of how her mom used to decorate before they moved; walls covered in memories. Every inch of the old hallway and stairwell, even the kitchen and dining room had been full with their family's history.

Iylah made her way around the main floor admiring the Gibson's photos. Before long, she unknowingly found herself *inspecting* the house. If a light was off, she switched it on; a door closed, she opened it and examined what was on the other side.

Her cell phone flashed 7:55 when she pulled it out of her pocket. She typed out a text to her friend Erica and hit send. She puffed up her mouth and let out a slow breath, glancing around the quiet home, bored. She considered taking Mrs. Gibson up on her offer to order takeout but finally forced herself to go and start cooking.

She looked through the fridge at the items she brought, noticing several other ingredients that might be good instead. When she closed the freezer door, the wine rack on the wall came into view. "Ooo!" It helped that both her parents were wine fanatics—well, were *once* wine fanatics, back when they could afford to be.

In no time, she assessed every bottle—recognizing many of them—and pulled one from a vineyard she'd never heard of. "Cab Sauv it is," she said, sliding it from its holder.

An electric wine opener was sitting on top of a waist-high cabinet in the corner. Iylah knelt and pulled open the front two doors to reveal several bottles of premium gin and tequila. "Jackpot." She Snapped a photo to some close friends captioning it with *Um, yes please!* at the top and *#Weekendvibes* at the bottom.

Iylah opened the bottle of wine and inspected the label: an open field with a young girl reclining in the grass, her back to the camera. Underneath the picture: *VA Gina Cabernet Sauvignon.* "Vagina?" Iylah remarked. She pulled the cork out and examined the bottle again. The address of the winery was Loudon County, Virginia. "Oh." She chuckled. "Got it—"

"Is it true about you?"

Iylah sucked in a sharp breath at the sound of Cole's voice. "Jeez!" Cole was standing in the kitchen staring at her. She put her hand over her heart in surprise. "I don't do too well with jump scares."

"I'll try to walk a little louder next time," Cole mumbled back, looking at his phone.

She noted his appearance: loose, black athletic shorts with a gray, faded Murray High Tigers t-shirt, and hair in the style of careless towel-drying. Despite the fact that it was late at night, she figured this was how he went to school. He nodded awkwardly, maybe waiting for her to say something. "What's up?" She finally asked.

"I recognized you—I mean, I recognized your name. You're that girl, aren't you? The one who . . . had the thing happen last year. Right? Is that you?"

"Well, you haven't really identified me as anything other than a girl who had a thing happen last year. So, not sure how to answer that question."

"Is it true?" Cole asked.

"Is what true?" Iylah was afraid of this but explaining herself to a fifteen-year-old was better than a parent. Still, she was a little agitated that Cole would bring it up. He started to answer her, and she cut him off. "Look Cole, I'm gonna be honest with you, this is not fun for me." Cole's face crinkled as if she'd insulted him. "I don't mean that being with you isn't fun, I mean that given everything that's happened, it's pretty hard—mentally—for me to do this job tonight. I'm a lot more on edge than I thought I'd be, and honestly, I'm kinda wondering if I'm gonna make it the entire weekend."

"That'd be great for me," Cole said with a grin, slouching against the counter.

"I bet it would," Iylah replied, with an eye roll. "Anyway, if it's alright with you I'd prefer we not talk about what happened last year, or anything, really, to do with Shelby Gray, okay?"

"Holy crap," Cole said, stunned. "It is you. Man, people talked about that for months after it happened—"

"Cole," Iylah interrupted, "as fascinated as I would be to hear about how you and your friends analyzed that night—that none of you were at, by the way—I would really love it if we could just share the house in silence. I'll work on my paper; you do you—won't even know I'm here. That work?"

"I knew her, ya know?" Cole said. "Shelby. She and I were friends."

Iylah could now feel herself tensing up. "Then I'm sorry for your loss. Now, can I get you something to eat?"

"Did you actually see it happen?" Cole cut in. "Or did you find her that way—"

Iylah lowered the wine bottle to the counter with a harsh *thunk* and exhaled. "Can you stop, please?"

Cole put up his hands in surrender. "Sorry. It was just a question." He checked his phone and then typed out a text before putting it back in his pocket. "Probably doesn't mean anything, but I'm sorry for, ya know, what happened to you guys. I'm sure that was pretty scary, huh?"

Iylah studied him. His apology seemed genuine. "Thank you. And it was, but like I said, I don't wanna talk about it." Iylah could feel her face becoming flush. Cole's expression suddenly morphed into one of confusion, then intrigue. She saw his eyes slowly look her up and down. They drifted back down to her shirt—or her chest, she couldn't tell. *You've got to be kidding me*, she thought. He parted his lips as if he was going to say something but stopped and closed his mouth. "Hmm."

Iylah glanced down at her shirt, pulling it from her skin. A cartoon llama in sunglasses was standing over the words, *My llama don't like you and she likes everyone.* Cole's head slowly cocked to the side. "What are you looking at?"

"Were you . . ." Cole began. He shook his head and breathed out a soft laugh. "Never mind. Definitely thought you were wearing a different shirt when I saw you earlier."

"Oh." Iylah checked her shirt, again. "No. Just this. Are you hungry? I was gonna make some dinner."

"Nah I'm good." Cole lifted a banana out of the fruit bowl and went to leave. "I'll eat later." He paused and eyed her suspiciously. The wine bottle was back in her hand. He smirked. Iylah thought he was looking at her nails. She'd just had them done with her mom; her favorite color, daphne blue with sparkles. "That bottle is my mom's favorite," he said. "And it was her last one."

"Oh," she muttered. "Shoot. Is she gonna be pissed I opened it?"

"I mean, probably. She can't buy it in Kentucky. Only gets it in Virginia."

Iylah clicked her tongue and set it back on the counter.

"But," Cole continued, "she did buy a couple of bottles for my friend's dad. I'd be happy to call him, see if he can sneak one out and bring it over here. If . . ." Cole stopped. Iylah raised her eyebrows; she knew where this was going. "You let me have some."

Iylah laughed. "No way. I'm not that cool."

"Suit yourself. *That* bottle is a pretty big deal to her though. It was a gift from her mom just before she passed away. Mom even had Mee-Maw's ashes scattered at the winery where they make it because it was her favorite place."

"Oh my gosh. I didn't know. Wow. I feel really bad about this. Do you really promise not to tell if I let you drink this?"

"Promise. I'll call my friend now and have him bring over another bottle."

"Okay, that's good. Because . . ." Iylah shook her head in relief. "I'd hate to have to tell your mom I drank the treasured bottle that her *dead* mom gave her. That's . . . wow . . . that's heavy." Cole nodded, with a face that suggested constipation rather than sympathy. "Especially since her mom is still alive in Alexandria, Virginia, and just got published in the *Washingtonian* for having one of the ten best restaurants in DC." Cole's face went slack. "I mean, that would really kick her in the balls, right? To know her mom was *actually* dead?" She smirked. "Nice try. But I do my research on the families I babysit for—make sure I'm not gonna end up in someone's wall or sacrificed in some weird sexcapade."

Cole rolled his eyes and mumbled something to himself as he stepped over to the refrigerator.

"Thought you weren't hungry," Iylah said.

"No, I said I'd eat later. I'm just looking around."

"I brought a really good dinner—it's my grandfather's recipe. He used to own this restaurant in Louisville—" Cole lifted out two Tupperware containers as she was talking. "I was gonna make a marinara chicken—a healthy version, at least. That's edamame in the other container. It's pretty freakin' delicious. I think you'll like it. You wanna help me make it?"

Cole's mouth turned down. "I'll take your word for it." He eyed the money on the counter and picked it up. "How much did my mom leave you? Why don't we just order a pizza?"

"Because I brought food," Iylah replied.

"Yeah, but I don't want to eat *your* food."

"Then . . . I guess you won't eat," she said sternly, offering an insincere smile.

"Gonna starve me, huh? That'll be great for your reviews," Cole mumbled.

"Oh. And what would your review say? My babysitter—keep in mind you're fifteen, it's a little embarrassing—didn't let me eat pizza and whatever I wanted? Instead, she made me eat super moist chicken and vegetables with some killer rice?" She pulled a wine glass from the cabinet and began pouring into it from the bottle. "Good luck with that."

"Eh, you're right. Probably safer to just eat it. Wouldn't wanna get pushed in the pool."

A dull tightening suddenly gripped Iylah's stomach. The glass paused at her lips, sloshing wine into her mouth, and some down onto her chin. She wiped it and tried to swallow but ended up coughing instead. "What did you say?"

"Nothing . . ." He replied, fingering out the bills on the counter.

She wanted to walk over to him and slap him. Maybe even to smash the wine bottle over his head. No. She wanted to go home. Why was she even here? She didn't need this money. She didn't need this stress. But maybe her mom was right. Maybe it was more about emotional growth and getting past this fear. Not letting her mind use anxiety and the past to control her future.

"Don't bring that up around me ever again. You don't know anything about what happened—"

"Whoa, whoa. What are you talking about? I said I would eat it." He started to chuckle and went back to counting. "Sorry. It was a joke. I call people *tools* all the time, don't take it so personally."

Iylah didn't reply at first, but her mind was put at ease. She'd misheard him. She could feel her heart starting to settle, but she didn't like how on edge she was. Memories of that night were beginning to come back and take over her perception.

"Call me when dinner's ready."

"Put the money down. Now." Her voice was firm again.

He groaned and dropped the money onto the counter with a smack. "Did you bring anything else besides chicken?"

"No," she replied, coldly.

"We had that last night. I'm really not in the mood to have it again."

Iylah tilted her head to the side. "Awww," she muttered. She put her hand over her heart. "Tough shit."

Cole shook his head and produced a nervous laugh. "You definitely seemed a lot nicer when I met you outside."

Iylah didn't have time to reply before he disappeared through the French doors. "What an asshole," she said to herself.

The search for cooking utensils and pots and pans did little to quell her uneasiness. Her patience was thin, focus limited, and temperament unpredictable. No wonder people didn't want her watching their kids—she was unstable. But she had good reason to be, right? Accident or not, what if she wasn't ready to be in this position again? What if something happened tonight? Could she protect Cole if she needed to?

As she was about to slide into another dark and tumultuous mental trance, she shook her head and said her own name aloud, commanding herself to calm down. Several minutes passed while she leaned against the counter, scrolling through her social media. She reached to retrieve her wine and noticed the cash still there. She fanned it out with her finger: two twenties were missing. "Son of a bitch." She'd approach him about it later. Thankfully, this sort of petty theft was not new to her. Then, something else hit her: "Nicer when I met you outside?" Iylah took a sip of her wine. "He didn't meet me outside." She considered this in her head. "Shit. Cole!"

One Year Ago
Shelby Gray
Part 1

*I*ylah clicked *end* on her cell and sent a short text to her friend recounting—bragging, maybe?—the conversation with Devin. She rounded the corner from the living room into the hallway, toward the kitchen, and was startled when she heard a glass bang against the counter. The basement door was open, and Shelby Gray was standing at the sink with her back to Iylah, filling up a glass of water. *Was she up here the whole time?* "I thought you were downstairs."

There was no response from Shelby as she cut the water off and began drinking. *Shit.* "Shelby?" No response. "Are you okay?" Still nothing. Shelby chugged the whole glass and then let out a big breath before filling it up again. "Just to be clear, I wasn't talking about you in there. I'm supposed to watch my niece next weekend—she's a nightmare."

Shelby turned and straightened in surprise, appearing to be shocked to see Iylah standing there. She removed an earbud. "Whoa. You scared me. Did you say something?"

The tension in Iylah's mind faded with a relieved exhale. "I didn't realize you had your earbuds in. Just saying hey, and that *you* scared *me*. I thought you were in the basement still."

"I just came up for water. That wasn't my mom, was it?" Shelby nodded to the phone in Iylah's hand.

"No," Iylah replied, slipping it into her pocket. "Not that time. She'll call in about an hour, I'm sure. And then again at ten to make sure you're in bed." Iylah shook her head playfully.

"Yeah . . ." Shelby muttered, finishing her glass.

"So . . ." Iylah opened a bag of Tostito chips that she'd brought over. "Anything you wanna do tonight? I brought my Firestick over. My friend jailbroke it so we can watch just about anything."

"Eh." Shelby shrugged.

"I could do something scary if you want. As long as it's not super gory."

"I don't know," Shelby replied. "I'm not really in the mood for a movie." She walked over and stopped beside the sliding glass door going onto the back deck.

"Since when are you not in the mood for a horror movie?" Iylah ate a chip. "You wanna have people over? Do like a girls night kind of thing? Order some pizza?

"Maybe. I don't know."

"You alright?" Iylah asked. Shelby shrugged and walked into the living room. Iylah put the chip bag down and followed to find her sitting on the couch and scrolling through her phone. "It's supposed to get cooler tonight. You wanna get in the hot tub later?"

"Maybe . . ." Shelby said softly, distracted.

"Okay . . ." Iylah nodded her head. "Or I guess we could just do our own thing. If you wanna invite your friends over and do something, I can hang out upstairs . . . ?"

"It's fine. I'm sure they're all busy anyways." She clicked off her phone and exhaled a long breath. "A movie is fine."

"Well, jeez. Don't get too excited." Iylah watched Shelby who wouldn't meet her eye. "What's wrong?"

"Nothing. Stomach just feels a little weird," she replied, getting up off the couch.

"Oh. We can start making dinner if you want?"

"I'm not hungry," Shelby replied, distracted. "You can go ahead. I'll eat later."

"Alright." Iylah threw up her hands. "Did something happen? You seem like you're in a bad mood all of a sudden."

Shelby looked at her for a brief second before lowering her eyes to the floor, almost as if she were embarrassed. "I'm fine. It's just, I'm sure the last thing you wanna do is hang out with a fourteen-year-old on a Friday night."

"What are you talking about? I'm the one who told your mom to call me if they ended up going out of town. I love hangin' out with you. Believe me, if I didn't want to be here, I wouldn't be. I figured you would be the one wanting to hang out with your friends tonight. Look, if you don't want to watch a movie, then let's do something else." Iylah stopped, waiting to see if Shelby's face showed any interest. "You wanna play a game?"

Her eyes came up to meet Iylah's. "What kind of game?"

"I don't know. What's that train game your mom was talking about?"

"*Ticket to Ride?*"

"Yeah. That sounded fun," Iylah said. "You wanna do that? We can play while we cook."

There was the briefest hint of concern in Shelby's eyes, but before Iylah could ask again what the matter was, Shelby said, "Okay. I'll go grab it," and left the kitchen, heading for the basement stairs. Iylah couldn't help but feel a ping of stress over her earlier conversation on the phone. *She must've heard me. Shit. What all did I say?* Iylah began walking around aimlessly, intending to lay out ingredients for dinner but instead just moving around the kitchen, distracted. She tried to mentally reconstruct the conversation she had been having on the phone but couldn't remember details, probably because the entire time she was in a nervous daze of infatuation with the guy she was talking to. *It's fine. She said she didn't hear you.*

There were two new texts waiting when she checked her phone: one from her friend Chrissy and the other from her crush, Devin. She read the one from the Devin first as it was most important. The content wasn't as exciting as she'd hoped. The message from Chrissy, however, instantly shook the butterflies awake in her stomach.

> 8:02 *PM CHRISSY:* Jasmine just snt me this. Lock those abs down!

She'd sent a screenshot of a conversation between Devin and their friend Jasmine:

> 6:44 *PM JASMINE:* We studying this weekend?
>
> 6:45 *PM DEVIN:* Maybe. Tryin to hit up someone. I'll let you know . . . ?
>
> 6:45 *PM JASMINE:* Who?
>
> 6:46 *PM DEVIN:* Girl we went to high school with. Iylah Maddox.
>
> 6:46 *PM JASMINE:* Oh shit! When that happen?
>
> 6:49 *PM DEVIN:* Hasn't yet. Just talked to her tonight. Tryna go out this weekend.
>
> 6:51 *PM JASMINE:* She normal now?

That's where the screenshot cut off. "Normal now?" Iylah whispered. "What?" She began typing a message back to Chrissy but stopped midway. Iylah was certain she knew what *normal now* meant, but what concerned her was that people way outside her circle of friends were talking about her that way. About what happened. A new text vibrated her phone. It was another screenshot with a message from Chrissy: *You didn't tell me he asked you out!*

> 6:53 PM JASMINE: Sorry. My text 2 spch is drunk tonight. She know about it? Not she normal now. I hope she normal. :) Let me know what night you do it and if you still wanna study.
>
> 6:54 PM DEVIN: Yeah I gotchu.
>
> 6:55 PM JASMINE: Can I at least get the notes from last class?
>
> 6:56 PM DEVIN: Your so needy

The nervous bubble in Iylah's stomach subsided. She read through the screenshots two more times. She took a step and almost slipped with a clown-like screech on the vinyl floor. There was a large puddle of clear liquid under her shoe. "What is that?" *Did Shelby spill water and just leave it?* The glass was still sitting beside the sink, empty. "Weird."

Iylah grabbed the roll of paper towels, wiped up the mess, and gingerly smelled the towels. "Definitely water." There was another puddle, a little smaller, maybe a foot from the one she just wiped. "Are you kidding me?" She inspected the ceiling for a leak, but it was clean. She wiped up the second puddle, checking to make sure that was all. That's when she noticed a large, discolored spot on the carpet in the TV room, just down the small staircase from the kitchen. "What is going on?"

She ripped off more sheets and soaked up the mess. Thankfully this one wasn't large. "Shelby?" Iylah called, "Did you spill something?" There was no reply. As she stood up to go back to-ward the kitchen, she saw it. It was sitting on the hearth of the fireplace, neatly on display as though just for her. Iylah sucked in a sharp breath, dropping the soiled towels to the floor. "No . . ." she said, stepping closer.

The object was a black, rectangular, three-dimensional tower that stood about eighteen inches. Iylah could see something like condensation dripping down the sides and felt a wave of nausea beginning to roll in her stomach. "No, no, no, no," she muttered again. She was so distracted that she failed to hear Shelby come up the basement stairs.

"Iylah?" Iylah jumped, grabbing the box and chucking it onto the couch, immediately pulling a blanket over it.

Shelby peeked from behind the door, over to where Iylah was standing. "Who are you talking to?"

"No one," Iylah said, trying to remind herself to breathe. "Just . . ." In a fluster, she bent down to pick up the towels.

"Did you spill something?" Shelby asked.

"No. I mean, yeah. I did. Just spilled my water. Sorry." She moved up the steps, brushing past Shelby and throwing the tow-els into the trash.

"It's okay," Shelby said. "It's just water."

"Yeah, it's fine. No big deal." Iylah replied. "It's just a little water." She washed her hands, shaking them out in a rush.

"You okay?" Shelby asked.

"Yeah, yeah. I'm good." She went to face her, feeling herself start to breathe a little faster. "Come on, let's play." Iylah mo-tioned toward the games in her hand. "What'd you find?"

"I got *Ticket, Mexican Train, Dominion,* and *Carcassome.*" She walked toward the stairs into the TV room. "You wanna play down here—"

"No!" Iylah cut in. She caught her burst and sank back. "I

mean, no." She motioned Shelby to the dining room. "Let's go in here."

"Oookay," Shelby said with a curious laugh.

They started to walk to the dining room, but Iylah hung back. "Go ahead and get one set up. I just need to check something real quick." She pulled out her phone again, waving it at Shelby.

"Oh," Shelby said quietly. "Alright." Iylah pretended to search on her phone, waiting for Shelby to be out of view, and then moved back toward the couch. The blanket-wrapped object was still there. She lifted it, holding it out as if it were a dead animal. "We're not doing this again." She opened the door to the garage, where there were two large trash containers. She opened the lid on one of them and tossed the box inside. "Fuck you," she said, closing the lid.

Iylah walked back into the dining room to see Shelby sitting at the table. "*Ticket to Ride* okay?"

Iylah nodded. She was still standing in the doorway. Her mind was racing with thoughts. She wasn't even sure what Shelby had just said; she couldn't focus. *Calm down, calm down, calm down.* Dread was beginning to bloom inside her lungs. She noticed she hadn't taken a breath in a while and stuck a hand out to the wall to steady herself.

Shelby seemed to notice something was off. "Are you okay?"

Iylah's heart was racing. "I'll be right back," Iylah said, exiting the dining room and moving quickly toward the main stairs, holding out her hands to the wall for balance. She needed to get herself under control before panic fully took over. Shelby asked what was wrong; Iylah stumbled over the first step and forced herself to say she was fine. "Just gimme a sec," she whispered, almost up the stairs. She burst into the bathroom, closed the door, and began running cold water over her arms. She took deep, controlled breaths, just like her dad told her, reminding herself she was okay. *In for four, out for four. In for four, out for four. In. Out.*

Shelby returned to the board to continue counting out the pieces, unsure about what exactly was going on. When she'd finished, she called up to Iylah. "Hey! I'm gonna go grab my phone from the basement. *Ticket to Ride*'s all set up, though. I'm ready when you are!" She was at the basement door when she heard someone behind her whisper, "Hey Shelby."

4

NOW

"Cole?" Iylah clicked on the light at the top of the stairs. It had the same sort of country feel as downstairs: wooden signs with scriptures and feel-good quotes lined the walls. She scanned both ends of the hall. Aside from the bathroom, every other door was closed. There was a low hum of a voice, and then a door at the other end of the hall clicked and opened, only to immediately close to nothing more than a hairline crack.

"What are you doing?" Cole asked, staring out at her.

She walked toward him. "Can I come in? I need to ask you something?"

The opening lessened. "I'm kinda busy. I've got a ton of homework."

"Did you say you met me *outside*?"

"I don't know. Maybe. It's fine. I wasn't tryin to be a jerk. I'll eat chicken."

"No, no, no. That's not . . . did you say that because . . ." She wasn't sure how to ask this. "This is gonna sound really weird. Did you open the door for me, or did your mom?" Even though it was only one eye, she could see it narrow in interest.

"I did," he replied. "Except I thought you were wearing a different shirt." Iylah went still. "Maybe. I don't know, I wasn't paying much attention. My mom had on a black shirt, so that's probably what I was thinking of."

Iylah felt her mind begin to spin. She exhaled a troubled sigh. "Crap." She went in a sudden rush down the stairs.

"What happened!" Cole yelled, but Iylah was too flustered to answer.

"No, no, no, no, no, no," Iylah chanted to herself, along with a slew of curses. She got to the main floor and stood still, intently studying her surroundings. "You can't be here. You got what you wanted," she said to herself in a whisper. "Can you hear me? What do you want?" *Maybe Cole was mistaken. Or maybe he was messing with her. That was it—it had to be. But why would he say it? Of all the things he could say, why that? Why would he make up that someone else came to the door?* She crept through each room, inspecting every inch of space for what she feared would be there.

The foyer was clear, as was the adjacent reading room and her bathroom. The kitchen, and the living room; nothing. She peeked in the laundry room just off the kitchen and into the garage—she felt like she was playing a game of hide and seek. "I swear to God if you're here . . ."

"Who are you talking to?" Cole said, coming down the stairs. Iylah turned to him; her hands pressed together like a prayer, fingers tapping on her mouth. "What's going on?"

"I'm trying to find something."

"What is it?" Cole asked.

"A box."

"Like, you're trying to find a box you brought or just any random one?"

"Neither," Iylah replied, and left it at that.

After several seconds: "Neither," Cole repeated. "You need help?"

She rolled her hands nervously around one another, as if the sweat on her hands was lotion. "It's a long, black, wooden box."

"But you didn't bring it here?"

"No." She hopped, looking on top of the refrigerator. "It may not even be here." She went back to her room and dumped the contents of her bag onto the floor. A couple of games, clothes, and various items spilled out.

"Is that a flashlight?" Cole asked, stopping it from rolling with his foot.

"Where do you keep your games?" Iylah asked.

"Like, my Xbox games?"

"Your board games." Iylah began stuffing her clothes back into the bag.

"Oh. I don't know," Cole replied. "There's a chest in the living room." Iylah didn't wait for him to finish. "If we have any they'd be in there."

She spotted the antique cedar chest immediately and opened it. Cole was right. Underneath a stack of blankets, there were a few board games: *Life, Risk, 13 Dead End Drive, Sorry!* and *Trivial Pursuit.* Iylah sighed.

"Hey," Cole called. "Is that it?"

She followed his voice. He had moved into the sunroom where Iylah had been working, just off of the dining room. He stood in the doorway staring at the chair where Iylah's laptop was sitting under a stack of papers. "Did you spill something?"

Those words, and what she saw when she entered the room, tightened her insides. Resting neatly beside her things was the black, oblong box, beaded with droplets of water.

One Year Ago
Shelby Gray
Part II

$\mathcal{S}$helby darted back up the basement stairs toward the kitchen, shoving Iylah hard against the wall. "Get away from me! What the *fuck* is wrong with you?"

Iylah felt something pop as her spine and head hit the wall, just before she lost her footing and began to tumble. The side of her hip smashed against the edge of a stair as she reached out for the handrail to stop herself from crashing all the way down. She winced at the shooting pain now going down her leg. "Shelby! What happened?!" Shelby didn't answer. Iylah pulled herself up the stairs and back into the kitchen, closing the door. "Ow! Shit!" She bent down, rubbing on her hip bone.

"Fuck you, psycho!" Shelby screamed. "I'm calling my mom!"

"Wh—What happened? Are you okay?" Footsteps were the only response, thunderously stomping across the floor above her. Iylah stood for a moment, mentally assessing the situation. She'd been in the bathroom trying to calm her nerves when she thought she heard a scream and a series of thuds. The sound was barely audible over the running water and vent. Iylah called for Shelby and almost instantly heard an outburst of howling. She darted to the basement stairs where she saw Shelby at the bottom, curled into a ball on the ground and holding her head. Iylah hurried down, but in a frightening burst of movement,

Shelby shot up and bounded up the stairs in hysterics, slamming Iylah against the wall as she went.

"What the hell happened?" Iylah asked herself, looking around. Her head had begun to throb from the fall, and she discovered a welt the size of a golf-ball that made her wince when she touched it. No blood though.

A *thud* echoed in a room above her, snapping Iylah out of her confusion. "Shelby!" She walked up the main stairs to Shelby's room and hollered for her a couple more times. A click sounded from the other side of the door—Shelby had locked it. Iylah tried to turn the handle just to be sure, and then proceeded to knock.

"Are you okay?" Iylah asked. No reply. "Shelby, can you please open the door? At least tell me if you're hurt?" There was an abrupt movement toward the door. *BAM!* Shelby must have kicked it—or punched it?

"Go away, you psycho! Get out of my house!"

"Shelby, what happened! I was in the bathroom the whole time—"

"Yeah, right!"

"Did you fall down the stairs? I heard you scream. Then you started going crazy, and you shoved me into the wall—"

"*I* went crazy?" Shelby interrupted. *BAM!* "I could have been killed!"

"How? Did you slip? Or, miss a step or something?"

"Oh, you are so dead for this! My parents are gonna make sure you go to jail for this!"

"You called your mom?" Iylah asked.

"Not yet. But if I were you, I wouldn't be here when I do."

"Shelby, I'm not leaving—"

The door flung open at once with a loud crack as the knob struck the wall. Shelby was holding out a baseball bat, pointing it threateningly at Iylah's chest. "I need my cell phone. Get back." Iylah stood her ground. "I said get back—"

"I heard you, but I'm not moving until you tell me what the hell is going on," Iylah snapped. "I've asked you like ten times if you're okay, or what happened, and all you do is tell me to F off."

"What do you expect?" Shelby jabbed Iylah's chest with the end of the bat, forcing her back. "You pushed me down the fucking stairs!"

Iylah froze, her eyes never leaving Shelby's. "I did what?" Iylah asked. "I didn't push you down the stairs."

"Don't play stupid. I saw you."

There was a nauseating dip in Iylah's gut. "Shelby, that wasn't—" She stopped herself, knowing there was no way to explain what might be happening. "Shelby. Look at me. I did not push you down the stairs."

In the quiet between them, something ticked—a door opening, perhaps?—from the main floor. Shelby's head followed the noise, giving Iylah the distraction she needed. In a swift movement, Iylah ripped the bat out of Shelby's hand, causing her to lurch forward and fall to the ground. Shelby's glasses flung off her face and skidded across the wood floor. Her hand began instinctively feeling around for them. When Iylah advanced, Shelby scampered back in a crap walk, squinting. "I need my glasses, I can't see," Shelby said.

"Are you gonna calm down and tell me what happened?" Shelby just stared back at her, panting. Iylah knelt and slid the glasses over to her. Shelby put them on and frantically started crawling toward the stairs to make a run for it, but Iylah blocked her.

"Move!" Shelby yelled, grabbing at Iylah's legs to push her away.

Iylah made sure to hold the bat away from the two of them.

"Shelby! Listen to me!" She said back, forcefully. "I didn't push you down the stairs! Would you stop and just let me explain!" She dropped the bat and seized Shelby by the arms, yanking her up—the girl was lighter than she expected. "Look at me!" Shelby continued struggling and commanding Iylah to let her go. Her voice was hard and enraged, but her face was nothing but fear. Iylah finally raised her voice to a deafening growl, screaming at the girl in her arms. "Shelby! Stop!" The shock from the noise took them both by surprise. Neither moved, only stared at the other. Iylah exhaled. She could see Shelby's eyes flooding. "Listen to me. I. Didn't. Push you. Okay?"

Shelby sniffed, looking like she was about to have a full-on breakdown.

"I know this is going to sound crazy—"

Shelby screamed, calling her insane, and jerked away again, this time freeing her arms and shoving Iylah away.

Iylah grabbed her by the wrist and snapped Shelby back close to her. "You want to call me insane, fine—maybe I am. But I need you to *calm. Down.*" Iylah's voice was sharp. "I know you saw someone that looked like me. But what were they wearing? Was it a red shirt, like this one?" Shelby eyed Iylah's outfit with uncertainty. "It was black wasn't it?" Shelby nodded. "And she had a ponytail, didn't she?" The shocked glimmer in Shelby's eyes was all Iylah needed to confirm what she feared. "Shelby, I need you to tell me what happened. I promise I can explain—"

"God! You can't explain that! I saw you, Iylah!" She yanked herself free, falling back against the wall. As the tears came, Shelby began to shudder, keeping her eyes on the floor. Iylah stepped forward, holding out a sympathetic hand but Shelby knocked it away, stepping farther from her. "I heard you on the phone."

"On the phone?" Iylah asked, trying to hide her guilt. "Oh. No, Shelby, that wasn't about you."

"Oh yeah? It was about some other 'cock-eyed girl' with 'sickening BO and the social skills of a piece of toast?' Really?"

"I didn't say you had sickening—" Iylah caught it as soon as it slipped from her mouth. "Shelby, look, I'm really sorry—"

"Please just go home," Shelby whispered sadly, hugging herself tight, unable to look up. Iylah saw tears cascading down her nose and onto the floor. Shelby sniffed, loudly, yanking her glasses off and hiding her face with her hands. "I just want you to go home."

"I didn't mean what I—"

"Get outta here!" She screamed at the top of her lungs. Iylah drew back at the noise. Shelby's face was wet and blotched with red. Her lip quivered as she took in a breath. She slumped against the wall again and collapsed helplessly to the floor, shaking her head. Iylah didn't know what else to do so she apologized one more time and stepped away to go and get her things. "Did you know you're the only one who's ever encouraged me to do theater?"

"What?" Iylah asked.

"My mom hates it. My dad thinks it's a waste of time," Shelby replied, taking in a snotted breath before wiping her nose with the back of her hand. "You're the only one who's ever pushed me to do shows. Did you know that?" Iylah didn't speak. "You know in all the shows I've ever done, my parents have only come to one performance? Just one. And you've been to, what? All of them? Since I was five?" Iylah could feel her head nodding. "You know why I still ask you to look at my monologues before I audition?" Shelby paused. "It's not because you know how to make it better. It's because . . ." She stopped, her face scrunching with anguish. "It's because I trust you when you tell me it's good." The emotions choked back Shelby's words, making them harder for Iylah to interpret. "Or that it's not good. It's because if I make you laugh, I know it's real. It's because if I see your head start nodding, and that tiny, thin smile come over your mouth, I know I've impressed you.

"And let's be honest, getting *your* approval for someone like *me* is a pretty big deal." Shelby let out a short burst of laughter. "You're popular. You're confident." Shelby looked Iylah up and down. "You're gorgeous—I mean, you're just babysitting, and you look like *that*—it's sick." The words made Iylah unintentionally smile. "And the best part was that you seemed genuinely interested in me." A pause. "But then, to hear you say those things tonight . . ." Iylah's smile faded. Shelby's hands were crossed in front of her as if she were holding an imaginary teddy bear. Her mouth opened, but the words didn't come. She sat there, appearing as if she might be choking or about to vomit. "It hurt so much." She cried for a moment, and then, "you tore apart every bit of trust I've ever had in you. And with that . . ." She paused, knocking the back of her head against the wall.

"Shelby . . ."

She shook her head, raising her hands. "Every shred of belief I ever had in myself." Iylah could feel her cheeks going pale. After a long, agonizing silence, Shelby turned her head to Iylah and said, confidently, "You're an awful human being, Iylah."

The words felt so much like a punch that Iylah's body lurched forward. She wanted to speak, but there was nothing to say. Shelby was right: there was no way to explain what she'd said, or even why she'd said it. Iylah knelt beside her and tried to engage but Shelby shoved her off, demanding that she leave. Iylah swallowed, got to her feet, and walked regretfully down the stairs, into the guestroom.

Her bag was still on the bed from when she arrived. She

thought for a moment if she'd gotten anything out, but her brain was submerged in a dense fog. She could still hear Shelby at the top of the stairs struggling to get a hold of her breathing through the anguish. It crossed her mind to stay, hide out downstairs and wait for Shelby to calm down. They could talk this out. Plus, how would it look when Mrs. Gray came home tomorrow morning? What would Shelby say happened? The sound of Shelby's cries grew with intensity and heartbreak. So unsettling that Iylah felt compelled—or pushed—to leave the house at once.

Iylah turned into the RacerFan gas station on Hwy 121 and idled in the parking lot. After a few minutes of weighing concern, she called Shelby's cell phone; no answer. This was stupid. There was no way she could spin any of this. Scenario after scenario ran through her head as she tried to conjure up some way to explain her absence when Shelby's mom called later, or when she arrived home the next morning. Or why Shelby had been crying all night—Iylah gasped. Her cell phone was vibrating in her lap; Shelby.

"Hey," Iylah answered, a little frantic. "Are you okay?" No response. "Shelby?" Iylah checked the screen; the call had connected. "Hello?"

"Hello?" A voice came back.

"Shelby?"

"Shelby?" It repeated.

"Can you hear me?" It echoed back. She checked the screen again and started to talk but a crackled sound cut through, silencing her. She spoke again but the noise continued, growing in consistency, like the sound of running water. "Hello? Shelby?"

Something sputtered through—a distant voice. Iylah could have sworn she heard her name. "Shelby?"

"I—ah."

"I'm here. Can you hear me?"

"I . . . id . . . o . . . ee . . . me?"

"I can't hear you," Iylah said back, plugging her other ear.

The voice broke through again, like a song going in and out of range on the radio. "I . . . did . . . you . . . eev . . . me?" Iylah paused, trying to make it out. "I . . . did . . . oo . . . leave me . . . ?"

Iylah sat straight up, throwing the car in drive. "Oh my gosh. I didn't leave you. I'm just down the road. I'll be right there—"

The static swelled in her ear making her jerk the phone away. She tried to speak over it but it became more severe as she drove back toward the house until finally cutting off with a double beep. The call dropped. "Shit!"

Iylah sprinted up the walkway to the Gray house, checking her phone to make sure Shelby hadn't tried to call again. Forgetting that she locked the front door she nearly crushed her face when it didn't open. She knocked and at once began fumbling with her keys, using the illumination from the headlights before they timed out. "Shelby!" She knocked again, with urgency. "It's me!" A piercing shriek from somewhere inside made her heart leap. "Oh my God!" she whispered, darting around the side of the house, calling Shelby's name. "Where are you?"

She flung open the gate to the back and followed the light spilling out from the garage's entry door. It was open. "Shelby?" Iylah moved carefully around the Jeep Wrangler and back into the house where she saw Shelby standing in the family room—

the room where Iylah had found the black box—slack jawed, frozen, staring back at her. "I heard you scream—"

"Why were you just standing in my garage?"

Iylah's brow crinkled. "I was around front. I heard you scream and thought something was wrong."

"I screamed because you were standing in my garage." Iylah advanced toward her as Shelby retreated into the kitchen. She stopped beside the glass sliding door to the porch. "Don't!" Shelby snapped. "Don't you come near me! Get out of my house!"

Iylah held out her hands. "Can we at least talk?"

"I don't want to talk. I want you to get the hell out of my house!"

Terror blanketed Shelby's face, like an animal who'd been backed into a corner with nowhere to run. "Shelby." Iylah lifted her palms. "It's me. I'm not going to hurt you, okay?" Iylah couldn't help herself and took two steps toward her. Shelby, in true threatened fashion, spun around, flicked back the dead bolt, and ran out the door, down the porch stairs into the backyard. Iylah dashed after her. The flood lights switched on illuminating the patio and covered pool. With every call of her name, Shelby would scream for Iylah to get away.

It took hardly any time for Iylah to close the distance between them. Shelby cut away toward the pool. Iylah followed close behind her, demanding that she stop, when at once Iylah reached out and grabbed her by the arm. She yanked her back and Shelby began screaming in hysterics. "Shelby! What is the matter with you? It's me!"

In a raw and powerful fit of rage, Shelby grabbed at Iylah's hand and ripped herself out of the grip, shoving her away. The movement sent Iylah back, but when Shelby turned, she tripped over her foot, and lost her balance, tumbling over the edge. She landed with a sickening *thud* onto the tarp that covered the kidney shaped pool. The drop reverberated into a death like grip over Iylah's heart. She sprang to the pool's edge with a shriek, reaching out to try and save Shelby from falling but the effort was fruitless.

Shelby thrashed over the cover, attempting to get back to the pool's side, but the tarp quickly began folding in on itself—over her—sinking down into the water. Confused and in a panic, Iylah tried reaching for a portion of the tarp to drag it back—to try and pull Shelby out—but she couldn't secure a grip. It felt as if the water was pulling it away from her. Shelby's cries grew even more dreadful, pleading for Iylah to help. Iylah darted around in a frenzy, looking for a pool net, or anything she could reach out for Shelby to take. There was nothing! The cries became choked as the water flooded around her. Iylah rushed back to the pool, screaming for Shelby, tears welling up in her eyes as she knelt down, and hopped into the water. She waded toward Shelby, who was now fully enveloped underwater, struggling wildly to free herself. Iylah screamed for help and tried taking hold of the tarp, but every movement seemed to entangle her more. Through it all, she kept calling Shelby's name and reassuring her that she was coming.

The next memory Iylah's brain chose to keep of that night was her lying poolside, staring transfixed as others drug the tarp out of the pool as if it were some mythical sea creature. Lights were flashing around her. At one point she was ushered to the swing under the back deck and given a towel. There were voices and faces coming at her from all sides, but her mind couldn't process what was happening. All she could see was Shelby.

Shelby pushing her away. Yelling at her to leave. Falling. Thrashing.

And all she could hear were the choked, panicked cries for Iylah to help.

5

NOW

Iylah held her cell phone up against her ear. "Come on. Come on. Come on. Pick up. Pick up." It was the fourth time she'd called Erica Lang, and no one was answering. She hit end and clasped her hands together, gently bumping them against her mouth. Her legs were anxiously twitching.

"Who you trying to call?" Cole asked.

"A friend."

"You're not sick or anything, are you?"

"No."

Cole gave her a thumbs up and started to leave. She stood with her hands in her hair, unsure of what to do. "Cole!"

"Yeah?"

Iylah sighed. "Shelby Gray. This is what killed her."

It took Cole a beat or two to respond. "This being . . . that thing right there?" She opened her eyes to see him pointing at it.

"Yeah," she nodded.

"You're telling me that little black box killed Shelby Gray?"

"I know how it sounds. But I'm gonna need you to play it with me."

Cole's eyes narrowed. "Play it? Play what?"

"It's a board game."

"Wait," he chuckled, leaning against the door frame. "You just said it killed her, and now you want me to play it. Wow! You're babysitter of the year—"

"She didn't die playing it!" Iylah cut in, her body sagging in submission. "I think she died because we *didn't* play."

Cole nodded, inspecting around the room with pursed lips. Finally, he clicked his tongue and pushed himself off the frame. "Okay then, well, on that note, I'm gonna go back upstairs."

"Cole. Wait!"

"Look, I'm all for shock humor and jokes and stuff, but this is a little dark." Iylah tried to interject, but he continued. "Plus, I'm really not a huge board game fan, so I wouldn't be the best competitor—"

"You don't have a choice."

"Oh really? Is that because you're in charge? And I have to do whatever you say?" Cole said mockingly.

"No," Iylah said, shaking her head calmly. "Because I don't want what happened to her to happen to you."

Cole's eyes flashed a momentary glimpse of shock. He stepped back, away from her. "Okay, using what happened to Shelby as a threat is definitely not cool," he said carefully. "Especially considering people say you're the one that did it—"

"I didn't do a thing to Shelby. Do you hear me?" Iylah snapped.

"I don't think you did but do you really expect me to believe that some board game pushed Shelby into the pool?"

"She wasn't pushed. She slipped—it was an accident!" Iylah exclaimed, defensively. "She was scared. Something was in her house that night, and she tried to run. And I think it's because we ignored her."

Cole's head tilted with interest. "*Her?*" Cole asked.

Iylah paused.

"Wait, who's her? Ignored who?" Cole asked. Iylah, again, said nothing. "Look, I'm not doing anything until you explain why you're freakin' out over a box."

"It's not a box." She timidly picked it up, holding it by its silver handle with her thumb and forefinger, and walked it over to the dining room table in the next room. "Look. I'll show you."

Cole let out a long breath, letting his head fall back. "This is ridiculous." He followed and stared, uninterested, at her and the object on the table. "Can we at least eat dinner first?"

"No."

"Mmm," Cole mumbled. "Of course not." He got closer to inspect the box. Dangling from the handle was a small key. Just underneath the handle was an unfamiliar script of white symbols.

$$\text{ʕ⊰ʔI}$$
$$\text{ʔI⊿⊱' ∏ʔ'Ⴑ⊦⊿ʕʕ}$$

"What is that, Japanese?" Iylah shook her head no. "Maybe Serbian?" Iylah didn't reply. "What's it called, then? The game."

"I don't know," Iylah said impatiently. She removed the key that was tied to the handle and inserted it into the tiny lock just underneath the script.

"Why is there a key?"

"Because that's how she made it." Cole was in the midst of asking "who is *she*" again, but the twist of the key cut him off. With the turn of Iylah's hand, there came a sequence of four clicks—clasps on each of the four sides. As if shedding its skin, the box released each of its four sides, dropping sequentially with a loud *thud* onto the table. Left standing in the center was a thinner version of the tower, etched with ornate designs.

"Not bad," Cole said, running his hand along the center tower. "The carvings are cool." Iylah grabbed the silver handle and lifted off a thin lid from the tower, exposing a fist-sized hole in the top. Cole reached out toward it when Iylah abruptly snatched his wrist. "Don't touch that," she said calmly, gently moving his hand away.

"Oh sorry," Cole said dryly. "Didn't realize the thing had teeth." He pulled his hand away from her. "So, that's all this thing is? Just . . . a board game?"

"There's not a name for what this thing is," Iylah said, surveying the cross-shaped board.

Cole took in a long breath and held it before finally saying in a mockingly empathetic tone, "Okay well, as fun as this seems, I'm gonna say hard pass." He made for the kitchen. "With how you were building it up, I was expecting something a lot cooler."

Iylah gave a frustrated growl and went to follow him into the kitchen, but something moved out of the corner of her eye, in the direction of the foyer. She stopped and stared through the hall, toward the front door. Though it wasn't clear, she could make out the shape of someone peeking out from around a corner, watching her.

The crinkling of a chip bag tore away her attention. Cole was in one of the pantries scavenging for food. When she looked back toward the front hall, the figure was gone. She shuddered and stepped into the kitchen. "I'll give you your mom's money if you play," she said abruptly. His expression was dumbfounded and before he could respond she walked over to the counter and thumped at the wad of cash on the counter. "There should be two hundred dollars here. It's yours if you play."

"Are you bein' serious right now?" Cole asked.

"Mmm hmm." She nodded, nervously, peeking out toward the foyer once more.

Cole grinned. "Nah, I'm not buyin' it." He squeezed past her to leave the kitchen, digging into his pocket for his phone.

"Three hundred!" Iylah called out. That stopped him. "I'll um . . ." She patted her pockets, then darted around him to the guestroom, leaving Cole open-mouthed. She brought her backpack in and dropped it at Cole's feet, looking for her wallet. She slipped out a stack of bills. "Here. I've got . . ." She counted out the bills in her purse. "Shit. I've only got forty dollars." She held it out to him. "Here. It's yours. As long you play."

Cole clicked his tongue. "Yeah, I don't know. I feel like there's a trap here . . ."

"It's not a trap!"

"How'm I supposed to explain suddenly ending up with two hundred dollars?" Cole asked.

"What do you mean how do you explain it? Don't you have a job or get an allowance?"

"No . . ." Cole replied. "I'll do odd jobs for neighbors or for my dad. That's how I make money. And I just spent everything I had on a gaming chair, so they'll definitely be suspicious if I suddenly have—"

"Oh my gosh, I'm offering you two hundred forty dollars, and you're not gonna take it?"

"I'm tellin' ya. I know my mom. She'll ask questions. Thanks, but that money won't do me any good after this weekend."

"Then I'll leave," Iylah added. "Okay? You play the game with me, I'll give you the two hundred forty dollars—you do with it whatever you want—and I'll leave before your mom comes home."

Cole squinted at her, considering her deal. "When?"

"Tomorrow morning."

Cole crossed his arms. "Tonight."

"I can't do that."

"Then no deal."

"Fine!" Iylah groaned. "Tonight."

"Yes!" Cole made a fist and shook it in front of him.

"But only *after* we play. Deal?

Cole snickered, rubbing his hands together. "Deal. Though I'm sure we'll have to call my mom later tonight. Just to make things sound normal, ya know?" He walked back into the dining room and over to the table where the game sat. He popped a chip into his mouth and spoke, while chewing, "I get anything else if I win?"

"Yeah," Iylah mumbled, taking a seat. "Nightmares."

Two Years Ago
Erica Lang
Part 1

It was a holiday weekend, and Iylah was back home in Murray, Kentucky on break from Belmont University. The first thing she noticed when the Uber pulled into the gravel driveway of her parents' home was that her mom's car wasn't there. She straightened up next to the window and scanned the property.

"What's wrong?" Erica Lang asked at seeing her friend become instantly distracted. Erica, who'd been Iylah's best friend since senior year, attended Vanderbilt University and had driven Iylah back home from Nashville for the weekend.

"My mom's car isn't here."

"Maybe they moved and didn't tell you," Erica quipped.

The driver careened his neck forward to get a look at the place as if he could offer insight. "This is the address you gave me."

"No, we know," Erica said back. "I was just kidding."

"Plus, my parents would rather die than leave this house," Iylah said, opening the car door. Other than the red lights of the Uber, darkness swallowed up the area around them; there were no streetlights or nearby houses to help illuminate the road. Erica pushed open the door with her shoulder and fell at once onto the rocks, catching herself with her hand.

"Whoa!" Iylah said. "Someone's gonna feel great tomorrow."

Erica couldn't stop laughing as Iylah helped her out of the car and to her feet. "I'm good, I'm good," Erica said, brushing off the debris from her hand.

"Sorry," Iylah said, waving at the driver. "We're okay." He asked if they were at the correct address, and she assured him they were. The driver maneuvered around—somewhat awkwardly on the narrow road—and drove off into the night.

"You good to walk?" Iylah asked.

Erica made a motorboat sound with her tongue and swatted her hand. "Please. I could run a marathon if I wanted to. Though, probably not in these heels—hold up." She motioned Iylah toward the grass and steadied herself on Iylah's shoulder. She reached down to slip off her shoes. "There we go." The two of them walked up toward the house, thankful for the tiny dim lanterns lining the walkway. The motion detector at the front door triggered the porch light. "Wait. You have a key to get in, right?"

"Yeah." Iylah scanned the barely lit driveway. "Where is her car?" She mumbled.

"Could it be in the garage?" Erica asked.

Iylah walked over and peeked in through the square window. "Not unless my dad got a supernatural urge to clean it." She maneuvered her head around the window, trying to see inside, but it was too dark. Plus, she was fairly certain it hadn't changed since she left for Christmas; a wreck—boxes piled floor to ceiling amid traces of woodwork and power tools. "You gotta be kidding me."

"You sure they didn't take it?"

"They wouldn't take both cars," Iylah replied.

"Good point," Erica said. "Alright well, no big deal. I'll just Uber back up to Vitellos tomorrow and pick mine up."

"Yeah, but how'm I supposed to get around?"

"Just take mine. I'll use my parents," Erica replied, relaxed.

"Really?"

"Yeah, it's fine. Drop me off at home tomorrow and pick me back up Sunday," Erica said. "There. Crisis averted." She winced, crossing her legs, and drawing a hand quickly to her stomach. "Where's your key? I forgot I had to pee."

"How do you *forget* you have to pee?" Iylah opened the door to her house and switched on the foyer light. Erica came in, dancing from one foot to the other. "What? Go to the bathroom."

"I don't know where it is!"

Iylah pointed her over to it. "You've been to my house like a hundred times," she laughed.

"You've been to *my* house a hundred times! I've been in here like twice," Erica said, hurrying past her and not bothering to close the door.

"What are you talking about? We hung out all the time."

"We did," Erica called from the bathroom, "at *my* place."

Iylah thought about this for a second. "Really?"

"Yeah. My parents had the hot tub, remember?"

"Oh yeah!" Iylah replied. "I forgot about that. That was like, every day after school, almost." She started walking through the house, switching on the lights, when she heard Erica let out a euphoric purr from the toilet immediately followed by a steady stream of pee emptying into the bowl. "You having an orgasm in there?" Iylah asked.

"Sure feels that way. Had the eye roll and everything," Erica yelled back.

Iylah checked the thermostat on the wall. "Makes sense that we would hang out at your place," she yelled out to Erica. "I mean if you had a hot tub, why would I be here?" The temperature read seventy-five degrees, and she considered whether or not to switch on the air. She knew there was a chance she'd forget to turn it back off before she left. Her parents were sticklers for not leaving anything running while they were out of town, even the air conditioner in the middle of summer. Every summer vacation of her childhood was practically overshadowed by the first night home, lying sleepless and sweating in what felt to be a sauna. Her mind instantly went back to her 12th birthday party at the house when the air conditioner went out the morning of the party. The group of them stayed up nearly half the night misting themselves with water from spray bottles.

She clicked it on, moving the temp down to sixty-nine, willing herself not to forget to turn it off before they left. It was a risk, but otherwise, it would soon be reaching 80. Erica walked into the foyer with her pants unbuttoned, rubbing her wet hands on her jeans. "If by hot tub you mean your morbid infatuation with my older brother, then yes, that's why you were always over at my house."

Iylah could feel herself immediately blushing. Her brain signaled for a nervous laugh, which she tried to convert into ignorance. "What are you talking about—"

"Bitch, I know you were trying to sleep with my brother. Don't even lie," Erica cut in. "I know you better than you think." The two of them walked into the kitchen for water. "You have any PJs I can borrow?"

"Yeah. I got a ton upstairs in my room." Iylah motioned for Erica to follow her.

"Where'd your parents go again?" Erica asked, sticking her head through one of Iylah's tank tops.

"Gatlinburg. They get a cabin up there every year." Iylah was sitting on the bed in her underwear, reading a text.

"You didn't want to go? Or they just didn't invite you?"

"No, I normally go. I love it up there," Iylah replied. "But I um . . ." She typed out a message and hit send, flashing a devious grin to Erica as she bit her bottom lip.

"What?"

"Jeremy called me last weekend and asked if I'd be home—"

"Oh my gosh," Erica cut in. "Are you serious right now?"

Iylah put her hands over her head and dropped back onto the bed in embarrassment. "I know!"

"*Jeremy* Jeremy? Like, Katie's Jeremy?"

"Yes . . ." Iylah said. "To be fair, they broke up."

"Like a week ago. Does Katie know?"

"Noooo!" Iylah replied, almost laughing. "She'd be pissed."

Erica's eyes squinted. "And you don't see a problem with that last statement?"

Iylah sat up, shoving her hands underneath her legs. "I didn't say I was gonna do anything. I just said he was home," Iylah replied.

"Mmm hmm," Erica hummed. "You're an idiot."

"Whatever. I probably won't even end up seeing him," Iylah said. Her phone chirped and she reached for it instantaneously.

"You have any coffee?" Erica asked, putting her hair up into a ponytail.

"Yeah. There's a Keurig downstairs."

"You want me to make you one?" Erica asked. Iylah muttered "uh huh" while typing. "You plan on coming down any time soon or you just gonna talk with Jeremy all night?"

Iylah stuck out her tongue and her middle finger.

"Alright. I'm goin' down." Erica left the room. "Try to hurry it up will ya?" She called from the stairs.

Iylah threw on a pair of light blue pajama pants and a tank top. It took a while because she kept going back and forth on her phone trying to figure out a response to send to Jeremy after he texted her, asking if she wanted to meet up. Erica's irritation weighed on her conscience. She knew that her friend Katie would most certainly not be okay with it and that there would be no way to explain it if word ever got out to her. After several minutes of typing out a response, correcting it, deleting it, re-typing and re-wording, she finally clicked her tongue, opting to simply leave him on read for now. "You're making this way too complicated," she said to herself. Iylah cut off her light and closed the door.

The second floor was a large loft with an open view of the main floor below. Erica was sitting on the living room floor, leaning up against the coffee table, typing something on her phone. She looked up, registering that Iylah was coming down the stairs. "Gosh! How is your hair still perfectly straight? Mine started frizzing up as soon as we started dancing," Erica said.

"Magic," Iylah replied, switching her phone to silent so she would stop looking at it.

"You get cold?" Erica asked.

"What?"

"You took your shorts off," Erica replied, typing something into her phone.

"Shorts?" Iylah mumbled to herself, examining her legs.

Erica examined her for a brief moment before returning to her screen. "Didn't wanna look like the rest of us ponytailed peasants, huh?"

"What are you talking about?" Iylah said with a laugh.

"Nothing." Erica scooted a mug of coffee across the table. "This is yours."

Iylah noticed the milky color. "Did you put stuff in it?"

"Just Baileys and Jameson."

Iylah was impressed. She wasn't even sure *she* knew where her parents kept the Jameson. She walked to the refrigerator to get some carrots and humus. "You talkin' to that guy from tonight?"

"What? Oh. No. Just playin' *Words with Friends*. It's stupid. Also, super addicting."

"Did you end up giving him your number? He seemed really into you."

"I'm sure he was. He drunkenly told me Asians were his favorite because he lost his virginity to one."

"Great opener."

"Least he was honest, right?" Erica called back. "We made out while you were in the bathroom."

Iylah snapped a carrot with her teeth. "Are you serious?"

"Yeah," Erica replied. "Kind of a crazy kisser, too. Pretty sure he drooled on me. I'm over it."

Iylah shook her head. "And you give me shit . . ."

"I give you shit for messin' with other people's boyfriends."

"They're on a break," Iylah replied. Then together, the two of them shouted the line from *Friends*, "We were on a break!"

Iylah poured more Baileys into her coffee and then checked around the counter. "Where's the Jameson?"

"Oh. Sorry. I guess I put it back," Erica replied.

"Back where?"

There was a slight pause. "Where you told me it was . . . ?"

"What?" Iylah whispered to herself.

Erica got up and came into the kitchen. "Did I not put it back?" She opened the cabinets above the microwave. "Yeah. Right here."

Iylah stood perplexed, studying the bottle. Erica began adding some of the liquid to her mug. "Hey, just out of curiosity, what did you mean when you said 'where I told you it was?' The Jameson."

Erica's eyebrows raised with an expression of awkward confusion as she screwed the cap back on. "When you came down you told me to add some of the Jameson to the coffee and said it was over the microwave." Iylah could feel herself looking perplexed. "You sure you need more to drink?"

"Erica, I've been upstairs the whole time."

Erica glanced around suspiciously. "You're saying you didn't come down and tell me to put Jameson in my coffee?"

"No," Iylah laughed. "You sure that guy didn't drug you?"

"I mean, I'm pretty sure," Erica replied. They both stood quiet for a moment.

"Are you being serious right now?" Iylah asked.

"Yes," Erica chuckled, moving back to the living room.

Iylah grabbed the bottle and went to follow her. "But how would I have told you if I didn't know—" She stopped dead in her tracks. Sitting on the floor beside where Erica had just been was a tall, black, oblong tower. At the base were four slats, one at each side of the tower. "Where did you find that?"

"What?" Erica followed Iylah's gaze down to the object. "That?"

Iylah stepped closer to it.

Erica's eyes narrowed. "You're joking, right?"

Iylah knelt to pick it up. She moved one of the slats up, and then lowered it back. It sat stable at a ninety-degree angle from the tower. "Holy crap," she said with a smile. "Blast from the past." She ran her fingers down the sides. "Where did you find this?"

Erica looked up at her strangely. "Okay, Iylah—"

"Was it sitting out?"

"How much have you had to drink?" Iylah said nothing, only

stared back transfixed. "I can't tell if you're messing with me or if you're legit going crazy."

"What? I just wanted to know where you got this from."

"Iylah! *You* brought that in here!" Erica replied in an agitated voice. "I was sitting on my phone, and you just walked up and said you found a game. Put the key in, made all those things fall . . ." Erica flicked one of the slats. "Even explained how to play it."

Iylah's smile faded. A queasy feeling churned inside. She began recalling the first time she ate edibles. She took too much, resulting in a response that she called time jumps—where her brain felt like it was skipping time. One second, she'd be sitting on a couch, and all of a sudden she was standing in another room, no recollection as to how she got there. She hated it. But even if that were the case now—even if she'd somehow blacked out upstairs—it didn't explain the box itself. It was just like the one she knew as a kid, except more refined. "You didn't find this—I mean, this wasn't just sitting out somewhere?"

"Okay. What's going on . . . ?" Erica said, standing back.

Iylah couldn't muster a response. There had to be a rational explanation. Maybe her parents did it. *That's it! They had it made, or they must have touched up the original. Wait!* "You said I brought this over here?"

"Yeah."

"You saw me bring it here?"

"Holy shit! Yes!"

"But how! I was upstairs—"

"Iylah! I saw you! I was standing at the Keurig and you were right here, holding this," Erica tapped the game. "Plus, I'm pretty sure your hair was in a ponytail, which kinda pisses me off about you. I put my hair up like that for five seconds, and it's a mess. You do it, and it's still as put together as it was before we left—"

"Did I say anything else?"

"You said it was a new game and that you wanted to try it out. And then you told me where the Jameson was." Erica pointed up toward the kitchen.

It didn't make any sense to Iylah. She started to speak calmly, cognizant now of her heart beginning to pound. "Erica. I promise you. I didn't come down here until you saw me. And I didn't bring *that*. That's my . . ." She stopped for a moment to collect herself. "I don't even know how that could've gotten here."

"Then who brought it?"

"I don't know. But it wasn't me."

"Okay, well," Erica chuckled, "I didn't dream it."

"You said I had shorts on?" Iylah asked, more of a realization than a question.

"Yeah. Like, yellow or a light orange maybe?" A sharp shiver shot up Iylah's back with such force that she nearly gasped. "What?" Erica asked, startled. "Iylah, what? You're scaring the shit out of me!"

Iylah broke eye contact and moved abruptly toward the hallway. Erica called out her name, but Iylah ignored it, disappearing around the corner. She flicked on the lights; the long hallway was covered with dozens of framed photos, meticulously placed along the walls. Iylah began inspecting them, running her finger up and down, side to side, desperately scanning over each one: family, church and beach photos, old timey pictures from Gatlinburg, Christmas group shots—the infamous one where their dog Fanny jumped up and accidentally scratched Iylah's mom in the boob just as the camera snapped.

"Iylah. What are you doing?" Erica asked, staring at her from the hall's end.

"Come on, come on, come on. Where are you?"

"Iylah—"

Iylah came to a sudden halt, dead still staring at one of the pictures. "You said yellow shorts, right? Were there black lightning bolts on 'em? Like Harry Potter-esque?"

Erica nodded. "Yeah." She moved over toward her.

Iylah tapped her long nail against the glass of the frame. "Like, this color yellow?" In the photo a girl, probably thirteen years old, was standing beside William Shatner. The expression over the girl's face was nothing less than overjoyed. She was wearing a pair of yellow shorts with two lightning bolts down the sides and a white Star Trek t-shirt.

Erica peered at it. "Yeah, that's it." She chuckled. "Gosh, how old were you?" She leaned closer. "Wait! Is that the guy from *Miss Congeniality*?" Iylah confirmed that it was. "Man, you were a little hottie back in the day," she grinned, elbowing her friend in the side. "How'd you meet him?"

"He was in Nashville for a Comic Con, but I didn't meet him. You've got the wrong twin," Iylah said softly. "That's Josephine."

6

NOW

Cole picked up the board game's key lying beside him. He placed it on his thumb and forefinger and flicked it into the air, catching it in his palm. "Any idea where it came from?" He did it again, this time fumbling it onto the floor.

"Let's just say it was left for me. And leave it at that." Iylah gently took the key from Cole's hand. "Now, before we play, there're some things you need to know. No running off on your own, that's most important. Second, we have to finish."

"Is this like that Catan game where it takes four hours to play?"

"I sure hope not," she said, maneuvering the board so one of the four slats faced them. "This is where we play." Along the black surface of the board were twenty-four fingerprint-sized indentions that went toward the tower in the middle. "We both start here at the beginning." She pointed to a light gray, glossy square at the slat's distal end. "And move whatever spaces our die says."

He pointed to the other slats around the tower. "We don't use these?"

"Nope. Just this one."

"Mmm . . . thrilling. Where are the pieces?"

"Right here." Iylah lifted up the detached box lid by the handle and turned it over to reveal a mesh pouch. She fingered at it to produce a few marbles—green, blue, and black—along with a die.

"I'll take black," Cole said.

"It's not ours, we don't use it." She put the green one back.

"Oh. Okay . . ."

Iylah shifted in her seat, unsure of how to say this next part. "There's something else." Cole raised his eyebrows in anticipation. "Stuff is going to start . . . *happening* . . . once we start."

"Stuff? Like, what kind of stuff?"

She pointed to one of the indentations on the board. "You see those little white hands on some of the spaces?"

Cole leaned closer to inspect the slat. Inside some of the indentions, with no discernable order to their placement, was an etching of a hand. Cole ran his finger over the spaces. "What are those?" He asked.

Iylah spoke this next part slower, making sure she had his full attention: "There are . . . *situations* . . . in the game. Some of them are bad; some are *really* bad."

"Ooo. Sort of like a truth or dare situation?" Cole winked.

Iylah's eyes narrowed. "No. Please, just listen." She bit her lip and shook her head. "Everything you see once we start, it's all real. Okay? You *have* to pay attention." Cole seemed to be pitying her with his eyes. "Ugh, never mind. Let's just start. You'll see what I mean." She dropped the black marble into the hole at the top of the tower.

"Wait, why'd you put it in there?" Cole asked.

"Because that's where it goes. Do you need to go to the bathroom?"

Cole gave her a quizzical look.

"It's best if we don't separate once we start. If you have to go, I'd go now."

"Otherwise, we'd have to go together?" Cole asked with a devious smile.

Iylah's face scrunched. "Gross."

"I think I'll be fine," Cole replied. "How do we start?"

She went to hand the blue marble to Cole but drew her hand back sharply. "Don't forget. You have to do *exactly* as I say, okay?" She paused.

"Psh. So, let you win? Where's your marble?"

"This is our marble. We're not playing against each other; we're a team."

"What? Are you serious? Then what's the point? How do you win?"

"We win when we place our marble in the box and pull it out along with the black one. Sort of like a rescue game."

"That's it?" Cole asked, disappointed. "Sounds a little amateurish. There's no challenges, or anything? Something to make it a little harder?"

Iylah averted her eyes toward the tower. "My sister. She's who we're playing against."

"Your sister?" Cole asked, perplexed. "Is she coming over?"

Iylah's eyes were fixated on the daphne blue marble rolling between her fingers. "You said you met *me* at the door when I got here?"

Cole gave an audible affirmation.

"Yeah, well, that wasn't me. That was my sister. Josephine."

Cole's brow wrinkled.

"Looked a lot like me, didn't she?" He nodded again. "She was my twin. And she died three years ago."

"Wait. What?" After a long pause, Cole let out a laugh. "Screw off." He continued looking at her, perhaps to see if she'd break. "You're being serious right now?"

"Yeah." Iylah could see Cole biting back a clever comment. "Like I told you, you don't have to believe me. You're gonna see it soon."

"So, you've played before?"

"This version? Yes. Twice—well, once. The other time we didn't get to start."

"That was with Shelby?" Cole asked.

Iylah nodded.

"What do you mean, *this version*?" Cole asked. "There's more than one?"

"My sister used to make games. Board games mostly. She loved 'em. She made something similar to this when we were little. It was for a class project."

"What happened to her?" Cole asked. "Your sister, not Shelby."

"It doesn't matter," Iylah replied quickly, almost anticipating the question. "Look, I'll try to explain what I have to as we go." She handed him the marble and Cole sat quietly, staring at it. "We need to start."

"You're telling me your dead sister rang our doorbell and had a conversation with me outside?"

"It wasn't me."

"You think maybe because I invited her in, that's why she's here?"

"No. That's vampires."

"Oh . . . vampires. Of course." Cole rolled his eyes and placed the marble on the glossy gray *start* square. There was an immediate disturbance upstairs; a thunderous boom rattled across the ceiling.

Cole jumped and cursed. "What the hell was that?"

Iylah wasn't as fazed by the disruption. "Come on. You need to roll."

Cole backed up, studying the ceiling as if looking for a spider. "Did you not hear that?"

"I did. That's what I've been trying to tell you. It's the game."

Cole ignored her and backed up toward the foyer. "I need to go check something."

"Wait, wait. Where are you going?" Iylah shot back.

"I just need to go upstairs and make sure something didn't break. That sounded like it was in my parents' room."

"Cole," Iylah said as he quickly walked away toward the stairs. "You have to roll."

"Fine!" He snatched the die and threw it onto the table. There, *three*—"

The surface of the starting square at once glowed with a dim, silvery hue. "Whoa." Half of Cole's mouth perked up. "I didn't realize that was a light." He moved the marble three spaces and darted off. "I'll be right back, okay?" Iylah shot out of her chair and called for him, but he yelled back for her to quit freaking out. No way she was letting this happen again. She followed him to the stairs and stopped, remembering that the marble landed on a marked space. It made her uneasy to think about having to reach in there by herself but maybe she should before anything happened. Cole's bedroom door closed above her.

"It was the one thing I said," she complained to herself. "Don't run off."

Two Years Ago

Erica Lang

Part II

*E*rica took in the features of the girl in the photo. She clicked her tongue against the top of her mouth. "Man, you guys really did look alike."

"Yeah," Iylah said almost inaudibly. "Twins."

"Okay . . ." Erica said back. She waited for Iylah to say something more. "So . . . what?"

"Erica!" She said, as if Erica should already know the answer. "The ponytail? The shorts? That wasn't me!" Iylah moved past her, toward the living room. "We don't even have those shorts anymore."

"So, what are you saying?" Erica asked, following. "Jo came in here and told me to make a drink? Explained how to play a board game?" Iylah tried to say something but was cut off. "You're saying I just had a full-on conversation with a ghost?"

"Well, it wasn't with me," Iylah said, squatting to examine the board more closely. "She told you how to play it?"

"Yes. *She* did." Erica held up finger quotes for sarcastic emphasis. Iylah took a seat on the couch and shifted the board over to her. "So, we're just gonna keep this going? The whole Josephine thing?" No reply. Erica shrugged and took a seat. "Fine." She explained everything she had been told about the game: that it was co-op, and the two of them would work against the game—she wasn't exactly sure what that meant in terms of how the game would play against them. She explained that they would swap out their actions; the one who rolled couldn't be the one who reached in the box.

"We have to reach in? What's in there?" Iylah asked.

Erica gave her an unusual look. "I don't know. *They* didn't say." Erica winked. "But we only reach in if we land here—on any of these." She pointed to the hand images inside the indentions. Erica picked up the blue marble and black marble that were sitting motionless on the carpet. "This one is ours, and this one goes inside. Said the black one has to go in before the game starts."

"Why?" Iylah asked.

"Supposedly, getting it out is how you win. We start here, roll the die, move up the slat, and once we get to the end, put our marble in the hole and then pull them both out. Something about a rescue mission."

A dreadful wave washed over Iylah. *Oh my God*, she thought. Her face must have shown distress because Erica asked if she was okay. "Yeah," Iylah said in a whisper, nodding. *Get it together, Iylah. Come on!*

"You wanna go first?" She handed her the die and blue marble.

Iylah took them delicately in her hand. "This is crazy," she said softly, looking at Erica. "I've seen this game before."

"You don't say?" Erica said back with playful sarcasm. Iylah tried to say she was serious, but Erica cut in, "We're also not supposed to cheat. Apparently, the game will know." Erica waved up jazz hands as Iylah studied the layout of the board and counted the spaces from start to finish.

"Do we have to work our way back?" Iylah asked. "Or do we win when we put our marble inside the box?"

"I think that's it," Erica said, with a shrug. "It's supposed to light up if we finish, so I'm sure we'll know. That should be entertaining." She reached her hand over the hole and dropped the black marble inside.

"Wait!" Iylah exclaimed. "What are you doing?"

"I thought we were gonna play," Erica replied. Iylah brought her knees to her chest, hugging them. The clock on the wall said 1:02 a.m. "Oh, come on. We got nothin' to get up for tomorrow. Let's play. Did I miss anything? Any special rules you forgot to tell me?"

Iylah's eyes communicated nothing short of annoyance. "It wasn't me." Erica smirked. "Whatever." The die felt heavy in her hand as she eyed it.

"You good?" Erica asked.

"I guess . . ." She dropped the die onto the coffee table. **Six**. The square under the marble glowed silver. "How did it do that?" Iylah lifted up the slat to investigate underneath, then scratched at the surface. It faded back to its original dark gray color within seconds. She knocked on it. "Weird."

"Good start, though," Erica said.

Iylah picked up the blue marble and moved it six spaces up into the appropriate hole, one marked by a hand. "Okay, so, we have to reach in now, right?" Iylah asked.

"Yeah," Erica replied. "Well, I do. You rolled, so it switches."

Erica raised her hand up. "What'd you put in there?" She grinned.

"Oh my God—"

Erica laughed. "I'm kidding. I'm kidding." She peeked in the hole. "Kind of." Her hand hovered over the hole for several seconds. "I'm kinda scared to reach in. Is that weird?"

"Would you hurry up?" Iylah exclaimed. She had not intended for her voice to sound so agitated, but everything about this was making her very uneasy.

"Calm your tits, I'm goin'," Erica said back. She lowered her hand inside and paused. The look on her face became confused. "Hunh."

"What? What is it?" Iylah asked.

"I don't know. It feels like a . . ." She slowly pulled her arm out of the hole. "Oh. Not what I thought. A party popper?" Iylah cursed to herself, watching Erica handle it with care. "Weird." She tried to hand it to Iylah, who promptly sat back as if the item were poisonous. "What is your deal?"

"Did you do this?" Iylah spoke nervously. "I'm serious, is this yours?"

"Iylah." Erica laughed. "Holy shit! What is going on? One minute you're excited for us to play it, and the next, you act like you're about to start crying. Is this part of the game?"

"This isn't my game!" Iylah said back sharply. "Okay? I never said I wanted to play it. That wasn't me!"

Erica's smile slowly faded. "You really believe I talked to Jo?"

"I don't know! Maybe I blacked out or something. Honestly, it's really starting to freak me out that maybe I did come down here, and I just don't remember."

"Okay, okay, okay," Erica said, putting her hands up in peace. Iylah could feel her breathing start to pick up. "It's fine. Let's say we call it quits, and uh . . ." Erica picked up her phone to check the time. "We'll play something else. Or, we can just chill and watch *Parks and Rec*—" She stopped abruptly, looking curiously at her screen. She started typing on it and swiping at the screen. "Hunh."

"What?"

"My internet's down." She swiped and tapped a few more times. "Yeah. Nothing."

Iylah picked up her phone. "Looks like mine is too." Both of them sat trying to troubleshoot their devices. Erica asked for the Wi-Fi but there were no options in range to choose from.

"That's odd," Iylah said back softly, restarting her phone.

"Maybe a cell tower is down."

Iylah went to the kitchen where a house phone hung on the wall. She picked up the receiver and held it to her ear. Nothing. She tapped the switch hook a few times, trying to restart it, but the line was dead. The cordless phone in the dining room offered nothing different. "The house phones aren't working either," she called.

"Okay," Erica said. "Well, maybe there are a *few* cell towers down." Iylah reentered and started up the stairs to the loft. "What are you doing?" Erica asked, following her.

"We have two wi-fis. At least we used to. The other is my mom's private one for work when she has to teach online." She began rummaging around the floor and knelt beside her mom's work desk. "Got it! Ugh." Iylah paused. "It's blinking red. No service." She stood up and sighed. "That's nuts. Why would everything just go off?"

Erica's gaze was beyond Iylah's shoulder. She nodded in the direction of her stare. "Is that Jo's room?" Iylah turned to see the door standing wide open and was caught for a moment in surprise. She was sure that door was closed when she went down earlier. Erica noticed the hesitation. "You good?"

"Yeah, I just . . ." Iylah walked wearily over to it. The room was dark except for the light from the loft's ceiling fan streaming in. The instant Iylah could make out that the room remained untouched since her sister's death, she grabbed the knob and went to close it. "It's just . . . I don't like to look in there." She began to shut the door, but something blocked it from closing. In its way was a bright pink shirt laying on the floor, half hanging out of the room. Iylah knelt, taking the shirt into her hand. "No way . . ."

"What is that?" Erica asked.

Iylah unfolded it, letting it hang in front of her to admire. "We um . . ." The front read *Maddox 12* in sparkly letters. "I haven't seen this in forever." She sensed Erica coming up beside her. "We made these—well, *she* made these—for our twelfth birthday party. I haven't seen them in . . ." She stopped. A memory emerged into her mind, one she'd rather not think about. She shook her head and folded the shirt, throwing it back on the floor inside Jo's room. She closed the door and headed for the stairs. "I was just surprised to see it."

Erica went to open the door once again. When it clicked, Iylah spun around. "No!" Erica froze. "Please . . . it's really hard to look in there, okay?"

"I didn't say you had to," Erica chuckled nervously. "I just wanted to see—"

"Erica, stop!" Iylah called out. Erica stiffened, shocked by the noise. Iylah felt a sudden cold and piercing sensation in her arm. She had folded her arms so tight against her chest that her long blue nails were digging into her skin. "Look," she continued, trying to appear calm. "We haven't changed it since she died, okay?" Iylah pleaded. "It's just . . . weird."

"Okay." Erica shut the door and threw up her hands. "I won't open it." She followed Iylah back down to the living room, reaching into her pocket to check her phone. "I really don't get this," Erica said, tossing her phone on the coffee table. "Maybe there's a storm somewhere." Iylah was standing at the other end of the room looking on, rigid and hunched with her arms folded. "Are you cold?"

"Let's put this away, okay?" Iylah said. She walked anxiously over and knelt beside the board to pry up the marble from its space. It wouldn't budge. Erica watched her for a moment before ridiculing her. "It's not me," Iylah shot back. "It's stuck in there."

Erica bent forward and tried to pick it up with the same result. She flipped it upside down and shook it. The piece didn't move. "Probably stuck to the paint or something. Just leave it. Get me the key." Erica lifted up the other three slats to their original position. The one with the marble wouldn't go fully back into place for the top lid to secure them. "Whatever." She let go of them, each slat falling with a loud crash back to the table.

"Don't forget the die," Iylah said, sliding it toward her. "Just throw it in there."

Erica held open the mesh pouch on the lid and scooped the die but immediately made a noise of disgust, letting it slip through her fingers. It bounced off the coffee table and onto the floor. "Uwgh! Gross."

"What?"

Erica ran a hand down the front of her shirt. "It's wet."

"What is?"

"The die. Like, really wet." She rubbed her fingers together, her face going sour. "Almost like, goopey."

Iylah picked it up. "It's not wet."

"What is *this* then?" Erica said, displaying the mucusy strands stretching between her thumb and forefinger.

"Feel it. It's not wet," Iylah said. "You must have put your hand on the table or something."

Erica scanned the surface. "In what?" She poked the die with her dry finger. "I swear it was slimy. That's why I dropped it."

Iylah ignored her, holding the die carefully in her palm and then placing it gently on the table as if it were a delicate gem. Iylah's stomach felt as if she were in a free fall and her mind was racing through a hundred memories a minute. The rational explanation was the alcohol, no sleep, excitement over Jeremy.

And of course, talking about Jo. No wonder she felt sick, she still couldn't bring herself to walk into Jo's room for God's sake. Jo must've worked on finishing the game while she was away at school. That's it! Her parents had it sitting out upstairs, and she must've blacked out and brought it down.

As much as she wanted to believe that faulty logic, the dread in her mind confirmed otherwise. Her twin sister had been here; talked with Erica; brought out this game. It wasn't the actual game Jo made for school. Jo couldn't have installed a lock mechanism, or lights inside the board, or even made the carvings along the sides. But it was eerily close. And Erica couldn't have known—let alone guessed—about those yellow shorts with lightning bolts. The thought of her sister being back in this house terrified her, but not as much as wondering why she was here. Her mouth had suddenly gone dry as she eyed the game. *Maybe the die really was wet. If it wasn't wet, Erica would have put the game away.* Erica went to take the die, but Iylah reached out, pushing the hand away.

Erica went still. "What's wrong?"

She doesn't want us to put it away. "Try and move the marble now," Iylah said.

Erica reached over and pinched the marble with her finger. It moved effortlessly out of its place. She held it for a moment, then looked at Iylah with unease. "Fuck off," Erica breathed. "How'd you do that?"

Iylah swallowed. "*You* did. You rolled a **six**."

"I didn't roll that," Erica said. "It fell out of my hand."

Iylah counted out six spaces before taking the marble cautiously from her friend's hand and setting it inside its new space. "I don't think it works that way."

"You don't think it works what way?" Erica asked.

Iylah's knee was starting to tremor as she stood there, hugging herself, trying to form her thoughts. All she wanted to do was leave. Go back to Nashville, wake up and not have to think about any of this. Something compelled Iylah to look up to the loft. That's when she saw it; fear all but paralyzing her. "I think . . ." Iylah began. "I think something wants us to play this game." Erica followed Iylah's gaze up to the loft. Jo's bedroom door was standing wide open. "And I don't think we have a choice."

7

NOW

Cole slid the latch on his door and opened it. A cloud of smoke hovered near the ceiling. "Are you crazy!" He waved his hands to clear the air. "I can smell that stuff out here."

Sherry Martin was sitting on Cole's bed wearing an extra-large Murray State University hoodie, the hood scrunched in tight over her face. She was typing on her laptop and pulled out her earbuds to ask what he said. Cole repeated himself. "You can smell that?" She asked. "I opened the window." Sherry straightened up and rifled through her sweater pocket to pull out a lighter. She lit the candle beside her. "Sorry 'bout that."

"Thought you quit smoking," Cole said.

"I did. Last week," she replied, narrowing her focus toward the screen. "Yearbook stuff is stressing me out. How's the babysitter?"

"Super weird. She's making me play a board game with her. Actually, she's *paying* me to play a board game with her, like two hundred dollars."

"Why is she paying you two hundred dollars to play a board game?" Sherry asked.

Cole's eyes bugged as his shoulders shrugged. "She's lonely?"

Sherry scrunched her eyebrows. "Seems suspicious."

"Oh, it's definitely suspicious but I'm not passing up easy money."

"How long you gonna be?"

"I don't know." Cole peeked his head out the door then

closed it again. "Hopefully not long. Hey, try not to drop anything else, okay? I don't want her telling my mom someone was here."

"I didn't drop anything," Sherry said. "I've *literally* been lying here since you left."

Iylah's voice called out from downstairs followed by the sound of footsteps coming up the staircase.

"Ooo!" Sherry said, pulling off her hood and giving animated eyes. "She misses you already."

"Shhh!" Cole hissed. He leaned his ear onto the door and waited to see if she came toward his room. "Pretty sure she's a little nuts," Cole whispered. "On the upside though, since I'm playing, she said she'd leave early tonight. Thinkin' about inviting some people over. Wha'd'ya think?"

"Yeah, sounds great." She paused and started typing. "You gonna invite Jared?"

"Of course. Why wouldn't I?"

"You think it's a good idea?"

"I mean, it'd be a little dickish if I didn't. Right?" Cole said. "No pun intended." Sherry didn't smile at his attempt toward humor. He cleared his throat. "I doubt he'll come."

"Well, if you invite him, I probably shouldn't be here . . ."

"What? No. That's dumb." Cole waved his hand at her. "I'll figure it out—"

"Wait. What just happened?" She clicked a few keys. "You've gotta be kidding me."

Cole was about to ask "what?" but Iylah's voice from the hallway cut him off, calling his name. He tensed and held up a finger for her to hush.

She mouthed, "Your internet went out." She typed something out and scanned the screen before flipping her laptop around. "Your wi-fi isn't showing up."

"I'll check it out," he whispered, and put a finger to his lip. "No smoking. Or moving."

She flashed a thumbs up as Cole quickly slipped out, careful not to reveal Sherry. "Iylah—" He tensed, giving an audible gasp. Iylah was standing at the other end of the dark hallway. "Shit!—I mean . . . sorry." He whistled and laughed. "You scared me." She didn't reply; only stared back. "What are you doing?" He walked toward her. "I didn't mean to leave you hangin'. I thought I heard something break up here and wanted to—"

"Cole!" Iylah called from the bottom of the stairs. Cole sucked in a breath and jumped back, hissing another curse word. He looked down and saw Iylah standing with her hands on the rails, staring at him. "Who are you talking to?"

"Um . . ." Cole moved his head back toward where he had just seen someone standing. "What?" He whispered to himself. His hand snapped up to flick on the light. No one was there, and his parents' door was open.

"Cole! Who were you talking to?" Iylah asked, sounding more concerned.

"No freakin' way," he said.

Cole moved toward his parents' room at the end of the hall, and before he could take two steps, the door began inching shut. He stopped and felt his skin go cold.

"Cole!" Iylah said, now behind him. "What? What did you see?"

He shook his head and blew out a breath. "Man, I don't know. I thought I was talking to you. But one second, you're here," he pointed up toward his parents' room, "and then I hear *you* call me, and whatever I saw over *there* is gone." He forced a chuckle and started down the stairs. "I'm losin' it."

He took a seat at the dining room table again. "I'm kinda

hungry now. You still up for making that chicken?" Iylah didn't reply. She was still looking up the steps. He said her name again.

"I think it's best if we don't go upstairs anymore," she said, her face one of grave concern.

"Why not?" Cole asked.

"Because you're not losing it," she answered, returning to the table. "There *is* someone else here."

"Excuse me?"

"Trust me. You can't go back upstairs by yourself—I wouldn't go up there at all."

He pulled out his phone. "Then I'm calling the cops." He had dialed 911 and brought the phone to his ear before she could even get a word in.

"You can't," she said back. "The phones—"

"Seriously?" He asked. "There's no service . . ." He got to his feet and moved toward the kitchen.

Iylah scrambled to her feet to follow him. "Cole. You can't call the cops!"

"Is someone really here?" Cole asked, agitated. "Like, for real?" Iylah couldn't speak; she stood with her mouth agape. "Is someone here?" He yelled.

"I—Yes. Maybe . . ." she replied.

He spun on his heel and continued walking. He picked up the cordless house phone on the wall. "Then if someone's in the house, I'm calling the cops." Cole typed in a series of beeps and lifted the phone to his ear to wait for the other end to pick up as she said, once again, he couldn't call anyone. There was no ringing. There was nothing. "Holy crap!" He checked the screen which was lit up with the numbers he dialed. He clicked it off and back on. No dial tone. "The phone's dead."

"That's what I'm trying to tell you! We don't have phones right now."

"Did the power go out?" Cole asked. "Where's your cell phone?"

In a flash, Iylah stripped the phone from Cole's hand, throwing it against the wall. The battery pack popped off and shot across the floor. The sudden outburst shocked him into silence and rigidity. Iylah was now in his face, standing a hair taller than him. She spoke slowly, nearly a whisper: "The Phones. Don't. Work. Okay?" He nodded his head and swallowed. "I need you to pay attention now and take a deep breath." He did. "Good. Now," she pulled out her cell phone and tapped the screen. "As I said, you can't call anyone. See? No bars. No service. The *game* has turned everything off."

Cole stumbled over his words before he finally got out, "Okay, so, now what?"

"You said you thought you were talking to me up there?"

"I mean, I thought I was . . ."

"Yeah, well, you didn't *imagine* it. That was *her*. My sister."

"Yeah," Cole said. "I stopped believing in ghosts when I was like ten."

"Would you like to go back upstairs and take a look for yourself?" Iylah asked.

Cole froze, bent over to pick up the phone off the floor. He straightened, looking uneasily from Iylah toward the foyer. "How do you know it's her?"

"Well, one, because I never went upstairs. Two," Iylah sighed, "I've played this before."

8

NOW

The colorful object in Iylah's hand got Cole's attention when he finally sat down at the dining room table. "What is that?"

"A party popper. It was in the game. We landed on one of the hand spaces, and I reached in after you went upstairs."

"What do we do with it?"

Iylah handed it over for him to see. "I don't know. All these spaces," she began, pointing at the hand-marked indentions, "mean that something is going to come out—or happen, I guess. So, I *think* whatever you pull out is supposed to help you. I'm still a little unsure about that part."

"How is *this* supposed to help us?"

Iylah shrugged. "I never figured that one out. It came out first last time too." She took it back and then shoved it into her pocket. "I never used it."

"So, all we're trying to do is get to the end?"

"Before she gets us, yeah."

"How does she *get* us?"

Iylah shook her head, staring at the gameboard, lost in her own thoughts. "I don't know," she confessed. "But I promise, I'm not gonna let anything happen to you, okay? We're not gonna lose."

Cole nodded, appearing in a daze. "How do we lose?"

"It's a co-op game, so, it's us against the game. We lose if we don't win."

He reached a finger toward the tower's top. "Alright. Marble in the hole, game's over."

"The lights," Iylah said with a snap, as if just remembering a dream. "At the end, we have to put our hands on the spots that light up. That's when we finish it. And we both have to be there for it, so," she grabbed his hand, "stay together. Okay?"

"You said that popper came out first last time. Maybe it'll be the same. What sort of things happened when you played before?"

She released him from her grip, still holding his eyes. A dull discomfort flashed in her stomach; an echo of that night. "You *really* don't wanna know." The concern over Cole's face told Iylah that even if she hadn't fully convinced him, he seemed worried enough to at least give it a go.

"What was next—" A knock rapped against the front door, startling the both of them. Cole jumped from his chair, readying himself, as Iylah let out a mouse-like yelp. Cole looked back at her, and then the door. "Is that her?"

Iylah stood up, moving warily toward the door, hushing him. The porch lights had come on, highlighting the silhouette of a tall figure in the door's tempered glass. "Are you expecting anyone?"

"No . . ." Cole followed behind her. The two of them stood still in the foyer, Iylah's hand on the door, unsure what to do—

"Bro, I can see you standing there," a voice from the other side called. Iylah drew her arm back.

"Jared?" Cole said. He opened the door.

"Yeah—oh! My bad." He looked from Cole to Iylah, back to Cole. "I didn't realize you had company. I can come back." He stepped back, waving his arms in apology. The boy looked like he was easily on his way out of college. His tan arms bulged out of the black Murray High Tigers baseball uniform which was partly unbuttoned to highlight a chest that had no business being on a high schooler. Iylah noticed his cleats had left a trail of dirt clods up the walkway from his car. Around his neck was a silver chain with a sort-of curved, guitar pick shaped pendant.

"No, it's fine, come in," Cole said.

Iylah's head turned in surprise. "Wha—no, wait!" She blurted out. She slid into the doorway, blocking Jared from entering. "I mean, sorry, but your mom. She told me you couldn't have anyone over."

"It's fine," Cole said, giving a nervous laugh. Iylah could see the embarrassed glare he was giving her. "He won't be here long." His wide, direct eyes were definitely saying, *move!*

"I just came to pick up something. You got my *Star Trek: Into Darkness* DVD right?" He asked Cole. "I was gonna watch it with—" Jared stopped, his eyes bouncing between the two of them as if he wasn't sure what to say. "I was gonna watch it with my *brother*. He hasn't seen it yet. We were gonna watch it tonight."

Cole and Jared had been friends since they were in kindergarten, which made Jared's cryptic attempt almost laughable. Cole bit back a grin. "Yeah, yeah, come on, I'll grab it." Jared stomped his feet on the porch and stepped inside, immediately removing his shoes. "You want something to drink? Soda, or something?"

"You still got ginger ale?" Jared asked.

"Always," Cole said, cutting through the reading nook and into the kitchen. Jared followed.

"Cole. We have to—" Iylah cut herself off with a growl when she realized he wasn't listening. She instead went around to the dining room and picked up her phone. Still dead. A soda can popped and she entered to see him pouring Jared a drink over ice. "Hey! Sorry to be a killjoy, but he has to leave. Like, right now!"

"What are you doing?" Cole griped. "He's just getting a DVD."

"Actually," Jared said, taking a sip. "It's a bit more than that. Kinda wanted to talk about what happened." He looked at Iylah. "In private, if that's okay. It's about Sherry," Jared said. "I kinda just wanna clear the air. At least between me and you."

"Have you talked to her?" Cole asked.

He shook his head with a face that read, *why would I talk to her?* Iylah was about to speak again but Jared noticed her and spoke instead: "Maybe we can go outside . . . ? Is that cool? That way I'm not technically in the house." He opened his hands to Iylah, looking for grace.

"Look, you really can't be here right now. I know it sounds stupid, and I wish that I could be the cool babysitter but—"

"Babysitter? Bro, for real?" Cole tried to interject that she wasn't a babysitter, but he cut him off. "Where're your parents at?"

Cole sighed, obviously irritated at Iylah. "They're on some trip for their anniversary—"

"Cole!" Iylah called, threateningly, holding up her phone. "Either he leaves, or I call your mom."

"Oh my Gosh!" Cole's hands flew up, pressing against the sides of his head. "Can you just stop, for like two seconds?" He turned to Jared. "Let's go outside."

Iylah cut in front of them. "Okay. What are you not hearing? Do you want me to call your parents? He can't be here!" She was really emphasizing her words, hoping he could read her mind, and tilting her head just slightly toward the living room where the gameboard still lay.

"That's why we're going outside," he said back, just as slow, as if she was deaf. "And you can't call my parents, genius, remember? The phones are out."

Iylah sank forward, having now lost her only leverage. They exited through the French doors, walking back toward the front door.

"Why're your phones out?" She heard him ask.

"We don't know. She thinks it's part of some game—"

"Hey!" She cut in. "Don't."

"Game?" Jared asked. "What kind of game?"

"It's a board game she has. Supposedly it's haunted." She could see he was trying to act cool now, despite his previous worry.

"What?!" Jared exclaimed. "Lemme see. Where's it at?" Iylah called Cole's name again, but he ignored her, leading Jared through the hallway past the guestroom, into the dining room. At the end of her patience, she stormed around the island in the kitchen toward the other set of French doors, and into the dining room. Jared was about to reach and pick up the die when she snatched his wrist.

"Get out. Now." She saw him wince at her grip and then quickly try to hide it. Cole called her name now, attempting to step in, but she shot him a look. *Back off.* Then to Jared, "I was told to not let anyone in this house, and I'm not losing out on making money so you two can discuss your bullshit high school drama. Get your ginger ale and go. You can talk tomorrow when I leave." Iylah could feel her grip starting to shake. Jared's wrist felt like the size of her calf. She let up, but not on her stare.

Jared was noticeably shaken as he stepped back. "Okay, alright, calm down. I'm goin'. My bad. I wasn't tryin' to be rude—"

"It's fine. Please, just go," Iylah said.

He nodded at Cole. "Call ya tomorrow?" Jared started down the hallway to the front door.

She could hear the disappointment in Cole's "yeah."

"Alright. I'll hit you up." He bent to grab his shoes and nodded toward Iylah. "Try not to piss her off." He chuckled to himself and closed the door.

Iylah turned to Cole. She could see the utter humiliation over his face. "I know that was a bitch thing to do, but it's too dangerous for him to be here."

"Whatever," he huffed, plopping down onto a chair. "God, I'll be glad when you leave."

"That makes two of us," Iylah muttered, picking up the die. "I'll go this time. You reach in the box." There was no pause for discussion. Iylah dropped the die onto the table. Six.

Cole looked on with lazy eyes. "Well, I guess that's good." He counted six indentions up. There was no hand. "Even better." No enthusiasm. He reached down to pick up the blue marble, but it wouldn't move. He straightened, regripped, and tried again. "It's stuck." Iylah attempted while Cole grabbed a bottle opener from the hutch and began trying to pry it up with no success. "Alright, so, what now? Is it broken?"

"No . . ." Iylah said quietly, studying the box. Then she cursed under her breath, dropping her head in her hands. "Oh no . . ."

"What?" There was a knock at the door. Cole whipped around. He could see it was Jared's silhouette. "I got it. Probably wants another ginger ale."

Iylah sat frozen as she stared at the black tower of the board. "He's gonna have to play," she whispered to herself.

Footsteps walked toward them. "Hey, Iylah?" Cole said. "He says his tire popped. We're gonna change it real quick, okay?"

"You can't," she said dazedly, sitting back in her chair to look at them. "He has to play." Cole either didn't hear or understand her because he asked her to repeat it. She stood. "Jerry?" She called.

"Jared," Cole said back, sharply.

"Jared! Can you come here for a sec?"

"Yo, it's not a big deal," he called from the doorway. "I'll just have my dad call AAA—"

"Please," Iylah cut in. "Can you just come back here for a second?" She heard him walk back, still in his socks. She handed him the die and looked at Cole. "He has to play. It's why the marble won't move." She fished out another marble from the mesh bag: orange. "It's why I didn't want him coming in."

"What's goin' on?" Jared asked.

"Can you roll that please?"

"I don't think board games are his thing," Cole said.

"And I don't think he has much of a choice," she replied, placing the marble on the start space of a different slat. "Go ahead." There was a distinct *crackle* in the walls and ceiling, as if the house were settling or experiencing high winds from outside. Cole was the only one who seemed to notice.

Jared's eyes danced suspiciously between them, trying not to smile. "Sure . . ." He let the die fall on the table. *Five*. "Okay. Anything else?" The starting square produced a faint glow. "Whoa. That's cool. How'd you do that?"

"Move that piece up five." Iylah said, pointing to the marble, as Cole watched.

"Oookay." Jared, with ease, popped the marble up from its hole and moved it five places into a marked space.

"Now, try to move ours," Iylah said to Cole. It remained stuck. He rolled the die, just in case, coming up with a four. The marble wasn't budging.

"There, see?" Cole said, stepping back. "It's not him. Obviously, it's just stuck in—

"Wait," She stopped him. "He landed on a hand. He has to reach in before we go."

"Reach in where? In there?" Jared pointed to the hole. "What's in there?"

"We don't know," Iylah said. "That's the point."

Jared looked on the verge of laughter, but he shrugged it off and reached in without hesitation. "It's empty."

"What?" Iylah said. She picked up the board and gave it a light shake. Nothing.

"What's supposed to happen?" Jared asked.

Iylah's shoulders fell in surrender as she put the game back on the table. She sat down in the chair and let out a sigh that became a helpless laugh.

"There's supposed to be something in there," Cole replied, making air quotes, and moving his eyes over Iylah as if she were crazy.

"You alright?" Jared asked her.

Iylah shook her head, massaging her temples. "I don't know what to do. It let you role—but why can't you pull anything out?"

"How would she know someone else was here?" Cole asked.

"I told you," Iylah said. "it's *her* game. She knows! She's who you saw at the door—she's who you saw upstairs. She knows you're here, know he's here! We all have to play!" Iylah's head fell back in exasperation. "I just don't know what we're supposed to do. We can't roll, we can't move—"

"Who are y'all talkin' about?" Jared asked.

"Oh man . . ." Cole sighed, leaning onto the table with both hands, his head shaking.

"What?" Iylah asked.

"There have to be *two* players. You said it yourself. One has to roll, the other has to draw."

"Yeah. But we don't have another player," Iylah said.

Cole looked at Jared, and then turned around toward the foyer. "That's not entirely true."

9

NOW

The moment Sherry appeared on the stairs, Iylah felt suddenly closed in, as if the air had turned murky. Her therapist loved to talk about human energy—Iylah's especially—believing that he could read one's disposition just by them walking into the room. Months ago, she would almost cringe with skepticism whenever he spoke like that. Recently, however, as her parents began to struggle with financial changes and the move, she was starting to sense what Dr. Boyd had been talking about. The energy in the room had at once become dark—troubling, almost. She could practically feel Jared tensing beside her at the sight of this girl.

"This is Sherry Martin," Cole said. Iylah was speechless, biting back the frustration that someone else was now a part of this. "Sorry. She was upstairs working on homework when you came over. She wasn't gonna stay long, but then we started playing and—"

"What are you doing here?" Jared asked.

"We were working on the yearbook," Sherry said back meekly.

Jared watched her for a long moment and then made for the door. "Screw it. I'm out—thanks for telling me she was here, by the way," he yelled back.

"Dude, I tried—"

Jared spun around. "You tried?! When was that? When you invited me in for a ginger ale, or when you offered to help me change my tire?"

"Hey . . ." Iylah spoke.

"What was I supposed to say?" Cole replied. "I'm not the one mad at her."

"You would be if you really understood what she did—"

"Hey!" Iylah yelled. "Stop!" They all looked at her in surprise, likely forgetting she was there. "I need all of you to come in the dining room." Her voice was full, stern.

"Yeah, no thanks," Jared said back, getting ready to open the door.

"She won't let you leave!" Iylah called out. That stopped him. "I promise it's not only your tire. You fix that, she'll just disable your car—probably already has." Jared faced her, puzzled; looking almost like Iylah was the one responsible. "Trust me. You're stuck here."

Jared took this in, eyeing the three of them, and finally said, "Did you mess with my car?"

"Check your phone," Iylah said. "Both of you." They did. "No internet, right? Can't get a call out? It's not a service problem. They've been shut off."

"What're you talking about?" Sherry asked, finally coming down off the stairs.

"Apparently, a ghost is haunting my house," Cole sighed. "And she wants us to play a game."

"She?" Sherry asked.

"All of you, come with me," Iylah directed. They followed her back to the dining room and stood around the table. "This is gonna sound really stupid, but he's right. I need the two of you to play this game with us." She nodded toward the tower, and then attempted moving her blue marble. "We can't move unless the two of you play. You'll have to be a team, so—"

"Yeah, that's not happenin'," Jared said, stepping away. "I don't know what's goin' on with the phones or what crazy, voodoo shit you're doin' here, but I ain't interested. I'll call a tow or walk."

"Check the box again," Iylah said. "You don't believe me. Check it again. Put your hand in, see what's in there."

"I did."

"So, do it again. You both do it," she signaled to Sherry. "And if you both come up empty, feel free to go. But if she pulls something out . . ." Iylah trailed off.

"How's she gonna pull something out if I don't?" He asked. Iylah started to respond but he cut her off. "Whatever. Look." He reached in coolly. "See? Nothing." He knocked his hands against the inside, and scraped his nails along the sides. He even turned the tower and board upside down and gave it a light shake. Neither marble moved, and nothing rattled. "Yeah. Empty. Can I go?"

Cole tapped Sherry with his hand. "You try it."

Sherry straightened and raised her hand to the box's mouth. She moved it toward the hole, letting it hover just above it for several moments before finally pulling away. "What's in there?" Iylah shrugged. "If there's nothing in there, then why do I have to—"

"Just do it," Cole blurted out. He tucked in his lips like he hadn't meant to say it.

"If you're in such a hurry, you reach in!" She said back fiercely.

"He can't," Iylah cut in and nodded at Jared. "He rolled, so we can't see what's inside until you reach in." Sherry complained that nobody was making any sense and tried to ask how it would know who was reaching in, but Iylah cut her off: "Trust me. Please."

Sherry's arm danced over the box until she finally thrust it inside with a deep inhale. She closed her eyes as she moved her hand around. Then, her eyes opened, looking immediately to Cole in shock. "There's something in here . . ." She whispered.

Iylah looked at Jared though there was nothing triumphant in her eyes.

Sherry delicately lifted her hand out of the hole, pulling with it a long, meaty, oily stick.

"Ew!" She let go at seeing it, dropping it onto the table. "What is that?"

"It's a stick . . ." Cole replied. He poked at it and then picked it up with his thumb and forefinger. "It's squishy." He smelled it.

"Is that beef jerky?" Jared asked.

"I don't know . . ." Cole leaned forward, sticking out his tongue to the immediate revulsion of the group. "What? It smells like jerky."

"Can I see it?" Iylah held it up, bending and sniffing it. "I don't understand," she whispered, placing it on the table for everyone to examine.

"Yo," Jared said, folding his arms. He had a grin over his face. "Hey man, be real. How'd you do that?"

"Do what?" Cole replied.

"How'd you get that in there?" Cole continued in his confusion. "Man, there was nothing in that box. I wouldn't've missed that." He peeked under as if to try and catch the silent partner who fed it from the bottom.

"Dude, I didn't put anything in there!" Cole said, scooting back, holding up his hands with innocence. "This thing's messed up."

Jared paused, twisting his mouth in skepticism. "So, the next time someone rolls, something else is gonna magically show up in there?"

"If someone lands on one of these hand spots, yeah," Cole replied.

"How did you know that was gonna happen?" Sherry asked Iylah, her voice unsteady. "That he wouldn't pull anything out?"

"Because that's how the game works. One person rolls, the other has to reach in," Iylah replied. "We play as teams, and the fact that you pulled that out," she eyed the stick, "means you're playing with us."

There was a disgusted hiss from Jared. "No. Uh-uh. I'm not playin' with her. I'll be with Cole, you take her—"

"We can't switch teams!" Iylah said sharply. "We've already started. The faster we get through it, the faster you both can leave." She picked up the die and started rolling it in her hand.

ᕦᕊ𐐒I
ᐟᕊᑎᕬᐣ Ꮅᕭᕊ𐐒ᕬᕦᕤᕊ

Sherry noticed the box top with the foreign script going across it. "What's this?" She asked.

"She doesn't know," Cole replied. "Might be the game's name or something."

"Is it another language?" Sherry asked. Jared leaned over for a glimpse.

"Nothing familiar to me," Iylah said. "I've looked. I think it's something made up—"

"That's Klingon," Jared interrupted. There was a momentary pause as everyone's gaze fell suspiciously on him.

"Oh my God," Iylah whispered, more to herself than anyone.

"What's Klingon?" Cole asked.

"Star Trek," Iylah said. "Klingon is a language they speak in Star Trek!" Her eyes met Jared's. "How did you know that?"

He jiggled his wrist in the air to show his silicone bracelets and pointed to his necklace. It wasn't a guitar pick. "Starfleet Command, baby. Trekky nerd all the way."

10

NOW

"Oh my gosh," Iylah gasped. "Can you read it? What does it say?"

"I mean . . . I'm not like fluent or anything. I learned it from my dad." He moved the script toward him and started humming to himself for several seconds, putting sounds together. "Hmm. Okay, I recognize that one." He pointed to the first set of characters, then the next. "But this one I have no idea. I think this one is *nar*. N-A-R-GH." He moved his finger across each character. He paused. "I think—don't hold me to it—but I think that's the word for *Escape*."

"Great," Cole said, sarcastically.

"This one though . . ." He read the characters as letters, and then sounded them out. "O-GH-T-A. Ohrta." Jared spoke the words forcefully, making the same sort of gargled noises that Iylah remembered from her sister. "I think that means *for*. Or maybe *by*. J. Jo. Jo. Joseh . . . vi . . . n. Joseh . . . veen. Josehveen? Escape For Josehveen? By Josehveen? Josahvine? Maybe? Don't know what a Josavine is."

"Josephine," Cole whispered, a face of unquestionable shock. "Escape *by* Josephine."

"As in, *made by*," Iylah continued. "Holy crap."

"Ohhh! I see it now," Jared said, rescanning the characters.

"How did I not see that before?" Iylah said to herself. "Star Trek was her favorite show!"

"I mean, don't beat yourself up, no one but Trekky nerds

like me would be able to recognize this, let alone read it. Who's Josephine?"

"Hang on," Sherry said, holding up her hand, and pointing at Iylah. "Is your last name *Maddox*?" Iylah froze, staring at Sherry. "Are you the one who . . ." She paused, looking as if she was waiting for Iylah to finish the thought; Iylah didn't. "That stuff with Shelby Gray." Iylah's lips tucked between her teeth.

"Whoa! That was you?" Jared asked, arching his brows in surprise.

"Guys, hold up," Cole interrupted. "She doesn't want to talk—"

"That was an accident—" Iylah cut in.

"Wait, wait, wait," Sherry cut in once more. She pointed at Cole. "You said *ghost*. Is that who we're talkin' about? Shelby?"

"No, no, no" Cole said. "It's not Shelby. It's Josephine."

"Oh my God," Sherry said slowly. "*Josephine*. The boating accident. At Land Between the Lakes. That was your sister?"

"Who?" Jared asked.

"That girl we heard about—the reason why they wouldn't let us be on the lake at night."

"Oh shit," Jared said. "Yo, I'm so sorry—"

"Guys!" Cole said, putting his hands over the table. They gave him their attention. "Look, there's something really weird happening here, alright? With the phones, and the internet, and this girl's name being on the box in Klinger—or whatever. I think we should probably listen to her. Like, now . . ."

"He's right. We're in more danger here if we don't play," Iylah echoed.

"How did she drown?" Sherry asked. "I mean—"

Cole said her name in what sounded like an exasperated tone and Iylah put her hands on her head, dragging them forcefully down her face, "We don't have time for this—"

"If your sister is haunting us, I think we ought to know what happened," Jared said.

Iylah groaned. "We're never gonna get through this," she said to herself. She took a deep breath. "Fine." She shook her head. "On our nineteenth birthday. We um . . ." Iylah stopped, in disbelief that she was about to recount this story. She bit her lip, feeling uneasy. "We asked a family friend of ours, Mark, to take us out on his boat, just us and some friends. He used to own the bar where Vitello's is now. Surprisingly, he said yes. We went out to LBL, sat on the boat in the middle of the lake all day; did the whole birthday thing." Iylah's arms crossed, her nails digging into the skin around her bicep. "That night, we were playing games, and uh . . ." Her face was tightening. She averted her gaze to her lap. "Jo wanted to go in the water. Everyone else was too drunk, so I told her she couldn't go—told her to stay on the boat. And so she, Mark, and I are all playing a game, and then Jo says she's gonna go to the bathroom." Iylah stopped again. She hadn't told this story in over a year—not since Dr. Boyd. "Me and Mark sat and talked. Jo never came back. After a while Mark tells me we better go. I went to check downstairs in the cabin to make sure everyone's asleep." Iylah clutched harder at her arms, feeling the pinch of her skin between her nails. "I saw Jo's clothes—" Her voice cracked as tears began to run down the side of her nose, onto her shorts. She quickly wiped them away and took another breath. "I saw her clothes and her float, and I figured she was passed out with everyone else."

"Oh my God," Sherry whispered.

Iylah continued talking toward her lap, not daring to look anyone in the eyes. "She'd apparently gone for a swim, and we didn't realize until it was too late."

"You didn't hear her screaming at you? Or see her in the water?" Sherry asked.

Iylah shook her head. "It was pitch black. If she was calling for us after the motor turned on . . ." She shrugged, weakly. "We didn't hear anything." Iylah's head lifted, locking a gaze on the game in front of her. "It was a couple hours before we realized. They found her two days later, still partially submerged, tangled up in a mess of vines. She was nowhere near where the boat had been. Likely, she tried to swim back, but there would have been no way for her to see out there in the dark."

After a few beats of silence, Jared mumbled, "I'm sorry."

She nodded. "Yeah. Me too" She sniffed up the snot in her nose and wiped her eyes. "Anyways, a short time after she died, I came home with my friend Erica one night, and *that* was waiting for us." She motioned to the board. "We beat it. But then it showed up again. At Shelby's." There was an unsettling pause. "I don't know what you've heard, but I had nothing to do with Shelby's death. It was an accident—"

A loud, dull *thud* sounded from somewhere upstairs, jerking their attention toward the ceiling.

"That's the same sound I heard earlier," Cole whispered. "She's upstairs."

"Yo man, can you not say stuff like that," Jared muttered.

"I don't believe in ghosts," Sherry said, confidently, though Iylah could tell her belief was *currently* being challenged.

"Cole saw her," Iylah said. It was as if she'd frozen time. Everyone sat still, dumbfounded. She was about to explain, but Cole cut her off and recounted everything that had happened so far: meeting her outside, finding the game, the noises, the person upstairs.

Iylah spoke up afterward and explained the rules of play. "We're working together against her, so it doesn't matter who gets there first." She scanned their faces, anticipating another question or maybe even a smart-ass response, but nothing came.

Jared was nodding, perhaps letting everything sink in. Iylah could feel a slight tremor in the table under her arm and realized that it was coming from Sherry's leg, bouncing on the ball of her foot.

"What happens if we don't get to the end?" Jared asked.

"There're two teams. I'm sure we'll make it to the end," Iylah replied.

"But what if we don't?" Jared asked. "You said it yourself; we're playing against her. What happens if she wins?"

Iylah didn't have a response.

"No . . ." Sherry muttered. "Mmm mmm." Her chair scraped against the hardwood and fell to the floor when she stood up, startling all of them.

"You alright?" Cole asked her.

"I'm going home. I don't wanna do this anymore."

"You have to," Iylah said back.

"No. Sorry," she said with sarcastic empathy. "I don't. You're not *my* babysitter, and this isn't *my* house."

"Sherry, not playing the game is what got Shelby—"

"I don't care about you and Shelby! And I don't care about you and your sister! I'm not playing this—"

"Hey!" Iylah yelled. Sherry froze. "You're not listening. You can't leave the house. We're all stuck here until it ends."

"Is she deaf?" Sherry said, looking at Cole. "Listen. I'm not fucking ten, oh-kay—"

"Wait!" Iylah said, holding up a finger. *The board*. She looked down at where Sherry's marble had moved and then frantically scanned the room. "Where's your thermostat?"

"Over by the front door." Cole pointed. It was still sitting at sixty-eight degrees. She moved back toward the dining room. "What's wrong with the thermostat?" Cole asked.

"I don't get it," Iylah said to herself, ignoring him.

"Don't get what?" Cole asked.

"When I played this before, something happened every time we landed on one of those hand spaces."

"It did already. The phones, remember?" Cole said.

"No, that was for us," Iylah replied. "They got that meat-stick thing which means something should have happened." She walked through the French doors into the kitchen, then into the family room to look at the TV, still staying within sight of the group. Nothing. No sounds, no strange noises, no heat. Just an eerie feeling. She moved to the foyer again and opened the front door, peering out into the darkness. The front porch light came on, illuminating the walkway. Streetlamps were on along the road. She could see people moving in the house across the street through a well-lit window. "Something's not right." She closed the door and locked it. Sherry stomped up the stairs behind her. "Wait! Sherry!"

"You don't listen very well, do you?" Sherry replied, continuing up.

Iylah was about to call her again, but Cole shot out of the dining room. "Hey," He held out a hand to Iylah. "I got it. Let me go talk to her."

"We can't separate. We have to come with you." Iylah grabbed her backpack out of the kitchen where'd she'd left it sitting on the counter, and they all walked up the stairs together. Cole blocked Iylah from coming into his room. "Hey, look, she's not gonna listen to you. Just, give us a second, okay?"

Iylah and Jared stood still against the wall. She could feel her heart beginning to pick up as sweat was forming on her palms. She rubbed them together close to her chest, reminding herself to breathe.

11

NOW

Cole's attempt at convincing Sherry to stay failed. After nearly ten minutes of arguing, she still wasn't budging.

"Look, please stay! What if something's really going on here?" Cole asked.

"It's not. And if there was, you're not gonna solve it by playing some demented board game."

With nothing left to stand on, Cole asked: "Is this about Jared? Because I feel like if you just talk to him about what happened you guys can figure out whatever's goin' on."

Sherry sneered at him blowing out an air of disgust. "Of course, you'd take his side."

"I'm not taking a side. I'm just sayin' maybe if you talk to him—"

"You're right, Cole. It was all my fault, and he did nothing wrong." She threw open the bedroom door and shoved past Iylah and Jared who were waiting in the hall. "Never mind that he could be the one to talk to me first!"

"Sherry! Would you stop!" He followed after her, down the stairs. "I didn't mean to bring it up, okay? I'm sorry."

"Yeah, well, you did bring it up, so I'm leaving. The two of you can sit here and talk about how much I fucked everything up, and how it's all my fault."

"Maybe it's because you *did* fuck everything up," Jared said back bleakly, from the top of the stairs.

Sherry stopped cold in her tracks.

"Dude," Cole said, shooting a glare at Jared.

"What? I mean, if she has a version of the story that doesn't involve her forwarding a pic of me to all of our friends," Jared took each step with a menacing pace, and then took a seat at the bottom. "I'd be happy to hear it."

Her face tightened in a heart wrenching pain.

"Sherry," Cole pleaded.

"Fuck you," she whispered, turning to the door, on the verge of tears.

"Sherry," Iylah said, stepping forward to grab hold of her arm. "Please. I'm begging you, just stay for a little while, it's not safe to go out—" Sherry jerked her arm away and slammed the door in Iylah's face.

"Damnit!" Iylah said. She opened the door to run after her, but Sherry waved her off, yelling more curses at all of them. Sherry walked down the driveway, and turned the corner onto the sidewalk, out of sight behind the shrubs that lined the Gibson house.

"Couldn't just keep your mouth shut, could you?" Cole asked. Jared shrugged. "You know how bad she feels?"

"*She feels bad*? Are you kidding me, right now? That girl ruined my life." Jared made his way into the kitchen and got his ginger ale. "Feeling bad isn't good enough."

Cole was about to say something when Iylah stepped hurriedly inside and shut the door. She fell back against it, closing her eyes, and putting her hands over them as she took several deep breaths.

"You okay?" Cole asked. She shook her head. "What does that mean for the game? Can we just do a team of three?"

"No. She has to stay. Shit, shit, shit!" Iylah thumped her head against the door. "I don't know what to do . . ."

"Why did you ask for my thermostat?" Cole asked.

Iylah exhaled, looking up at him. "It's from the last time I played. The thermostat; it went crazy. After the phones went off, we tried to put the game away, but it wouldn't let us."

"What does that mean, *it* wouldn't let you?" Jared asked.

"When we—my friend Erica—picked up the die to put it away, she said it was covered in something, and she dropped it. Like a . . . goop—or something. But to the game, that counted as a roll, and when she moved the marble, the thermostat cranked up the heat. Hot air started blowing through the vents as if the furnace was on fire."

"Screw that," Jared said.

"Within two rolls, we were locked in. Had no choice but to play."

"What did it give you? With the heat, I mean."

"Fans," Iylah replied. "Little, miniature fans." She swallowed and took a seat on the wooden bench beside the door, putting her head in her hands. "That's what I don't understand. That jerky has to mean something about whatever's about to happen. What am I missing?"

"Was that all that happened?" Cole asked. She shook her head. There was an uncomfortable quiet, prompting Iylah to glance up and see both boys staring at her with grim concern. Cole started to speak but the words got choked. He cleared his throat. "Was it the worst thing that happened?" Iylah hesitated, then shook her head. Cole's body sagged.

"What was next?" He asked, sounding like he really didn't want to know. Iylah ignored him. "Iylah."

"Music," Iylah finally said. "Loud, ear-splitting music. From every speaker and device that could produce sound. TVs, speakers, phones, radios—even my mom's noise canceling head-phones—they all had the same song playing."

"Which one?" Jared asked.

" 'These Boots Are Made For Walkin',' " Iylah replied. "By Nancy Sinatra. It was one of her favorites."

Jared gave a optimistic nod, looking between the two of them with a hopeful grin. "Hey, alright, that doesn't sound that bad."

"Easy for you to say," Iylah said gravely. "We couldn't turn it off. Tried flipping off switches, unplugging things; nothing worked. Every device was playing the song, getting louder and louder."

"What'd she give you?" Cole asked. "How'd you stop it?"

Iylah nervously laughed. "We couldn't stop it. But the game gave us a rock." Iylah noted the confused look on their faces. She held up her fist. "About this big. It was painted and decorated to look like a Treasure Troll. Jo and I made it when we were kids. That's the moment it clicked for me. That's how I knew this was Josephine's game."

"Why that?" Jared asked.

"Because I threw that rock away when I was twelve," Iylah said back, matter-of-factly.

"Okay. So, maybe there's a connection. Do these things mean anything to you?" Cole asked. "Like, why the rock? And the heat, and the music? The phones."

Iylah averted her gaze to the floor. "Not to me."

"How does a rock help with loud music?" Jared asked.

Iylah sat motionless for several seconds, holding her gaze on the area rug beneath her feet. She was about to reply when from outside the door came a blood-curdling scream.

Two Years Ago
Erica Lang
Part III

"Finally!" Erica yelled. She was standing on the other side of the room.

Iylah was still cowering in shock from the object whizzing past her head and smashing the TV screen. "Erica!" She yelled. She had ducked out of the way when she saw Erica launch something toward her. Now, trembling on the floor with her hands over her ears, she surveyed the damage. The cracks worked their way from the point of impact all the way across the screen in a web-like fashion. The rock that Erica had thrown dropped onto the hardwood floor with a *thud*. Even with every device playing, she could tell that the music from the TV had stopped. Iylah snapped out of her trance. Confusion over the rock's strange return suddenly faded into alarm over her parents' reaction. "Why did you do that?"

"I don't know," Erica replied. "That's what the thing gave me." She pointed in the direction of the living room where the game still sat. The TV flickered and let out another attempt at the song before skipping, then popping, and finally going dead. "See. It worked."

"My parents are gonna kill me!" Iylah screamed. "They just bought that TV."

Erica didn't look at all remorseful, giving her a look that said, *what was I supposed to do?* "Sorry," she said, throwing her hands up. "But in case you didn't notice, that rock was *in* the box!" Iylah ignored her, still transfixed on the TV. "Iylah. Did you not hear me?" Erica stepped forward.

"I heard you," she cut in, practically screaming. Two of her mom's clay Willow Tree statues came toppling to the floor beside her, having been shaken off the shelf by the bass' subwoofer. She moved the other statues onto the couch. As if the stabbing pain in her ears wasn't bad enough, the beat knocked against her chest like a sledgehammer. She knelt to pick up the rock.

"What is that?" Erica called out.

"How would this have gotten in that box?" She shouted over the music still coming from every other device in the house, the same song starting up for the fifth or sixth time in a row.

"Iylah. How would *anything* have gotten in there? This game is messed up!"

The noise from the surround sound seemed to go up even more, prompting Iylah to scream and drop the rock to cover her ears. Erica grabbed her by the arm and led her out of the family room into the hallway. There were no speakers here but with the deafening volume, it wasn't much better. "We need to get out of here!"

"And go where?" Iylah called, feeling the bass *thump* even against her cheeks and eyes.

"I don't know! Somewhere!"

"What am I supposed to do about the TV?" Iylah asked. "I can't just leave it like that." They spoke inches from each other's faces, still yelling to make themselves heard.

"Call the police!" Erica shouted.

"And tell them what?" Iylah yelled back. "Plus, how am I gonna explain that you threw a rock through my parent's TV?"

"Oh my God! I'll buy you a new TV!" Erica snapped, frustrated.

"Maybe we should try and finish the game," Iylah said. Erica's expression was blank. Iylah wasn't sure if she'd been heard. She pointed to the gameboard on the couch. "The game! Maybe we should—"

"I heard you!" Erica cut in. "I'm not playing anymore." Iylah's face scrunched in surprise, a look that no doubt communicated, *what?!* Erica looked around in a frenzy and then spotted something. She grabbed Iylah's arm once again and drug her into the laundry room, slamming the door. It was a little better; enough for Iylah to uncover her ears. "Unless you're playing a really good trick on me, there's no way I'm messing with that thing anymore." There was a loud squeal from somewhere in the house, followed by a static interference that cleared into music. Another unit had come on. Erica started pacing, and fanning herself, nearly hyperventilating. "We need to get out of here!"

"How?"

"Uber!"

"We can't call anyone, remember?" Iylah shot back.

Erica opened the other door, leading to the garage, and flipped on the light. "Then we need to walk. I'm not staying here. I'll knock on a neighbor's door or something. Come on." Erica started down the steps, but Iylah grabbed her hand.

"Erica! We don't have any neighbors. This house is in the middle of nowhere."

She could see the realization droop over Erica's face. There was a flash of despair at the understanding that the two of them were starting to become trapped by whatever was plaguing this house. Erica closed the door and leaned against it. "What do we do then?" She could see Erica's face becoming flush, beginning to tear up.

They didn't have a choice, but maybe that's all *she* wanted; for them to just play the game. Erica spoke again, but Iylah cut her off, instructing her to hang on before rushing out of the room. She ran to the game on the couch and grabbed hold of the central tower by the top, lifting it and the slabs into the air. On her way back to get Erica, she caught sight of the thermostat, and stopped dead. It read ninety degrees.

Iylah led Erica down to the other end of the hall to her dad's home office. Even with opening the windows, it seemed as if little could be done to cool them off. It was as if the furnace sensed an attempt to thwart its efforts. It rattled on, pumping out even more hot air. The two of them moved the standing antique radio—somehow blaring "These Boots Are Made for Walkin'" through its dead speaker—to the hallway and shut the door.

The noise was loud, but tolerable. Iylah set the gameboard on the floor and wiped the sweat from her face. "Okay," Erica said. "How many more spaces?" Had the house not been sweltering, Iylah would have thought Erica was trying to get warm by the way she was hugging herself.

"Eight. Are you okay?"

"I just wanna get outta here," Erica replied impatiently. "What if we walk? How far is the closest neighbor?"

"Little more than two miles away." Iylah paused. "Plus, again, what do I tell them? We found a haunted board game and now a bunch of weird shit is happening at my house?"

"Yes! Say that!"

"No one's gonna believe that! Not to mention, I don't want my parents knowing—."

"I don't give a shit about your parents, Iylah! I think we're past that point. If it's between getting out of here and your parents finding out you lied to them, then it's not much of a choice."

"Can we just try it my way?" Iylah asked, frustrated. "We can probably finish in two rolls. If it doesn't get better, we'll go for help."

"If it doesn't get better?" Erica exclaimed. "What do you think is going to happen?" Erica waited for Iylah to respond, but neither had an answer. "You think all of this stuff is just gonna magically disappear?"

"It wouldn't be the most surprising thing that's happened," Iylah replied. "If all this shit is coming from that game, then it only makes sense to finish it, right?"

"Nothing about tonight makes sense," Erica replied. She switched on the mini fan they'd gotten earlier from the game and exhaled. "Fine. Gimme the die." Erica squatted down over the gameboard. There was a brief moment of hesitation as she clutched at her belly.

"What's wrong?" Iylah asked.

"I need to pee."

"Are you serious?"

"What? I had a lot of water! Here." She dropped the die onto the floor. **Two**. "Shit."

"Now we have to get six. Hurry and go. I'll move."

"Can you go with me?" Erica asked.

"It's right there," Iylah replied, aiming a finger at the wall. "Just leave the door open."

Erica stood up and opened the door. Music flooded in as she scanned the area before walking toward the bathroom nearby.

Iylah watched and then picked up the marble and moved it two spaces. Another marked square. "Great," she mumbled. She lifted her hand and reached into the center tower through the hole on the top. Whatever was inside felt soft. Delicate, almost. Like flower petals. She took hold of what she could and began to pull it up. Flowers always reminded Iylah of a girl her sister used to be friends with when they were younger: Gwendolyn Potts. Gwen and Jo were practically inseparable. They had somehow managed to make it into every class together until middle school. In the fourth grade, Gwendolyn was diagnosed with leukemia. She passed away in the summer before high school. Flowers usually reminded Iylah of her because Gwen always wore a—

"Holy shit!" Iylah gasped, jerking her hand away from the box. Dangling out over the side of the hole was a decrepit and tarnished floral crown. There was no doubt in Iylah's mind that it was Gwen's floral crown. She wore the same one practically every day to school: an arrangement of yellow, red, and purple flower petals.

It was also on her head when they buried her.

12

NOW

The door burst open, slamming into the wall, and punching out a knob-sized dent. The large, framed painting nearby fell to the floor with a shuddering *crash*. Sherry tumbled in, tripping over the threshold and fell to the floor.

"Sherry! Holy crap! What are you—" Cole began, jumping up, shocked from the sudden destruction of his mom's picture.

"Close the door! Close the door!" She frantically yelled.

Cole stood motionless as Jared brushed past him hurriedly and dove to close the door.

"There—there—there's something—there's something—it was behind me!" She was hysterically pointing at the door.

Her obvious terror shook Cole out of his concern over the hole and broken glass. He knelt beside Sherry, attempting to calm her down.

"It's okay, it's okay. What happened?

"There was a—a—there was—a dog! Big dog!" Sherry tried to catch her breath. "It—it tried to bite me—"

"A dog?" Jared asked. "What are you talking about?"

Sherry swallowed, shaking her head. "It's out there!"

"You're fine. You're inside," Cole said, his hands caringly at each side of her head, trying to get her to look him in the eyes. "Are you hurt at all? Did it get you?" She shook her head, tears beginning to form. "It's okay." He hugged her close, scanning over her body for blood. Cole turned to Iylah. "What is she talking about?"

Iylah stuttered, now on her hands and knees in front of Sherry. "I-I-I don't—I don't know." She inched closer to look at Sherry. "Are you sure you're okay?"

"Iylah, what are we supposed to do?" Cole asked, his voice heavy with concern.

"I don't know!" She replied. "There wasn't a dog last time."

"Well, there's one now!" Cole yelled back.

"Hey," Jared said. "For real, this shit can't hurt us, can it? Like, it's a game. Right?"

Iylah looked at Jared for an instant before noticing that Sherry was visibly shaking. "Damnit! I told you, stay together! Don't go outside—"

"Iylah, come on," Cole interrupted.

Jared walked to the door. "What did it look like?" He cracked open the door and peeked out.

"Don't—don't do that," Iylah said, trying to grab hold of Jared's leg.

"It—it was huge," Sherry stuttered out. "I—I kept hearing this noise, like a crunching, or something behind my car and when I shined my light, there it was, just—just standing there by my door. It looked like it was trying to eat the gravel. It walked toward me snarling and twitching it's head like something was biting it. When I tried to back up, I tripped over the curb and fell—"

"You don't know what kind of dog?"

"No—no. I've never seen anything that big. It practically towered over me when I was trying to scoot back." She was still trying to catch her breath. Iylah looked at her quizzically. "It was black, long hair."

"One of your neighbors got a dog?" Jared asked. "It sounds like it might have rabies." Iylah's attention turned, at once, to the outside. She shot up, moving behind Jared to get a peek into the night.

"The guy across the street has a lab, I think," Cole said.

"That wasn't a lab," Sherry said. "It was hideous. It's hair was all matted and stringy with mud or something."

"Was there a collar or anything?"

"No, I—I don't know. There was something over it's neck, like a . . . a . . ."

Iylah turned to her. "A bandana," she spoke, though it wasn't a question.

"Yeah. Maybe. How'd you know?"

Iylah ignored her. "Fanny . . ." she said, inaudibly.

"What'd you say?" Jared asked.

Her heart skipped as panic dropped in her chest. "Close the door." The words in a whisper, choked. She said it again and went to move Jared's arm out of the way.

He stiffened. "What're you doing—"

"Shh!" She hissed. "Wait!" She clutched his arm tight, not daring to move. Everyone listened. There was a faint rumbling noise coming from the side of the house: a single prolonged tone. The sound was almost gurgled, or scratchy. A growl. "Close the door! Close the door!" Iylah exclaimed, finding her breath, and shoving Jared aside to slam the door closed. As soon as it latched, something lunged forward and pushed on the other side, forcing the two of them back. Jared cursed and pressed his shoulder into the door.

"Holy shit!" Jared said. "What is that?"

Iylah steadied herself against the door, as the creature on the other side continued to scratch viciously against it.

"Don't let it in! Don't let it in!"

"Gee, ya think?" Jared replied, holding the door with his

hands, and flicking over the dead bolt. "What are we supposed to do?" Jared asked.

"We have to finish the game. We finish the game, it might go away—"

"Wait! That's it!" Jared exclaimed. "The game! It gave us the stick, remember?" He pushed off and hurried toward the gameboard in the dining room and returned holding the jerky. Iylah stepped back, watching the monster through the tempered glass chomp its teeth. When she took more steps back, the dog seemed to lose interest, dropping down to all fours. "You said they're supposed to help, right?" He was holding up the meat stick. "Maybe if we give it to the dog, it'll go away." The group didn't have much time to consider. Iylah was about to say she wasn't sure when Jared flicked over the dead bolt, and cracked open the door, sticking his hand out with the meat stick. He whistled in a friendly tone. "Here boy."

"No, no, no! What're you doing!" Iylah yelled, extending out an arm to grab him. "Jared!"

The black dog seemed to materialize out of thin air from the darkness, as it pounced forward, snatching the stick out of Jared's hand. He cursed, yanking his arm back in, and slamming the door. "Damn, that thing's fast!" He said, shaking his hand as if he'd been burned.

"What the hell is wrong with you? Why did you do that?" Iylah scolded.

"You said whatever comes out of the game is supposed to help!" He shot back.

"Yeah, but we don't know how! What'd you think, it would just magically go away?"

"I don't know, maybe," Jared replied. He turned his head, as if listening for movement outside. There was calm for several seconds before a smirk appeared on Jared's face. "See. What'd I tell—" The dog threw itself against the door once more, snapping its teeth and clawing at the glass. "You gotta be kidding me."

"We could've used that to distract it or something," Cole said. The dog started to bark at them. Iylah could feel herself go lightheaded as she watched it's shape on the other side. In the instant it snatched the stick from Jared's hand, she got a glimpse of it in its full form. "You idiot!" Cole yelled. He and Jared squabbled over the poor decision while Iylah found herself barely able to stand and leaned against the wall. She didn't want to say it, but this wasn't just any dog; it was *her* dog from when she and Jo were kids.

Aunt Fanny. Fanny was a black Newfoundland. A giant of a dog that always wore a checkered bandana around its neck. There wasn't a mean bone in its body until she got sick. Fanny had stayed a weekend with family friends while Iylah's parents went out of town. The couple had two small kids that loved the dog and kept her occupied. A week after their return, Iylah's dad got a call that there was a fox in the neighborhood where Fanny had been staying. While the boys had been playing with her, a fox sprung on them in the yard before Fanny came between them and chased it off into the woods. She apologized for the late notice but had no idea until she overheard her sons telling their friends what happened.

Her dad had not noticed anything unusual in the dog's behavior over the week but was certain they were up to date on her shots. Unfortunately, they were not. It had been nearly four years. They scheduled an appointment for the vet the next afternoon, but by the morning, things had taken a tragic turn for her. Twenty-four hours later, the day of Iylah and Jo's nineteenth birthday, they put her down. *Why Fanny? What are you trying to tell me—*

"What if that thing gets inside? Then what, dumb ass!" Cole fired at Jared. And that's when the realization clicked for Iylah, her stomach sinking.

"It won't come inside," she whispered, letting out a breath and taking a seat on the stairs.

"What?" Cole asked, holding up a hand to cut Jared off.

"That's why," she muttered to herself, her head shaking slowly. "It's not supposed to come in. I think . . ." She reclined back, pressing her hands against her eyes. "I think its job is to keep *us* in. She wants us to feel like we have no hope of getting out."

Two Years Ago
Erica Lang
Part IV

*I*ylah and Erica pressed their backs to the wall inside her bedroom closet. Despite the noise, Iylah could make out the ragged, panicked breathing from the both of them. The spot wouldn't be a bad place to stay except the heat was almost unbearable.

Erica had burst out of the bathroom in a frenzy, running up the stairs. Iylah grabbed the game and followed close behind, right into her bedroom and into the closet. Each now tried to breathe quietly and slowly, finding it difficult to catch their breaths. Between them was the gameboard. Iylah stared at it by way of the miniature flashlight that was once attached to her keyring as Erica leaned forward and tried to peer out through the louvers on the door. "Are you gonna tell me what happened?" Erica didn't answer. "Erica."

"I saw someone."

"Yeah, I gathered that. What does that mean?"

"There was someone in the bathroom with me," Erica replied.

Iylah wasn't sure if she heard right but Erica kept going, trying to get the words out. "She—she—she was all . . . petrified. She was—she was just standing there." Erica seemed to be losing her breath. There were several stutters as she tried to form the next sentence. "I-I-I finished peeing, and when I turned to get the wipes from the back of the toilet, I could see—it was like . . . it looked like someone was standing in the shower. Behind the curtain. I-I thought it was you—I thought maybe you'd snuck in before I got in there, but there was no way. And so, I said your name and then . . . they—whatever that was—spoke back. Her voice was garbled like her mouth was full."

Pinpricks began to creep over Iylah's back.

"She—she said something, but I couldn't make it out, and then I—I pulled the curtain back. She was just standing there. Her skin looked like it had wasted away around her bones. She was holding out her hand, moving her jaw up and down as if she was trying to talk."

Iylah could feel a tremor in her hands. Terror was racing through her veins. Her mind didn't want to believe it. There was nothing rational about what Erica had just seen. Even more irrational was who Iylah knew the girl in the bathtub to be.

"What do we do?" Erica asked. "She's down there. She's down there waiting for us. I saw her trying to get out of the shower." Erica spied through the door once again.

"We have to finish the game."

"I can't, I can't, I can't," Erica chanted, as if pleading. "You didn't see her."

"It's . . ." She paused and considered. It would be pointless to tell her friend that what she just saw was more than likely Jo's dead best friend. *How would that even be possible?* "When you were in the bathroom, I pulled something out of the box. Something that I think belongs to them."

"Who? That girl?" Erica asked.

"Yeah, I think so," Iylah replied.

"Where is it?"

Iylah held up her clenched fist and opened it. Erica leaned

in. "It's a flower crown. It belonged to a girl we knew when we were kids. One of Jo's friends. Gwen. She wore this every day." The terror over Erica's face made it apparent she knew where Iylah was going with this. "Gwen died the summer before—"

"No, don't even say it!" Erica said back quickly, putting her hands over her ears. "I don't wanna know!"

Suddenly, there was a *thud* nearby. Something banging. Iylah went still and switched off the flashlight. Erica continued chanting something to herself until Iylah snatched her arm, yanking it away from her ear. She held a finger over her mouth and pointed at the door. "Shh!" Erica twisted around as another *thud* broke over the music, this time right outside Iylah's bedroom. The two of them scooted back against the closet wall, covering their faces with hanging clothes. "No, no, no, no . . ."

Iylah noticed the crown dangling from her hand.

Then came a series of *thunks* against the bedroom door. "Oh my God, oh my God, that's her," Erica whispered.

"Shh!" Iylah leaned forward and crawled delicately over the floor. "Maybe if we give her this . . ." Iylah whispered.

"No! Iylah, please don't open that door! Please!"

If they didn't think of something quick, there was no way to keep it from getting in the closet. Iylah wadded up the crown and shoved it into her pocket. She clicked on her key chain light and scooted closer to the game. "We have to finish this now. Look, all this happened when we started playing. Maybe it'll stop if we get to the end."

"And what if it doesn't?" Erica asked.

"Then we face whatever's behind my door and try to get the hell out of here." Iylah held out the die in her hand.

"How many more spaces?" Erica asked.

Iylah counted. "Six," she whispered. "Hey, at least the music's not so loud in here, right?" Iylah gave a strained smile, but it was lost in the darkness.

Another stream of weak, dreadful knocks rapped against the door. "At this point, I'd take the song if it meant not having to see that again."

"You ready?" Iylah asked. Erica nodded, and Iylah dropped the die on the floor. "**Five**. Shit." She moved the light up toward Erica's face.

"It's fine. I'll roll as soon as you move," Erica said. "Hurry!"

Iylah picked up the marble and moved it five spaces forward to another marked space.

Erica seemed like she was anticipating something to happen, but after a few moments of no surprises, she picked up the die off the floor and rolled it. "Four!" There was a pause. "Holy shit! We did it!" She reached for the marble but couldn't grab hold of it with her fingers. She fingered it from other angles, trying to pry it off the wooden slab, but it wouldn't budge.

"I landed on one of the hand spaces. You gotta pull something out."

Erica breathed out a curse. She reached into the box without apprehension. The light illuminated enough of her face for Iylah to notice the immediate perplexity that suddenly draped over it. "What the . . ."

"What is it? Take it out."

"There's no way . . ." Erica whispered to herself, slowly drawing her hand out of the box. Clutched in her fist were several long, white, cottony tubes. Strings were hanging out of her hand like small tentacles. "What the hell?"

What felt like a knot began forming in Iylah's stomach. "Tampons," she said. It came out in a straightforward tone because Iylah finally understood what was happening. She understood the meaning behind the game—it was a twisted reminder.

A pain in her stomach suddenly grew sharp, provoking an audible gasp. She clutched at her side, dropping the flashlight to the floor.

"What's wrong?" Erica asked.

"I don't know." A stabbing ache began to pulsate in her gut, causing Iylah to wince and double over. "What's happening?"

"Are you okay?" Erica asked, shifting her legs to scoot closer.

"I don't know." And that's when she noticed it. The beam of the light was directed along the floor, highlighting Erica's open legs. It took Iylah's mind only a split second to recognize the dark red splotch, showing through the pajama pants. Before Iylah could say a word, Erica felt it. "Oh shit," Erica whispered, rolling over and onto her feet. She snatched up the flashlight and pointed it at her pants. "What the fuck?"

The gooey, warm sensation of blood suddenly struck Iylah, who immediately brought a hand to her crotch to check, but the sharp pains took hold again, distracting her mind from the liquid forming in her pants. There was another audible wince of pain as Erica began cursing over and over to herself in a whisper. "What's happening?"

"We have to roll."

"Iylah, I'm not on my period. Why the fuck am I bleeding?"

"It's happening to me too! Just do it." But before Erica could reach for the die, light from the hallway flooded into the darkness and underneath the closet door. A shadow materialized through the louvers. Both girls sat still, not breathing, or taking their eyes off the outline of the crooked figure standing on the other side. Finally, something pushed against the door. And then came a sound. A garbled noise. Erica sucked in a gasp behind Iylah.

The pushing of the door became more forceful. Iylah lifted up a hand and pulled at one of the louvers to see what was on the other side. It was barely visible in the dark, but there was no mistaking the pair of bare legs. She yanked her hand away, instantly cupping her mouth and inched back. The mangled noise came out again, only this time it was followed by a trickling of something onto the floor, just under the gap of the closet door. Iylah shined a light and reached forward to inspect the crumble.

Dirt. "Oh my God," she whispered. The pushing against the door became even harsher as whatever it was began trying to turn the knob.

"Roll the die!" Iylah whispered, staring tensely at the door. "Roll it! Roll it!"

Erica picked up the die and dropped it on the floor. "**Two.** Two!"

"Move it!" Iylah said through her teeth.

"Move it where? There's nowhere else to go—oh! I forgot. It goes inside!"

Iylah registered the marble hitting the wood with a hollow *thud* as she saw the knob on the door begin to turn. Immediately, a portion on each of the game's four slabs began to illuminate.

"Iylah!" Erica whispered. "The lights. We have to put our hands on the lights. This is what she told us to do at the end."

Iylah could hear Erica talking, but her mind was too troubled to understand. The closet door was now slowly creaking open. Iylah pulled up the flower crown, clutching it in her hand as if to appease whatever was on the other side. It continued to make indecipherable hums and groans. Iylah wanted to scream but couldn't. Her body went rigid and cold as the door opened wider, inch by inch, allowing the music to flood in around them. She felt the strength in her legs begin to fade as she dropped down to her knees. She felt Erica take her hand and jerk at her fingers, pushing them onto the gameboard and yelling at her in the process. A bone thin leg under a long, tattered gown came into view as the door continued to inch open. Iylah shut her eyes; she didn't want to see it. She chanted to herself for whatever it was to leave them alone. She could sense light increasing in front of her eyelids as the door opened wider. More. And more. And—

Darkness. The music in the house came to a screeching halt.

Iylah opened one eye. The light pouring in from outside her bedroom was enough to show that whatever stood behind the door had now vanished. The door squeaked open to a stop, bouncing against the wall. She stared ahead, realizing she was holding out her hand in front of her with the crown clutched tightly in her fist.

"Iylah!" Erica whispered. "The music!"

Quiet had suddenly overtaken the house.

"It stopped!" Erica slid across the floor, knocking the gameboard aside, and crawled over to the door. There was a metal vent on the floor. Iylah watched Erica stick her hand over it. "There's nothing! I mean, it's hot, but there's nothing blowing out anymore!" Instantly, she peered behind the closet door into the bedroom as if someone might be hiding behind it or lurking elsewhere out of sight. She sat there, on all fours, still, just watching out in the direction of the hallway. "Iylah," she whispered. "I think it's over." She began to laugh, but those noises quickly melted into sobs as Erica fell forward, onto her arms, and cried.

Iylah, on the other hand, continued to sit on her knees, completely stunned. She couldn't take her eyes off the closet door. Erica was mumbling something incomprehensible into the floor. Iylah could feel her mind getting foggy, a sudden wave of vertigo was breaking the restraints on her equilibrium. Adrenaline was rushing through her body like a deadly rapid. She wanted to cry, or maybe even laugh, but all she could do was rock, and breathe, now clenching the floral crown to her chest.

"Iylah." Erica said, softly, shifting back to her. Iylah didn't reply, only stared out into her bedroom. "Iylah. Did you hear me?" Erica whispered. "Iylah, can you look at me—"

Iylah could no longer suppress the adrenaline rushing through her body. Without warning, she clutched at the shirt over her chest—instantly feeling a nail crack off—as her body forced out a primal scream. She held it until there was nothing left, and then did it again, ringing out every last ounce of energy she could muster. With one final howl, the floral crown intertwined between her hands snapped into two pieces.

Erica leapt forward, wrapping her arms around Iylah from behind and bringing her close. Iylah continued to scream and struggled against her for an instant before collapsing into her friend's arms. The cries had robbed Iylah of her breath, forcing her to hyperventilate. Erica held her tight, taking deep breaths against her back, whispering for her to follow the rhythm.

The two of them lay together on the closet floor for nearly half an hour, crying into each other's arms. Though the panic in Iylah's mind had subsided, the constriction in her stomach was unchanged. The pain was searing through her abdomen, shooting into her back. When she felt Erica shivering against her, she pulled her close, though with Erica's height Iylah had to scoot up to eye level. Erica's arms were curled close to her; the heat from them brought some relief to Iylah's stomach. They both continued to lie quietly, neither saying a word. When Iylah could feel herself slipping from consciousness, she heard Erica whisper: "You still awake?"

Iylah opened her eyes and nodded.

"You okay?"

Iylah nodded hesitantly. "My stomach's cramping really bad."

"Mine too," Erica said. "Do we need to go to the doctor?"

Iylah shook her head. "Mine are always this bad. Just need some Ibuprofen." Her eyes picked up the faint glow of a dawning sun coming in through the window. She tucked her chin, curling herself tighter, certainly not ready to begin a new day.

"What do we do now?" Erica asked. Iylah didn't reply, and Erica put an arm around her. She moved her hip to get closer to Iylah but drew back at once at the cold ickiness in her pants. "Ugh. Sorry. I guess changing would probably be best, huh?"

At the mention of clothes, the dull ache in her stomach briefly gave way to the gooey sensation around her pelvis. Iylah moved her legs, feeling the stickiness inside her pants. "Yeah . . ."

"You okay to move?"

"I think so." They continued to stare at each other, Erica running her hand through Iylah's hair. "Thanks for helping me," Iylah whispered. "With the breathing."

Erica nodded. "It's okay. I was freaked too. Helping you took my mind off it." She sat up slowly and rubbed a hand up and down Iylah's back for comfort. "You think it's over?"

Iylah hugged herself tighter, grimacing. "Sure doesn't feel over."

"You sure you're okay?"

Iylah nodded again. "I'm fine." Erica helped her sit up. "Like I said, mine are always painful. Just need medicine."

Erica did not stop rubbing her back. She spoke in hushed amazement: "So random."

"What is?"

"Everything. That game," Erica said, nodding over toward the box. "All that stuff: your sister, the heat, that song. That girl! What was the point? It all just kinda seemed to be super random."

Iylah, still staring at the black board game in a daze, nodded. "Yeah," she whispered. "Super random."

13

NOW

The group took a seat at the dining room table. Sherry looked on from the hallway, occasionally checking behind her at the front door. The moment they decided to continue playing and head back to the game was the moment the dog receded into the dark. "You gonna sit?" Cole asked Sherry.

"No."

Cole's eyebrows arched as he mouthed "okay" to himself. "Here we go." He rolled a *four* and moved the marble up. It was an empty space. He let out a sigh.

"So, nobody reaches in, right? Nothing happens?" Jared asked.

"Right," Iylah said. She scooted the die in Sherry's direction. "You're up."

Jared leaned over the table and swiped the die, not bothering to wait for Sherry to walk over and pick it up. He shook it, then dropped it onto the table: *Three*. He counted the spaces before he moved the marble, and tapped the marked indentation where his piece would go next: "Crap. What does that mean? What's next?"

"I don't know," Iylah said.

"How do you not know?" Jared moved the marble up three spaces. "Haven't you played this—" At once, the house went dark. "Whoa! What the hell?" Jared yelled, jumping up.

Sherry cursed. "Guys. What's going on? Cole?"

"Yeah, I'm here. Power must've gone out. Anyone got a cell phone?"

"I have mine," Sherry replied, quickly. She clicked on the light and shined it on the tower, then on Iylah, who at once covered her eyes.

"It's okay," Iylah replied. "It's just part of the game."

"You have to reach in, Sherry," Cole said.

"I'm not reaching—" Her phone suddenly went off. "Damnit. My battery's dead," Sherry groaned. "Is there a flashlight?"

"Yeah. I think there's one in the basement." He scooted his chair back. "There's a box of emergency stuff down there. I can go get it—"

"No! We stay together," Iylah cut in.

"It's just down the steps," Cole replied. "It'll take thirty seconds—"

"Cole. We stay together. No matter what," she said sternly.

"So, what does that mean? We all go down together?" Jared asked.

"Sherry, maybe try reaching in," Cole encouraged. "There might be a flashlight in there or something."

"Good idea," Iylah said. "Sherry, go ahead."

"Ugh," she moaned, agitated at Jared. "Next time, I roll." The group waited.

"Are you in yet?" Cole asked.

"Shut up!" She hissed. "God!" Movement could be heard on the board, skin scraping against the unsanded wood of the hole's rim. Sherry pulled her hand back. "There's nothing in there."

"Yes, there is," Iylah replied sympathetically. "Come on, it's in there."

"Ahh! Fine!" She reached in again and began feeling around.

"Oh. I got something!" There was a collective yell to hurry, and Sherry yanked her hand out of the box. A thin square box rested in the palm of her hand. "What is it?" She asked. The group of them leaned in to try and see what was in Sherry's hand, willing their eyes to adjust in the darkness. She shook the object and then fingered the top to try and open it. "Oh," she uttered. She turned it upside down and emptied the contents onto her hand. "It feels like birthday candles. And a box of matches."

Jared took a candle from her hand and lit it using a match. "Yeah, these will *really* help," he said, mockingly, moving it around the table. "How we supposed to see anything with these?"

"Wait!" Iylah said, springing up. She'd forgotten what was in her backpack. "I have a flashlight!"

"Where you goin'?" Jared asked.

"Just over here." Iylah moved carefully across the floor of the dining room, into the hall. Light from the streetlamps streamed in through the windows enough for her to find the foyer and then the entrance to the guestroom. She checked the group; total darkness except for the tiny dancing flame that Jared was holding. She paused at the threshold, eyeing the emptiness in front of her. With a shaky voice she called them: "Can y'all come here? Please?" They did. "Sorry, I don't want to go in alone. Just in case." She walked into the guestroom with the others and knelt on the floor, feeling around. "My bag's not here. Do you guys see it?"

"I can't see a thing," Jared said.

"You brought it upstairs," Cole said, snapping. "When we were up there with Sherry. You had it, didn't you?"

Iylah's tongue clicked. "You're right. Come on," she whispered.

"Wait, wait, hold up," Jared said. "We're goin' upstairs?"

"We need a flashlight, don't we? Would you rather go looking in the dark basement?" She asked.

"Good point. Your basement's scary as hell," Jared said to Cole.

The group felt their way toward the stairs and began walking up carefully, Iylah in the lead.

"Hey, I just thought of something," Jared whispered. No one bothered to ask what. "Didn't your twin die on your birthday?"

"Can we please stop talking about her dead sister?" Sherry asked, a tremor in her voice.

"You think that's why she's giving us this stuff? She wants us to have another birthday for her?" Someone swatted his arm. "Ow! What?"

The group had latched themselves to Iylah's shirt and arms, huddling tight against her to fit up the narrow stairway. She kept a hand against the wall to help navigate but also for balance. One of the wooden signs got knocked off the wall and bounced down the stairs to the floor. There was a collection of screams and abrupt tugging. "Hey, Hey! Calm down!" Iylah said. "It was me. Sorry, my hand hit it."

They got to the top, and Iylah felt her way along the wall toward Cole's room. The rest of them stayed put. "It was right here," she whispered. "Where is it?"

"Maybe you dropped it on the other end of the hall," Cole said, moving toward the other side.

"I didn't go over there," Iylah said. She moved her foot around, hoping to feel it, but there was nothing.

A soft *creak* cut through the quiet. "What was that?" Jared asked.

No one said a word.

"Cole, where are you?" Sherry asked.

"I'm right here," he replied.

"Was that you?" Sherry asked.

"No. Sounded like it came from my parents' room . . ."

"Of course it did," Jared whispered.

A door began to creak open.

"Yo, who is that?" Jared asked.

"Everybody, get back, now!" Iylah said abruptly, reaching for the group. The door screeched open for several seconds before finally coming to a stop, the knob gently touching the wall. Iylah could sense Cole moving toward it. "Cole, don't go in there!"

"I'm not. I'm just looking—" Cole stopped. "Whoa . . ."

"Whoa what?" Jared asked. "Don't do that shit, man."

Cole spoke barely above a whisper. "There's someone standing in the room."

"Cole, get away from the door," Iylah said, finding Cole's arm and yanking him behind her. She stood now, facing inside Cole's parents' room. Though it was pitch black inside, against the far wall was a window with a thin curtain over it. In the moonlight, it looked as if someone were standing at the window's edge.

"Oh wait," Cole whispered. "Sorry. Never mind. It's a lamp."

"Are you sure?" Iylah asked, loosening her grip on the bunch.

"Yeah. It's my dad's reading lamp. False alarm," Cole replied.

"Man, y'all, quit playin'," Jared said, grabbing tight onto Cole's shoulder.

Cole shrugged him off. "What are you doing?"

"Shut up, I don't like this stuff. Man up and let me hold on to you." Jared inched forward, shifting Cole enough for him to lose his footing.

"Whoa!" Cole said, grabbing onto Iylah's arm, almost tearing her down. He tripped over something.

"Would you guys stop!" Iylah said, agitated.

"Sorry," Cole said. "I think I found your bag, though. It's right here."

Iylah knelt down, feeling around the floor. "Thank God."

There was a gasp from someone, but Iylah couldn't tell who. She unzipped the bag and began feeling around.

"Guys . . ." Sherry whispered.

Iylah ignored her. "I got it!"

"Guys!" Sherry hissed more intensely. "I don't think that's a lamp." Iylah froze. "It's moving."

"Fuck this, y'all. I'm out," Jared said, backing away.

"No," Cole said sharply, holding on to his arm. He looked inside again and paused for a moment. "I don't see anything moving. Are you sure?"

Iylah switched the flashlight on, and sure enough, there was a lamp beside the bed, in front of the window. "See? It's fine. Come on, let's get back down." She clicked off the light.

Sherry gasped. "Look!" Sherry breathed. "That's not a fucking lamp! It's coming toward us."

Iylah switched on the flashlight again and pointed it at the lamp, trying to calm Sherry down. "See?" Then she clicked it off and took a few steps into the room. "You're just looking at a weird angle. It's definitely a lamp—"

In a flash, whatever had been standing there darted away from the window. The sudden movement set forth an eruption of screams from everyone as they fell over one another in their haste, darting down the stairs. The cries stunned Iylah into paralysis. She stood, staring blindly into the room, feeling that something was about to attack her. But nothing came.

Sherry shrieked downstairs, and it was followed by a thundering crash with an accompanying shatter of glass. The noise broke Iylah from her daze. She sprang back to follow them in a run but was cut short when something smashed into her face. In the instant before she passed out and fell to the floor, a warm sensation flooded her mouth, as her vision—despite the deep blackness around her—began flashing with bursts of white.

Three Years Ago
The Visitor

*S*omeone was crying outside.

Iylah sat up in bed and peered out the window. The mesh of the screen blurred her view. It didn't help that there were no lights along the road. She sat still and listened. The sound was unmistakable; a girl was crying. It was getting louder, not because it was getting closer but because the person sounded in evermore anguish. Choked, guttural groans held back only by a need to breathe.

She knew that sound. Her heart fluttered. "Jo?" Even in the darkness there was no mistaking that someone was standing in the road in front of their house. "Oh my God," Iylah whispered. "Jo!" She rushed down the stairs as gently as possible as not to wake her parents. She wasn't sure *how* it was Jo but if it was, she felt it was in her best interest to be the first one to speak with her.

Iylah peeked outside the door, scanning the yard. "Jo!" She whispered. She closed the door softly and began down the walkway. The porch light flicked on. "Jo!" She stopped to listen; there were words stuttered between the breaths and sobs.

"Iylah," she heard the voice say.

"Jo!" Iylah said, a little louder than she intended. "Oh my God! Jo, I'm here. Where are you?"

There was a response, but the words were incoherent. The cries sounded like they were coming from all around her. She moved down to the road, checking for any sign of movement. "Jo?" She could hear a mild breeze picking up through the trees.

"Iylah!" the voice whispered sharply, right behind her. She whipped around in the direction of her house. The front door was open and in the light she should make out someone standing just inside.

"Jo!" Iylah exclaimed in a whisper, running to the doorway, stopping only a few steps from the house. The person stood rigid, their back to Iylah, arms wrapped around themselves and practically convulsing as they continued to sob in short breaths.

"W-W-Why d-did you l-l-leave me?"

"Jo," Iylah whispered.

The figure twisted around. Iylah gasped, her hand leaping up over her mouth. It was her twin sister. The sister that no one had seen for nearly 48 hours since she'd gone missing. She said Jo's name again, but it came out stifled as tears welled up in her eyes. She lunged forward, throwing her arms around the girl. "Jo! Oh my God! Oh my God."

Iylah pulled back, placing her hands on either side of Jo's face. She stared at her sister, eyes darting back and forth over her features fighting the notion that this encounter wasn't real, that it was a dream. The thick, curled hair; the unkempt, bushy eyebrows. The acne scars. Iylah rested her forehead against her sister's, closing her eyes, and in tears thanked God she was alive. Jo, in all this, said nothing, standing statue still in her sister's embrace. Finally, Iylah turned her head and rested it lovingly on Jo's shoulder, still not letting go.

Despite hugging her, the emotional surprise of seeing Jo had numbed Iylah's mind to the coldness of the body under her fingers. As her mind began to clear, she started to feel Jo shaking under her. Iylah straightened, noticing that Jo wasn't hugging back—her hands were limp. That's when she noticed the icy chill now tingling her chest. Iylah's shirt was damp. "You're soaked." Jo's head, along with her body, was quivering as she stared back at her sister. Iylah reached to touch the chilled flesh beneath the sleeve of Jo's arm. "Shit, Jo. You're freezing! Come on, let's get you inside."

Iylah led Jo into the living room, still careful to be quiet. She clicked on a table lamp and was unable to suppress a gasp when she saw her sister's body in the light. It had a pale tint of blue—almost gray. Were it not for the tremors, Jo could have easily passed for a corpse. Her half-open eyes watched Iylah, devoid of any life. She was wearing her favorite shirt—the one Iylah had gotten her at a Faith Hill concert—and a pair of bright yellow shorts with lightning bolts on them.

Iylah ripped two blankets off of her mom's easy chair and began to pull up on Jo's shirt. "Here, let's get you out of these clothes and get warm." Jo's arms lifted cautiously, her body still trembling. She never broke eye contact with her sister.

Iylah wrapped a blanket around Jo's shoulders and then pulled down her shorts to cover her legs with the other. "There. It's okay." She hugged her once more, rubbing her hands up and down Jo's arms before resting her on the sofa and picking up the clothes. These were the clothes Jo had been wearing days ago on their birthday, when Iylah had last seen her. Iylah tried to reason how Jo could have gotten home. Something didn't feel right but her brain wouldn't chase it down.

Iylah chucked the soiled clothes into the laundry room to be washed the following day and sat beside her sister. She took her hand—it was warming, thank God—and rubbed the back of it. Jo sat, her mouth slightly open, as if in a trance, staring across the room at the mess that had taken over the living room. Clothes left unfolded or thrown over furniture, pillows and blankets cast to the floor, plates and bowls crusted with old food left out on side tables. Iylah followed the gaze, surveying the house's distress. "They're gonna lose their shit when they see you're home," she said, stifling back the urge to cry with a laugh. "Everyone's been looking for you for the last two nights—"

"Why did you leave me?" Jo cut in, emotionless, her gaze unmoved.

Iylah's mouth hung open as she began stammering over her words. "I-I-I didn't mean to—Jo it was an accident, I swear. I didn't mean to leave you. We were all in the boat; I thought that everyone was downstairs—I thought you went to bed."

"You left me," Jo said softly, her lips turning down as her eyes welled up once again. "You left me alone." Jo's head fell, tears dropping on Iylah's hand. "You left me alone, Iylah. I was so scared." She leaned into her, practically collapsing against her chest. Iylah wrapped her sister in her arms, comforting her as the sobs broke into muffled howling. Iylah tried to reassure her and keep the noise down. She didn't want her parents to wake up. "I screamed for you to come back, and you left me. I was so scared."

"Shhh," Iylah whispered, running her hands through Jo's icy hair. "It's okay. You're here now. You're okay. I've got you." Jo sat up, her pale face blotched with red, and her eyes as gray as a storm. "You're here now," Iylah said, raising a hand to stroke the side of Jo's face.

"But you didn't want me to be," Jo said, dejected.

The words sliced Iylah's heart. "No!" She swallowed, suddenly feeling nauseated by her sister's harrowing stare and shot forward to hug Jo tight once more. "Don't say that. Please, you have to believe me. I didn't know . . ." Tears streamed down her face.

"I was so scared, Iylah," Jo whispered, almost inaudible in Iylah's embrace. "It was so dark. And I couldn't breathe." Iylah at once sat back, wiping an arm across her eyes to clear her vision. "Something grabbed me in the water, and I couldn't get out. I called for you, and you—you n-n-never came b-back—" Iylah took Jo's head in her hands. "You never came back . . ."

"I did! We did! As soon as I knew you were gone, we came back and searched everywhere. We've been looking for you for days. Mom, Dad—the police—everyone."

"How did you not see me?" Jo asked softly, staring deep into her.

"I thought you'd gone down with everyone else. We thought you were asleep. That's why we left." Jo's eyes studied Iylah, almost as if she were waiting for her to say something else. All that came out was, "I swear." With those words, Jo's gaze suddenly fell away from Iylah's. She appeared to slump forward. "Jo, you have to believe me. You know I would never do anything to hurt you like that."

Jo gripped her sister's hand and squeezed, taking a deep breath. "I wanna go to bed, now," she muttered. Her eyes rolled slowly up to meet Iylah's.

"Okay," Iylah whispered, nodding. "Okay." She hugged Jo close again, assuring her that everything was okay now that she was home. Iylah stroked her sister's head for a long while before maneuvering it to rest atop her shoulder. "I want to go to bed."

Iylah stood up, helping Jo get to her feet. She could hear Jo's teeth chattering. "Here. Let's get you into the shower." She held her close as they walked quietly up the stairs to the loft and into the bathroom. At first, Jo was hesitant, but she didn't resist. Iylah turned on the showerhead and quickly retrieved two towels from under the sink before closing the door. She hoped her parents were still out cold. Thankfully, their room was downstairs, at the other end of the house.

Jo, still wrapped in the blankets, stood motionless against the wall.

"Perfect," Iylah said, flicking water from her hand. "Here." She waved Jo over, leaving the shower door open. Steam was beginning to rise out. "This should warm you up." Iylah removed the blankets from her sister, causing Jo to suck in a sharp breath and immediately begin shivering again. "Almost there, almost there," Iylah whispered. She helped her gently remove her bra and underwear, and wearing only a t-shirt and shorts herself, stepped into the shower before taking Jo's hand to follow.

Jo winced when her bare feet hit the tile floor. Iylah detached the showerhead from its holster, and beginning with Jo's legs, started gradually moving it up Jo's body. Jo took in a deep breath and closed her eyes. Her hands, which had been previously locked under her armpits, began to slacken. Iylah could see the rigidity of her body begin to break down as her shoulders slumped. She let out a soft, ecstatic breath and then shook with a chill as the warmth engulfed her. Iylah smiled.

Iylah ran the warm water all over, using the loofah to wash her sister's body. The light tile floor became streaked with a dark, sludgy substance running within the water toward the drain. Iylah hadn't noticed anything on Jo's body before and thought it strange for a brief moment, wondering where it was coming from. Jo put her head down and sighed.

Iylah shampooed her hair and held the water over her head for a long time. Jo seemed to relax even more under it. Iylah glanced down once again and noticed several strands of something greenish-brown gathering at her feet and now sticking out of the drain, forcing shampoo suds to start pooling. Jo nearly slipped when she tried to turn, but Iylah caught her and quietly chuckled. Before she knew it, she'd completely cleaned her sister and was cutting the water off. She checked the drain once more;

whatever was there must have finally run down with the soap and water.

Iylah got her sister dressed in a clean set of clothes, then wrapped her back up in a blanket. She switched on the bedside lamp in Jo's room across the loft and plugged in a hair dryer. She closed the door and put a towel underneath to help drown the noise. Jo sat on the floor in front of her while Iylah did her best to dry the wet hair. "That should be okay. You think?" Jo nodded weakly, not even bothering to feel it.

She helped her sister into bed, tucking her tightly into the sheets. Jo lay there staring at Iylah for a long while. Her face had regained some of its color, and the soul in her eyes was beginning to awaken. After a long moment, Jo rolled over and faced the wall.

Iylah knelt beside the bed, tickling her back and running a hand through her hair, waiting and hoping that Jo would fall asleep. When she noticed a faint change in her breathing, Iylah leaned back and stood up. "Night, Jo." There was a fleeting moment where she wanted to wake up her parents, but Jo needed to rest. So did her parents. They could all reunite in the morning.

Iylah considered going straight to bed herself, but there was no way she'd be able to sleep. She made her way back downstairs and cleaned up where she and Jo had been. She folded and put away the blankets and started the wash with Jo's clothes and the towels they'd used. Still wide awake, she found herself hand washing the stack of used dishes that had been left out in the living room.

The clock on the stove read 3:09. Drowsiness was suddenly starting to take over. She crept back up the stairs and stopped outside Jo's door. It was closed. She was sure she'd left it open. Something squirmed in her stomach—a feeling. *Tell me this wasn't a dream*, she thought. She reached her hand out to open the door. "Please, no," she whispered. Iylah peered into the darkness and stepped in to get a closer look. She sighed with relief. Jo was still curled in the sheets, facing the wall as Iylah had left her. She touched where her sister's shoulder would be and stroked down her arm before leaving her once again.

Nestled finally in her own cool sheets, Iylah scooted her body toward the window and exhaled in satisfaction. She closed her eyes and felt her body begin to give way to rest. A creak in the floor snapped behind her. Iylah's eyes opened, bringing her out of what she felt to already be a deep sleep. "Jo?" She turned her head, seeing the silhouette of a girl standing in the doorway against the loft's night light. The figure didn't move. "Jo. You okay?"

It stepped closer, and then whispered in a strained voice, "Can I sleep in your bed?"

"Yeah," Iylah replied. "Come on." She moved the covers and scooted closer to the wall. Iylah felt Jo crawl in beside her and nuzzle close, placing a hand against her back, like she did when they were kids. Iylah had always found this idiosyncrasy annoying when they shared a bed—always having Jo's hand somewhere on her—but tonight she understood the calming effects. It brought a smile to her face as she drifted off, feeling Jo's light breaths against the back of her neck.

It wasn't long before she heard the strained voice again. "Iylah," it said. She stayed still. She had definitely been asleep this time and could feel exhaustion's grip still holding her. "Iylah."

"Mmm." She could feel something rubbing her arm, gently rocking her. "I said it's fine," Iylah mumbled into her pillow. "You can sleep in here." The rocking continued. Iylah's eyes opened slightly, finally sensing the light outside. She moved the blanket up over her head. "It's too early. Go back to sleep—"

"Iylah, sweetie," the voice said again. It was her mom. Iylah's eyes shot open. She spun sharply to see her sitting on the bed, triggering a sudden concern that Jo was being squished beneath. Iylah sat upright and tried to pull the covers from under her mother, who promptly stood up. "What's wrong?"

Iylah threw back the sheets. No one. The suddenness of being awake was making her mind foggy. She searched the room, trying to get her bearings. "Where's Jo?"

"Iylah . . ."

Iylah stood up, pausing as her eyes adjusted to the light and her brain's equilibrium became more stable. She looked around the room and then walked toward the door. "Did you see her?"

"Iylah, sweetie," her mother tried to cut in. "Come here." Silvia advanced on her cautiously, bringing up her arms as if to take her daughter in.

Iylah stood still, staring, until an uneasy feeling flashed over her. She hurriedly went into the loft toward Jo's room and opened the door, reasoning that Jo had gone back to her own bed at some point during the night. It only seemed natural that her parents wouldn't open Jo's door—why would they? She peeked in, careful not to wake her, but there was no point. The bed was perfectly made, just as it had been the day Jo disappeared.

Iylah pushed the door open, saying her sister's name and looking around. She felt her mother come up behind her.

"Iylah," she whispered, touching her shoulder. "The sheriff called earlier this morn—"

"No, no, no, no, no," Iylah muttered rapidly, scanning the room, running both hands through her hair in confusion. "She—she—she was here. She came home. Jo. She was here last night."

"Iylah . . ."

"Mom. I'm not . . . I promise, I'm not making this up. I saw her. I-I-I touched her. I woke up last night and heard her crying outside—she was there."

"Iylah sweetie, you couldn't have seen her—"

"It wasn't a dream, Mom! She was here. She came in, she was crying—we sat on the couch downstairs. We sat here! Right here!" Iylah pointed at the bed. "I dried her hair!" Her mother reached out and tried once again to embrace her, but Iylah jerked away and took off down the stairs. "I swear to God, mom," Iylah called, choking back tears. "She was home." Iylah darted toward the laundry room, where she opened the washing machine lid. "Look, see?" She reached in and pulled out a clump of wet clothes. "She was—" Iylah stopped when she noticed that the clothes in her hand were her dad's. "What?" she whispered.

"Iylah . . ."

She took off back up the stairs to the bathroom, where she opened the door and at once noticed that everything was as it had been the day before—before Jo's arrival. The hand towels were untouched; no soap bottles moved. The loofah was still hanging over the faucet. She inched closer to the shower and knelt over the tile floor, running her finger along the cold rock. Dry. "I don't understand," she said to herself. She could hear her mom behind her, now standing in the doorway. Iylah turned to address her, "Mom. I swear, she was right here—" Iylah paused, staring at the drain. Something was poking out, barely visible. She grazed over it and noticed the water on her finger. She pulled on it slightly, but whatever it was broke off. A tiny piece of a stem.

"Sweetie, they found your sister early this morning." Iylah could feel the muscles in her face beginning to tighten as her eyes remained locked on the drain. She sensed her mother step closer. Iylah's head began to shake slowly in hopes that denying the truth would somehow change it. "She was here," she whispered. "We stood right here. I washed her. She was home." Her words became strained as she stood up and moved down the stairs into the living room. Her mother followed her, coming around to face her and placing her hands on either side of Iylah's head. "Mr. Taylor found her when he went fishing this morning." Iylah felt as if she was starting to lose consciousness. "He says he found her just a couple hundred yards from where you said she jumped in." Instantly, Iylah reached out for the table to her right, beside her mom's easy chair, and noticed its surface. It was clean. The dishes were gone. Iylah collapsed into the chair, urgently scanning the room. Everything was as she'd left it after getting Jo in bed.

With this realization, a choking snort escaped her mouth as she threw her hands up over her face and gasped, trying to hold back the tears. Her chest was on fire. She wanted to cry, but the tightness in her lungs prevented her from drawing a full breath, allowing instead only short gasps of air as she sunk onto the floor, clutching at her stomach. The pain seared as if someone was cutting into her belly. It wasn't until her mother knelt to embrace her that she completely broke down.

14

NOW

The three of them rushed into the garage.

Cole shut the door and moved carefully away from it, making sure to hold onto Sherry's hand in the dark. "What broke?" He whispered, barely audible over the panting between them.

"I'm so sorry," Sherry said, trying to catch her breath. "I tripped over something and accidentally grabbed the wine rack on the wall."

"Fuck!" he whispered. "Like, the whole thing came down?"

"Yeah. I'm so sorry. I'll clean it up. And I'll pay for it."

"You can't pay that back. Those wines are super expensive. And hard to find. My mom's gonna kill me."

"What the hell was that up there?" Jared asked, still trying to calm his nerves. "You saw that right? It wasn't just me?"

"No, I saw it. Something was in there."

"We need to get the *fuck* out of here. Like, now!" Jared said.

"Good thinking genius; how're we gonna do that?"

"Don't get snippy with me. It was an idea. You're obviously not gonna come up with anything."

"Of course, you turn this around on me."

"Guys! Really?" Cole attempted.

"You turned it around on yourself the night you sent that picture."

"Oh my God!" Sherry snapped. "I *told you* I didn't mean to send it."

"Guys!" Cole interjected.

"Oh. You didn't mean to send it?" Jared paused. "Well, shit, I guess that makes everything better."

"Jared," Cole said pointedly.

"God! You are such a prick!" Sherry exclaimed in a hushed voice. "It was an accident. I didn't see you back there. You really think that little of me to believe I would send something like that out intentionally?"

"Hey! That's enough!" Cole attempted again.

"Um, for a girl who never takes selfies, it seems a little suspect that you just happened to send *that* picture out," Jared said. "To every one of our friends, by the way."

"Okay, you know what? Fine. What do you want from me, Jared? I've tried to make this right. I've tried calling you, texting you. I even went by your house yesterday. You won't give me the time of day—"

"Because I don't want anything to do with you!" Jared fired back in a whisper.

She stood stunned; the words hanging in the air, echoing in her brain. Sherry at once felt nauseated. After a moment of quiet, "You don't mean that."

Cole tried to say something, but Jared continued. "You think you can make this better by simply telling me it was an accident? You *don't get it*, that's the problem. This isn't something you just fix, Sherry. You have no idea how much you messed shit up with me. At home, at school, baseball . . ." He paused, holding back his words.

"Jared, I know it doesn't make it better, but I had no clue you were back there—"

"And why would I believe that, Sherry? Huh? You've already lied to me. You texted me the next morning saying someone hacked your phone when you knew—you fuckin' *knew*—you were the one sent that shit out!"

"I didn't know what to say, I'm sorry."

"Oh, you're sorry about *that*, but not about sending it? You realize you've never apologized to me? Not once."

"Yes, I did!"

Jared fired something back, but Cole couldn't make it out due to Sherry not letting up with her speech. The two of them went back and forth in hushed tones over each other as Cole began to hear a shuffling inside the house. He focused his hearing, leaning closer to the door, and that's when he realized. "Oh crap," he muttered. Iylah wasn't in the room with them. "Guys!" Finally, he felt his way in the dark until he got close to them and grabbed them both by the shirt and ordered them: "Shut up!" He couldn't see them, but their silence told him he had their attention. "Where's Iylah?"

"Wasn't she behind us?" Jared asked.

"I thought she was. Iylah?"

Another noise came from behind the garage door. "Shhh!" Cole hissed. Someone was walking around in the kitchen. "Iylah?" Cole called, louder than he anticipated.

"Dude," Jared swatted him. "What if it's that other chick?"

The door handle of the garage clicked and turned. "Cole?" She said.

There was a collective sigh of relief. "Iylah! Holy crap. Where did you go?" Cole asked.

"I slipped on the way down. Sorry. Are you all okay?" She stepped down, closing the door behind her.

"Yeah, we're fine. How about you? You hurt?" Cole asked.

"I'm okay. We need to hurry and finish the game."

"What was in that room?" Jared asked. "Was that her? Your sister, I mean."

"Yes."

"Screw that," Jared exhaled. "I'm not goin' back in there."

"What's the alternative? Staying out here?" Cole asked.

"What about your parents' cars?" Jared asked. "We could open the garage and just gun it, maybe even hit whatever's outside."

"They took them. Dad took his Camaro this morning. Probably thought I'd drive it."

"Our best bet is to finish," Iylah said. "That's the only way to make it stop."

Cole felt around for the knob, easing the door open to listen for anyone else in the house. "What about your sister? What if she's down here now?"

"Yeah, I ain't goin' back in there without protection," Jared said, beginning to rummage around the garage.

"There's no one else down here," Iylah said. "As long as you're playing the game, she won't bother you."

Cole stepped inside the house, looking around the darkness. "The flashlight. Did you bring it?" Iylah didn't reply. "Iylah?"

"Yes?"

"Where's the light?"

"Oh. I guess it's still upstairs. Sorry. Must've dropped it."

Cole breathed a curse. "Come on guys, let's go."

"We're goin' back upstairs?" Jared asked.

"We need that light." Cole could hear Jared fumbling around, moving things, and talking in a frantic search.

"Here we go!" Something rubbed against the tall oil drum that held the yard tools, followed by a raspy grating of metal prongs against the concrete floor.

"Is that a rake?" Cole asked.

"I guess . . ." Jared mumbled.

"Dude, put that back. You're just gonna knock shit over," Cole said.

Jared's tongue clicked. "Fine. But I'm not goin' in first."

The three of them walked in through the garage door into the laundry room. Cole, with Jared latching onto his arm, felt his way awkwardly around the wall into the kitchen. Something splashed under his foot, and then crunched. "The wine. Holy crap, it's all the way over here?"

"I'm sorry," Sherry whispered.

"It's alright. I'll clean it up when we're done." Glass snapped under his foot as he moved on. "Jared, watch your feet, man. Glass everywhere." Jared commented that he had thick socks when Cole stopped suddenly.

"What?" Sherry asked, almost tumbling onto him.

"My mom's rugs." He stood still. "We can't track over the carpets."

"Seriously, bro?" Jared muttered.

"Just shut up and follow close, alright? Don't step on the rugs."

They crept into the foyer. "Should we grab the game?" Jared asked.

"Nah, we'll come back down," Cole replied. "Everybody okay? Iylah? You good?"

"Yuperoo," she replied in a voice that could have either been sarcastic or cheerful. They began their ascent up the main staircase. "Everybody be careful."

"Wait, hold up. Do we really need that light? What happened to those birthday candles?" Jared asked.

"I'm not lighting candles all night. We'll be quick," Cole replied. Bunched together as if stuffed inside one set of clothing, they all moved slowly up the stairs. None of them made a sound until they reached the top. "Where'd you leave it?"

"I don't know," Iylah replied from behind them. "Maybe check over by your parents' room."

"Yeah, we're not goin' over there," Jared muttered.

"It might've rolled somewhere when she fell. Everyone feel around," Cole said. He squatted, running his hand along the hardwood floor. Both Sherry and Jared detached, but stood close by.

"Got it," Iylah said. She was on the other side of the hall, near Cole's room. "I guess it rolled over here—"

Sherry gasped and stumbled.

"What! What happened?" Cole asked.

"I'm fine. Just tripped," Sherry replied. "Found your backpack. Jeez it's heavy. What did you put in here?"

"Here, I got you," Cole said, taking it from her.

"Alright. Let's go. I don't like bein' up here in the dark," Jared said.

"Iylah, can you turn the light on?" Cole asked.

"Here. You take it," she replied. There was a low rumble as it rolled across the floor toward him.

"Ooo!" Jared stumbled. "What is that? I just stepped on something. Sorta feels like . . ." Jared paused about the same time as a horrible shriek shot out around them. In conjunction, Sherry screamed, and Jared began yelling, "Shit! Shit! Shit!" leaping over the floor toward Cole, who abruptly stooped to feel for the flashlight on the floor.

There was a sharp gasp as something on the floor started to breathe rapidly.

"What is that? What is that?" Jared nearly pulled Cole down the stairs with him before Cole steadied himself on the wall. "That's her sister, man. Come on. Let's go! Let's go!" Sherry screamed again and began clawing over toward the two of them.

"Guys! Stop!" Cole said, finding the light, and clicking it on. The beam opened onto Iylah, who was sitting up, holding the side of her head. The bottom of her face looked as if it had been painted with blobs of red. Lines of it ran down her neck, streaking and spotting the top of her shirt. "Iylah?" He at once shined the light toward his bedroom. The girl that had been with them a second ago was gone.

The Last Day
of Sophomore Year
Part 1

*I*ylah felt her phone buzz in her hand as Mr. Wheeler readied his computer to show her final chemistry grade. She glimpsed at the phone. It was Jo calling. She rolled her eyes and hit ignore. The last day of school was always Iylah's favorite: time to sign yearbooks, no formal classes, and no expectation to stay. Unfortunately, her twin sister Josephine did not share her excitement.

Iylah's plan was to collect her final grades, add a few more signatures to her book, and then meet up with her friends to walk over to The Varsity—a restaurant owned by her friend, Mark—for a slice of pizza, or Dairy Queen for ice cream. Or both! It *was* summer; they could do whatever they wanted. That was the plan until Jo asked if Iylah could walk her home after school.

"Iylah Maddox," Mr. Wheeler said, announcing her name with gusto as if he hadn't seen her in years. "Give me just one second to pull yours up. Don't want you to see the others . . . and . . . there. Come on around." He motioned her around his desk and pointed at blocks on the screen. "Final quarter, final exam. Final grade."

"I got a ninety on the exam?" Iylah asked, shocked.

"You got a ninety?" he replied, just as surprised. "That can't be right." She swatted his shoulder, making him laugh. "Great job, Iylah. You really turned it around after second quarter. Proud of you." He paused and looked at her with sincere eyes. "Unless I need to investigate this ninety."

She shrugged. "You can try," she replied, getting another laugh. The phone buzzed in her hand; Jo again.

"You happy with the grade?"

"Happy? I've spent the morning trying to come up with how to tell my parents I bombed this class. And not only did I get an B on the exam, I got a B in the class? They're probably going to think I paid you."

He smiled. "Well, you earned it."

"Can't say I had much of a choice there," Iylah replied. "It was either a better grade or no phone for the summer."

"Your sister help you out?"

Iylah sighed. "Of course." The phone in her hand buzzed again. "What'd she get?"

He clicked out of her report and turned toward her with a look of derision. "You know I can't tell you that."

"It was the highest grade in the class wasn't it?"

"Can't tell you," he said back in a slightly melodic tone. Two guys walked in and said "hey" to Mr. Wheeler. One of them threw what looked to be a squishy ball at him which he promptly caught, and threw—playfully harder—back at them, smacking the thrower in the crotch. The kid doubled over and let out a surprised "Ahhww!" as Mr. Wheeler threw up both hands and yelled "Boom!"

She looked at her phone: four missed calls from Jo. "Oh my gosh," she huffed, agitated. "Alright, I gotta go. Thanks again, Mr. Wheeler."

"Great having you in class, Iylah. Your sarcasm was always a ray of sunshine. Let me know next year if you want to start tutoring my AP students."

"Oh yeah," Iylah said, "Count me in for that one." She left the class and was just about to text her friend that she was done and ready to meet up when Jo called once more.

"Holy crap, Jo! What? What!"

"Iylah?" Jo said, sounding distressed. "Are you still here?"

"Yes. What do you want?"

"Um . . ." There was a long pause. "Can you please walk home with me after school?"

"Jo, I'm not staying at school all day. Just have mom or dad come get you?"

"I asked mom, but she said to tell you not to leave without me."

"Wait. You didn't tell her I was leaving early, did you?"

"No I—"

"Did you tell dad?"

"I didn't tell them. I just said you were going with your friends after school and asked if they could come and get me. Mom said for you to take me home first."

"Why don't you just come with us? We're walking over to Mark's place for a pizza," Iylah said. Then, in a cheery, slightly teasing tone, "He might be there."

"I can't leave early. We're playing my game in Ms. Bellamy's class. I said I'd be there."

"Jo, it's the last day of school, I highly doubt Ms. Bellamy will care if you're not there. I'm sure *she* doesn't even want to be there—"

"No, it was her idea. There's gonna be a lot of us there. It's students vs teachers. We're gonna have pizza and stuff. You could come. We're playing that game I made over Christmas break; the one where you have to—

"Yeah, I'm not stayin' for that," Iylah cut in. "Look, if you wanna go with me, we're leaving now. Otherwise, you're on your own."

"But Iylah—"

"I gotta go. And hey! You better not tell mom or dad that I left early, alright?" She waited for Jo to reply. "Okay?"

"Okay . . ." Jo replied. "What am I supposed to do about Maggie? What if she's still here when I leave?"

"I don't know, maybe trying standing up for yourself!" Iylah said, irritably. It came out a lot louder than she'd intended but the hallway was a symphony of student conversations and loud annoying chants. No one seemed to notice.

Maggie Burbank had been one of Jo's and Iylah's closest friends since kindergarten. The three of them had grown up sleeping over at each other's houses on weekends, trick or treating together, even having birthday parties together. Then, somewhere along the way in middle school, for reasons unknown to either sister, Maggie became not only distant toward Jo, but in many instances, hostile. The relationship with Iylah changed as well but only in that it became stale: they lost touch, neither really engaging with the other anymore, drifting instead toward a different group of friends. Their mom chalked it up to normal middle school drama while their dad humorously reasoned that she'd likely been bitten by a tick. Jo tried for a while to mend the relationship, but Maggie found more joy in Jo's humiliation than her friendship.

"If she tries to start something, which I'm sure she won't because by the time you leave here, no one will be around, but if she for some reason is still here, and tries to start shit, then . . . I don't know . . . kick her in the shins."

Jo was quiet again for such a long time that Iylah was about to ask if she was still there when Jo finally spoke and said, "Please. Can you just walk me home?"

She sighed. "Jo. If you don't do something about Maggie, she's just gonna keep doin' it next year. You gotta stand up for yourself sooner or later." Iylah waited for Jo to reply. "Okay?"

"Okay . . ." Jo said, barely audible. "Bye."

Iylah had just sat down with her Blizzard when a sequence of hums buzzed over the wooden table she and her friends were sitting on at Dairy Queen. One of her social media accounts flashed on the screen with a notification. "Cheers to summer!" Janelle said.

The rest of them yelled cheers, clicking their plastic spoons together. "What kind did you get, Iylah?" Janelle asked.

"Cookies and Cream. What'd you get?"

"Just a chocolate cone. So good," Janelle replied in an erotic whisper, licking the side where it was dripping. She was really selling the lick as she moved her tongue from side to side, making a face that crossed from sexy to overly creepy. The girls laughed.

"What kind is that?" Iylah asked Katie. Katie was staring at her phone, trying to shade the screen with her hand. Everyone turned to her, noticing the sudden quiet and a look of disgust over her face. Dark cream was running off Katie's cone onto her finger. "Something you wanna share with the rest of the class?"

"Oh no . . ." Katie replied. There was a collective murmur among them. "I think it's Jo. She's on Maggie's story. Look." They all crowded around, leaning with their elbows on the table. Their shadows helped to block the light. The picture was of a girl's backside, but Iylah knew instantly that it was her sister. She was wearing a yellow t-shirt and a blue skirt with a mesh overlay. She had her backpack on and appeared to be carrying something in the school hallway, but just beneath the pack, her skirt was tucked into her underwear, revealing a pair of white panties and the first letters of the word Tuesday written across the bottom. Beneath the photo in pulsating, bright pink letters: "Happy Friday! I wondered what that smell was." To the side was a floating head animation; someone sticking their tongue out in disgust.

"I fuckin' hate that girl," Janelle said.

Iylah stood, her appetite for sweets gone. She picked up her phone to call Jo and noticed the notifications: *xxMagPiexx has sent you a picture* and beneath it, *xxMagPiexx has started a live video*. "Shit." She clicked on the picture. "Did all you guys get this?" They checked their phones and confirmed. "Oh my gosh! She probably sent this to everyone—"

"Guys," Katie said with a troubling tone. "She's live." She turned the phone toward them, but they opted for their own, cupping hands over their phones to see.

The video was live. A group of girls were standing outside. It looked like the parking lot just outside the gym and one of them was encouraging the others to hush. "Here she comes, here she comes." The camera zoomed in on someone walking toward them. This time there was no denying that it was Jo. She was carrying what looked like rolled up poster boards in her arms and appeared to be struggling to keep them from slipping out. "Ok, ok, get ready." Jo turned down the sidewalk in front of the school, walking toward the path home. Iylah closed her eyes in shame. Jo's skirt was still tucked into her underwear.

Maggie held up a red kick ball, quickly passing off the camera to someone else. The others in the group, all unshown, began telling her to hurry. "I got it. Shut up," Maggie hissed. "Three. Two. One." The camera caught a sudden movement on the side as someone strode up and launched the red ball up into the air.

Iylah screamed for Jo to move, thinking she would somehow hear. The throw was dead on, smashing right across Jo's face and knocking her down. There was a faint shriek as the camera went haywire; the group of girls began screaming with joy. Maggie yelled, "Direct hit, son!" as they took off running the opposite direction. The feed cut off shortly after.

"Fuck that," Janelle said, taking a bite of her cone. "Come on."

"What are you doing?" Iylah asked.

"We're gonna go get your sister," Janelle replied, snatching her lanyard of keys off the table. "And then if we're lucky we're gonna beat the shit out of Maggie."

Janelle sped down 16th St., turning way too fast onto Sycamore St., which ran right in front of the school. Iylah, who had not said a word since Dairy Queen, held on for dear life. She didn't know what to say. On the one hand she should have just made her sister come with them, but on the other, her parents were gonna be pissed when they found out Jo got hit. That would mean that Iylah left without her—left early—and she'd most likely be grounded for a week. Janelle turned violently into the nearly empty parking lot, her tires screaming against the road, and then slammed to a stop. "Get that ball," Janelle said. The red ball that hit Jo was lying against the curb.

"For what?" Iylah asked.

"Just grab it." Iylah did and got back in. Janelle shifted into first and began creeping through the parking lot, leaning over the vestibule and scanning the area.

"There she is!" Katie shouted, scooting up and thrusting a hand between Iylah and Janelle. "There's Jo!" She was right. Jo was walking up ahead, the opposite way of before, still carrying her poster boards. Janelle sped up, coming to a stop beside her and getting out of the car. The abrupt action made Jo recoil and drop her boards. She looked like she was about to run.

"It's me! It's me! It's us!" Janelle said.

"Jo! Are you okay?" Iylah asked, getting out from the passenger seat. Jo looked around, trying to take in what was happening. She likely had no idea that what just happened had been recorded for everyone in their small town to see. There was a large, dark blotch across the left side of Jo's face. She sniffed the snot back into her head and swallowed. "I'm fine," she whispered, looking up to see her sister.

Iylah stepped forward and tried to take her sister by the arm and offer a comforting voice, but Jo jerked it back. "I said I'm fine! Leave me alone!"

"Okay, okay," Iylah said, stepping back. "We just wanted to help."

"You've been enough help to me today, Iylah. Just leave me alone." Jo's voice wavered, obviously wanting to cry. She stooped to once again pick up her boards and Iylah noticed that one of them was ripped across the top.

"Why don't you come with us? We'll give you a ride home." Janelle asked.

"No thank you," she replied. "I can walk." She stood, awkwardly trying to keep hold onto her things, and shot a glance over to Iylah: "Gotta stand up for myself, right?"

"Guys look!" Katie said. "There she is."

Jo's eyes got noticeably wide just before Iylah turned to see Maggie and two of her friends standing at the far end of the lot.

"Bingo," Janelle whispered. She went and retrieved the ball from her car.

"What're you doing?" Katie asked.

Janelle was rummaging in the back, bending inside for a brief moment before coming out with a yearbook in her hand. She began walking away from them, toward the other girls.

"Janelle!" Katie called, and then to the others, "What is she doing? Janelle!"

Iylah and Katie followed in quick pace, trying to figure out what was going on, even though Iylah had a pretty good feeling where this was about to go. Finally, Janelle stopped, and handed the yearbook to Iylah who promptly asked, "what are you doing?"

"Payback," Janelle said confidently. Iylah had only seen her angry once before. It was during their tennis game, the day Janelle found out her mother had cheated on her dad. Despite the earth-shattering news, her dad still came to the game—he never missed one. He sat alone, in the corner by himself, in sunglasses. Iylah remembered occasionally glancing up from the bench and seeing him sorrowfully trembling. At one point, in the middle of a set, Janelle's mom showed up and attempted to sit next to her father. One could tell there was a heated discussion happening until finally, the dad got up and moved down, putting himself into a crowd of people to get away from her. It was hard to ignore. The words weren't audible but in the quiet of a tennis match, it was easy to tell that whatever was coming out of Janelle's mom's mouth wasn't cheerful. And then, as if Janelle had a slip of the eye or wrist, she tossed up the ball and served it into the stands, square onto her mother's chest. There was a loud pop as her mom fell back, yelling obscenities at the other girl, thinking she had carelessly served. No one said a word, except for the official who called "fault." Janelle stood her ground, glaring a hole into her mother. Everyone in the stands stared quietly with her. The woman eventually made eye contact and at the moment when Janelle seemed to believe her mother understood what was going on—that this was the wrong time to have a discussion and she was the wrong daughter to lie to—she began bouncing the ball and readied herself to serve again.

This moment would blow that one out of the water. Janelle narrowed her eyes and seemed to square her shot before she shouted out Maggie's name. Iylah had barely a second to react. Janelle drew back and fired the red ball at an alarming speed. It cut through the air with deadeye accuracy, and leveled Maggie right in the face, making a hollow *Doink!* Iylah heard herself curse.

"Thank you," Janelle said merrily, taking the yearbook from Iylah's grip. She sprinted over to Maggie who was still sitting on her butt, pressing her hands to her face. When she noticed Janelle coming toward her, the bewildered, pained look vanished into lip biting fury. Maggie pushed herself off the ground and held up her fists in defense as Janelle, who was now running at full speed, cocked back the yearbook as if it were a baseball bat. In an unexpected, smooth, violent motion, she cracked the book across Maggie's face, sending her back down to the pavement. The friend on Maggie's right made a sudden move to flee, but Janelle took it as a threat. She swung the book back once more at face level but stopped when the girl shielded her face with her hands. Taking advantage of the opening, Janelle flipped the book on its side and drove the spine forcefully into the girl's gut. The hit forced out a sickening bellow as she dropped to her knees. Iylah and Katie both yelled and rushed over to try and step in.

Janelle put her sights on the third friend who at once began backing away, frightened and holding up her palms in surrender. Maggie was screaming in misery, and the other one was making dreadful noises attempting to recapture her breath. Janelle looked down and noticed a phone beside Maggie and picked it up. "This hers?" She asked the only friend still standing. There was no answer until Janelle stepped toward her, hands ready to strike. "Are you deaf? Is this her phone?"

The friend nodded. Maggie looked up at what was transpiring. "Good." Janelle ripped off the case and slammed the phone to the ground. It bounced up only once before Janelle began stomping her black Chuck Taylors feverishly on top of it. Maggie sat up in protest but didn't dare try to stop her. Janelle gave the phone one final smash with the yearbook and whipped an arm over her hair to throw it back.

"It was a joke!" Maggie yelled. "What is your deal?"

She moved toward Maggie, standing over her with absolute power: "If you ever do that shit again to any of my friends, I'm gonna stomp those lopsided tits of yours back through your *fucking* ribs. You understand me?"

Iylah could see the terror in Maggie's face as she nodded from behind her hand.

"I don't hear you," Janelle said.

"I understand," Maggie said back in a strained voice.

"Apologize to her," Janelle said, pointing back to Jo.

"I'm sorry."

"Bitch, she can't hear that." Janelle kicked at her, connecting with the side of Maggie's butt.

"Stop!" Maggie screamed, scooting back. "Okay. I'm sorry!"

Janelle shook her head. "Yeah, I know you don't mean that." She reared her foot back once more.

"I'm sorry! I'm sorry!" Maggie screamed, holding up her hands. "Please!" Tears began to flow. "I'm sorry."

"Fuck yeah, you're sorry," Janelle said. She turned back to Iylah and winked, moving back to the car with a magical strut in her step. "Let's go."

Chills exploded over Iylah's body. *That was freaking awesome!*

"That was the most bad ass thing I've ever seen," Katie whispered. "Holy shit." Janelle nodded to Jo and took the boards from her before throwing her other arm around her. The look on Jo's face was one Iylah hadn't seen in a long time; total admiration.

15

NOW

Cole and the others stood in fixed dismay, staring at the empty hallway where someone had most certainly been present not more than five seconds ago. A sharp wince from Iylah brought him back to reality. He knelt beside her. "You okay? What happened?"

"I—I don't know. I must've hit my head. Ow . . ." Cole glanced up at the others, who had their eyes locked on him. Iylah noticed the blood on her hands. She began moving her jaw as if testing to see if it worked. "Ahh," she muttered. "My nose." A hand went to touch it and sprang off with another wince.

"Is it broken?" Cole asked.

She laid her fingers over it softly at first, and then with more pressure, finally pinching it gently with both fingers. "I think it's fine. I can breathe, at least. Hurts like hell, though." She noticed her shirt in the light, and made a moan of disgust, pulling it away from her skin to examine it. "Great." She sucked in a breath and tried to stand up.

"You sure you're okay?" Jared asked. "You screamed pretty hard just now."

"Yeah well, it felt like you were ripping the hair off my head."

"Sorry," Jared said. "We didn't see you. Couldn't see anything really. We just came back up here for the flashlight and—"

Cole helped Iylah steady herself, and she quickly shoved him off.

"Whoa—what was that for?" Cole asked, backing off, raising his hands in innocence.

"You left me behind! That's the one thing I asked you not to do."

"Hey, hang on a second. We didn't realize you weren't there. Sherry screamed and we all thought something was coming at us, so we bolted to the garage."

"Yeah, and as *he* already pointed out," Iylah said, throwing a finger over at Jared, "you only came back up here because you needed this." She ripped the light out of Cole's hand. "Glad to know I take precedence over a flashlight." She lowered the light and cradled the bridge of her nose.

"Well, no, that's the thing; you weren't gone," Cole said. "You were with us." Iylah looked at him curiously. "We all ran to the garage, and you came down probably five minutes after. Followed us all the way up here."

"Wha—how? I couldn't've. That wasn't me."

"Yeah, we know that now," Sherry said.

"You couldn't tell it wasn't me?"

"Iylah, the whole house is pitch black. I can't even see you now," Cole replied. "At least not without that." He pointed to the light.

She felt the neck of her shirt. It was sticky between her fingers. "Did she say anything?" Iylah asked, examining the blood.

"Not really," Cole replied.

"She *did* say something," Sherry cut in. "She said if we finished, everything would stop."

Iylah raised the beam to their faces. They were standing bunched together beside the wall, now shielding their eyes.

"Wait, hold up. How do we know this is her?" Jared asked. "Like, what if she's the bad sister and the girl who followed us up is Iylah? Quick, what's your birthday?"

"Dude," Cole said in a voice of exhausted frustration, "they have the same birthday. And would you really know if she was right? Do you know their birthday?"

Jared slouched, deflated. "Good point."

"It's me," Iylah said. "I was with you all when we saw whatever was in there. I just must've hit a wall when you all ran."

"For real though, I feel like you need a bandage or something? Maybe get you a new shirt?" Jared said, pointing toward her.

"I'm fine," Iylah replied with a harsh tone. "Let's just finish this."

Iylah made the others walk with her into the guestroom. They all stood in the doorway, waiting as she rifled through her bag. When she clicked off the light, it was dark enough for her to change shirts without closing the door.

Iylah flipped the light back on and moved past them into the foyer. "From now on, Everyone. Stay. Together." They each walked back into the dining room and situated themselves back at the table. The contents of the game were as they'd been left. Jared found the matches and lit two of the candles.

"These're gonna last like thirty seconds a piece," he muttered.

"Then save them," Cole said, blowing it out. "She has a flashlight."

Iylah shifted the light around the table. She reached across toward Cole and picked up the die. "We ready?" She asked.

"No . . ." Jared mumbled.

She dropped the die onto the table and watched it bounce

around. "*Two*." Then, she moved the light down to the board for Cole to see the spaces; no etching. "Yes!" Cole whispered.

"Lucky," Jared said back.

Cole moved the ball up two and motioned toward Sherry. "You're up."

Sherry reached for the die, but Jared swept under her hand and took it. She protested, saying that she wanted to roll.

"You think I wanna reach in there?" Jared said back.

"I've done it twice already; it's your turn," Sherry replied, agitated.

"You said earlier that you didn't want to roll!"

"No, I said I didn't want to *play*," Sherry replied. "Obviously I'd rather roll than put my hand in there."

"Fine." He held out his palm for her to take it, but just before she took hold of the cube Jared dropped it on the table: *six*. "Sorry. But if it makes you feel any better, it was just an accident."

"You're such an asshole."

"I promise. I didn't mean to," Jared said without emotion, standing up.

"Where you goin'?" Cole asked.

"I need to go pee." There was a collective sound of disgust from the table. "What? The bathroom's right there; I'll be two seconds."

"You can't go by yourself," Cole said.

"What do you want me to do, pee in a bottle here at the table?" Jared replied.

Sherry mumbled something in disgust as Cole scooted his chair out. "I'll go with him. Just go ahead," Cole said.

"No!" Iylah cut in. "Guys, we can't split up. If he goes, we all go." She could sense some pushback about to come and continued. "We'll do what we did with me; just leave the door open."

"Not sure I'm comfortable with that," Jared said.

"Neither are we," Sherry added.

The three of them crowded inside the doorway. Jared asked for the flashlight. "You don't need a light to pee," Iylah replied. "Just go."

"Are you kidding? It'll get everywhere. You guys turn around, or something."

"I'm not standing in the bathroom while he's peeing. That's gross. I'll be over here on the bench." Before Iylah could protest, Sherry had already walked away and sat down in the foyer.

"Fine. Cole, you stay with him. I'll go with her." Before she left, she shined her flashlight toward the shower, and hesitantly peeked behind the curtain. Nothing. She could sense the look of puzzlement coming from the boys. "Just checking," she muttered. "Be quick, okay?"

The Last Day
of Sophomore Year
Part II

*J*o's adamance to go home after the incident with Maggie was squashed by Janelle's stubbornness to keep her with the group. After Jo relented—with the help of a Blizzard from DQ—they drove around town, crammed in Janelle's convertible. They cat-called pedestrians at the town square and hit top speeds on open roads going toward Kentucky Lake, screaming with their arms held high. Iylah hadn't seen her sister laugh and make this much noise since probably the sixth grade, when they went to Kentucky Kingdom together and Iylah had to force Jo to ride the roller coasters with her.

On the way back into town, Iylah suggested going to the movies later and Katie recommended they kill time at her place. She was house sitting for her neighbors—the Grays—who had a pool. Iylah knew the Grays well, as she would occasionally sit for their daughter, Shelby. They had always encouraged the girls to come and use the pool whenever they were in the neighborhood.

Being that it was the end of May, the water felt hardly warmer than an ice bath. It didn't matter, though. School was over, they had a pool to themselves—plus two six packs of Mike's Hard Lemonade to share—and they'd witnessed their friend pummel someone they all greatly disliked with a yearbook. Iylah stood on the edge with Katie and suggested they jump in together. She counted to three and went to jump before slipping her hand from Katie's grip, watching her takie the plunge alone. Everyone laughed as Katie emerged, screaming at Iylah and the water's coldness. Janelle came up behind Iylah and shoved her in, to the amusement of everyone. She went to go lie out on one of the chairs, while Jo sat on the edge with her feet in the water.

The four of them recounted what happened to Maggie: her look of shock after she got hit, the sound the ball made when it bounced off her head. They regretted that no one filmed it. At one point, while Jo was so distracted with describing the game she made that was played after school, Iylah went underwater and pulled on her foot to drag her in.

The group played *Marco Polo*, fought on each other's shoulders, and at times simply lie quietly around the pool, taking in the afternoon.

Jo sat up from the lawn chair and went over to the pool, sitting down on its edge beside Janelle who was reclining on a raft. "Thank you," Jo said softly, "for today; for helping me."

"It was nothin'. That girl's a tit bag. She's had it comin' for months."

"Yeah. Guess I should've listened to her," Jo nodded toward Iylah who was submerged beside Katie under water. "She told me to come with you all."

"Well, yeah, but then I wouldn't have gotten to bash her face in." Janelle smiled.

There was a quiet moment between them. Nothing but the air around them brushing through the trees, birds chirping, and water lapping up against the side of the pool. "I wish I could've just stood up for myself. Do what you did."

Janelle's raft had turned away from Jo, so she flipped her

hands in the water to right herself. "You don't do what I did without having reason."

"I got a ball thrown at my face and a picture taken of me with my underwear out. I think that's plenty of reason."

"No," Janelle replied. "I mean . . ." She sighed and sat up, sliding off the raft and into the water. She pushed the raft away and rested her arms on the concrete, next to Jo. She spoke in a hushed voice, as if she didn't want the others to hear. "Maggie had two friends with her—two girls I don't even know. It's one thing to do that to *one* person, but three? I could've gotten my ass kicked. Granted I had those two vaginas on my side," she thumbed over to Iylah and Katie, "but what're they gonna do? I've never seen your sister hit anyone."

"She hits me all the time," Jo laughed.

"Well, yeah, of course. That's what sisters are for," Janelle replied. "What about you? You ever hit anyone?"

Jo shook her head. "Just her, I guess. And I wouldn't call that hitting."

"What if Maggie walked up to you after she hit you? What would you have done?"

Jo thought about it. "I don't know."

"Would you have fought her?"

"I'd like to think I would've tried." She rolled it around more. "But I'm not really a fighter. So, I guess I just would've walked away."

"And that's what I'm sayin'. Bullies like that, you handle one of two ways. Walk away, or engage. You walk away, you're generally safe. You engage? You're not always gonna win." She paused and elbowed Jo's leg. "But eventually you will. And after a while, it becomes instinct. Someone does you wrong, or messes with someone you know, it's nothing to respond because it's what you've had to do. It's been beaten into you." She looked out at the yard. "It's who you are." Janelle turned around and extended her arms behind her.

"Is that what happened to you? It was . . ." Jo felt uncomfortable even saying the word. "Beaten into you?"

Janelle reclined there, letting her legs gently rise and fall in front of her. "You could say that, yeah. There was no thought in what I did today; it was just . . ." She snapped her fingers. "Instinct. I hate that stuff—people like Maggie. People whose self-esteem is built on degrading others. Fuck them. And that's the silver lining of having a bully; eventually, they will get fucked." She took a swig of her drink and tapped the bottle against Jo's shoulder. "You either do it yourself. Or you find a crazy bitch like me to do it for you." Janelle crossed her eyes, and smiled, making Jo laugh. "Look, in all honesty, it's nice that I can *do* that—take care of myself, and my friends, and stuff. But I'll tell ya, it came with a price." She likely noticed the confusion on Jo's face. "A safe childhood," Janelle finally said. "I'm the result of what happens when you grow up frightened of the only person that's supposed to love you."

"I'm sorry," Jo said.

"Is what it is," Janelle said with a shrug. "I'll tell ya though, there're very few feelings that can top hittin' someone in the head with a hard back book." They laughed as they looked across the pool, where Iylah and Katie both inhaled a large breath and went under water. "But I'll tell you this, I'd trade that feeling in a heartbeat if it meant having a better . . ." She bit back the words, her lips sliding between her teeth. "Eh. It doesn't matter. It's not gonna change; no point in wishing it would." Janelle's eyes became distant for a brief moment as if she were lost in her own mind. Jo had known Janelle since she could remember. While she didn't know the extent of it, she knew there was something cruel in her home—something with her mom. But

Janelle never talked about it. Bruises along with unplanned absences from school or events were always explained away with rational excuses.

At once Janelle took another swig of her drink, draining it. "So, what happened with you two anyways? Weren't all you guys like super close?"

"We were, yeah, back in middle school," Jo replied. "I don't know what happened. It was like all of a sudden, when we got to middle school, she just . . ." Jo waved her hand as if knocking away a fly, "she was done with me. The two of them still talk, I think." Jo nodded over toward her sister. "Not close or anything, but civil. More civil than she is with me."

"You think it has something to do with what happened at y'all's birthday? When was that? Sixth grade? Seventh?" Janelle asked.

"Summer before seventh," Jo replied, in a grim voice. The mention of that night made her stomach twist. "No. I don't . . . I mean it could. I don't know why that would have anything to do with it."

Janelle put her bottle beside the pool, but not before tipping whatever remained into her mouth. "I don't know how you both stayed friends after that. I'd've beaten my sister's ass for that shit."

"Wait . . . what?"

"Her," Janelle nodded over to Iylah. "If my sister did something like that to me, I'd've disowned her. Shit was messed up." She let out a chuckle. "You're better than I am."

Jo could feel her forehead creasing in confusion. "Iylah didn't do that. It was an accident."

Janelle looked at Jo as if she'd just asked what year it was. "Are you sure?"

Jo sat fixated on Janelle for a bit and then said with uncertainty, "Yeah. She said it must have been there from when we ate."

Katie sprang out of the water, surprising the two of them, sucking in a life-saving breath, and throwing her arms as if to reach for safety. Iylah emerged soon after, not even out of breath. "Told you!" Iylah said, holding up her hands in victory.

Janelle turned back to Jo and shrugged. "If you say so."

Katie moved to the side and wiped her face as she caught her breath. She cursed with a laugh. "To be fair, I don't think vaping is helping."

"Anyone else?" Iylah said.

"What're y'all doin?" Janelle asked.

"Holding their breath," Jo said.

"You wanna try?" Iylah asked Janelle.

"Hell no! I'm not gonna win that."

"Jo?"

Jo shook her head. "I'm good."

"Oh, come on! You scared I'll win?" Iylah taunted.

"Yeah. That's it. Because you winning happens so often," Jo said dryly. "When's the last time you beat me at . . ." Jo paused, tilting her head like she was doing math in her head, "anything?" Jo could see a twitch in her sister's cheek. "I just don't want to get wet again. Aren't we leaving soon—"

Iylah gritted her teeth and threw her hand forward, sending a wave over Jo's body. Jo sucked in a stunned breath, going rigid from the ice-cold water. "You jerk!" Jo yelled, rubbing water out of her eyes. "You are such a turd!"

"Guess you have to get in now," Iylah replied with a devilish smile.

"Oh, you're dead," Jo said, moving toward her in the water.

"Who can normally hold their breath longer?" Janelle asked.

Both Jo and Iylah called back, "me!"

"Don't listen to her," Iylah said, "She's only beaten me like twice."

Jo rolled her eyes. "She's never beaten me. Why do you think she's so stubborn I do it?"

"How long can you do it for?" Janelle asked.

"I used to go for a minute and a half. Now? Probably a minute . . . ? Maybe . . ."

"You could *not* hold your breath for a minute and a half," Iylah said back.

"Yes, I could," she fired back, defensively. "Mom timed me."

"Alright, alright, who cares?" Janelle cut in. "First one up loses, okay?" They agreed. "No cheating."

"I don't cheat," Jo said.

"You definitely cheat," Iylah came back.

"No, I don't. You're the one who cheats."

"Oh, BS! When have I ever cheated?"

"Are you kidding me!?" Jo yelled, with a laugh. "Uno? Last night! You kept—"

"Oh my God! Shut up!" Janelle called out. "Just go."

They both took in a breath and exhaled. "I don't cheat," Jo said again.

"Mmm hmm," Iylah mumbled, a face of skepticism. "Ready? Go!" They took in a breath simultaneously and went under. After a bit, Iylah poked her head up a tiny bit—enough to open her eyes and see Jo was still under—and then went back down. After several more seconds she came up and breathed. "Damnit!"

"She's good," Katie said.

When Jo continued to stay under, Iylah put a finger over her mouth for quiet and put her hands on the surface of the water, just above Jo's head. She stood there, still as could be, biting her lips to keep from laughing. When Jo came up, Iylah pushed her back down. Jo reached up her hands to check for the obstruction, but Iylah knocked them away. She tried again, only to get pushed down more. Jo at once threw her hands up out of the water and gripped on to Iylah's wrist, trying her hardest to wiggle away and out of her sister's force. "Come on, you got it, just a few more seconds!" Iylah yelled, laughing. Jo began kicking and clawing at her sister, trying to break free when finally, Iylah let go, and dove back out of reach. Jo came up, pulling in a breath with such intensity it sounded like a scream. She beat her arms in the water, desperately trying to pull herself to the ladder, where she grabbed a hold of the metal rungs and crawled up, scrambling out and onto the ground. She sat on her hands and knees, breathing as if she'd just run a marathon, trying to calm her nerves. "Why did you do that?" Jo said, through terrified breaths.

"I was just playin' around. You won, anyways," Iylah said with a laugh.

"Yeah, you went a really long time. How do you do that?" Katie asked.

Jo didn't answer. All she could do was breathe furiously.

"Jo, you okay?" Janelle asked. Jo shook her head. Her eyes were closed, as she sat back on her feet. She put her hands over her head, trying to get control of her breathing.

"I'm ready to go home," Jo whispered.

"Oh, come on," Iylah said.

"You scared the shit out of me, Iylah! I could've died!"

"You weren't gonna die, give me a break. I didn't hold you under that long."

"I wanna go home," Jo said again.

Iylah shook her head. "Whatever. God, you're such a baby."

"Iylah. She's freaked out, come on, give her a break," Katie said.

"Lemme get dried off, and I can take you home." Janelle

said. Jo nodded, feeling her nerves start to calm. "Actually we should probably go ahead and go. The movie starts in like thirty minutes." They all got out of the water, as Janelle threw Katie and Iylah their towels. Iylah stood in the sun to stay warm while she dried off. Jo was still sitting on the other side of the pool, on the ground, enveloped in a towel, appearing to be lost in thought.

"Hey, if it's any consolation," Iylah said cheerily, bending over to let her hair fall. She started to wrap the towel around her head. "You made it to a minute-fifteen." She laughed again.

That childish snicker. It wasn't the laugh Iylah used when something was funny. It was the one she used when she made a joke and wanted others to know she'd made one. Jo wasn't sure if it was the laugh, the comment, or the nerves from almost dying—maybe all of the above—but something melted inside of her. Blood was either rushing to or from her head, producing an almost dizzy sensation, and she could feel her teeth beginning to pierce through her lips. She watched her sister wrap her hair in a towel, and straighten up, looking around to see who else was laughing. The others weren't, but they smiled, appeasing their friend.

An empty Mike's Hard bottle came to a stop against Jo's leg. She eyed it, feeling a sudden peace come over her, as if she'd found the solution—the missing puzzle piece—to fixing this problem.

She picked it up, hearing the glass scrape against the concrete, and feeling a wave of euphoric pleasure as she held the bottle's neck. In a flash, it was like her body switched to auto pilot. She straightened up and launched the bottle as hard as she could across the pool. She heard Katie yell "look out!" just as Iylah turned around and tried to get her hands up. The effort was too late, as the bottle clunked dead center of her face, crushing her nose. It fell to the ground, shattering on the stone as Iylah screamed a hideous growl and covered her nose. As Jo watched the blood gush through her sister's fingers, she couldn't help but hear Janelle's voice in her head: *There're few feelings greater than hitting someone who deserves it.* Jo exhaled, feeling the release in her cheeks as they drew back into a smile. She's right—

"Jo!" Janelle called.

Jo took in a sharp breath, looking around. The glass bottle was still in her hand. Janelle and Katie were standing on the other side of the pool, looking at her with anticipation. "You okay?" It took her a moment, but Jo nodded. "You mind grabbin' the other bottles over there?"

"Are we going or what?" Iylah asked. She was sitting on the swing that hung from the rafters under the deck, typing on her phone. "Jo, you gonna go with us, or are you still doing your panic thing?"

Jo stood up, clutching the bottle so tightly she felt it might crush it in her grip. She saw Janelle swat at Iylah's arm. Katie held open a plastic shopping bag for the trash. "I'll go home," Jo said, dropping the bottle—and the exhilaration of what could have been—inside the bag with a miserable *clank.*

16

NOW

Iylah walked away from the bathroom and clicked the flashlight on once more to assess the foyer. Though the boys were only maybe four or five arm lengths away, Iylah couldn't shake the feeling that it was just far enough for Jo to do harm. She saw Sherry shimmy out of her hoodie and fan herself for a moment before putting her hair up into a bun. She took a seat next to her on the bench beside the front door, instinctively reaching for her cell phone, and sighing when she realized it was dead. "So, what's the deal with you two? You and Jared?"

"I don't wanna talk about it," Sherry mumbled.

"Okay . . ." Iylah replied. She then realized that Jared may be right about the flashlight's life being cut short, so she turned it off.

"This is crazy . . ." Sherry said softly to herself.

"I know," Iylah whispered. She wasn't sure what else to say, so she didn't. Iylah contemplated how feasible—and effective—it would be to move the bureau across from her against the front door, or even the window so the dog couldn't see them moving around—

"Earlier, you said . . ." Sherry began. "When I was on the floor after the dog, you said '*that's why.*'" Iylah paused to remember what she was referring to. "You said it before you told us about the dog keeping us in." Iylah could feel Sherry staring at her. Or maybe she was just paranoid. "What did that mean? *That's why?*"

Iylah didn't respond with anything coherent, just a couple of mumbles.

Sherry cut her off. "You know why she's doing this, don't you?"

"I . . ." Iylah stopped.

"What does she want?"

"I think there might be something . . . like a . . ." She trailed off.

"A what?" Sherry asked.

"I think there might be a connection. Like maybe she's trying to tell me something."

"Something bad? Something good? What?" The sound of Jared peeing seemed to really carry through the darkness. "Gross."

"I don't know yet. It was just a passing thought, that's all."

Silence stretched between them as Iylah began rolling the flashlight back and forth in her palms. Neither spoke for a long moment until Sherry exhaled. "About a week ago," she paused. "I accidentally sent a picture of myself at the movies to a few friends. I didn't know it at the time, but *he* was in the background."

"Okay . . ."

"You asked what was going on. That's why he's pissed at me."

"Was he doing something? I don't get it."

"I probably shouldn't say any more than that. I don't wanna get yelled at anymore, ya know?"

"No worries. I figured you guys had dated and one of you cheated on the other."

"Well, no. At least not that I know of. We haven't really talked since all this happened. We used to date. Broke up about two weeks ago."

"Oh. Ohhh," Iylah hummed. "So, that photo at the movies; it wasn't just *him* behind you . . ."

"Nope," she replied. "It wasn't."

"Picture was that bad?"

It took Sherry a moment. "I mean, in the grand scheme of things? No. But it got out. That's what made it bad." She paused. "You'd think that with us dating and having been best friends for . . . ever . . . that this would be something he could talk with me about—something I should've known." Her voice had become barely audible. "He won't even look at me now."

Iylah was starting to put the pieces together. "Can I ask a question?" Iylah asked. "Between you and me. Was it intentional?"

Sherry sighed. "It almost was. He'd broken my heart a week earlier. I'd be lying if I said it didn't cross my mind. But I decided against it. Took another one instead and when I went to send it . . ."

"You sent the wrong one," Iylah finished.

"Yeah," Sherry breathed.

"You guys okay?" Cole asked from across the hall.

"We're fine," Iylah said back.

"We're almost done," Cole said.

"The worst part is," she said with a hushed voice, "that I have so much going through my head: the breakup, what's going on with him, how . . ." She stopped, words becoming stifled, "how humiliated I was by all this. And it sucks because I want to be there for him, but I also want to tell him how much this hurt. Being together for all this time to find out that I was . . . what? A cover?" Iylah could sense her leaning forward to wipe the tears away with her shirt. "I just want my friend back."

Iylah had no words for this girl. It was horrible what she was going through; what words *could* comfort? "You know, not that you asked, but I've been where you are. Not with the phone thing but I've done my fair share of things to make people not talk to me." She tapped Sherry on the leg. "Just keep apologizing. Make sure he knows you're not leaving his side."

"Well, he's made it very clear that's exactly where he doesn't want me."

"It's definitely gonna take some time. But if you guys were as close as you say, you can't let him forget that. He'll come around. Take it from a girl whose biggest regret is a relationship she ruined. Never let those you love believe that you think life would be better without them. Because, if you wait long enough, if you don't continuously try, that's exactly what you'll find. A life without them. You were friends for a reason. Don't let a five second mistake ruin years of what y'all have had."

"It was a pretty shitty five second mistake," Sherry whispered. "What if he never does?"

Iylah shrugged. "I don't know. But you can't go at it that way. All you can do is make sure he knows how you feel; that this relationship means too much to throw away. And that there are some things you both need to talk about. Start there, and don't let up."

Sherry wiped her face again, as Iylah leaned out, trying to listen for the boys. It occurred to her that she hadn't ever heard the toilet flush. "Cole?"

"Sorry, y'all. He had to poop," Cole shouted.

"Dude. Don't yell that out," Jared tried to say quietly.

They were taking too long. Iylah stood up, a thought suddenly sparking in her mind. "Hey. What did he roll?"

Sherry thought for a moment. "I don't remember."

"Jared," Iylah called. "What'd you roll?"

"Uh. I don't know. Six, I think."

"Did you move?" Iylah asked.

"Yeah—er, wait. No. That's when we left."

Iylah grabbed Sherry's arm. "Come with me. Guys, stay put."

"Where're you goin'?" Jared asked.

"To get the game."

"You think it's safe to get it? What if something happens to them, or us?" Sherry asked.

"Something's *gonna* happen if we don't move soon," Iylah replied, pulling Sherry along through the hallway. She grabbed the board and the die and set it down next to the bench in the foyer, shining the light on top. "Go ahead."

"Six, right?" Sherry asked, squatting.

"Yeah," Jared replied.

"Okay," she said, counting the spaces. "Shoot. It's marked."

"It's fine. Just go," Iylah said.

Sherry picked up the marble and scooted it up, counting the spaces as she went. The moment she placed it onto the board, several loud, deafening *slams* rang throughout the house. Sherry jumped up and Iylah dropped the flashlight onto the floor. "What was that?"

Cole yelled and began cursing in pain.

"I don't know," Iylah said, bending over to grab the light. "Are you okay?" Cole didn't answer. "Cole!"

"Yo, what happened?" Jared called.

Cole winced in pain. "Holy crap, that hurt!"

"What?" Sherry asked.

"The door slammed right on my shoulder. Pushed me out."

"Why'd you close the door?" Jared shouted.

"I didn't," Cole replied. Iylah took Sherry's hand again and moved toward the bathroom door.

"The knob won't turn—ow! Shit!" Jared said.

"What? You alright?" Cole asked, trying to open it.

"Yeah." He paused. "Just burned myself with the candle wax. Did you lock the door?"

"No," Cole said. "I didn't do anything." He tried once more. "It's stuck." Iylah moved him aside, turning the knob herself. "You didn't believe me?"

Cole was right. The knob wouldn't budge. "Did you accidentally lock it?" Iylah called out.

"I didn't touch the door!" Jared yelled. "This ain't funny, man. Open up!"

"I can't! It's stuck!" Cole stepped in again, this time shoving his shoulder vigorously against the door to no success.

"It's the game," Iylah said. "She's locked the doors."

"Why?" Sherry asked.

Locked doors, Iylah thought. She didn't have an answer for Sherry.

"Well, this is awesome," Cole said sarcastically. He knocked on the door. "Game locked you in, bro."

"So, what am I supposed to do?"

"Wait a second! *The game!* What did it give you?" Cole asked Sherry.

"Nothing. I mean, I didn't reach in."

He took the light from Iylah and knelt beside the board. "Maybe it'll have something." He shined a light inside the hole. "Go ahead."

Sherry came and sat beside him. She held her hand up over the top of the hole, cautious for a second before lowering it down. To Iylah's surprise, nothing came out. Sherry tried again. And then again. "What's going on?" Jared called.

"We're trying to get the thing out of the box!" Cole yelled back. "Come on, Sherry."

Sherry pulled her hand out once more and sat back in agitation. "There's nothing in there."

Cole lifted the game off the floor and shook the tower. There was the faintest of rattles inside. "There's obviously something in there."

"Then where is it?" Sherry asked, tilting the tower toward her. She put her arm as far down as it would go, slamming her knuckles around the inside. Once again, she came up empty. Cole shined the light toward Iylah. "What do we do?"

Iylah was leaning against the wall to halt the anxiety-inducing vertigo from toppling her over. Memories had suddenly started flooding back into her mind. *Locked doors . . . locked doors . . . what are you trying to say . . . ?*

"Iylah . . ." Sherry said.

Iylah gasped. *A locked door!* It finally hit her. "Hang on!" She knelt to the floor and picked up the tower, inspecting it. For a moment she sat still, thinking to herself, unsure if she wanted to say what she knew to be true. Finally, she shook the board with force, drawing forth another rattle from deep inside. "Iylah?" Sherry said again.

"It's a paper clip," she replied softly. "That's what she's giving us." Iylah thought to turn the board upside down but figured it wouldn't work. "Go ahead and reach in," she said, putting it back on the floor.

Sherry did. Perhaps this time it would be a little easier, knowing what she was looking for. Something scraped inside, and in the beam of the light, Iylah watched her pull out a tiny, red paperclip. The look on Cole's face was either one of sheer surprise or offense.

"How did you know that was in there?" He asked.

Iylah swallowed. Her throat had gone bone dry. "I—I didn't."

"Bull shit," he muttered. "How did you know what she was gonna pull out?"

"I didn't *know*," she shot back. "I just . . ." She shrugged her shoulders.

"This happened before, didn't it? In the last game you played," Cole said.

"No. That game was about something different," Iylah replied.

Cole seemed to consider her words. "What does that mean?" Iylah didn't reply. Her head fell in shame. "Iylah! What does that mean?"

There was a beat of silence between them. "She said earlier that she thinks the game is trying to talk to her," Sherry said. "She . . ." Sherry stopped, her eyes meeting Iylah's. "She said she knows why her sister is doing this."

"Okay, so why—" Cole began.

"No, I didn't say that," Iylah cut in. "I said there was a *connection*. Maybe. And it's just an idea, okay? I don't know for sure."

"Well, then, what's the connection?" Cole asked.

Iylah took the paper clip from Sherry's hand. Whether or not it was a good idea to tell them, she knew she had to. "I think the game is centering itself on the night Josephine died."

The 19th Birthday Party
Part I

A party popper exploded into a shower of pink and green confetti. "Say nineteen, bitches!" Iylah draped an arm over her boyfriend, Bryce, and her friend, Erica Lang, as they stood over a crouched Josephine and Mark Matheson—the owner of the boat. The group echoed her as the cell phone let out a series of faux, old-fashioned camera clicks. After the fifth click and a pause, "Is that it?"

"That's it," Jo replied. "Just five." She brushed paper dots off her shoulder.

"Finally!" Iylah exclaimed. "Who's up for shots?"

There was a raucous cheer from the group as Iylah grabbed her boyfriend, slid his cap backwards and kissed him. The two of them went to the cooler and dug out a stack of mini red cups while Jo instead walked over and picked up her phone to scroll through the pictures.

Mark walked up behind her. "Any good ones?" He startled her. "Sorry. Just me." He laughed.

"You scared me." Jo suppressed the smile trying to spread over her face. "Yeah, I think so." She swiped through them, seeing Mark's reflection in the phone. At one point, she saw his eyes drift over to her. "This one's good," she muttered, trying to quell the nervousness in her stomach. Jo suddenly realized that her eyes were closed in the shot. "Oh, wait, never mind." She swiped. "Here's a good one. Everyone's smiling." Iylah's eyes were squeezed shut with her tongue hanging out. One hand made a hang-ten sign while the other held up a bottle of tequila. "Well, almost smiling," Jo said.

"I think it looks good," Mark said. He leaned in closer, holding his hand over the screen to shield the glare. "Send me that, will ya?"

"Yeah, sure," Jo replied, attaching the picture to a text. She could still feel Mark standing next to her. The butterflies inside her were going haywire.

"Why don't you ever smile?" He asked.

"What? I *am* smiling," she replied, re-checking the photo.

"You're grinning," Mark said. "You've always done that, I feel like."

"I don't know," she replied. She had stopped typing and was staring at the screen, unsure now if she wanted to send it to him.

"I didn't mean it looks bad," Mark said, swatting her on the arm. "I think you look great." Jo caught herself biting on her thumb nail and at once dropped her hand. "It was just something I noticed. Seriously, I didn't mean anything by that." He leaned in once again and tapped the screen. "It's a sexy-ass grin."

Jo's heart skipped. She couldn't tell if the spots now burning on her neck and cheeks were from her blood rushing or from sunburn. She didn't know what to say. *Thanks? Stop? You look good too?* She stood nervously quiet for so long that she'd forgotten to breathe, and instead of saying anything, on her next breath in she accidentally snorted. Her hand flew up to her mouth in embarrassment. "I'm so sorry!" she exclaimed.

Mark started laughing. "Did you just snort at me?"

"Oh my God, I have no idea how that happened."

"It's fine," Mark said happily. "It was cute." Jo's head was shaking in shame. "Seriously."

"I'm gonna go to the bathroom," Jo said.

"Oh, come on!" Mark called, holding his arms out. "It's not a big deal. It was just a snort." Jo walked below deck, toward the bathroom. "Don't forget to send me that pic!" He yelled after her.

She slid into the bathroom and shut the door. "Idiot!" She whispered to herself. She stared at herself in the mirror, testing her grin and her smile. She never liked her smile; always thought it made her look like a victim of the Joker. It was as if her smile was too big for her face. She went back and forth from it to her grin, comparing them. *I think you look good.* The text on her phone was still up, and she clicked send on the message, immediately regretting her decision. Her phone made a Star Trek laser blast sound indicating the action. Mark almost immediately sent back a hot pepper emoji and said, "Thanks." Jo smiled. Her reflection in the small mirror caught her eye, sluggishly discouraging her face back to neutral. She hated that smile. She brought her mouth to a grin, then showed a little bit of teeth. Then she went full, the edges of her lips nearly stretching off her face. "Ugh." She shook the frustration out, picking her phone back up.

She scrolled through the photos once more and filtered the best one with her Instagram app before posting it to her account. She was sure that Iylah would hate it but she didn't care—

A loud run of *bangs* sounded on the door.

"Somebody in there?" Iylah yelled from the other side.

Jo clicked off her phone and slid it into her shorts. "Just a second," she called back.

"Jo? What are you doing in there?"

"Peeing . . . ?" Jo looked at herself once more in the mirror, inspecting her ponytail. She reached behind her and pulled out the band, shaking out the tangles and teasing her hair with her fingers.

"Hurry up! I gotta go!"

"Just about done." Jo flushed the unused water. She stared

self-consciously at her face, touching the acne scars along her cheek and forehead. She turned her head from side to side, peering at herself while running her hands down the sides of her head and hair. At once, the sliding door to the bathroom was thrown open, prompting Jo to gasp. Iylah was standing there, looking at her quizzically.

"What are you doing?" Iylah asked.

Jo quickly put her hair back up. "Nothing. How did you get in here?"

Iylah laid a red paper clip on the counter. "You were taking too long." She nearly knocked her over as she slid past, lowering her bikini and falling onto the toilet. She let out a sigh of exhilaration as the urine began hitting the bowl. "God, that's amazing!" She sighed. Jo didn't say anything and started to close the door when her sister asked, "You okay?"

"Yeah. I'm fine."

"You having fun?"

"I guess. Yeah. I'm a little peeved at Mallory and Logan for not showing up, but it's okay. I have my book if I get bored."

Iylah groaned. "You did not really bring a book, did you?" Jo tried to respond, but Iylah cut her off. "Jo, please do not sit up there and read. That's super weird."

"How is that weird?"

"Because it's our birthday, and we're in the middle of a lake. Everyone else is drinking and jumping off the boat, having a good time, and there you are, sitting in the shade reading books. Everybody's just gonna think you're miserable." Iylah stood up and rinsed off her hands.

"Who is gonna think I'm miserable besides you?" Jo asked. Iylah looked to be pitying her. "What? I'm having fun! I like sitting and reading."

"But not at your own birthday party." Her expression scrunched. "What were you doing with your hair?"

Jo felt like a turtle trying to go into its shell. "Nothing. I was just massaging my scalp."

"Jo, come on. We have twin powers, okay? I know when you're lying. Lemme see."

"No. I wasn't—"

"We're not leaving here until you take your hair down. He'll love it."

"Iylah. Stop! I don't like Mark, okay? Besides, I don't want to take it down. It'll get all gross looking in the water."

"You don't have to leave it down in the water. Put it up before you get in. But I think you should keep it down for now." Iylah gave a devious grin. "You know? Let him see it first . . . ?"

Jo felt herself flush. She looked down, trying to hide her smile. "I knew it. See? Twin powers?" Iylah stepped closer and released Jo's hair from the band. "I don't know why you don't show these curls off more. Guys love this stuff—girls too." She winked at her, over a thin smile. Iylah scrunched and raked at Jo's hair with her fingers, shaping the way it fell.

"I'm gonna look ridiculous . . ." Jo trailed off.

"If by ridiculous you mean hot, you'd be correct. What are you doing? Open your eyes, goofball."

Jo did. She hardly ever saw her hair out of a ponytail, unless it was getting out of the shower and even then, she didn't pay much attention to it. Iylah had brought the hair to one side, letting it fall over her shoulder. Jo lifted her hands to feel the curls; taking in how it fell over just a part of her face. She moved her head back and forth, her eyes stuck on her face in the mirror. It looked good—great, actually. It was the sort of look that would make her jealous of Iylah.

"Not bad, right?" Iylah asked. "Here." Iylah made Jo face her again and picked up a small bag lying in the corner.

"What're you doing?"

"Shhh," Iylah replied. She lifted mascara out of the bag.

"No, no. I don't want makeup—"

"Jo. Relax. Just trust me." Iylah began carefully touching up Jo's eyelashes, speaking slowly as she did. "You may not realize this, but I think I have a pretty good idea about how to make this face pop." She and Jo abruptly spoke in unison: "Twin powers." They both chuckled lightly, and Iylah instructed Jo to be still while she worked. Iylah gave a pleasant smirk, shaking her head.

"What?" Jo asked.

"Nothing." Iylah smirked. "I've missed you. I'm glad you came home. This is nice."

"Yeah. Wish it was under better circumstances."

"You don't like having a birthday party?" Iylah asked.

"I didn't come home because of our birthday."

"Oh, *that* circumstance. Right," Iylah said, her face sinking. "Still. I'm glad you came home. And that you got to see her before she died."

"Actually, that part I could've done without. I don't wanna remember her that way," Jo said. "But you're right, this has been nice. I'm glad I came." She watched her sister back up and study her.

"Hmmm." Iylah's eyes bounced around Jo's face as if she were admiring a painting. Finally, she reached for a tube of lip gloss. Jo asked Iylah if she was kidding, but Iylah ignored her, telling her to pucker.

"And, done." Iylah stepped back and grinned happily. "Perfect. Take a look."

Jo turned to face herself in the mirror. "Wow." She couldn't help the giggle. The change was subtle but enhancing. Her eyes were cheerful, bright. Or maybe it was the glowing lips. It was the first time in a while she didn't immediately notice her flaws.

"Gorgeous," Iylah said, picking up the lip gloss and applying it to herself. Jo studied their faces in the mirror.

"You don't think he'll find it odd that I'm wearing makeup all of a sudden?" Jo asked.

"I promise he won't notice the makeup. But he *will* notice *you*."

Jo let out a laugh—almost embarrassed—suddenly bringing a delicate hand over her mouth. She blushed. Her eyes found Iylah's. "Thanks."

Iylah shrugged. "Eh . . . what are sisters for?" She put everything back in the bag. "Plus, you were wearing sunglasses earlier, right?" Jo nodded. "Then make sure you don't put them back on until he sees you."

"I may not get in at all now," Jo said.

"Oh, you're getting in," Iylah said. "It's waterproof. Have you had anything to drink?"

Jo thought for a second and then sheepishly mumbled that she'd had a beer.

"That's it?" Iylah exclaimed. "Okay. Come on. We're doin' a birthday shot!"

Jo pulled her hand back. "Iylah, you know I can't do shots. I throw up."

"No, you throw up when it's cheap liquor. Mark brought Patron. I promise, stuff goes down like ice-water, come on." Jo, with her hands tucked under her armpits, sunk away from her sister in hesitation. "Jo, that was like four years ago, and you had a lot more than one shot. You'll be fine. Come on."

Jo stood still for a moment and then gave in. "Fine. One shot."

"Oh, no, we're definitely doing like five. This is gonna be the best night you can't remember." She took Jo's hand and began leading her up the stairs, then stopped abruptly to face her. "Seriously though, if I see you reading *Star Wars*, I'm throwing it in the water."

"It's *Star Trek*, and I don't read it; I watch it. I'm reading *Death Note*. Which I actually think you'd like. It's about a high school girl who—"

"Is it Mangus?"

Jo's face scrunched. "Manga? Yeah."

"Then I will *definitely* throw it in the water." She pulled Jo up the stairs onto the deck of the boat. "Just promise me you'll try to have a good time. Okay? No reading or drawing or sitting by yourself watching *Star Wars* reruns, okay? Be fun! Not weird."

Jo gave a half smile and nodded, speaking dully, "Okay. No reruns of Star Wars. Be fun, not weird. Got it." Her fingers had just touched her lips when Iylah slapped them away from her mouth. "Ow. What was that for?"

Iylah took Jo's hand and held it for her to see. The nails were all chewed down, despite the black nail polish on top. "How do you even bite them with polish on?"

"I don't know," Jo mumbled.

"You think Mark's gonna find that hot? A girl who's constantly chewing on her hand like a piece of corn? *Tck-tck-tck-tck-tck.*" Iylah mimicked gnawing on her own hand. "At least try not to do it around him."

"Okay . . ." Jo nodded. They walked back to the group. Iylah's friend Erica was lying back, tanning on the seats. Bryce was sitting beside her on his phone, scrolling. Mark, who was in the captain's chair, got up and came over to them.

"Wondered where you guys were. Y'all good?"

"Yeah, we're fine. Just twin talk in the bathroom," Iylah replied.

"Cool cool cool," Mark replied. He was wearing glasses, but the pause over his face as he looked at Jo was unmistakable: mouth slightly agape, head shifting a touch to the side. "You um . . ." He paused, seeming to settle over her as if staring at someone he wasn't sure he knew. "You—you guys wanna do something? Drive around? Jump in?"

"Sure—"

"We're gonna get a drink first. You want us to bring you anything?" Iylah interrupted her sister.

"Yeah, that'd be great. One of the Miller Lites is fine."

"Ooo, get me another beer will ya, babe?" Bryce shouted.

"We'll be back," Iylah said, ignoring her boyfriend, and wrapping her arm around Jo's to turn her around and pull her toward the cooler. "Look'a that," Iylah said playfully. "He was checking you out."

Jo smiled childishly. "He was not."

"Yeah, he was. Did you see him stare at you?"

"Iylah. He was wearing glasses; how do you know what he was staring at?" Jo opened the cooler.

"You want me to talk to him?"

"No!" Jo yelled, slamming the lid and catching the volume of her voice. She reached to cover Iylah's mouth. "No! Don't you dare."

"You sure? I don't mind." Iylah was walking toward Mark, still looking at Jo. "It's no big deal. Here, I'll just do it." She walked toward him. "Mark. Jo wants to—"

Jo didn't wait for her to finish that sentence. She ran toward her sister and shoved her through the open gate, off the boat, and into the water. It would have been a rare win for Jo, except that Iylah was able to grab her sister's wrist and pull her in alongside her. Iylah laughed, repeatedly trying to yell out for Mark, who was in the middle of a conversation, but Jo kept shoving her back underwater. The rest of the group noticed the laughter and promptly joined in on the fun. For the next hour, as the sun was getting ready to go down, everyone was in the water having the time of their life.

The sun's absence didn't deter the group from swimming in the lake. After dinner they drove back to Mark's favorite spot and dropped anchor. For a while, they floated on rafts around the boat then alternated between chatting together and Marco Polo. At one point—Jo wasn't sure when—she and Mark somehow abandoned the game and were floating next to each other, talking. Mark, hanging by his arms on the side of Jo's avocado raft, had been probing her about her interests and her art.

"Wait. You mean, like, tabletop games?" Mark asked.

"Yuperoo," Jo replied, instantly biting her lip, and wishing she could take that phrase back. "What did you think I meant?"

Mark chuckled. "Man, I'm here thinking that you're talking about video games."

"Oh," Jo said. "I mean, that'd be cool. But not really my thing. I mean, I like to play them. Sometimes. I don't *not* like video games if that's what you're thinking . . ." she said in a fluster. *Stop rambling!*

"No. It's cool, I'm not a big gamer. Played a lot of *Goldeneye* and old-school *Mortal Kombat* back in the day, but that's really it. I still have my SNES and 64 at home. Great party games."

"Yeah, we have a Wii still. Don't play it much anymore."

"So, what kind of board games are we talkin' about? Heavy strategy? Something like *Candy Land*?"

They both laughed. "Not quite," Jo replied. "I really like engine-builders and push-your-luck games. I've written a couple of those. Funny you say *Candy Land*, I did a roll-and-move style game a long time ago that I've recently gone back to working on. I made it for our math class back in sixth grade, but it turned out to be really fun. It's called *Zombie Escape*. You had to escape from—"

"Let me guess," Mark cut in. "Russians?"

"Of course." Jo giggled. "Zombies, obviously. It was a co-op game."

"What's co-op mean?" Mark asked.

"All the players work together. Against the game."

"I've never heard of that. But then again, I've never heard of the other things you said: engine something?" She corrected him, offering a very brief explanation.

"Okay, that doesn't seem too complicated," he replied. "But let's go back to this co-op thing. How do you know who wins?"

"I mean, if you can beat the game, everyone wins. They're super fun."

"That seems a little . . ." Mark paused. "Easy?"

"Oh, No way! *Definitely* not easy. I've probably played my zombie game a hundred times and only won maybe a third of them. They're a lot harder, which is why I like them. You can design it so the game changes every time it's played. And with most of them, you can play by yourself. But it's usually better if you play against the game with multiple people."

"You make it sound like they have a mind of their own—the games."

"If you design them the right way, they do." Jo regretted how corny those words sounded as soon as they came out.

"Jeez," Mark said.

If you design them the right way, they do? Ugh! What am I

doing? Don't be such a nerd, Jo! "Sorry," she whispered. "I can get kind of carried away with game talk. What do you like to do?"

"Actually, I was gonna say that sounds pretty fun," Mark replied. "Maybe if you get a free night before you head back to school, gimme a call. I'd love to try it."

Jo went still, unsure of how to respond. "Um. Sure. Yeah," she mumbled.

"Yeah?" Mark said, smiling.

Then, gaining a touch more confidence, "Yeah. That'd be cool. I've got a ton," Jo said happily. "The closet in our basement is full of—"

"I meant the one you're working on now. The zombie game."

"Oh . . ." Jo stammered. "Okay. Um . . . I mean, *that one's* not fully ready yet. The basic game play works fine, but I've been trying to incorporate this idea where the game can sort of trick the players given the right scenario . . . I don't know. It's been hard to write in because I'm not sure when it should happen—or how, for that matter—or even if it'll work . . ." She stopped. *Holy cow, stop rambling—*

"I've never met anyone who wrote board games before. Have you always done this?"

Jo nodded with an audible confirmation. "I love'em. It was my childhood, basically. My parents introduced us early. I remember for a while they went on some kick of buying a new game almost every week. We'd finish dinner, and my dad would pour over the rules for a bit while we cleaned up and showered, or whatever, then he'd make popcorn and we'd all sit down and play. Didn't matter what was going on: he could be in the middle of grading finals, they could have just had an argument, or been stressed at work, or maybe me and her got in a fight—that happened quite a bit—didn't matter. No matter what, every Thursday night, we'd all sit there and eventually, whatever was going on just sort of . . . vanished, ya know. And we just played as if it was the most important thing: laughing, working together, trash talking, of course." Jo stopped, feeling a warmth begin to wash over her. "I miss that. That's what I want my games to do. Encourage people to put it all aside—disconnect, ya know? No phones or anything. Just play."

"How have I known you all this time and you've never mentioned it?"

Jo felt a touch embarrassed for talking so much about this. This was the longest Mark had ever talked with her. *He won't make that mistake again. All you can seem to talk about are your stupid games!* Then, she felt awkward that it had grown so quiet and mumbled, "I don't know."

"Well, you've definitely inspired me," Mark said pleasantly. "If yours isn't ready, teach me a different one. Maybe one of those engine games." Jo corrected him again. "I'd still love to see *your game* though. At some point. It sounds pretty cool."

Jo was thankful it was pitch black because there was no way she was able to stifle her goofy smile now. At a loss for words, she managed to say, "Cool beans." Then bit her lip, shaking her head in annoyance. She could hear Mark breathe a laugh through his nose.

"Cool beans, indeed," he replied.

"What about you?" Jo asked. "Interests? When you're not running your bar, of course. Which is really cool."

"Oh, right. What do I like to do?" Mark sighed. "Good question. If I ever do have free time—it's gonna sound stupid—I like to read."

"That doesn't sound stupid. I love to read. What are you reading right now?"

"That's the problem. I never have the time. Plus, I'm so behind. I literally just finished the second Harry Potter book." Jo gasped. "So good."

"I love Harry Potter," Jo replied.

"Yeah, I sort of got that impression by your Hufflepuff bathing suit. I'm not making fun, by the way. It's cute. I just noticed the symbols. That is Hufflepuff, right?"

"It was the only one I had." She nodded her head toward the deck. "She swiped my other one, which I should have expected. I come home for a day and she's already conning me out of my own stuff."

"Hey, so what's up with you guys anyways? Y'all okay? Y'all don't seem as close anymore."

"We're okay. Just . . ." Jo stopped, moving her hand delicately back and forth on the water. "We drifted apart a while ago. I mean we still talk and stuff, and I see her during breaks when we come home, but about halfway into high school we just . . . sort of lost touch, I guess. Or maybe it was me. I don't know."

"How often do you come back?"

Jo paused. "Honestly? As infrequently as I can. I'm only here now because of our dog Fanny. Otherwise, I'd have stayed in Virginia."

"Yeah, I'm sorry about that. Your dad told me. He said they had to put her down on your birthday." Jo nodded. "Man, that's hard. They ever find the fox?"

"Yeah. Euthanized it yesterday," Jo replied, staring out over the water. "She was a good dog."

"Yeah, she was a sweetheart," Mark added. "Sorry about your sister too. If I'd have known you guys were on the offs, I wouldn't have suggested coming on the boat. Not much space."

"Oh, no! It's fine. This has been fun. Really," Jo said, fondly. "It's not like I can't be around her. We're still friends. Plus, it's actually been nice celebrating with her. We haven't done a birthday together since we were twelve. We just don't have a lot in common. I mean, except for our bathing suit preference, obviously." She smirked.

"Well, I think you made a good choice with Hufflepuff. It looks good. Honestly, I'm sort of proud that I recognized it." Mark adjusted himself on the raft. "Let's see. What else am I reading? I have a bunch sitting by my bed. I just bought *The Martian*, which I heard was really good."

Jo perked up. "It's amazing! You have to read that one first."

"Then I have *Ready Player One*, which I also heard was amazing," Mark said.

Jo's mouth dropped. "Holy guacamole! You haven't read *Ready Player One*? Read *that* one first! It's so fun. And it's one of the few movies that actually measures up to the book!" She sensed she was practically yelling at him. "Sorry." She sunk back a little, calming her voice. "It's really good. You should read it."

Mark laughed. "Okay. I'll bump it up."

"I didn't mean to yell at you," Jo said, sheepishly.

"You're fine," Mark chuckled.

When he flicked his wrist, Jo felt his hand brush hers. Because of the darkness, she hadn't noticed that both of their hands were floating in the middle of the avocado core. "Sorry," she said.

"It's okay," Mark replied. There was a pause. She could see his silhouette begin to look around. The raft suddenly bumped up as he adjusted his body, and then she saw his head go down and rest on it, leaving a hand in the middle, letting it float beside Jo's in the water. "I haven't been on the lake at night in forever. I always feel like the water is warmer when it gets dark." She could feel the warmth of his hand grazing close to hers. Jo moved her hand away slightly, readjusting herself on her side of the avocado. She couldn't remember what he just said. *Crap. Something about the water being warm?* "Yeah," Jo mumbled.

"The stars too," Mark said. "They always look better on the water for some reason."

Jo looked up for a moment. She felt his hand again, this time not just grazing but practically against hers. Her stomach blossomed with butterflies. She could feel her heart beginning to dance happily. She'd forgotten to breathe and suddenly tried to regain oxygen without awkwardly gasping for air. Jo didn't move her hand this time. She just let it sit there, more out of shock than anything. And then it happened; his hand drifted *onto* hers. At first, just a finger and then what felt like two. Jo sucked in a breath as she went still, her mouth hanging open. His touch was light but confident as he gently stroked the top of her hand. And by way of what could only be magic or the Force—because Jo was scared shitless—her hand, almost like a magnet, drifted atop his. She couldn't stop her body from responding. It was as if the water itself was molding them together. She could feel him run his fingers under her palm. *Was* it him? The movement was so soft, maybe it was the water doing it. Maybe he can't feel it.

"Did you really bring an avocado for a float?"

Jo had been trying to calmly control her breathing for so long that Mark's question caught her off guard. Instead of saying anything, she remained quiet, over-thinking whether she should laugh or answer.

"You okay?" Mark asked.

"Mmm hmm," Jo mumbled. She realized her hand was awkwardly stiff and lifeless. About the time she got up enough courage to engage, a voice came from the boat.

"Jo!" It was Iylah. Mark's hand slipped away, and Jo felt herself virtually deflate. When Jo answered, Iylah called back, "We're gonna go up and play a game. You seen Mark?"

"I'm right here. Sounds good." Mark yelled. Jo could see him turn back to her, though she couldn't make out his face. "You ready?" He didn't wait for a reply before maneuvering the float back toward the boat.

They reached the ladder, and Mark grabbed hold. Jo took his hesitation as a sign that he was letting her go up first, so she too grabbed onto the rung except Mark wasn't fully out of the way for her to go up. She could see his head look up toward the deck and then come back down to face her. "I was serious about that game. If you're free tomorrow, let me know." He maneuvered away, allowing her the room she needed when she felt her leg cross against his in the water and could feel that he was probably inches away from her body. She lifted her head. Their hands were on the same rung. His finger gently caressed hers as they floated there together. "I'm an excellent judge of what's entertaining."

"Oh yeah?" She asked, followed by an unfortunate response of another snorted laugh. She instantly covered her face again in surprise. "Oh my god," she whispered, shying away. Mark couldn't keep back his delight. She immediately tried to go up the ladder, but Mark held on to her wrist, stopping her. "It's okay. Like I said earlier . . ." she could feel a slight pull on her arm; nothing forceful, but certainly noticeable. "It's cute." As she eased fully back into the water, she felt a hand come up on the side of her back, onto her ribs, and then gracefully run down her arm. Jo was in a trance. She wondered if he could hear her heart beating. A quivered breath escaped her mouth.

"You cold?"

Jo shook her head—it was more of a brief rattle. "Mmm mmm," she shivered out. She felt a hand come up against her face and shift her hair back. She closed her eyes, feeling her body begin to draw closer—

"Jo!" Iylah called again. Jo's eyes shot open; Mark pulled

quickly away. "Oh. There you are! Hurry up! You guys wanna do *Cards Against Humanity?*"

"Yeah, sounds good," Mark said casually. Jo reached for the avocado and started up the ladder. Iylah grabbed her arm once she got to the top and pulled her away toward the others, excitedly. "What was that all about, you little slut!" She whispered enthusiastically, smiling brightly at her sister.

"What?" Jo replied. "We were just talking." She could feel her cheeks flushing.

"Talking, huh? You realize that people on land could probably see your goofy smile right now, right?" Iylah asked.

Jo didn't say anything. She threw a towel around herself and turned away from the group to begin drying off. Her sister was right; she was absolutely beaming.

17

NOW

"Hello?" Jared yelled. "What'd you guys find?"

Cole seemed like he wanted to say more. Instead, he grabbed the paperclip out of Iylah's hand and jetted to the bathroom door. He straightened out the paperclip, and began jabbing it into the door's handle.

"Shine the light here, will ya?" Cole said.

"What are you doing?" Sherry said.

"Trying to open the door, but I can't see the hole to stick this in."

Iylah scooted in and knelt to feel the handle. "There's nothing here." She knocked on the door. "Jared, is there a tiny hole in the knob on your side?"

After a few seconds: "No."

"I thought you knew what to do with it," Sherry said.

"I never said that," Iylah replied. "All I said was that it was a paperclip—and *that* was a guess."

"Damnit." Cole sighed and collapsed onto his butt. "My dad just redid this bathroom. He must have bought new knobs. Most of ours have a little hole where you can stick something in to pop the mechanism." They heard Jared struggling on the other end to open the door, but it wasn't moving. "Sorry, man." Cole began frantically searching his pockets. "Anyone got a credit card?"

"Forget the credit card! Kick the door—something! You don't have a hammer or a crowbar?"

"Maybe out in the garage—" Cole started, but suddenly, grotesque barking could be heard from outside, followed by a violent scratching at a nearby window. Iylah and Cole crept through the foyer and peered at the window in question. What little light there was from the streetlights illuminated the black dog standing on its hind legs and trying madly to bite and claw through the glass of the small reading room. "Are you sure that thing is supposed to stay outside?" Cole whispered.

"No . . ." Iylah replied. The beast's teeth scraped against the window, urging her to grab Cole by the arm and move without its notice back to the bathroom.

"Alright, we have to get him out—like, now!" Cole said, bending to inspect the knob once more.

"Actually, if it gets in, he's probably safer in there. We should finish the game," Iylah countered.

"Forget the game! Get me out!"

"It won't get in if we finish," Iylah replied.

"You know that for sure?" Jared called out.

"Maybe she's right," Cole agreed. "Seems like our best shot."

"We'll stay beside the door in case something happens. Here, I'll go." Iylah rolled the die and shined the light: *four*. Cole knelt and counted the spaces, letting out a groan when he saw the hand marking. "There goes our streak of sixes." He placed the marble in its spot and sat idle on his heels, looking around him.

The dog outside was still scratching at the glass, its nails and teeth made a sickening chorus of high pitch scrapes. Jared started pounding against the bathroom door, saying something, but it was hard to hear over the dog's barks.

Cole wasn't sure when it happened, but suddenly every noise seemed amplified, like each was trying to outdo the other. He swallowed and noticed there was no saliva to go down. The intense banging reverberating in his chest turned out to be the banging of his heart. At that point, an overwhelming sense of dread began to envelop him. He sensed his mind starting to erupt in waves of heat and confusion. He could feel his body hunching forward though he wasn't sure why. He realized he was breathing faster, in and out more quickly through his mouth.

"You okay?" Sherry asked.

"I don't know," Cole whispered.

"Reach in," Iylah said. Cole sat unresponsive for a moment. "Cole."

"Hang on . . ." he whispered and let out a breath, reclining back on his hands. He felt nauseated; his mind clouded. Iylah, again, told him to reach in the box. Cole raised his hand and stuck it in the hole. He felt something—a rag, perhaps, or a shirt—and pulled it out. He held it, staring blankly, trying to get his breathing under control. Sherry finally took hold of it and held it in the light.

"A shirt?" Sherry said, trying to make out the lettering. "Is that Faith Hill? What does that say? Just . . . B . . ."

"Just breathe," Iylah whispered, dropping the flashlight and scooting back on her hands toward the front door.

"Fuck . . ." Cole whispered, standing up and reaching for the wall. He missed and knocked over the coat rack. Something on one of the rungs snapped—likely now broken—but he didn't care. He felt like he was on the verge of passing out.

"Cole . . ." Sherry said. He ignored her. The dog, Jared, the game—none of it mattered. He needed to get out of here. He needed air. He went toward the garage, but his foot clipped the door frame as he walked into the dining room, almost tumbling before he caught himself on the wall.

"What's wrong?" Sherry asked. Cole continued not to answer. He paced back into the foyer, starting to hyperventilate. "Cole!"

"I can't breathe . . ." He took in several deep breaths and then stood still, doubled over, resting his hands on his knees. He stood back up and then leaned against the wall, before slowly sliding down onto the floor, where he sunk and curled into a fetal position.

"Cole!" Sherry darted over to him. She kneeled and put her hand on his arm. "What can I do?"

"I don't know," he replied, covering his eyes with his hands, and trying to catch his breath.

"What happened?" She asked.

"I don't know . . ." *breath* "Just . . ." *breath* "All of a sudden . . ." *breath.*

Sherry shined a light over to Iylah, who was backed up against the wall, visibly terrified. "Iylah?" She said. "Help me, please. What's going on?"

"I-I-I can't. I can't." Iylah sounded like she too was having a difficult time breathing.

"What do we do?!" Sherry exclaimed.

"I can't move . . . I can't move . . ." Her breathing intensified, eyes pooling with water.

"I think I need to go to the hospital," Cole said, between breaths.

"Okay," Sherry said, rubbing his arm. "We'll get you there. Just hang on. I'll call an ambulance—" She was reaching for her phone when she remembered it was dead. "Shit!" She threw it down on the floor. She could feel her jaw tightening. "I don't know what to do . . . I don't know what to do . . ."

"You guys okay?" Jared called out.

"Something's happening to Cole!" Sherry shouted, her voice breaking. "Jared, please help!"

"I can't!" The hammering on the door grew louder and more violent.

She spun back toward Iylah, who looked like she was frozen. Sherry furiously crawled over to her and grabbed her arm, yanking her forward. "Iylah please! Do something!" Iylah took a sharp breath, and finally looked at her. "We need to get him out of here!"

It took a moment for Iylah to come to, but she wiped the water from her eyes and drug herself toward Cole. "Here," Iylah said. "Lift up." She pulled Cole by his underarms onto her lap and then maneuvered around to put her back to the wall. "I want you to breathe with me, okay. Big breath in. Slow breath out." She took hold of his hands and wrapped her arms around him, then began to take deep breaths. "Try to tune everything out and focus on your breathing."

She motioned to Sherry and nodded her head toward the bathroom: "tell him to be quiet." Then to Cole: "Come on, do it with me, breathe in. And then breathe out." After a few moments, Cole began to breathe with her. "Try to feel my breaths. In. And Out." Cole tried. "Okay, now breathe in for two seconds, and then out for two." Cole did. "Now breathe in for four, out for four." Cole did. She increased the exhale to eight. Then twelve. Then sixteen. By this time, Cole could feel the sensation of dread begin to subside. The two of them sat on the floor for a couple of minutes in silence before Iylah finally asked if he was okay.

"I think so." He let out a long breath. "Man. I don't know what happened. It was like, all of a sudden, those noises got louder, and then I could feel my heart racing. Just . . . freaked myself out I guess. I felt like I couldn't catch a breath and then that shirt said *breathe,* and it got worse." He felt his hands twitching and rubbed them. "That shirt. I think it's the same one I saw earlier when you came—I mean, when *she* came to the door."

"I got it for her at the concert. We were supposed to go together but she got sick. She wore it the night she died."

"You okay?" Sherry asked, and to Iylah, "How did you do that?"

"She used to get panic attacks when we were kids. My mom and dad used to do that to help get her out of them."

"Is that what that was?" Cole asked.

"Yeah," Iylah said. "You'll be fine." She tucked her knees to her chest and placed her head between them, taking a deep breath.

"But was that him or the game? It was him, right? The game couldn't do that. Could it?" Sherry was working herself into a frenzy.

"It was me, okay? I just got worked up." He grabbed her hand. "I'm fine, now." He took note of Iylah. "What about you?"

Iylah nodded, continuing to breathe deep. "When I was a kid, I always thought she was faking. Then I started to get them a couple years ago." Another breath. "Miserable." Breath. She motioned for Sherry. "Can you come here for a second?" Her voice echoing off the floor. Iylah took hold of her hand and pulled her closer. "Can you just, like, rub my back, or something?"

Sherry did. She held Iylah's hand with her own, and with the other she gently slid her nails over the top of Iylah's back: up and down, back and forth. She even started to take long, slow breaths herself, in case that helped. Cole watched them, feeling his own breathing grow steadier. "It always helps to breathe along with someone." She raised her head from her knees. "Thanks . . ."

"Thank *you*," Cole said. "Worked for me too." He sat up and scooted over to them. "Let's get this over with."

"Just try to stay calm, okay. We're not out of the woods yet, unfortunately. If you feel it start to come back on, count your breaths again." Iylah said. "Maybe remind me to do the same."

A *thud* reverberated through the dark house, and a subsequent snap followed, startling all of them. Cole cursed and moved toward the sound. Though it was too dark to get a clear picture of the outside through the window, he could make out that the dog was still pawing violently against the glass. Upon closer examination, he saw that a crack had formed in a windowpane. The dog reared its teeth and began chomping at it, barking incessantly.

"We have to change rooms." Cole went back and carefully picked the gameboard up.

"All the doors are locked, remember," Sherry said.

"No, wait!" Iylah said. "The paperclip."

"Maybe we can open one of the other doors?" Cole said.

"But we need to stay by Jared." Sherry said. "We'll need him to roll, won't we?"

"Try my room," Iylah said.

Cole ran a finger over the knob and felt a small hole. "Bingo." It took hardly any time to activate the mechanism inside. The lock clicked, and Cole turned the knob. "Yes!" He whispered. "Come on!"

18

NOW

The three of them crowded around the gameboard on the floor of the guest bedroom. It gave them proximity to Jared and on the dreadful chance that whatever was outside broke in, they could barricade themselves behind the door. For now, the door remained open, granting them a bit of illumination from the streetlights streaming in from the front door window. Cole noted that the flashlight may get the dog's attention, so he closed the curtains. Sherry was about to roll the die when Iylah stopped her. "You can't roll; it has to be Jared. Otherwise, we'll have to break him out to get him to reach inside."

"Unless she rolls on an open space," Cole said.

"You wanna take that chance?" Iylah asked.

"Good point," Cole replied.

The dog's clawing and barks had subsided, likely due to the lack of movement and noise inside the house. Sherry and the others maneuvered quietly toward the bathroom. "Hey," she whispered. "You need to roll. Here." She tried to push the die through the opening under the door. "Damnit," she whispered. "It won't fit."

"So, now what?" Jared asked.

"You have to roll," Iylah whispered. "There's no other way."

"But if it's marked, we're screwed," Sherry came back.

"Then pray you don't land on one," Iylah replied.

"Hey man," Cole said, tapping the door. "We're in the guestroom, okay? Like, five steps away. Door's open. We'll get you out as soon as we can but if something happens, just yell. Alright?"

They went back to the guestroom. "Hey," Cole said, placing his hand over Sherry's. "Don't screw it up, alright?"

"Yeah. Thanks." She took a deep breath and dropped it on the floor. *Two.*

Each of them at once counted the spaces and let out a collective sigh. "Finally," Sherry whispered.

Iylah picked up the die and noted the spaces needed to win or avoid markings. There were two blank spaces, a hand space, and then three blank spaces. "Come on . . ." She shook the die in her hand before dropping it on the floor. "*Three,*" she said with disappointment.

"Of course," he said. "All those blank spots and we land *there.* Seems a little unlucky." Cole held the marble over its new space, contemplating.

Iylah noticed his hesitation. "What's the matter?"

"Nothing," Cole whispered. "Just thinking."

"Don't," she said back.

"Don't what?"

"Put the piece where it goes," she replied. "I rolled a three. No cheating."

"I know, I know," Cole said, lowering the marble prudently. He set it down and started to reach into the hole when a faint, muddled *whoosh* began above them as if someone had turned on a shower.

Sherry grabbed his wrist. "What is that?" They each sat still, listening as the noise increased, growing more powerful by the second.

"It sounds like . . ." Cole stopped. "Like water."

"Hey, guys!" Jared yelled. "Shit! Shit! What the f— Guys!" Jared's voice had reached terror. Cole sprang up.

"What's going on?" Cole asked.

"Everything just suddenly came on in here! The sink, the shower! The *freaking* toilet is overflowing! What'd you do?" Cole could hear water splashing onto the floor. "Ooo! It's on super high too. Shit's freezing!"

Cole moved to leave the room, but Iylah grabbed him by the arm. "This is what she wants. Stay together."

"Hang tight, man. We'll be right back," Cole tried to assure him.

Jared was not pleased with this decision and demanded they not leave him. Cole hollered back to "just wait a second" and led them through the dining room, into the kitchen. They didn't need the flashlight to know that the sink was on. Its pressure was beyond normal, almost jet-like. Water *splished* underneath their feet as they walked. It was even pouring out of the dispenser on the refrigerator door. Cole pushed the lever in and out to try and get it to stop.

"Your sister," Sherry said, coming to a stop and squeezing Iylah's hand. "You said she drowned, didn't you?"

Iylah was a step ahead with that connection. She felt herself nod but couldn't speak.

"You were right, weren't you? She's trying to tell us something about that night."

Iylah felt something drip onto the tip of her nose. She brought a hand up to check and shined a light at the ceiling. Another drop fell into her eye. "Ouch!" She said instinctively. "Something's dripping up there."

"That's my parents' bathroom," Cole said. "Crap! The guestroom!" He rushed them back to the room and shined the light to the ceiling, cursing immediately. Water was coming down in healthy trickles, collecting in several spots on the floor, notably beside the gameboard. Cole promptly bent to pick it up, wiping the water off the bottom with his hands. "It's coming from my bathroom upstairs. We have to turn it off."

"But we can't go upstairs," Sherry said. "She's up there."

"I'm sure that's what she's wanting us to do," Iylah added.

"Then, what? Just let it keep coming out?"

"We have to! Look, if we finish the game, it should stop," Iylah called back. "That's our only option."

"Easy for you to say," Cole fired back. "She's not ruining your house. My mom's gonna kill us! I at least need to shut it off down here—" Cole stopped, cursed, and snapped his fingers. "I didn't reach in, did I?" He didn't seem to need an answer because he handed the light to Iylah and put his hand inside. Though, in a flash, he yanked it out.

"What?" Sherry said.

"It's . . . gooey." Cole said. He lowered his hand back in. "Ooo. Weird. It's like sludge."

"Pull it out!" Sherry yelled.

"I'm trying. I don't know what it is. It's hard to grip. Maybe something's buried in it . . ." Cole slid his hand around and took a handful of the gooey substance. Iylah moved the light toward him as he set the gameboard down and pulled his hand out. "What is this?" Cole drew back his hand—and somehow took the whole gameboard with him! "Whoa!"

Iylah tilted the light toward the box. It was now hanging in midair with long, leafy stems coming out of the hole. She followed it with the light onto Cole's wrist and gasped. Cole raised his arm to try and get a better view. "What the . . ." he began. He tried to tug himself free, but whatever it was was connected inside the box.

"Wait, wait. Hang on," Sherry said. "I have a pocketknife. It's on my keychain." She patted her pockets. "Shit. My keys are in the dining room. I'll get'em." She didn't give Iylah time to object. "Come on, be a look out." Sherry snuck hastily into the dining room and retrieved them. "Here squat down," she directed, kneeling to stabilize the gameboard on the floor. She held his hand, not wanting to touch whatever it was that was holding him and tried to line up the blade.

"Wait, I got it," Cole said, holding out his other hand. "I don't want you cutting me."

He moved the knife toward the strange substance. With a little pressure, he was able to slice through a piece of it. "There we go," he said. The beam of the light was sinking to the floor. "Iylah! I can't see." She apologized and held it still with two hands. Cole took hold of the slimy strands with his other hand to move some out of the way. At once, they began constricting around his fingers and wrist and then working their way up each forearm, tightening, drawing his two hands together. "Whoa, whoa, shit! Shit!" The knife fell out of his hand.

"What are you doing?" Sherry cried. "Quit moving!"

"It's—it's not me! It's not letting go—" Cole was struggling to tear his wrists free of the cold, wet vines, but instead they felt to be moving up his arm and constricting with even greater force.

"Pull it out of the box!" Sherry yelled. She bent down and took hold of it. Cole pulled away. "Pull harder," she said, gripping tighter on the bottom. He tugged a little harder, not wanting to jerk Sherry down.

"Let's both pull," he said. "One, two, three!" Then, bracing himself, he drew his arms back, away from her, but this time whatever it was inside began retracting itself, pulling him toward the box. "Wait, wait!" Cole yelled. "It's pulling me! Hold up! Stop!"

Sherry instantly put the box on the floor and stood back. The pull from inside relaxed.

"It's not gonna let go," Iylah said.

"What does that mean? I'm stuck like this?" Iylah started to mumble a response, but Cole kept going. "I thought you said the things inside were supposed to help us."

"I—That's what I thought. I'm . . ." She could feel herself getting flustered at the fact that she really did have no idea how to process a way out. This was nothing like what she and Erica had experienced. *That* round was scary—terrifying even—but she never felt as if she were in real physical danger. On top of that, there were three others in danger; three children in her care. She had to protect them. If Jo was after them, Iylah would do everything she could to make sure this night didn't end up like Shelby. "Look, for now, just . . . I don't know . . . don't keep pulling. Just breathe and try to relax. If you don't move, maybe it won't do anything."

"Where's the knife?" Cole asked. He spotted it on the ground and kicked it over to Sherry. "Here. You should try."

"Sherry, no," Iylah said, with warning.

"I can't stay like this. How'm I supposed to play? Sherry, come on."

Sherry picked up the knife and stared at the collection of long feathery threads that had now wound their way all over Cole's arm like a tribal tattoo.

"I don't think it's a good idea," Iylah said. "It seems like if you just relax—"

"It's fine," Cole said. "Sherry, please."

"Okay," Sherry said, "just be still." She reached out and delicately grabbed hold of Cole's wrist with her fingers. "They're too many to cut at once. I'll try breaking up a couple strands at a time . . ." She went to readjust her hand and that's when Iylah saw the plant begin to snake its way onto her wrist. Sherry shrieked and dropped the knife back to the floor. "No! No! No!" Sherry screamed. "Get it off!"

Iylah stepped over as Sherry was about to make the same mistake as Cole and force it off with her free hand. She grabbed her wrist just in time. "Don't touch it!" Iylah said. "It latches on to whatever it touches. Just be still."

The three of them went still as it came to a halt midway up Sherry's forearm. "We can't take it off?" She asked.

"I don't think so. It seems to get worse the more you struggle."

"Lemme guess," Cole said. "Finish the game, and it'll come off."

"How're we gonna play like this?" Sherry asked.

"Just keep that other hand away, so you have something free in case you need it."

Cole careened his head to get a better look at the alien substance. "What do you think it is?" Cole asked.

Iylah didn't answer immediately. She drew back and sat on the bed, still holding the light on the couple. They were joined together by what looked like thick strands of sludgy hair protruding from the game's top; the board hung in the air between them. "It's milfoil," she said.

"Mill what?"

"Milfoil. It's a plant that grows in the water—lakes usually." Iylah paused. "It was wrapped around . . ." She paused, swallowing as if the words themselves didn't want to be said. "It was wrapped around my sister's ankles and arms when they found her."

The 19th Birthday Party

Part II

The group sat along the edge of the boat on the cushioned seats, each one huddled in a towel against the cool night breeze. Mark had slid a large cooler into the middle, providing a surface to lay down their *Cards Against Humanity* entries. At one point, Iylah called for a purge of unwanted cards, and the group cheered in gratitude.

"Jo. How many cards you want?"

Jo was chewing away on her nails, oblivious. *Tck–tck–tck–tck.*

"Ahem—Jo!" Iylah coughed. Jo's head shot up to see her sister giving a wide-eyed expression. She pulled her fingers down. "Cards. How many you want."

"I'm okay," Jo replied, wiping her hand on her yellow lightning bolt shorts.

"Here," Iylah replied, handing over five cards. "They're funny. Just give me five of your cards."

"I like these cards," Jo replied. "I'm fine."

"Well, you haven't won a round yet, so . . ." She put the cards back on the stack. "Just trying to help."

"Iylah," Bryce said. "She's fine; we're having fun."

"She just plays it so literal. It's not funny."

"I think her cards are hilarious," Mark said. "The humor is just more subtle. Balances out the dick and vagina humor that keeps popping up."

"I lean more toward drug humor with a touch of anything

Blue Man Group, personally," Erica said. Jo lifted her eyes to Mark. The soft glow of the lanterns showed his face enough for her to see him wink at her. Something churned in her stomach. A half grin perked up on her face as she averted her eyes and began pointlessly rearranging her cards.

As the night progressed, what sounded like a high, slow whooshing sound kept going off. "What is that?" Erica finally asked.

"My phone," Jo said. "Sorry. I didn't notice." She got up to retrieve it from her bag.

"What noise is that? It sounds familiar?" Mark asked.

"Star Trek. When they beam someone up." She pulled out her phone and typed in her password. *Nineteen texts!?* "What?"

"Jo, you're up," Mark said. Jo did not respond. "You good?"

"Yeah, sorry. Hang on," Jo replied, reading the messages. "Mallory and Logan texted me—they were supposed to come today. Sorry, I just wanna see what happened . . ." she trailed off. Then, to herself: "Wait. What?" Jo read each of her friend's texts carefully. Both were texting about the same issue, and though their responses were different in content, each was scathing in tone. Jo's skin felt tingly, her insides achy. She felt like she was going to be sick. Her eyes drifted over to her sister, who was counting down before taking another shot. She could sense her hand shaking as she walked over toward Iylah, with the phone held up for her to see the screen. The laughter came to an abrupt halt as Jo approached, standing inches from Iylah.

"Whoa," Bryce said, peering up at her. "You alright?"

"Did you tell my friends they couldn't come?"

Everyone now looked at Iylah who breathed out a chuckle. "What are you talking—"

"Mallory just texted me," Jo said, inching the phone closer for Iylah to read. "I put that pic of all of us on Instagram, and

Mallory says that *I* told her we weren't going today. Both her and Logan texted me, asking why we were having the party when . . ." Jo now read from the phone, " 'I told them this morning it was canceled'." Iylah held up her hands, attempting to take control of the conversation, but Jo cut her off. "Did you call my friends and tell them they couldn't come?" Jo normally lacked the confidence to engage in a conflict with Iylah, but not tonight.

"Jo . . ."

"Did you?!" Jo shouted, pointing a finger at her, startling everyone.

Iylah slapped the hand away. "I didn't call them. Mallory called you this morning while you were showering, and I picked up."

"Guys, can we not do this now?" Bryce softly interjected. "Come on, it's birthday time. Let's do a shot!" He picked up the tequila bottle as Erica agreed.

"Oh my God!" Jo exclaimed. "You pretended you were me? They both think I lied to them."

"Well, I'm sorry, Jo!" Iylah said back in a mix of sarcasm and frustration. "Jeez. I wasn't trying to make your friends think you lied to them. You don't ever post pictures—how was I supposed to know?"

"Alright, y'all getting too crazy for me," Bryce said. He tossed his cards onto the cooler and pulled back his cap to scratch his scalp. "Startin' to lose my buzz. I'm goin' downstairs for a bit. Y'all two get your shit straightened out." He nudged at Erica. "You comin'?"

"Yeah," Erica said, tossing their cards onto the cooler. "Seriously, you guys, don't kill the mood. Go jump in the lake or something." The group stood up and headed toward the stairs.

Mark grabbed his cell phone and called out that he would follow them, leaving the sisters alone.

"What are you doing? You gotta do this shit now?" Iylah asked, pouring more tequila into her red cup. "And ruin our birthday?"

"Me?" Jo scanned through her phone again. "You've already ruined it. You ruined it when you lied to my friends—"

"Oh, gimme a break, Jo!" When everyone was finally gone, Iylah took a breath and rubbed at the bridge of her nose. "You really think your friends would have gotten along with everyone here? Come on! The birthday parties with your friends were awkward when we were kids. You think things have changed?"

"What's wrong with my friends? What's so wrong with *them* that they can't be around yours? Or you?"

"Nothing's wrong with them, they're just . . ." Iylah paused and shrugged. "They're just weird. They don't mesh with anyone here. At least you get along with my friends. I can't say the same for yours."

"Because I don't have a choice!"

"What's that supposed to mean?"

Jo was about to respond, more agitated, but she stopped herself. She knew it was pointless. Her shoulders sagged, and she breathed out, "Nothing."

"Do you not like my friends?"

"They're fine," Jo replied. "It's whatever." She hung her head and started to walk past Iylah but was grabbed on the arm.

"You know why Mallory called this morning? She bedazzled shirts for us all to wear and wanted to know if she had the right count. And the best part is that each of our shirts had patterns of our favorite animals." She stared pointedly at Jo. "Our favorite animal? Are you kidding me? Plus, how the hell did she even know what our favorite animals were?"

Jo stood still, looking away from her sister, out into the darkness. "I told her you liked skunks."

"Really? And you wonder why I don't want them coming? Who bedazzles a shirt?"

"She was just being nice," Jo said softly. "You used to like skunks."

"Yeah, when I was fuckin' six!" Iylah exclaimed.

Jo shuddered at her sister's harsh tone, shying away as if about to be hit.

Iylah sighed. "Look, I wasn't trying to be a bitch, but come on, let's be honest, your friends and mine; it's like different worlds." Iylah stepped forward slowly. "I just told her the party got moved to tomorrow and to bring the shirts then." Jo looked away, feeling her eyes begin to moisten. Iylah continued, "I wanted to spend the day with you, celebrating our birthday and having fun without constantly feeling like I was stuck in an awko-taco." Jo nodded gently. "Just tell her my friends surprised us. You had no idea Mark was taking us out on the boat."

The Star Trek beam came through again, and Jo checked the message. "Okay," she whispered. "Whatever." She started toward the stairs to go down into the cabin.

"Are we good?" Iylah asked.

"I have to go call Mallory," Jo muttered back. "You guys play without me."

19

NOW

$\mathcal{S}$omething thundered against a nearby wall, followed by a curse from Jared. The three of them eased out into the hall, toward the bathroom; Cole and Sherry uneasily walking with the gameboard hanging between them like an unconscious alien lifeform.

"You okay?" Cole asked, knocking on the door.

"Almost got it," Jared said. Before Cole could ask, "what?" glass shattered above them in a piercing jumble of noise. The shock made Cole and Sherry nearly fall over trying to cover themselves, though they weren't sure from what. Glass rained down around them.

"Jared! What are you doing?!" Iylah shined the light above the bathroom door where there was once a rectangular window. It was now empty except for random jagged shards of tempered glass sticking out from the frame.

"I remembered you had a window above the door. I was gonna climb out."

"Dude!" Cole replied. "What am I supposed to tell my parents?"

"I think that window breaking is the least of your problems," Sherry whispered.

"Yeah, well," Jared said back, sounding as if he were jumping. "I'm not." *Jump.* "Going." *Jump.* "To stay in here." *Jump.* "Got it!" There was some audible struggling on the other side of the door.

In the light they could see Jared's head peek into view. "How're you gonna fit through there?" Iylah asked.

"I don't know," he huffed. "Maybe—ahh!" He dropped down and cursed again. "Alright, well, sorry. I couldn't see it in the dark. I thought it was bigger than that."

"Awesome," Cole replied. "Great. Yeah. Let's just trash the house, no biggie."

"At least he can roll now," Sherry said. "Iylah, can you grab the die? It's on the floor. Jared? You have to roll."

Iylah retrieved the die and pitched it through the now-smashed window.

"Where'm I supposed to roll? It's pooling water in here."

"Just do it on the countertop," Cole said. "Hurry up."

"Man! You hurry up! Get me out of here!" Jared replied. There was a rattle against the granite countertop. "*Five*," he said, chucking the die back over the door.

"Got it!" Sherry said, catching it.

"Alright, let's go finish, come on," Cole said, moving away.

"Guys! I'm freakin' out in here."

"We're trying, okay?" Sherry called back. Iylah took her hand but Sherry froze, turning to face the door. "Hey." She paused. It was the first time she'd spoken to him without fear of being yelled at. Getting terrorized by a ghost for the last hour seemed to direct their emotions everywhere else but against each other. "I just want you to know I'm really sorry."

"Sherry, we gotta go," Cole said.

"And I know that you want nothing to do with me right now, and I understand that. The other night at the movies, I wasn't trying to follow you; I promise. I went to Paducah, and just wanted to be alone. I was hurt. And when I took that picture and saw him . . . kissing you . . ."

"Sherry," Cole prodded again.

"It made me feel humiliated—not because of *that*, but . . . because when I saw you two together it made me feel," she stopped, unsure if she should continue. "It made me question everything about you and me—what we were. I felt used. I felt like it was all just a cover."

"Sherry. We have to go—" Cole tried again.

"In a second!" She exclaimed. "But that didn't give me the right to do what I did. To share your secret with people. I didn't do it on purpose—I wanted to—but you're right, at the end of the day, I did it. And I can never take it back. And I can never understand how that made you feel. But I *want* to."

"Sherry!"

"Cole!" Jared yelled from the other side of the door. "Shut up!"

"Fine. Whatever." Cole sagged.

Sherry continued. "I don't want to lose you as a friend, okay? We have a lot to talk about, and I don't anticipate you wanting to talk to *me* anytime soon, but when you're ready, I'm here, and . . . I'm ready to do whatever I can to earn you back. As a friend." Iylah squeezed Sherry's free hand. "I'm here when you're ready. I love you."

"Sherry," Iylah said softly. "We have to finish this . . ."

Sherry stood motionless for a moment, waiting for Jared to speak. When he didn't, she exhaled, her lips quivering. Finally, she nodded and turned away when Jared tapped the door. "Hey," he said back, over the sound of the water. "Thank you. That means a lot. I um . . ." Sherry stepped closer, pressing herself against the door to better hear him. "I'm sorry. Look, I never meant to make you feel used, or embarrassed. I promise I wasn't using you—" A shocking rumble came at the front door followed by a stream of incessant, rageful barking.

"Guys! Can we *please* do this later?" Cole yelled. "I'm sorry, man. We gotta move. We're almost done!"

Jared yelled "hurry" as the three of them awkwardly darted back to the guestroom. "You guys couldn't wait until this was over?" Cole asked.

"It's fine," Iylah said. "We're okay." Cole lowered the gameboard to the floor next to the bed and sat beside it. Despite the earlier struggle, there was still a considerable amount of slack in what was now tangled around their arms. "He's right. We're almost there," Sherry muttered, picking up her marble with her free hand. She counted out the spaces before placing it on a spot marked with a hand. "We need another five to win."

"Will things get worse as we get closer?" Cole asked.

"They won't get better," Iylah replied gloomily.

"Great," Sherry said, her hand above the box.

"Wait!" Cole whispered abruptly. "Use your other one. That way it doesn't latch on to both."

"Oh yeah," Sherry muttered. She slid the vine covered hand inside the hole. She had lowered her arm almost to her elbow, when something brushed against it. She tried to pull it back, but the milfoil around her wrist had expanded, forcing her to stay put. She screamed when something inside began moving in between her fingers. "Omigod, omigod, omigod. What is that! There's something in here!"

"Pull it out!" Cole yelled.

Sherry yanked her hand out of the hole, almost knocking herself in the face with the tower. Iylah positioned the light near Sherry's hand, which was empty. "What was it? Did you get it?"

"No, I didn't get it! It had hair!"

"Hair?" Iylah said. Iylah tried to illuminate the box's interior, but it was pitch black. It was then that Cole heard something move on the floor. He called for quiet. Something was shifting underneath the bed. Sherry knelt and lifted the bed skirt to peek underneath, holding out a hand for Iylah to give her the flashlight. There was nothing there.

"You guys hear that, right?" Cole asked.

"I hear it but . . . I'm not seeing anything," Sherry said. As the light made another pass, something shot wildly out at her. She screamed and flew backwards in surprise, jerking Cole and the gameboard with her. In a fit of terror, she threw the flashlight at what had darted at her. "A snake!" she yelled.

Iylah shrieked and jumped on top of the bed. Sherry swiftly followed but got yanked back before she could get her body fully on. Cole was sitting motionless on the floor, his hands cuffed in front of him, the gameboard hovering tightly between them. Sherry's arm and shoulder hung off the bed. "Cole, get up!" Sherry whispered, trying to pull him.

"I can't," he muttered back through his teeth. He was looking ahead at the wall opposite him. The flashlight was rolling back and forth, and in the beam, every time the light rolled right, it illuminated two large, brown snakes poised at the other end of the room. They were thick, each with a series of crossbands along its back. Cole inched his knee up to try and stand. The snake on the left reared its head back and dropped its mouth open, prompting the other to do the same. A disturbing hiss came from each of them. Cole recoiled back down, huddling lower to the floor. "That's a cottonmouth," Cole whispered.

After a lengthy and anxiety-filled pause, Sherry asked in a hushed voice: "Are they poisonous?"

"Extremely," Iylah replied.

"Iylah . . ." Cole breathed. He inched his hand over to try and get the light but stopped, noticing the snakes' heads moving in unison with his arm. "They're watching me. They won't let me move."

"Sherry, reach in the box," Iylah said. Sherry immediately protested. "You have to. Whatever is in there will help. Do it, or they'll bite him."

"Iylah, I can't do it," she whispered in horror. "Please. Please. Please. I can't do it. Please." Both girls were frozen, fearful that any sudden movement would prompt the snakes to attack.

"Sherry, the snakes aren't in the box—"

"I know, but something else is. Please don't make me reach in there."

"You have to!"

"Sherry!" Cole hissed. "Do it now!" One of the cottonmouths raised a little higher for intimidation.

Sherry began whimpering, muttering "you're okay" to herself over and over. She lowered the board onto the floor, careful not to make any sudden movement. She inched more of her body off the bed slowly and lowered her hand once again into the hole, wincing as she did.

Whatever was inside rubbed up against her. She sucked in a sharp breath and tried to pull back her hand, but this time it wouldn't move. The slimy plants protruding from the hole prevented her arm from backing out. The thing moving around inside began weaving its way in between her fingers rapidly. Something cold streaked across her fingertips before whatever it was started to make its way up her arm. Several sharp pin-like pricks crept up her skin, triggering Sherry to attempt jerking her hand free, fiercely cursing in a panic for someone to get the box off her. Her frantic movements bought Cole a window of time to snatch the flashlight, and dart onto the bed. The snakes lunged toward him at nearly the same moment.

Iylah helped him onto the bed and snatched the flashlight, pointing it down at the box where something the size of a golf ball was forcing its way out, over Sherry's arm. Her shrieks grew more desperate and frightful, urging Cole or Iylah to get it off, but Cole was in shock watching whatever it was peek out of the hole. Iylah reached down and carefully positioned her fingers against the skin on Sherry's arm. "Stay still! Don't move, don't move!" she began to whisper over Sherry's frenzied cries.

Iylah pushed the arm hard against the rim to allow whatever it was inside to crawl out. Sherry wailed uncontrollably as not one, but four shaggy black rats climbed up her arm toward her neck and head. As one of them began crawling on her scalp, her anxiety finally overpowered Iylah enough to yank her hand away and fling the rats onto the floor. A mixture of obscenities—directed at Iylah—spewed from Sherry's mouth as she began clawing at her arms and shirt. She screamed in a fit of terror, madly scratching at her head as if they'd buried themselves in her hair.

Iylah wrapped her arms around her, still careful not to engage the plants between her and Cole. "Shh. It's okay. It's okay," she whispered.

Cole pulled himself closer to Sherry. "They're gone! They're gone! You're okay." He and Iylah continued reassuring her until Sherry's fright grew less. She had begun to cry and put her head onto Cole's shoulder, shivering.

Iylah heard scurrying across the floor and pointed the light down off the bed. "Look!" In the light, two of the rats scampered across the floor, the snakes following close behind them.

Cole steadied himself and motioned to Iylah. "You told me it wouldn't be like this."

"I know . . ."

"You said we would be in more danger if we didn't play than if we did—"

"I know."

"Those are cottonmouths, Iylah! Like, really poisonous snakes! If one of us gets bit, that's it!"

"Cole! I heard you, okay? What do you want me to do?" Cole shook his head in disgust, scooting away from her. Sherry straightened, wiping her eyes with her free hand. "I didn't know it was going to be this bad. This wasn't what happened the last time I played, and I wasn't about to let something bad happen to you if we didn't do what she wanted."

"Why is she doing this?" Sherry asked. She could sense Iylah was about to deny knowing and cut her off. "No! You said it seemed like she was trying to tell you something, and that it was centering around the night she died. The water, the snakes, the freaking panic attacks! What does she want?"

Iylah didn't have words at first. She sat open mouthed, wondering how much she should say. "The night she died we got in a fight. The fight was because I embarrassed her. Truth be told, it wasn't *just* that night. We fought all the time and I humiliated her constantly. I didn't always intend to, she just . . ." Iylah took a breath. "There wasn't anything she couldn't do. Or learn. And I *hated* it. No matter what we did, she was the one that got the recognition—*she* was the one that got the *attention*.

"And despite my parents' intense belief that I was overreacting, she was the one that always got her way. And . . . I don't know. I just, I hated her for it. So, as we got older, if I couldn't beat her in sports or games or at school, I would beat her in other ways. I would belittle her because it was the only way I could actually come out on top. I used whatever I had: strength, yelling, my looks. Most times, I would just use her feelings for me and manipulate her. And I did it all the time: parties, with boys, in front of my friends—her friends." Iylah exhaled, feeling the weight of her agony begin to flood out. "And yet, despite everything I did, she . . ." The words became choked in Iylah's tears. "No matter how I treated her, she was like a freaking lap dog. We'd fight and not five minutes later she'd come barreling into my room asking me to braid her hair like mine, or to play, or to watch a movie." Iylah took a pause.

"It's funny. There were so many times she'd tell me how much she wished she could *be* me. She thought it was the other way around—that I was the one who got all the attention. That I was the confident one because I had all the friends, or the cute one because I could talk to boys." An anguished chuckle escaped her. "I'd say, 'Jo, we look the same—you can talk to a boy.' And she'd say, 'yeah, but they talk *back* to you.' I wanted nothing more than for her to go away and she wanted nothing more than . . . *me*."

Iylah could feel herself curling forward to rest her head on her knees as she did in therapy when Jo came up. "She never saw how smart she was, or how talented she was. *Everyone else* did, though. Jo, the good painter; Jo, the really good swimmer; Jo, the smart one. She freakin' designed board games! I mean, come on, how cool is that?" She sighed. "And as popular as she thinks I was, or how confident she thinks I was, it was a facade. People didn't talk about me the way they talked about her. Iylah Maddox. Jo's sister. Second place. The rebellious daughter. The girl who wears too much makeup. The best partner to have in beer pong. The attention whore who is secretly so insecure with herself that she sits in the hot tub with her top off at parties." Iylah sniffed and wiped her cheeks with the back of her hand. "That's why we got into a fight on the boat that night. She was doing so well in school, and knew what she wanted to do, and everything seemed so in place for her. And I . . ." She cut herself off. "I did something to her that night. Not because I wanted to but because I could. Something to make me feel like I still had something over her. Like I still had value."

"What'd you do?" Cole asked.

Iylah shook her head. She sat, silent. "Of course, had I not done it, she'd . . ." She stopped again. There was no need to finish.

"So, you think that's why she's here tonight?" Sherry asked. "Because of what happened on the boat? Like a payback?"

Iylah shook her head. "No. She's been paying me back for three years. Cutting away at my life because it's what I did to her. I can't work, I can't sleep, I can't leave my house—I can't even take care of you three. It's why she wants *you*. To make *me* feel the way I made *her* feel. To make me powerless."

A moment of silence came between them. "Iylah . . ." Sherry said. "Look at me." She didn't. "We're gonna make it through tonight, okay?"

Iylah sobbed into her hand. This night was all her fault. Even in the dark, she couldn't bear to look at them.

"And when we do, we're gonna figure out some way to end this. Alright? We'll destroy the game, or find a priest, or something. Okay? Iylah!" Sherry called, clapping her hands. Iylah jumped, now looking toward her. She sniffed. "This is not your fault! And whether or not you *believe* that is irrelevant because we need you to get us to the end. You are obviously a good person. You're brave, you're compassionate, you're strong."

"You got me through my panic attack," Cole added.

"Yeah. And you're still here with us. And when we make it through tonight, you're gonna throw it in your sisters' face that she doesn't control you, and that you aren't helpless."

"Yeah, you definitely aren't the same person as what you just described. I wouldn't have gone up those stairs first, but you did. And I definitely wouldn't have gone in my parents' room like you did."

"He's right," Sherry said. "You've been on top of keeping us safe all night. So, you show us how to stay alive . . ." She reached forward, grabbing at the floorboards until she found Iylah's hand, and squeezed it assuredly. "And then we'll figure out some way to burn this *fucking* game to ash."

The 12th Birthday Party

*I*ylah stood against the wall, waiting breathlessly for her mom to get off the phone. No matter how many times Iylah tried to cut in and ask if *they* were coming, her mother continued to ignore her.

"Okay. Thanks again. Bye-bye." Silvia Maddox hung the phone back onto the cradle and fanned the collar of her shirt. Iylah could see sweat beading along her mom's forehead. "I'm sorry, sweetie. No one can get here until tomorrow."

Iylah groaned and pushed the back of her head into the wall, lightly pounding it in frustration. "Can you call someone else?"

"I tried. The only other one who can come can't get here until later tonight. And they're gonna charge me a lot more than I'm willing to spend."

"How much?"

Her mother eyed her with exasperation. "It doesn't matter because I'm not paying it. Someone will be here tomorrow before you all wake up."

"Can we go buy more fans?"

"We have two more fans in the garage."

Aunt Fanny strolled into the kitchen with her tongue out, not quite hyperventilating, and collapsed onto the cold floor beside Iylah. "See! It's so hot that Fanny's on the verge of dying." Her mother chided her, and Iylah continued to grumble, sagging her body to the floor. "No one is gonna want to stay, especially because my room is like, a million degrees."

"Oh, stop it," Mrs. Maddox swatted her hand as she moved to exit the kitchen. "You couldn't all fit in your room, anyways. Where would you all sit?"

"Not all of us. But what if my friends want to do something else?"

"Iylah, no ma'am. This is your and your sister's party. She already gave up one of her invites so Katie could come. I do not want to find out that you three went off somewhere and left Jo and Gwendolyn on their own."

"What?" Iylah was now sitting on the floor, leaning against the cabinet. "What were we supposed to do—" She was cut off by her mom motioning for her to talk softer. Iylah dropped to a harsh whisper. "Mom! My friends don't want to sit around playing board games all night."

"What's wrong with board games? You like board games," Silvia replied.

"I do, but not when Jo and her friends start quoting movies and discussing Star Trek trivia. It's gonna be awkward enough having Gwen here."

"Why do you say that?"

"Because she wears the same thing on her head every day to school, and I'm pretty sure she doesn't shower. I'm nervous everyone's gonna start making fun of her and make everything awkward."

"Perhaps you're making things awkward by being nervous *for* her. I'm sure she'll be fine. I want you and your sister to think of things to do together—*not* in groups."

Iylah moped. "But there's nothing we can all do—" She stopped abruptly when Josephine walked into the room, carrying a box of several paper bags. She slid the box onto the table, and then began speaking in a high-pitched tone to Fanny as she knelt and rubbed her belly. The tail rose and fell once; likely too hot to exert the effort. "Ooo," Jo said, holding out a hand to Iylah's head. "I like your braids. Can you do mine?"

"Sure . . ." Iylah said with a sigh, falling to the side to lie on the floor beside the dog. Fanny picked her head up. Her huffing stopped as she gave a concerned look to Iylah—perhaps making sure she didn't get hurt—then went back to panting.

"Is anyone coming to fix the air?"

"No sweetheart. Not until tomorrow."

Jo shot a worried look over to Iylah, and then back to her mom. "Are we still gonna have the party?"

"Yes," Silvia said breathily. Another dramatic groan from Iylah. "We're gonna put you *all* in the basement." She checked in with Iylah, who was lying on her back. "It's much cooler down there, and you'll have plenty of space. You girls can roll out sleeping bags and watch TV—you'll have the whole thing to yourselves. Your dad and I will just sack out up here." She paused and eyed Josephine. "How you feeling?"

"I'm okay," She answered. "Stomach hurts a little. And the . . . thing . . ." Jo pointed to her groin, "feels a little weird."

Mrs. Maddox gave a tight smile and arched her brows. "Great being a woman, isn't it?"

"How are you wearing pants?" Iylah asked. "Aren't you hot?"

"No," Jo replied.

"It's a hundred degrees in here," Iylah continued.

"I'm not hot."

"Maybe you could make it a pool party," their mom suggested. "I've still got three of the baby pools from your nephew's party. And all those guns. Everyone could bring bathing suits, that way you wouldn't have to be inside the whole time. You want me to fill them up?"

"Um . . ." Jo mumbled.

"Ooo. Yeah!" Iylah said, sitting up. "That could be fun. We could do like a water gun fight or something!"

"What do you think, Jo? You wanna do that?" Their mom asked. Jo looked to be hesitating. She clicked her tongue. "Oh. I'm sorry. I forgot. May not be the best idea."

"What?" Iylah protested. "Why not—oh." She paused. "Is that why you're wearing pants?" Jo hid her face. "So, you can't go in the water or put on shorts because you think you're gonna bleed on everyone?"

"Hey!" Mrs. Maddox cut in. "That's enough."

Iylah dropped back down to the cool floor and let out a breath.

"Alright, you girls decide what you wanna do. Jo, I think you'll be fine in the pool. I'll show you what to do if you decide to fill them up." Jo nodded. "I'm gonna go dust off the fans."

"Where's dad? Can we call him and have him pick up a couple more?" Iylah asked.

"Iylah, we have enough fans. Besides, he and Mark are trying to fix something in the car."

Jo sucked in a breath. "Mark's here?"

Silvia laughed. "No. Your dad brought the car over to him to see if he could help install something before he left for college. He did wish you both a happy birthday, though. Said he had a gift for each of you. He's gonna give them to your dad."

Jo's eyes beamed, which made Iylah smile. "Jeez. Calm down, love bug." Jo's cheeks flushed.

"Iylah. Don't tease her," Silvia said, leaving the room. Iylah closed her eyes, hearing Jo scrounge around the food plates on the counter.

Josephine scooped up a handful of grapes. "Hey Lala?"

"Mmm?" Iylah mumbled from the floor.

"If you want to do the pools, that's fine."

"No, it's okay, it's your birthday too." She thought for a second. "What about the water guns?"

Jo gently nodded, grabbing another grape. "That sounds fun."

"Perfect," Iylah replied, emotionless. She now understood why Fanny always preferred to lie in here. It wasn't so bad down here. Maybe she could even take a nap before the party— *Tck Tck Tck Tck*. "Ugh! Stop!"

"Sorry," Jo said.

"That's so gross. Go wash your hands."

"Okay," Jo said, walking over to the sink. "It's pretty cool we get the whole basement, huh?" Jo gleefully asked. "This is gonna be so fun! What games do you think everyone will want to play?"

Iylah opened her eyes. She stared at her sister for a long moment before rolling her head back to face the ceiling. "I don't know. Just pick out whatever you want." Iylah finally got to her feet and grabbed some fruit off the tray.

"Maybe mom will let us watch a scary movie," Josephine said. There was no reply from her sister. "Lala? You wanna do that?"

Iylah was staring at the box of paper sacks on the table. "What is this?"

"Oh! Those are the party bags. I made one for everyone who's coming."

Iylah repeated "party bags" to herself as she scanned them. There was a name written across each one in a different color of glitter glue. "What's in'em?"

"Lots of stuff: candy, trolls, a funny pencil." She started to rifle through the bag. "A bracelet; fake mustache." She pulled out an item. "And for Lala—"

"Can you stop calling me Lala?" Iylah exclaimed. "We're not five anymore."

"Sorry." Jo said softly. Then, pulling out a party popper, "I figured you'd like these." An apologetic smile crept over her mouth. "Mom will hate them." Then she reached back in. "And a ticket for a raffle that I'm gonna do. The winner gets a t-shirt."

"Let me guess; you made it?" Iylah asked dryly.

"Yupparooni," Jo replied. She scooped up the box of bags and said, merrily, "but the big surprise is that I made a shirt for everyone." She walked giddily toward the hall.

"Yay," Iylah sighed.

To Iylah's surprise, the basement was almost *too* cold. She had suggested everyone just wear their bathing suits because of the heat, but nearly everyone was back in their clothes, and two of her friends had borrowed hoodies from her.

"You guys wanna play a game?" Jo asked.

Iylah's head whipped around to her sister. "Jo, nobody wants to play a game." She gave a nervous smile, checking in with everyone in the room. "We're gonna eat soon."

"I meant when we're all done eating," Jo replied, scanning the room. "Do you all want to play a game?" There was a quiet in the room for a moment, and then Iylah's friend Katie spoke up. "Sure. Which game?"

"I've got lots!" Jo opened the closet door to reveal nearly seventy-five game boxes, all neatly stacked and in order by box size.

"Like, board games?" Janelle, another of Iylahs friends, asked.

"Yeah." She pulled one out and turned it around to show them.

"Oh. I'm not good at those," Janelle replied.

"I have all different kinds . . ." Jo said, scanning the shelves.

"What's that one?" Her friend Gwendolyn asked, pointing to a black tower on the middle shelf.

"Oh! This my project for Mrs. Abbott." Jo brought the tower and a yellow tote bag over to the bar next to Gwen.

"I haven't even started mine yet," their friend Maggie Burbank said. "You made that?"

"Yup!" Jo took out a plastic bag with pieces and cards inside.

"What's the project?" Janelle asked.

"You have to make a math board game. I call this one *Zombie Escape*. It's pretty simple." She pulled four slats out of the bag and attached them to the bottom of the tower, making a cross pad with the black tower in the middle. Then she took out a handful of colorful marbles. The slabs were beautifully painted to look like broken roads, filled with cracks, rubble, disabled cars, and broken street signs. Several makeshift indentions were carved out of the wood for the marbles to sit in.

"Man. Yours is so nice," Maggie said. "I was just going to cut up an old cereal box and put some squares on it."

"How do you play?" Gwen asked.

"Guys, it's the weekend. Do we really have to play a math game?" Iylah said. "Plus, she'll talk forever about it."

Jo's head sank and she started to put it away. "Okay."

"No, no. It looks cool," Katie said, reaching her hand over the tower's top, where there was a hole. "How do you play."

"It's pretty easy." Jo perked up. "There are two players per team. You roll the die, move up the board, and each time you stop, you have to answer a math question. If you land on one of these zombie hands," Jo pointed at the marked spaces on the board, "you have to draw a card from inside the tower." Jo then reached her hand inside to demonstrate. "Each card makes it more difficult to solve, so, like . . ." She drew a card from the stack nearby. "No using fingers to count. Or . . ." She pulled out another. "Opponents sing 'Row, Row, Row Your Boat' while you figure it out. Stuff like that. You work together to answer before the timer runs out. If you miss one, the person who rolled becomes a zombie, and moves two spaces back. Then you start playing against your partner. The cards don't affect them, but if they answer before you, *they* get to roll. If they infect you—by landing on you—or get to the safe zone inside the tower, here, you lose."

"That sounds so cool," Maggie said.

"Thanks," Jo replied. "We've played it a bunch. She loves it." She motioned to her sister.

"I didn't know you liked board games." Janelle looked at Iylah.

"I mean, sometimes. If I'm bored or whatever," Iylah replied, noting Jo's look of puzzlement.

"Can you make one of these for me?" Maggie asked with a smirk.

"She probably would," Iylah said.

"You guys wanna play?" Jo suggested, fishing out pieces from the tote bag.

"No!" Iylah said. "No math games! Come on, let's do something fun!"

"What about a blindfolded makeover? My sister and I did that. It's fun," Katie asked.

"We don't have any makeup," Jo replied. "Our mom won't allow us—"

"She won't let us use it for stuff like this. It's more expensive, is what she means," Iylah cut in.

"What about braids?" Gwen asked. The group seemed to answer in unison that they all wanted braids like Iylah and Jo, though Iylah seemed a little hesitant to do four people's hair.

"What about *Never Have I Ever?*" Janelle asked. There was a murmuring of hesitation and disapproval.

"Oh! We could play *Sardines*." Maggie suggested. A collective response of excitement from the others.

"We could do something outside," Iylah said. "Maybe *Freeze Tag?*"

"I like *Sardines*," Katie said. "What do you guys think?"

"I don't know how to play that," Jo said, sheepishly, taking her gameboard back to the closet.

"We'll teach you. It's super fun!" Maggie insisted. "Gwen, do you know how to play?"

"Mmm hmm." She nodded.

"How have you never played *Sardines?*" Katie asked. Jo shrugged. "You'll love it."

"Can we play music?" Katie asked.

"Ooo! I'll get my iPod!" Jo scampered to her feet and headed for the stairs.

"Wait wait wait!" Iylah called. "Just get mine. It's got more on there."

"No, it doesn't."

"Well, yeah, but no one wants to listen to the Beatles. You have all of mom and dad's music; it's old."

"I like the Beatles," Gwen said. Katie and Maggie agreed.

"Just get mine. There's a good mix on there."

"Can I bring both?"

"Jo, just get my iPod!" Iylah said, a little louder than she intended. "It's fine. I've got some of your songs on there too."

It wasn't two minutes later that Iylah was called upstairs by their dad. "Yes, sir?" He was sitting on the couch reading. Jo was standing beside him, chewing on her nails. She stopped when Iylah gave her a disgusted look.

"What's the problem?" He asked.

"With what?" Iylah asked.

"Why won't you let her listen to her music?"

"What?" Iylah's eyes widened as she threw up her hands. "I didn't say she couldn't listen to her music. I just said get my iPod. They wanted to listen to music. Mine has more of a mix."

"Iylah. It's both of your birthdays, please try to share—"

"Dad! I'm—" She stopped, catching herself for interrupting. "Sorry. I didn't say she couldn't have her music."

"All of hers are rap songs and country. Gwen and I don't want to listen to that," Jo said.

"How do you know what Gwen wants?" Iylah fired back.

"Girls. Stop." Their dad put his book beside him. "Either find a way to compromise or no music."

"How can I compromise? Whenever she doesn't get something she wants, she runs to one of you."

"You never let me choose anything," Jo said, looking at the floor.

"Are you kidding me?" Iylah exclaimed.

"You got to have *three* friends over."

"You said you didn't mind!" Iylah replied. "Besides, you've chosen the entire party. You decorated it. You made those stupid bags—" Jo looked instantly hurt by that. "I don't mean stupid; they're fine. But you chose those. You're choosing a movie later. And you chose the pizza."

"There ya go—problem solved. Jo chose the pizza. Iylah, you choose the music." Jo's shoulders slumped. "Your mother just left to go get the pizzas. Why don't you two go ahead and bring down the plates and napkins."

There wasn't a formal table in the basement, so the girls spread out on the floor. Jo sat with Gwen and Janelle, talking about TV shows, while Iylah sat near Maggie and Katie, giggling and furiously texting on Maggie's phone.

"I like your wreath," Janelle said to Gwen. Iylah glanced over.

"Oh," Gwen said shyly. "Thank you." She patted it with her hand and softly smiled back.

"Do you have any more?"

"Janelle!" Iylah cut in.

"What? I like it!" Iylah noticed Gwen suddenly look ashamed. "Seriously. I was just gonna ask if you had one I could have—or if you could make me one."

"Oh," Gwen muttered. "Sure. Yeah." She nodded her head excitedly. "I can make one for you. Just tell me what colors you like."

"Cool," Janelle said. They continued talking when Iylah heard "Ms. Jackson" by OutKast suddenly get cut short over the speaker. A new song began playing. She looked up to notice Jo standing beside the bookshelf where the iPod was plugged into the speaker, looking like she was innocently going through books. Iylah didn't say anything.

At one point, Jo snapped her fingers and darted off to get the gift bags. She passed them around to excited fanfare. Everyone laughed and seemed genuinely excited at the goofy stuff inside. There was also a communal shriek when Maggie used her party popper.

"My mom hates those things," Iylah said with a grin. "Use them well."

"And don't lose your raffle ticket. The winner gets a prize," Jo said. The group let out an "ooo." "And Lala, here's yours."

"Lala?" Maggie said, surprised. "I like that."

Iylah could feel the blood rush from her face. She snatched the bag out of Jo's hand, giving her sister a death glare.

"I'm sorry, I'm sorry," Jo whispered, flinching.

"I'm gonna start calling you Lala," Maggie said.

"Alright, alright. Shut up. It's what she used to call me when we were kids."

"It has a nice ring to it," Katie said. And then in a high-pitched, baby-like voice, she held the name out: "Laaaaa-laaaaaaa." Everyone giggled.

Iylah swatted Katie's arm playfully. "Shut up."

"I'm sorry, Iylah," Jo said, again, looking remorseful.

"Oh, Jo it's fine," Maggie said. "We're just messing with her."

Iylah pretended to laugh, all the while staring down her sister.

The girls were finishing up their dinner when Janelle suddenly said, "Alright. Never have I ever shaved my legs." It took the rest of them a moment to process the statement and then the purpose. Janelle held up three fingers. "Come on, never have I ever shaved my legs. Who's done it?" The others each held up their fingers; nearly all of them dropped one.

"You've never shaved? How?" Katie asked.

Janelle untucked a leg from under her and rubbed up her shin. "I don't know. It just doesn't grow, I guess." A few of them ran the back of their hand up her leg.

"I'm jealous. I started shaving at the beginning of the year. I feel like I have to do it every week," Katie said. There were some murmurings of agreement.

"Katie, you're up," Janelle said.

She sat in thought, and then smiled deviously. "Alright. Never have I ever kissed a boy." Each of them nervously checked the other, but no fingers went down. Then Maggie dropped one and the others yelled, "What?!" coupled with questions of "Who?" and "When?" And then Iylah dropped one. There was even more excitement and phrases of surprise and disbelief thrown around.

"You kissed a boy?" Jo asked, sounding offended. "You never told me. Who?"

"You don't know him. It was at school."

"Would I know him?" Maggie asked. "It was Andrew, wasn't it?"

Iylah shrugged.

"Who was it?" Jo asked again.

"She doesn't have to tell. That's not the game," Janelle said. "Gwen, you're up."

Iylah leaned over to Maggie and whispered discreetly, "Never have I ever taken off this head wreath." The two of them stifled a giggle.

"What?" Gwen asked, looking at Iylah and Maggie, then the rest of the group. "Did I do something?"

"No, no," Iylah said, calming herself. "You can pass if you want."

"Nope. Everyone has to go," Janelle said. "Come on, I know you have one. Give us a good one." They all watched Gwen in anticipation.

Gwen stumbled over some words and finally said: "Never have I ever . . . worn . . . a bra . . ." She lifted her eyes slightly to check in with the group. There was a pause as they took in her words, and then an eruption of laughter. At first, Gwen appeared to be taken aback by the response and a little embarrassed, but she quickly loosened up and joined in the laughter.

"How?" Maggie said, trying to get a breath. "How have you never worn a bra?"

"Not a real one. I wear those things." She pointed over to the couch where a sports bra was hanging over the back. "See?

There's nothing here." She straightened out, highlighting her chest.

"I promise, you're not missing anything," Maggie said. "Especially during volleyball. It's the worst. Iylah, you're up." They continued. When it got back to Janelle, the questions became more isolating. She said she'd never had a crush on a boy in their class which was a stab at Katie. Katie then said she'd never said someone's dad was hot, which was directed at Maggie. Gwen said she'd never owned a thong—her mother thought they were for prostitutes—which to Iylah's surprise, no one else had either. Janelle told a story about taking one of her mom's and wearing it out only to later discover it was actually her dad's, which had everyone nearly crying with laughter.

"Alright," Maggie said. "Lala, you're up."

"Ooo, Laaaaalaaaaa!" Katie said with animation.

Iylah's eyes darted to Jo, who immediately put a hand up over her mouth to conceal the snickering.

Iylah masked her frustration with a tight smile. "Hmmm." She peered at Jo. "I've got one." She held one finger back up. "Never have I ever. Gotten. My. Period." At the mention of the word period, Maggie made a gagging noise.

"Not me," Janelle said.

"What's the matter Mags? Don't like the word *period*?" Katie asked.

Maggie made another noise in her throat, hunching forward. "Two words I can't stand. That, and *moist*."

No one dropped their finger. Iylah scanned around. "No one's gotten it yet? Jo?"

Jo visibly swallowed, looking nervously back at her sister. She gently shook her head.

"Really?" Iylah asked. "Because I could have sworn I heard you and mom talking—"

"Shut up!" Jo said back.

"Wait, wait. You got your period?" Janelle asked. Maggie stuck out her tongue and shook her head as if she'd eaten a sour blueberry.

Jo's eyes were on the floor.

"Does it hurt?" Katie asked.

"I don't have my period!" Jo shot back, not bothering to look up.

Maggie made another gagging noise.

"Okayyyy," Iylah said. "Guess no one has to put a finger down. Jo, you're up."

Jo got to her feet, scooping up her plate and walking it over to the trashcan. "Can we just play something else?"

"But no one's lost yet," Iylah shot back playfully.

"Let's do *Sardines!*" Gwen suggested to everyone's excitement. Jo dumped her plate and started cleaning up the food that had fallen on the floor, appearing to be off in her own world. The girls threw their mess away and got ready. The parents allowed them to use the entire house, except for the bedroom where they were watching TV. The group went outside so Gwen could explain the rules. Jo at once asked to be it, but Iylah steamrolled that, cutting her off. "I'm gonna be it. You all count to sixty."

Iylah darted off toward the house.

She hid in the basement under the stairs, against the back wall; a place she knew no one would find, and Jo would never go for fear of bugs. Occasionally, someone would come downstairs and snoop around. Katie got close but never spotted her. At one point, Iylah was bobbing her head to Garth Brooks' "Rodeo" when suddenly it stopped, giving way to "Say My Name" by Destiny's Child. That one cut off too and skipped to Nancy Sinatra's "These Boots Are Made For Walkin'.'" Iylah rolled her eyes.

After ten minutes, Gwen was the first to find her. And then Maggie. After another ten minutes, Janelle found them. Soon after that, Katie heard snickering and surprised all of them. It had been nearly thirty minutes, and Jo was nowhere close to discovery. She would come downstairs, look around, make a weird noise or crack a joke to get everyone laughing, but no one was biting. She opened the door to the storage area and peered inside, shining a flashlight. "Milkshake" by Kelis came on the speakers. There was a sound of disgust followed by the door closing. Two of the girls started humming. Iylah nudged her elbow and shushed them when she heard her sister moving close by again. They waited quietly. Iylah was trying not to laugh when suddenly the song shut off with an accompanying *thud*. Something fell.

Then, after a long moment,: "Iylah," Jo called nervously. *Was it a trap?* "Iylah, come here. I did something."

"What should we do?" Maggie asked.

"Iylah. Something happened to your iPod."

"Man," Iylah whispered, trying to maneuver herself through the others and the boxes of Christmas decorations.

"What are you doing?" Janelle whispered. Iylah ignored her and threw open the door. Jo was holding the iPod in her hand. Iylah swiped it away from her. "What did you do?"

"I-I-It was an accident. I was walking by and tripped over something, and I fell."

"Then how did this happen?" She exclaimed, holding up the device. The screen was shattered.

"This fell on it when I tripped." Jo reached down and picked up a large rock—painted to look like a Treasure Troll—that normally rested on the shelf beside the stereo. "I went to catch myself and got caught on the wire. It pulled the iPod down, and then I accidentally knocked the rock off onto it. I'm so so so sorry. It was an accident."

Iylah lifted the wire coming out of the stereo system that was previously connected to her iPod. She analyzed the space: the console, the floor. "What did you trip on?"

"I don't know." Jo checked behind her. "Maybe the rug. I was just walking and-and-and something was on the floor. And I tripped."

"How would you have tripped on that rug," Iylah said, pointing behind her sister, "and ended up over here?"

"I don't know . . ." Jo said nervously.

Iylah's eyes continued inspecting the stereo. "You sure you weren't trying to change the song? Or take out my iPod?"

"No," Jo said back innocently. "I haven't even gone near it."

"Oh yeah? Then why is yours . . ." Iylah slid her fingers just under the stereo and pulled out Jo's black and red iPod, "sitting right here?"

"I, um . . ."

"Oh. What? You don't know? It just magically appeared there?" Iylah asked.

"I was using it earlier . . ." Jo said softly.

"No, you weren't. You know how I know? Because after we talked to Dad—when I got *mine*—*yours* was still plugged in. I know you keep coming over here and messing with it."

"No, I don't!"

"Then who keeps changing the songs?" Iylah yelled. Jo drew back at the noise. "You've changed, like, three of my songs. I saw you. We were all hiding in the storage, under the stairs. You looked in there, and when "Milkshake" came on—"

"It was an accident. I swear. The wire was hanging down, and I must have kicked it off. And then rock fell on it."

"You are such a liar!" Iylah screamed again. "You just said you tripped over the rug."

"Iylah," Janelle muttered. "Give her a break. She said she was sorry."

"Yeah, but she doesn't mean it. This is what she does. Plays the poor, little ole' me thing to get everybody on her side so she can get what she wants."

"No. I promise, it was an accident—" Jo tried to speak, but Iylah continued.

"Yeah, an accident that wouldn't have happened if you would just learn to not touch my stuff!"

"I swear, I didn't mean to . . ."

"I swear I didn't mean to!" She replied back in an impish, mocking tone. "You are such a little brat!" Iylah could see Jo's eyes welling up. "Aw. You gonna cry now? You break my iPod, and you're the one crying?"

"Iylah Maddox!" Their mom was standing on the landing, coming into the basement. "What are you doing!"

"She broke my iPod!" Iylah shouted.

"No!" Jo attempted.

"She didn't like the songs I was playing, so she tried to switch it out with her own. And in the process," Iylah held up the rock and her device, "this fell on top of it."

Mrs. Maddox scowled at the two of them and then pointed at Iylah. "You. Upstairs. Now."

"Why me?" Iylah shot back, instantly noting the threatening expression on her mother's face. She swallowed, shrinking back.

Silvia didn't take her eyes off of Iylah and allowed the tension to hang over the room for a long moment before she said, "Now."

Iylah's mom chewed her out for nearly two minutes for not only causing a scene but making Jo cry in front of everyone over an issue that could have been more appropriately settled by coming and discussing it with either herself or their father. Despite an unwillingness to listen to Iylah's side of the story, Silvia promised that Jo would pay for a new iPod. But Iylah was expected to go downstairs and apologize.

"Like, right now?"

"Yes. And don't say another word about that iPod. I will deal with Jo later, and we'll figure out how she can get you a new one. Do you understand?"

"Yes ma'am."

Iylah left defeated and moped into the bathroom. The situation played back in her mind as she sat on the toilet in a daze. She was so pissed. She wanted more than anything to slap her sister. There was no way Jo was going to buy her a new iPod, and if she did, she'd likely buy some crappy used one that didn't work. Jo was probably downstairs right now getting everyone to believe that it was an accident and that Iylah had overreacted. She wouldn't be surprised if, when she walked downstairs, Jo's iPod was hooked up to the stereo. "Ugh," she muttered. She washed her hands, looking at herself in the mirror and shaking her head.

And that's when she got an idea.

Iylah was right. The Beatles' "Here Comes the Sun" was playing, and everyone was singing along with the chorus. Iylah tried to look as peaceful as possible as she came down. They were sprawled on the floor. Maggie and Janelle looked to be going through a stack of DVDs as the others gave a positive or negative comment about each one. Jo, frantically biting at her nails, was the first one to notice her. She straightened up and smiled;

that huge, awkward smile. Iylah stopped, her face scrunched. *You little sneak.* And then Jo waved, timidly, the smile fading only slightly. It was a face of welcome, but Iylah couldn't help thinking there was a trace of victory in Jo's eyes.

"You think your mom will let us watch an R movie?" Maggie asked, as if nothing had happened.

"What?" Iylah asked.

"We wanna watch this." Maggie held up *Cruel Intentions.*

"Sure," Iylah mumbled. "We just won't tell her."

"Okay, cool," Maggie replied.

"Jo, you wanna go make some popcorn?" Iylah asked.

"Oh, yeah!" Jo replied. She connected eyes with Iylah and whispered that she was sorry. Iylah forced a smile, though it came only half up. "It's fine. I'll get the movie ready."

The girls laid out their sleeping bags and blankets on the floor. Iylah sat on Katie's bag and suggested Janelle sit next to her on Jo's. Then, when Jo came down, Iylah patted Maggie's black sleeping bag on the other side, suggesting she sit next to her. Jo beamed at the olive branch, handing out the bowls of popcorn to everyone.

"Mom and dad are in their room," Jo said to her sister, excited. She passed her a bowl.

"Cool," Iylah replied.

"Anyone need more to drink?" Jo asked. Everyone said they were fine, and Jo lowered herself down onto the bag. Iylah bit her lip in suspense. A tightness gripped in her chest. She had to remind herself to take a breath.

The movie played for a few minutes before Iylah began fumbling with the remote. She pointed it at the TV and started hitting it in the palm of her hand. "Can you guys hear it?"

"Not really," Katie said.

"Ugh. Remote's not working." She slipped off the back cover.

"Of course. No batteries. Jo, can you just turn the volume up on the TV?" Iylah asked. "Please."

"Sure." Jo swung forward onto all fours and crawled toward the TV. She moved a hand along the side panel, searching for the volume button.

"Um . . . Jo?" Iylah said, sitting up and shining a light on her sister. "I think you sat in something."

The reaction was instantaneous, just as Iylah wanted. Jo turned her butt away from the group and reached behind her to feel. "Oh no."

"Oh, wait. Is that . . ." Janelle stopped. "I think you might need to go to the bathroom."

There were murmurings of "ew" and "gross" as Jo hurriedly got to her feet, still feeling the back of her pajama pants. Iylah moved the light toward her. Jo seemed to have felt something because she was staring dreadfully at something on her finger.

"What? What is it?" Maggie said.

"It looked like she sat in something," Janelle said. The light shined onto Maggie's sleeping bag where Jo had been sitting. "Ew. Whose bag is that?"

"That's mine!" Maggie said, frantically. "Agh! What is that?"

Iylah leaned down toward a splotch of goopy, dark liquid. "It's red."

Maggie's throat made that gagging noise again as a hand went up over her mouth.

"I'm so sorry, I'm so sorry . . ." Jo began saying, standing against the wall.

Iylah cut her off. "Oh my God, Jo! It's all over Maggie's bag. It's everywhere."

The noise in Maggie's throat happened again, but this time her hand was unable to silence it. The gag brought forth a deep gurgle, and in an instant the contents of her stomach forced their way through her fingers and out her nose onto the floor. There was a loud shriek from the girls as they all scattered desperately away from the mess. Iylah could hear her sister still muttering, "I'm so sorry" repeatedly—this time in tears—as she darted across the floor and ran up the stairs.

Iylah slid the used ketchup packets into her pocket, trying her best not to laugh.

20

NOW

Cole and Sherry tensed when one of the rats scurried over the floor. It shrieked. There was a momentary, frenzied struggle before a sickening crunch popped below them. "Oh my gosh. We gotta get outta here!" Cole said.

"Hey! Hey! Whoa! What the hell is that?" Jared yelled. "Yo. Something's trying to get underneath the door—ooo! What is that! Guys!"

"Oh, no," Cole muttered. Desperate, frantic movement could be heard in the bathroom. It sounded like Jared was throwing whatever he could get his hands on. "Hang on man!" Cole shouted. "We're coming!" He searched the guestroom for movement with his light. "I don't see anything."

"If one of them went into the bathroom, then that snake won't be far behind," Sherry said.

"Yeah, or it's under the bed waiting on us," Cole replied. He positioned the tower between his fingers and lifted it up. "Iylah, are you okay?" She shook her head in several directions. "Hey. You're gonna get us through this. Okay? We trust you." Iylah nodded, again, a touch more confident. "Alright. Count of three, we jump off and run to the dining room table; get on top of it."

Cole thought for a second. "Jared?" He yelled. No response. "Jared!" Still nothing. "Shit. Alright, let's go, come on!" The three of them jumped off the bed and jostled out of the room. Jared must have heard the violent stomping because he started asking what was happening. Cole ignored him, pulling Sherry alongside him, the gameboard bouncing between them. They all leapt onto the dining table, a loud crack sounding out under the weight. They went still, Iylah checking the floor.

"Here. Go ahead and roll," Iylah said, passing him the die.

Cole lifted, and dropped it onto the table: *three*. It was a blank space. "Thank God!" Cole said.

Iylah placed the marble in its new spot, and there was an instantaneous crash back in the foyer, startling all of them. Cole stared at Iylah in a panic: "I thought we landed on an empty space!"

"Ooo! Shit! Shit! Shit!" Footsteps were pounding.

"Jared?" Sherry asked anxiously.

"I'm out!" Jared yelled. "Where are you guys?"

"We're in here!" Cole yelled back. Jared suddenly scampered in from the hallway, high stepping over the floor, and promptly leapt onto the table with them.

"How'd you get out?" Iylah asked.

Jared caught his breath. "Not gonna lie. May have broken your door," he replied. "Why didn't you guys tell me there were rats?"

"Rats are the least of our problems. There are two cotton-mouths around here somewhere," Cole said."

"Damn," Jared said, looking over the table. "Gotta be honest, I'm a bit more freaked out about the rats." The table creaked again, louder. "What now?"

Iylah handed him the die. "Now, you roll."

"How much more we got left?"

Before any of them could offer an answer, there was a shrill explosion of glass shattering in the front of the house. A thick *boom* with a frenzied skittering of clawed feet on the hardwood floor. "It's inside," Cole mouthed. "We gotta hide."

"Let's split up," Jared said.

"No!" Iylah whispered. "We all have to be together to end the game. We can't split up." She noticed the French doors and crept off the table, careful not to make a sound. The others hissed at her demanding to know what she was doing. She lightly pushed them open and checked to make sure the coast was clear. "Come on. In here," she said softly.

They slid carefully off the table, stepping quietly into the kitchen. Iylah closed the French doors shut behind her and leaned against them. She tried to listen over the water still streaming in the kitchen. It now covered the entire floor and splashed under their feet as they moved.

"We need to get upstairs," Cole said, inching toward the other set of French doors leading to the foyer and main staircase.

"Guys!" Iylah whispered, not wanting them to dart off.

Cole leaned in close to talk over the running water. "Be careful. There's glass everywhere. I think the dog's in the hallway."

"Maybe I can distract it over here and give you guys a break to run through the other doors, and up the stairs," Iylah suggested.

"You could if you had that meat stick," Cole said. Jared swatted his arm.

"What about you?" Sherry whispered.

"I'll be right behind you," Iylah said back.

"No. You've been telling us to stay together this whole time," Sherry said, a little louder. She was immediately hushed. "We're not leaving you."

"I can keep her attention here and give you guys a head start."

"How do you know it's a her?" Cole asked.

Iylah ignored him. "You're going to need enough time to unlock your bedroom. Just make sure it's open when I run up, okay?" Something toppled over in the next room. It sounded like the dog had pulled over the antique butter churner. Iylah steadied herself against the door. "You have a better idea?" Iylah asked. There was no reply. "Make sure you're quiet going up the stairs." They could hear the dog beginning to chew at something, hard cracks snapping under it's teeth. "I'll distract it; go. Please!" She whispered.

"Be careful, okay?" Cole said. "The glass."

"I got it," Iylah replied. She waited a few moments for them to get in position. "Get ready." She waited a little bit longer and then, finally, whistled the notes she'd always whistled for Fanny to come running.

The reaction was instantaneous. It was closer than she thought, throwing its heavy body against the door, knocking Iylah forcefully back. "Go!" she called out. She shoved herself back, holding the doors steady as it lunged again. Iylah heard a snap in the hinge. The dog took in several whiffs through its nose. "It's me, girl," Iylah whispered. She tried to whistle the notes again but couldn't. "Fanny," she cried. "Who's a good girl?" Undeterred, the dog let out several more violent barks. She could feel its teeth grinding against the wood. "Please, stop. Fanny, please . . ." Iylah remembered that the goal was to distract and run. She needed something to tie the knobs together. *My hair!* She ripped out the phone-cord hairband and wrapped it around the knobs. It would buy her a few seconds—it had to. She waited, took a breath, and then whistled again. Fanny gave one more jump—harder than ever—knocking her backward. In the light, the dog's snout pushed through the narrow opening.

Iylah moved back and saw it jump once more, pushing the doors almost enough to pop the band. She panicked, spun around too fast, and slipped on the wet floor. A sharp, white-hot feeling tore across her side, just below her ribs. She gritted her teeth, trying not to scream. She shined the light over to the door where the dog's head was caught in the opening. It was trying to jerk itself free, snapping and barking furiously. It was stuck! She had a break. Ignoring the pain in her side, she dropped a hand to the floor to push herself up and felt another fiery wave of agony shoot through her hand. The jagged edge of a broken bottle tore through her palm. The pain was immense, scorching up her arm.

She moved the light to see red spilling out into the water. When she tried to maneuver to her feet, her insides wrenched with fire, and she finally screamed. Sizeable chunks of glass were sticking out of her stomach and side; her shirt soaked with blood. "Oh no . . ." she muttered. "No, no, no."

The slashing and gnarling of the dog on the other side grew louder still. Iylah was certain it would break through at any moment, and then, in an instant, the terrifying noises of animalistic rage ceased. There was only the sound of the sink, and water from the refrigerator hitting the floor. Iylah shot the light's beam over to the door. The dog was gone but standing in the dark was a figure.

"Cole?" Iylah whispered, though she knew it wasn't Cole. Her mind conjured up images from that night with Erica. Gwendolyn Potts. The flower crown. The dirt on the floor. The figure stepped toward her, its feet sloshing in the water. She tried to stand but the pain in her side was excruciating. "Cole!" She cried, barely able to get her voice above a whisper. "Sherry! Help me!" That's when she remembered the party popper in her pocket. *They'd certainly hear that.*

Iylah dug it out of her shorts, her nerves almost fumbling it onto the floor, and pulled the string. Even with knowing it was coming, the pop startled her. She held her eyes shut hoping that whoever it was would somehow go away. When she opened them, the light in her hand shined on a pair of legs standing only a few feet in front of her. It wasn't Gwen.

Yellow shorts with black lightning bolts. A black t-shirt. At seeing the figure's face, Iylah dropped the light into the water and sucked in a ragged breath. She forced herself back in a crawl on her good hand, overriding the horrible sensation stabbing into her skin. She backed up into the cabinets and watched her dead sister step closer.

"I'm sorry. I'm so sorry. I'm so sorry," Iylah breathed, her vision clouding. "Please, please, please." The flashlight was out of reach, now shining its beam away from her. Nothing but a silhouette, the figure stood in front of Iylah. "Please. Please just leave me alone. Jo, I'm so sorry." She reached a hand out, hoping to touch her sister's leg, but she must have been too far away. She couldn't feel anything. Misery seized her throat. "I'm so sorry, Jo. Please."

The figure knelt in front of her and went still. Iylah felt something touch her wrist and draw her arm up. She tensed and began panting again that she was sorry, pleading with Jo not to hurt her. The touch on her wrist was cold. She felt her fingers become forcefully curled into a fist as if someone was wrapping their hand around hers. Then something pulled on her thumb, stretching it up. Iylah didn't know what was happening, but she continued to beg. "Please. I'm sorry, Jo. I'm so sorry. It was an accident. I swear, I didn't mean to . . ." She tried to pull away or scoot back, but she was pinned against the cabinets, and the shadowy presence held her wrist tight, fingers locked in a thumbs up position.

Iylah saw the figure's hand come up, casting a silhouette against the light, and make the same sign. Thumbs up. It didn't feel like contact, but there was a cold pressure against her knuckles as if the figure was pressing its fist into hers. Iylah finally fell quiet as she stared.

The figure leaned forward and spoke in a hushed voice, next to Iylah's ear: "All. Good."

The three of them nearly slipped on the top step. Water covered the hard wood. Jared didn't bother with the paperclip. Instead, he narrowed his shoulder and crashed into the bedroom door, nearly taking it off its hinge. Jared closed the door behind him as Cole and Sherry moved vigilantly to the bed and set down the gameboard.

What sounded like a firecracker went off somewhere downstairs.

"What was that?" Sherry asked. They stood, listening intently. "You guys heard that, right?"

"Maybe Iylah knocked something over," Cole said.

"Dude, that sounded like a gunshot. You think she had a gun this whole time?" Jared said.

"No. I'm sure something just fell over," Cole said. He stubbed his toe on the bed and cursed. "Where's the flashlight?" Cole asked.

"Iylah has it," Sherry replied.

"Are you kidding?" Jared fired back. "How're we supposed to see?"

"Guys! Shh!" Cole hissed. "It'll hear us."

"I can't see a freakin' thing," Jared said. There was a brief moment of quiet as they waited for Iylah to come running up the stairs. "Where is she?"

"I think we should go back down—"

"No way!" Sherry said. "We'll never get past that thing—" A frantic knock at the door cut Sherry off.

"Finally! Open the door!" Cole called. Jared did, and someone came rushing in, kicking up water. "Iylah?"

"Sorry," Iylah said. "Everyone here?"

"Yeah, yeah, we're here. You okay?" Cole asked.

"I'm fine," Iylah replied. "Just had a bit of trouble getting up."

"What was that pop?" Sherry asked. "Like a loud boom."

"Oh," Iylah said. "That was the party popper. When I tried to come up, the dog was by the stairs. I thought the sound might scare it. It worked. We can't go back down there. We need to finish this now. Go ahead and roll. I'll guard the door."

"Alright, how many spaces left for us to win?" Jared asked.

"Iylah, where's the light?" Cole asked.

"Oh shoot. I dropped it when I ran up," she said shamefully. "What about the candles?"

Jared snapped. "I got 'em." He shuffled around his pocket for a bit before there was a spark of light and a tiny flame. Jared held out one candle and lowered it to the board.

"Five," Sherry said. "We're at twenty. If we roll a five, we win."

"Whoa! What's up with your arm?" Jared asked, pointing to the tangled mess around Sherry's wrist.

"It's milfoil," Sherry replied. "It latched onto Cole, and when I tried to help, it got me too."

"What's milfoil?"

"We'll explain later. Where's the die?" Cole replied.

"Damn. So, you're just stuck together?"

"For now," Sherry replied. "I have it. We ready?"

"You can't just cut it off?" Jared asked.

"Dude! We'll explain later! Just go!" Cole exclaimed.

"Sorry. Here, lemme see the die," Jared said.

"Oh no! You've rolled the entire game! I had to dig out those rats last time!" Jared hushed her. She lowered her voice back down to a whisper. "I'm rolling this time." She shook the die in her hand when something crashed against the bedroom door, startling Sherry to drop the die onto the wet floor. "Shit. Where did it go?" She took the candle from Jared and searched around the bed. "Oh! Got it!" She whispered. "Um . . . six! It's a six! We win! We did it!"

"Hell yeah!" Jared yelled.

"You won?" Iylah asked.

"Yeah! We got six," Sherry replied, picking up the die off the floor and showing everyone. "See?"

"Okay. Hurry and move," Iylah said.

Jared leaned forward and pulled up the marble. He moved it up five spaces, coming to a dead-end at the tower. "Just put it in?" He asked.

"Yup," Iylah said. "Put it in and pull out the black marble that's inside."

"The black marble?" Jared started.

"We put a black marble in at the beginning. I'll tell you later! Just go!" Cole said, rushed. "Be careful not to touch the plant thing coming out."

Jared took the ball and warily lowered his hand inside the box. "Do I just drop—"There was a pause as his brain registered the sudden interruption. And then he screamed.

The Last Day
of Sophomore Year
Part III

Iylah walked up the stairs to her room where, according to her father, she would spend the foreseeable future. Jo's door was open; a soft glow from the lamp at her desk bled out into the loft. Iylah stopped, contemplating whether or not to engage, when she heard her father walk in from the garage, and slam the door. He stomped into the family room and looked up the stairs where Iylah was standing at the top. The two of them made eye contact. "Iylah!" She tried to interject that she was going but he cut her off, sternly. "I said in your room. Now."

She growled in annoyance, pounding the floor with each step, and to punctuate the moment with frustration, slammed the door to her room. The trophies on her dresser toppled over onto the floor, muffling whatever her dad was shouting up at her. She had always known her father to be stern with her when he was upset, but he'd never yelled at her as he'd done in the car coming home. It was a new sound for her. The echo of that gravelly, pained voice in her mind evoked a nauseating blend of shame and terror.

She ignored the fallen mess and sat on her bed, instantly reaching for her phone, and wiping her eyes. She had missed texts from Janelle and Katie, but when she went to reply, a data error popped up. She tried again with the same result. She clicked on the internet app and waited, only to be told "Something went wrong. Please try again later." Nothing worked: no internet, no texting, no social media. She exhaled, flipping the phone onto the comforter beside her, and fell onto her back. He'd already turned off her data.

She lay there, staring at the ceiling, running through the day's events that led to this. Scenes replayed in her mind, but they were overcome by flashes of her father's face: his eyes and cheeks red from earlier tears, and echoes of that distraught, exasperated voice.

A long moment passed before she heard a voice say "goodnight" from outside her bedroom. She opened her eyes and checked the clock on her nightstand. It'd been over an hour since she'd been home. She must've fallen asleep. She heard her mom yell something from down below, and then Jo replied with "Okay." Iylah sat up and opened the door. Jo stopped in her tracks, glancing back toward her.

"What did you tell them?" Iylah whispered at her.

Jo stared at her sister, emotionless, for a brief second before walking in and shutting her bedroom door to just a crack.

"Jo!" Iylah called, barely above a whisper. "Oh, you . . ." She bent forward to look out through the railing down into the family room. Neither parent was in sight. She cut the light and speedily tiptoed across the floor. Jo didn't bother to look up when Iylah came in. She was sitting at her desk, bent over what looked like a makeshift gameboard, painting a small piece with a fine tip brush. Aunt Fanny, who was sprawled out on Jo's bed, lifted her head slightly at Iylah's entrance, thumping her tail on the comforter. Iylah reached over and patted her.

"What do you want?" Jo mumbled, not even looking up.

"What did you say to dad?"

Something like a brief start to a laugh escaped through

Jo's nose as she shook her head. "Nothing, Iylah." She stopped painting and turned her weary eyes to her. "I didn't say a thing." Her voice sounded fatigued, uncaring almost.

"Bull shit!" Iylah whispered back. "He came and pulled me out of the theatre."

"I'm sorry . . ." Jo mumbled, putting the piece down, and studying something on the board.

"You obviously said something. How else would he know I was at the movie?" Again, Jo made no reply. "God! You always do this!"

"Yup," Jo said, in a monotone voice, going to draw. "I *always* do it. It's *always* my fault—"

"You know, next time if you're that pissed at me, maybe instead of running to mom and dad like a five-year-old, you could . . . I don't know . . . actually say it to my face." She could see something twitch in her sister's cheek. Jo wanted to fire back but she held it in, as always. The passive, quiet treatment was her M.O. "Can you stop being a baby for like two seconds?!" Jo's hand stopped. As Iylah's words hung in the air, her sister's head turned eerily toward her, almost doll like.

"Stop being a *baby*?" Jo said, straightening up. "Do you have any idea what happened to me today?" Jo kept her voice down to a whisper. "Do you have any idea how *embarrassing* that was for me?" Iylah said nothing. "And to make matters worse, you never did anything—"

"We came and helped you out is what we did—"

"No, Iylah. *Janelle* came and helped me out. Not you! I stood back there watching, you didn't do anything."

"What was I supposed to do? You—you think I'm gonna fight Maggie and her friends? Janelle's a psycho—"

"No, I didn't want you to fight Maggie," Jo replied, pausing as if to see if Iylah would get it without having to say it. Jo turned back to her drawing, picking up her pencil. "I just wanted you to care."

"What—what does that even mean?"

"I get why you didn't want to walk me home today. I do. You were right. I need to stand up for myself. But when you saw that I'd been . . . humiliated . . . that I'd been hit in the face like that . . . why was *Janelle* the only one who stood up for me?"

Iylah felt a sudden drop in her stomach. Stunned, she whispered, "Screw you." That shocked her sister into attention. Iylah held her gaze for a moment, shaking her head. "Maybe get your facts straight. After I saw that video, I tried to call you—"

"And yet I have no missed calls."

Iylah bit her lip. *Had she tried to call?* "Fine. But I believe, if memory serves me right, when we found you at the school, it was *me* who got out and tried to get you to come home with us. And again, if I'm not mistaken, it was *you* who shoved me off."

"You weren't trying to help me, Iylah," Jo said matter-of-factly. "You were trying to deal with me."

"Oh my God, self-pity-Sally ladies and gentlemen!" Iylah gave a detached laugh. "It doesn't matter what I say, you're gonna spin this to make me look like the bad guy, and that I don't care about you."

"So, you're saying what you did today, that was you caring about me?"

"I tried to—"

"You standing *nowhere near me* while Janelle beat up on Maggie, that was you caring? Or when you *didn't even* ask me if I was okay? If I was hurt? That was you caring?" Iylah had no reply. "You realize you didn't even say sorry to me today?"

"Sorry for what?" Iylah exclaimed in a whisper, still careful not to alert her dad that she'd changed rooms. "That I wasn't there to walk you home and take care of you—"

"For anything!" Jo cried. Her eyes moistened. "For what happened to me. For me getting embarrassed, or hurt . . . or you holding me under the water today. That really scared me, Iylah. You could obviously see I was panicking afterward and all you did was . . ." She paused, calming herself. She took a breath and poked at the dice cubes on her desk. Her voice became somber. "All you did was make fun of me. It was bad enough being humiliated at school, but to get it from you, too? 'Jo, are you still doing your panic thing?'" She mimicked in a lower tone. She picked up her dice and rattled them around in her hand, still unable to look at her sister. "It must be nice being you. Never having to be scared, or have your mind tell you you're helpless." She pitched the dice against the books on her desk. "Never having to be betrayed or heartbroken by your sister."

Iylah fell to sit on the bed and folded her arms. Fanny's tail thumped again, as she lifted her arm and leg, beckoning Iylah to rub her belly. Iylah did, and watched Jo turn back to her game, and wipe her eyes with her shirt. "You *did* betray me," Iylah whispered. "You came home and told dad that I didn't walk you home, and that I left school early. Then you lied and said I got in a fight with Maggie." Jo looked up at her. "Yeah. Thanks a lot for that. I get that sometimes my joke might backfire, or that I might say the wrong thing, but I would never go behind your back to mom and dad. It was one thing to do that shit when we were nine or ten but now?"

"Iylah . . ." Jo interrupted.

"No. Wait. You realize I didn't *actually* get in a fight, right? I didn't lay a hand on her. And thanks to you, mom and dad took away my trip to Louisville next weekend. So, you want to talk about betrayal—"

"Iylah," Jo held her hands out as if strangling the air. "I didn't tell on you." Iylah drew back, unsure if she'd misheard her.

"I never even told them about the fight. I said I got this from tripping on the stairs in the garage, trying to carry my stuff." She pointed to the cut over her eye. "I told mom and dad you walked me home and then went back out to Katie's and then to a movie." Jo stopped to let this sink in. "Did it ever occur to you that someone might have recorded you? Because that's what happened. Dad got a call from Maggie's mom when he got home. They have Janelle on camera, but Maggie said that all three of you jumped her after school."

"What?! How! I didn't do anything!"

Jo shrugged. "Janelle might be expelled. I told dad she was protecting me—"

"Did you not say anything about me? At least tell him *I* wasn't the one fighting?"

Jo shook her head. "He didn't ask me about you."

"Jo," Iylah said. "You have to tell him what happened. I didn't do anything! What if the school expels me too?" Jo swiveled around and picked up her pencil, drawing something on a piece of paper. "Jo."

"Our twelfth birthday. The ketchup packets." Jo continued scribbling. "You told me someone must have left them there. Was it you?"

"What?"

"The ketchup packets on the sleeping bag." She now stared intently at Iylah. "Did you put them there?"

"No. What . . . ? No. You've asked me this a thousand times—"

Jo then picked up her brush and spoke meekly. "Okay. I guess I don't have anything to say, then. Goodnight."

"Fine. What do you want?" Iylah asked.

Jo resumed painting one of her game pieces, holding it under the lamp. "I want you to admit that it was you. And I want an apology."

"Jo, that was like four years ago."

"An apology is when you say you're sorry about something you did that hurt someone else," Jo said softly.

"Are you going to finally admit that you broke my iPod?"

"I told you, it was an accident. I tripped," Jo said back, defensive. "Plus, I bought you a new one the next day. And *I've apologized* profusely ever since. All I want to know is if it was you."

Iylah opened her mouth to speak but nothing came out except a choked "I." There were no excuses; Jo obviously knew. "If I say it was me, you'll tell dad I had nothing to do with Maggie?"

Jo went back to dotting the game piece with her brush.

"Fine! Yes. It was me. I put them there." She held up her palms. "You happy?"

Jo froze, letting the brush hover slightly above its target. A short puff of surprised breath slipped through her nose, as her head shook slightly. "Goodnight, Iylah."

"I'm sorry. Okay? Now, are you gonna tell him or not."

"Please get out, now."

"Jo. You have to tell him I didn't do anything. And that Janelle was defending *you*—"

"Iylah Maddox!" Her father called harshly from the hall. "Get out here! Now!"

Iylah gave a hushed curse and leapt off the bed to the door. "Sorry, dad. She called me over to ask a question."

Jo appeared behind Iylah. "I didn't call her in here. She came in complaining about being grounded." Iylah turned in astonishment toward her sister. "I've asked her to get out twice, but she just keeps talking."

"Wha—no! That's not—"

"Young lady, you are pushing my patience. Get your teeth brushed, get to bed, and I swear if you so much as make a sound before tomorrow morning, you can kiss your camping trip in July goodbye. Do you understand me?"

"Yes sir," she replied.

"Goodnight." He said with finality and started back down the stairs. Iylah made for her room but stopped, turning to address Jo who was standing in the doorway. "What is wrong with you?"

"I want an apology from you. You don't just say 'I'm sorry' because your back's against the wall and you want something out of it. It needs to *mean* something. You have no idea what that day did to me—"

"You want an apology from me? Fine. Here goes." She stepped closer, keeping her voice to a barely audible whisper. "I'm sorry that my iPod got broken. And I'm sorry you took it so personal when I got you back for it. But am I sorry for doing what I did? No. I'm not. It was a joke. And I'll tell you something else." She paused, inching her head closer. "I'd do it again." She leaned back and grinned. "There's your apology." She turned, whipped her head back toward the bed, and snapped. "Come on, Fanny." The dog hopped off the bed and trotted off to Iylah's room across the loft.

Iylah flicked off the light when she came out of the bathroom. As she opened her bedroom door, she could make out the faint sound of whimpering. She stopped, turning back toward Jo's room to listen. The nightlight illuminated enough to show that her door was open. Jo was crying. For a brief moment, something flashed in her mind to go check on her, but as quickly as the thought entered, it vanished. Instead, she rolled her eyes. "I'm grounded, and facing expulsion, and you're the one crying. Of course, you are."

Iylah didn't bother turning on the lights in her room. She slipped on a pair of shorts and a clean t-shirt, and slid into bed, turning to face the wall. As she lay still, her hand rubbing Fanny's fur, she began to consider how she might get out of the grounding; what she could say to convince Jo to talk and clear her name. After all, the whole thing *was* because of *her*.

As Iylah felt herself begin to doze, the muffled moans and sobs from her sister across the loft became more clear in the calm night air. Iylah sat up in a huff and reached over to her night-stand to turn on her fan. It hummed to life, drowning out the obnoxious cries of her sister. The cool breeze blew over her neck and face, as her worries over a difficult summer faded into nothing, giving way to a restful night of sleep.

21

NOW

*J*ared jerked his hand out of the box, dropping the candle onto the floor, and bellowing with agony as the light sizzled out. There was a chorus of "what happened?" and "what's the matter" and "what! what!" but Jared couldn't answer. He scooted back across the floor toward the opposite wall—the only physical response his brain could muster—before finally curling into a ball. The screaming subsided into a slew of strained gasps and profanities. All the while, the dog had found its way up and was aching to get in.

"My fingers! Something bit my fingers—they're—they're gone! My fingers are gone!" He said through clenched teeth.

"Oh my God . . ." Sherry said nervously. "Guys." With her free hand, she dug into the candle box and lit one with her mouth like a cigarette. She moved it over his hands to see one wrapped over the other. Blood was gushing out through his fingers. "I need a towel—or something—"

"Over there," Cole said, motioning with his bound fingers toward the bed. "Grab that shirt. Wrap it around his hand."

"Did you roll a six?" Iylah asked from over by the door. Sherry ignored her. "Sherry. What did you roll?"

"Iylah. Can you give us a second here?" Cole said back, flustered.

"I rolled a six!" Sherry called out, struggling to get the shirt.

"No, you didn't," Iylah said back, matter-of-factly. "Sherry." Sherry whipped her head around to face Iylah, who was still standing beside the door, shrouded in the darkness. "You didn't roll a six, did you?"

"Guys, can we focus on getting this—" Cole began.

"Fine. No! I didn't roll a six. Okay? God!"

"What?" Jared cried.

She stammered. "I didn't think it would matter." Jared muttered something indecipherable. "We were only five away. I thought we could just toss it in and end it."

"It's a haunted game! You didn't think she would know that!" Jared yelled.

"Sherry . . ." Cole whispered. "Are you kidding me?"

"I'm sorry!"

"What happens now?" Cole asked Iylah, carefully picking up the die. "We finish the game, he gets his fingers back, right?"

"No," Iylah said, grimly. "I told you; everything is real. But if we can get this done, you can get him to a hospital."

"Wait. No, no, no, no! I can't lose my fingers! How'm I gonna pitch now?"

"Sherry, reach inside. You'll need to get the marble out." Iylah said.

"Me?!" Sherry countered.

"Yes," Iylah replied.

"Of course! Every time! This stupid box." She took hold of the candle with her wrapped hand and reached in with the other. She felt the marble instantly. It was resting near something else. "Ew! Ew! Ew!"

"What?" Cole asked.

She yanked her hand out of the hole. The marble along with Jared's index and middle fingers sat briefly in her palm before she dropped them with a dull *thud* onto the floor.

"Looks like you'll get to keep the fingers after all," Iylah said. "Put the marble back where it was."

"We'll need to get those on ice, right?" Cole asked.

"We'll do it after the game," Iylah said. "We're almost done. Cole, gimme the die." He tossed it over to her. She continued holding her body against the door and rolled the die away from her, toward Sherry, for light.

"It's a **five**," Sherry whispered to herself. "You did it!"

"We did?" Iylah said.

"Quick, what do we do?" Cole asked.

"Put the marble inside," Iylah called out.

Cole was slightly cautious. "You rolled a five, right?"

"Yes!" She yelled back. "Hurry!" Cole maneuvered his plant-tied hands to the floor and took the marble between his middle and third fingers. He held it over the hole, and dropped it inside the box.

"Now what—ouch!" Sherry asked. The candle had burned to its nub, burning Sherry. Darkness settled into the room once again.

"There's a black marble inside," Iylah said. "Cole, you need to pull them both out."

Cole, nervous that Jared's fate may be his own, shut his eyes and plunged his hand into the hole. He felt both marbles immediately, fingered them into his palm, and lifted them out. As soon as his hand emerged, a dim white light began to glow inside the starting squares at the four ends of the gameboard.

"Um . . ." Sherry leaned forward. "What is that?"

"It's the end of the game," Iylah replied. "Everyone has to put a hand on the lights."

"So, it's over?" Sherry asked. "We need to get him to a hospital, now!"

"No!" Iylah shot back, startling them. "We have to put our hands on the lights. That's how the game knows we're all here."

"What am I supposed to do with him? He won't let go of his hand," Sherry shouted, irritated.

"It's the game's final wave. If you don't put your hands on the board, it's going to leave you."

"Leave us? What does that mean?" Cole asked.

"It's going to kill you! Touch the squares, now!" Iylah shouted.

Sherry sat up and pulled the gameboard over to Jared, who was still lying on the floor clutching his hand. She put her free arm around him and sat him up beside her, encouraging him to put his good hand on the board.

"It won't take long," Iylah said.

Jared placed his free hand down, wincing. The light on the board grew a touch brighter.

"One hand on each square?" Cole asked.

"Yes," Iylah replied.

Sherry put her hand down. The illumination became stronger.

"What happens once we do this?" Cole asked.

"It all ends," Iylah replied. "My sister loses." She set her hand down on an open spot. Not only did the lights grow more radiant, but they also started to pulse softly. For a brief moment, Cole was caught off guard by the sight of Iylah's hand. In the light, her nails looked different. They didn't look blue or pointed anymore. They looked chewed down. "Come on, hurry!" Iylah said again, pleading. The thought, as quickly as it arrived, vanished from his mind. Jared moaned with excruciating pain, as Sherry comforted him. Cole took a breath, got down closer to the floor, and placed his interlocked fingers onto the remaining light square.

22

NOW

The brightness of the starting squares increased to a blinding level as each of them began flashing, at first in rapid succession together, and then, one by one, becoming out of sync. They decreased in brightness until there was no more than a faint glow in each; blinking slowly and softly until, finally, the gameboard went dark.

Jared drew his hand away and fell back onto the floor. He'd fainted from the pain. There was a distinct *click* and the light overhead came on. "Hey! Alright!" Cole said. He noticed a new calm in the room. "You hear that?"

Sherry looked around. "The water stopped."

Cole felt a sudden flow of blood shoot through his arm and looked down. A pile of black and green, feathery stems lay on the floor beneath his hand, trailing all the way back to the box's hole. "Check it out." Both of them had been released from the plant's tangled hold. He knelt, tapping the mess with his index finger. It was still wet. Then, for some odd reason, he began to laugh. A chuckle at first, soon developing into a hearty laugh.

"What's so funny?" Sherry asked.

Cole lost his balance and fell onto his butt. He didn't know why he was laughing, only that it felt good to do so. He tried to speak, raising his arms and shrugging his shoulders. All he could get out was, "I don't know." Sherry smiled, chuckling herself. Cole's laughter eventually turned to tears. He felt on the edge of crying and covered his eyes with his palms. Sherry wrapped her arms around him. She whispered something into his neck, but he couldn't make it out. Cole continued to sit there in her arms for a moment, laughing, crying—both.

"You sure you're okay?" Sherry asked.

"I just can't believe we did it," Cole said. "I mean, holy crap! What the hell was all that?" He spoke muffled into the top of Sherry's shoulder. He leaned back. "Were we dreaming? Like, did that really happen?"

Sherry looked down at the floor and ran her fingers over it. Water trickled from her hand when she brought it up. "Yup. It was definitely real." Jared jerked, letting out a muffled groan. Cole and Sherry crawled over to him in a flurry. The white t-shirt over the wound was covered with blood.

"Crap! We gotta get him to a hospital." Cole wrapped the wound with another shirt and tightened it. He placed Jared's other hand on top to hold it steady.

"God, I feel so stupid," Sherry said, kneeling beside Jared. "I can't believe I did that."

"You didn't know," Cole said. "He'll be okay." Sherry gave him a look that said, *you don't know that*. "Look at the bright side. He's talking to you again. The game wasn't a total train-wreck." It was a poor attempt at cheering her up, but Cole committed, offering a faint smile.

"Yeah. For now. Until he remembers it was my fault. Come on, let's get him out of here." She picked the severed fingers up off the floor, holding them far away from her. "Do you have any bags? I'll go put them on ice."

"Yeah. I can get it," Cole said, attempting to get to his feet.

"No, it's fine. Just tell me where the bags are."

He scanned the floor. "What in the hell am I gonna tell my parents?"

"Bags?" She said again.

"Oh! Sorry. Yeah. In the drawer by the fridge." He walked over to her and opened the door. "What should we tell the Doctor?"

Sherry sighed. "I don't know. I'll make something up." Then she paused. "Guess we should get on the same page, huh?" She pointed to the blood that was all over the floor. "And, yeah, your mom's definitely gonna kill you. Or Iylah."

"Who's gonna believe we all played a board game—" Cole stopped. "Wait. Where *is* Iylah?" He and Sherry scanned the room. The gameboard was sitting in the middle of the floor where they'd left it; Jared and Sherry's marble still in the same spot. The black and blue marbles were lying beside it. He called out Iylah's name, but there was no answer. The two of them walked out into the hallway. Cole flipped the light on overhead. Water was still seeping out from under the bathroom door. "Iylah?" Cole called again. No response. "Where is she?"

Jared moaned. "Shit. I'm so sorry. I'll go get some ice, and then I'll take you to the ER." Sherry went beside him. "We'll have to take his car. Not sure how I'm gonna carry him."

"I'll help you—" Several loud booms came from downstairs, making them jump. "What was that?"

They both froze. *Boom! Boom! Boom! Boom!* "That's your front door," Sherry whispered. A sudden, thick *snap,* followed by a thunderous *crash* rang out. Sherry and Cole quickly got to their feet and moved to the hallway.

"Iylah!" The person yelled.

A confused look came over Cole and Sherry. "Hello?" Cole asked.

"Where's Iylah?" The voice called back.

Cole rounded the corner, staring down the stairs. The person came into view; an Asian girl about Iylah's age. "Who are you?"

"Where's Iylah?" She asked.

"We don't know. We can't find her—"

"Shit!" the girl exclaimed, bounding up the stairs and brushing past Cole and Sherry. She continued calling her name, moving first to Cole's room—not fazed by the mess or blood—and then the room next door, ripping open the closet.

"Excuse me!" Cole said. "Who are you?"

She ignored him, hurrying down the hallway and into Cole's parents' room. He grabbed her shirt. "Hey! What are you doing in my house? How do you know Iylah?"

She tore away from him, throwing open his parents' closet. "I'm a friend of Iylah's. Erica. She called me tonight before she came." She shoved through them, back to the hall and into the bathroom. "She told me she would text me every hour, and if she didn't, to call." The trash can had tipped over in the water, covering the floor with debris: wrappers, tissues, used Q-tips. She looked back at them. "Nine o'clock was the last time I heard from her."

"The phones," Sherry cut in. "They went out a while ago."

"I figured. I left Nashville a couple hours ago when I stopped hearing from her."

"Probably a good thing you didn't get here sooner," Cole said. "You have no idea what's been going on here—"

Erica moved past him and started down the stairs hurriedly. "Believe me, I know exactly what's been going on here. Iylah!" Before Cole and Sherry could even process the decision to start walking down the stairs, there was a dreadful scream. They both almost tumbled down the stairs trying to move fast enough. Another shriek led them toward the kitchen, where Sherry immediately gasped and covered her mouth. Iylah was lying on her stomach, sprawled out on the floor. Her face to the side, eyes open, and a hand reaching up for the flashlight that was still on.

"No, no, no, no! Iylah!" Erica fell to her knees, flipping Iylah over onto her back. "Iylah! Come on, baby girl, wake up!"

"Iylah?" Cole mumbled. He walked toward her, around to the other side of where Erica was. The pallor of her face was what caught his attention first, drained of all life into a sort of blueish gray. Her mouth was slightly agape; her eyes stared up at the ceiling as if lost in thought. Lines of black mascara, like tears, had run down her face onto her neck. Next to her was a colorful array of wet confetti stuck to the watery floor. A blown-out, pink party popper lay beside her. Cole noticed the blood pooling around Iylah's midsection, his eyes finally falling upon the large pieces of glass sticking out of her side and stomach.

"Erica . . ." he whispered, pointing to her side.

Erica looked down, now seeing the blood. "Call 9-1-1!"

"I-I-I don't have a phone—"

"Just do it!" She screamed. Sherry recoiled at the noise and ran off to find a phone, hoping they were working again. "Iylah?" Erica started slapping her lightly in the face. "Iylah, come on, stay with me. Come on!" Cole could only stand frozen as he watched Erica lift Iylah up and hug her close, the two of them rocking back and forth as she pleaded with her friend to wake up.

The 19th Birthday Party
Part III

*I*t was over half an hour before Josephine came out of the boat's master bedroom. The conversation with Mallory and Logan had gone better than Jo had hoped. She did a three-way call to apologize to both of them together and explain the situation. In the heat of the moment, she had no problem heaping the blame on Iylah, though guilt was beginning to set in. Maybe she went a little too far. Mallory was already planning a way to get Iylah back when they had a rescheduled party.

On her way to the stairs, Jo spotted Bryce and Erica on opposite ends of the couch, both asleep. She heard Iylah's laugh pour in from somewhere above. She walked up to the deck, typing out a text to her two friends when she abruptly stopped. In a lamp's illumination, she could see Iylah sitting with her feet propped up in Mark's lap, holding a red cup. Jo could hear her talking.

"You need more?" Iylah asked, reaching for the tequila bottle.

"Nooo," Mark said, holding his hands out. "I'm good. I still gotta get us home."

"Oh, you're fine," Iylah replied. "Here." She took his cup and began pouring into it. "You mind rubbing my legs? They're freezing."

Jo gulped. She watched Iylah fake a shiver, and an achy sensation began twisting through her stomach. She watched Mark sit there with his arms crossed, still. Then her sister leaned forward and grabbed his hand.

"Like this." She rubbed his hand up and down her ankle. Mark kept his hand there and continued rubbing, though at a much slower pace. After a few moments, Jo could hear her sister begin to make audible signs of approval. Then, she watched Iylah put the bottle and cup down on the floor and lean forward. Iylah grabbed Mark's hands and began to move them up her leg. Mark, who seemed a little dumbfounded, lifted his head to meet Iylah's eyes, and Jo could see her sister slowly leaning in to kiss him.

Jo finally stepped out of the darkness toward them, though she couldn't bring herself to speak. Mark saw her first and swiftly pulled his hands back. Iylah's gaze followed Mark over to her sister. "Oh. There you are! Where've you been?" Iylah asked. She pulled her legs off his lap and stood up. "You want a drink?"

Jo started to feel light-headed. She hastily backed away from her sister and moved toward the cabin steps.

"Jo, where you going?" Iylah was coming toward her.

"To bed," she called out.

"Wait. Why?" Iylah grabbed her by the shoulder and spun her around. "We were gonna play another game." She hiccupped. "He wants to play that *Exploding Kittens* game you brought."

The tears that never seemed to be far away in Iylah's presence began to cloud Jo's eyes. She stayed locked on her sister for a brief moment, then glanced toward Mark. Finally, she let out a breath, letting her face fall. "I don't wanna play anymore."

Iylah looked back at Mark. "What? I thought you'd wanna play—" Jo's eyes slid coldly back up to her sisters. "Oh, give me a break. Nothing happened."

"I'm ready to go home," Jo said quietly.

Iylah laughed. "What is your problem?" Jo didn't respond.

Iylah lowered her voice. "Did you think he was into you, or something? Is that why you're mad?"

Jo's head sank in humiliation. "I need to go." She hurried back downstairs into the cabin, bursting into tears as soon as she reached the bathroom. Behind a closed door, she shoved her face into the hand towel to muffle the sounds of her heartache. Jo at first sat on the toilet, and eventually found herself beginning to curl up onto the floor, weeping uncontrollably. There was a knock on the door and an attempt to slide the panel back. Jo had locked it.

"Jo?" Iylah said. "Are you in there?"

Jo swallowed and tried to sound collected. "What?"

"Can you unlock the door, please?"

Jo stayed quiet, staring at the wall. "I'll be out in a second."

"Ugh. Would you just open the door? It'll take two seconds."

"Go away!" Jo put her hands over her face, reminding herself to take in deep breaths. Then, there was a faint clicking sound at the door, like a small animal eating on the other side. "Iylah!" Jo said. The sliding door jerked to its locked point, and then there was more clicking. "What are you doing?" Jo straightened and ripped open the door in a violent wave. Iylah was kneeling, holding a paper clip. Jo advanced, shoving her sister back fiercely against the wall. For a tense moment, she stared at her threateningly. "I said, I'll be out in a second." Jo grabbed the door handle and slammed it shut, locking it. She exhaled softly, her back pressed against the door. *Where did that come from?*

"Jeez. Calm down!" Iylah said. It was apparent that the sudden change in tone was just as surprising to Iylah because her response was more apologetic. "Look, I just wanted to talk." There was a slight slur in her words.

"I have nothing to say to you. Just tell Mark I wanna go home."

"Fine," Iylah sighed. Footsteps sounded from the other side of the door and then stopped. "Are you gonna be in there all night?" Jo didn't answer; simply shook her head, trying not to cry. She leaned on the sink, staring at her glassy, red eyes in the mirror. "Mark needs some aloe. Can you bring it up when you come back? There's some in my bag on the counter." No reply. "He's got a bad burn on his back." Silence. "Jo?"

"Okay! I got it," Jo yelled, "just leave me alone!" The shadow of Iylah's feet disappeared for a moment before coming back into view.

"Hey. I'm sorry if you took that the wrong way." Jo pressed a towel against her face. "I swear we were just talking." Jo cried into the towel, trying not to be too loud. She slid to the floor and then fell on her side. Iylah continued talking. "One minute we're sitting there talking, and the next minute he has my feet in his lap, rubbing my legs. I just . . . I don't know, I'll tell him to back off—"

"Oh my God! Go away!" Jo screamed, sitting up and yanking the towel off her face. Likely the whole boat was awake now. The shadow beneath the door moved away, and Jo heard her sister stomp up the main stairs. She fell back onto the floor, staring up at the ceiling. She could feel the tension rising in her chest, constricting her throat. She tried as hard as she could to hold it in, but the distress was too much. Her body began to shake with grief, pushing out all of the misery of the last hour, the last day—hell, the last several years. She brought her fists up to her face as if she could plug up the water, but it was no use. Warm tears ran out of her eyes, down into her ears and hair.

She didn't want to be around her sister anymore. She couldn't be around Mark. She was sure everyone heard her yelling. She wanted off of this boat. She took several deep breaths, reminding herself that she was okay, that she was not trapped.

Everything was going to be okay. They'd be heading back soon, and then she could drive home. *A deep breath in.* Back to school. *A long breath out.* Away from Iylah. *In for four; out for four.* Away. A peace began to settle deep within her chest, and she felt herself starting to sink into the floor.

She remained there several minutes. Everything had gone silent, save the soft *ticking* of her nails being bitten off. She'd worked them down so far that now she was biting skin. Jo surveyed her nails, Iylah's words from earlier about their appearance echoing in her mind. She sighed in frustration, wiping the saliva on her shirt. An object in her peripheral vision caught her attention, sitting beside the toilet. Iylah's bag. It was lying tipped open, some of the items had spilled out. Jo sat up and slid it over, immediately finding the aloe. She started digging through the pockets and found what she was looking for. She pulled it out and read the label.

It wasn't until she stood up and looked in the mirror that she realized she was grinning.

Jo came up the stairs to see Iylah and Mark still sitting in their chairs, though now they were on their phones. She tripped over someone's bag and had to catch herself, but not before stumbling and making an awkward entrance. Mark sat up, asking if she was okay. She stood quiet for a beat and then said, "Yeah, I'm fine. Sorry."

Mark stood and started to pick up the card deck when he suddenly moaned and dropped to one knee. "Whoooaaa," he mumbled. "Definitely got up too fast."

"Slow down, cowboy," Iylah said, coming over to him.

"I'm good, I'm good." Mark got to his feet, arms out at his

side, steadying himself against the rocking of the boat. Jo could see his face, an expression of either concern or nausea. "Nope, never mind. I need to sit." Both Jo and Iylah took hold of an arm when he tried to find his chair. "I got it, I got it," he muttered, waving them off. Had it not been for Iylah, he would have toppled over.

"There," Iylah said. "I'll get you some water."

"There's a Keurig in the cabin. You mind getting me a coffee?"

"Sure," Iylah replied, looking at Jo. "Go grab the coffee, will ya?" She asked.

"I don't know where it is," Jo replied.

"It's right on the counter as you walk down there. Can't miss it. Should be all good to go. I had a cup earlier. The coffee pods are in the box next to it. I'll stay here and make sure he doesn't kill himself," Iylah said sarcastically to Mark with a soft laugh. Jo stood and started toward the cabin when Mark called her name and thanked her. Iylah then asked, "Where's the aloe?"

Jo stopped. She saw her sister kneeling in front of him—not getting the water like she said. Iylah whispered something to him, and the both of them laughed, though he a little less than her. Iylah called for her sister. "Did you bring it? It was in my bag in the bathroom."

"Yeah, it's right here," she replied. Jo reached in her pocket and pulled out a white tube. "I thought you were getting water," she said coldly.

"Oh. You're right," Iylah replied, getting to her feet, and going to the cooler.

"Here," Jo said to Mark, holding out the tube. "Sorry. Her bag was really full. Took forever to find it. You feeling okay?"

"I'm fine. Just moved too fast, I think."

"Yeah, moving fast doesn't mix with tequila," Jo replied.

"Hey now," Mark said spiritedly. "In my defense, I'm terrible with peer pressure. Blame your sister. She's a pusher."

"Excuse me!" Iylah said from the cooler. "I didn't hold that cup to your mouth." She chuckled.

"Might as well have," he uttered to himself—or maybe to Jo. He wasn't taking his eyes off her. "Hey, um, that wasn't what you think it was. I wasn't . . ." He trailed off.

"It's fine." She shrugged self-consciously, not looking at him. "No big deal—"

"Finally!" Iylah called. "Got one." She closed the cooler lid. "Here you go." She forced a water bottle between them, moving Jo back. "You want help putting the aloe on?"

"Nah, I got it," Mark replied. Jo made her way back toward the cabin to make a cup of coffee for Mark. "Oh, wait," he muttered. She stopped and watched him. Mark held the tube into the light next to him. "You sure this is aloe?" He asked.

Iylah was pouring another drink. "Yeah. Should be," she replied.

"Um," Mark said. "What's imi . . . imiqui. Imiquimi." He paused, trying to focus his eyes. "Imiquimod?" He rolled the tube over and continued reading slowly. "Genital warts?" Iylah's head shot up, whipping around to Mark, who was now laughing. "I don't think this is aloe."

Iylah darted over and swiped the tube out of his hand. "That's not mine."

Mark looked to be trying to stifle his laugh, but it wasn't working. "It's okay," he said.

Iylah spun violently toward her sister and began advancing. Jo couldn't bring herself to move. She stared her down, teeming with pleasure over this moment but also with increasing fear. Before Jo could get her hands up, Iylah shoved her back, causing her to stumble over the pile of floats stacked behind her. She fell embarrassingly to the ground.

"What the hell is wrong with you?"

"Whoa!" Mark said. "Iylah, it's fine!"

"Huh?" Iylah demanded. Jo maneuvered herself to be ready in case Iylah pounced on her. She scooted back in a crab walk. Mark was trying to get their attention, but Iylah wasn't having it.

"I grabbed the wrong thing," Jo said apologetically. "I'm sorry."

Iylah let out a humorless laugh as Jo inched back to the edge of the boat. Iylah stalked threateningly toward her. Even in the dark, she could see that her face was seething with rage. Iylah glanced back at Mark and then to Jo, lowering her voice. "You're such a piece of shit."

"Iylah. I'm sorry. I didn't know—"

"Don't you talk to me!" Iylah shot back in a venomous whisper. She knelt and got in Jo's face. "Don't you *fucking* talk to me! To think, I actually missed having you around."

"Iylah!" Mark called. "Come on. Leave her alone."

Iylah stood, keeping her eyes on Jo. She started to walk backwards over to Mark but stopped. Jo got to her feet, steadying herself, keeping her head down. She suddenly felt sick over what she'd done. "Iylah. I'm so sorry—" The strike was so swift, Jo didn't have time to register the movement, let alone protect herself. Iylah's hand ripped hard across her face, knocking her back against the boat's side and onto the ground. She heard Mark scream Iylah's name as a crack sparked in her ear, igniting a strange sensation of low and high noises deep in her brain. She could sense her vision starting to tunnel as she maneuvered to all fours. Trying to stand, she kept her eyes on Iylah, balancing herself against the boat. Her head throbbed. Something along the side of her face burned—likely a scratch from Iylah's long nails.

She stood there, humiliated over what she'd done but mostly that Mark had watched. What had she hoped to accomplish by doing that to her? Whatever it was, Mark surely now thought of her as nothing short of a bitch. Her lips quivered as she exhaled; a tear running down her face.

Iylah began to walk away but stopped. She turned, spinning back suddenly to her sister, making Jo recoil and hold up her hands in defense. "Once we get home, you and I are done." Iylah's voice was no longer scathing or angry. "God, I hate you." It was calm. Resolved. "When we get off this boat, I'm done with you. I don't want to see you. I don't wanna talk to you. Ever. Again."

Something like a red-hot iron pierced through Jo's heart. It was true that they weren't as close as they once were. But as much as Jo wanted space from Iylah for the time being, she couldn't deny that she still loved her. How could she not? They had spent nearly every waking moment of their life together— until the middle of high school. A few rocky years couldn't erase a lifetime of cherished memories. The games they played, the secrets they confided, the experiences they shared, the trouble they got into together. The majority of her life was lived with her twin beside her. No one knew her more than Iylah, and Jo would argue that no one knew Iylah more than her. Granted, she was a pain in the ass, but she was still her other half.

After a lifetime of experience, Jo was used to her sister's anger: screaming, teasing, manipulating, bullying—even the occasional punch between them. It was part of their relationship. Disappointment, frustration; those were a given. But never *hatred*. The irritation she had just felt for Iylah suddenly vanished as Jo now only wanted to apologize. "Iylah. Please. Don't say that. I'm sorry—" She reached for her sister's arm, but Iylah smacked it away.

"Don't you *fucking* touch me!" She spat back.

"Iylah please . . . I'm sorry, okay? That was mean, and I don't know why I did it—"

She moved away. "I have nothing to say to you. Go away," she said coldly.

Jo didn't stand there long before she turned to go down into the cabin. She heard Mark call after her but ignored him. She'd already been embarrassed enough. She went down the stairs and stood frozen in thought for a few moments before going back up. Out of the corner of her eye, she could see Iylah sitting beside Mark once again. She wanted to look on but instead, stepped over the guard rail and sat down on the ledge beside the boarding ladder, letting her feet dangle in the water.

Iylah had been lying on the cushioned bench for nearly fifteen minutes, staring up at the twinkling stars when she heard Mark get up and go down into the cabin. No one had said a word since the argument. Likely he was going down to check on Jo. She would give him a sob story; somehow spin the aloe incident into an accident. She rolled her eyes and tried to force the thoughts from her mind. The sloshing of the water against the boat was actually soothing, as was the rocking. She could feel the muscles in her hands and arms begin to slacken as her body swayed back and forth. This was nice.

Iylah opened her eyes with a start. Mark was sitting in the captain's chair with a cup of coffee, staring at his phone. She never even heard him come up. She sat up and reached for her phone. Twenty minutes had passed. It was nearly two. "Jeez."

"We should probably go," Mark said, standing up to stretch. He took another sip from his mug.

"You okay to drive?"

He yawned. "Yeah. I'm good. I have a meeting tomorrow morning at the restaurant with a contractor. Don't wanna roll in looking like this," he motioned over his swimsuit and tank top. "You guys are welcome to hang and snooze out here or below deck until morning. That cool?" He stood and started digging through the cooler for water.

"Yeah. That's fine." She got to her feet, looking out over the black water. Clouds now covered the moon and stars. She could barely see five feet in front of her.

"We got everybody?" Mark asked. "I take it your sister went to bed. Is she okay?"

"Probably," Iylah mumbled. "I'll go check." She went down the stairs into the cabin. Bryce was covered up on the couch and Erica was in the master bedroom, passed out on top of the bed. Jo, on the other hand, was nowhere to be found. Iylah walked back up onto the deck where Mark was pulling up the anchor. Jo's avocado float was still on the pile of floats where it was earlier. "We good?" Mark asked.

Iylah didn't reply as she made her way to the boat's rear and steadied herself on the guardrail. The ladder was down. A burst of anxiety ignited in her stomach, but it quelled almost instantaneously. Iylah was more than confident in her sister's ability in the water. Jo was likely just out for a swim. Iylah tried to spot her or listen for any signs of movement, but there was none, save the sound of water lapping against the boat. *Maybe she's in the bathroom. She might've gotten sick.*

"Iylah! We good?" Mark called, shining his flashlight on her. Iylah shielded the light with her hand, holding up a finger. She scanned the lake once more, and probably ten or fifteen feet out she caught sight of something moving. Then, she heard a *splash*. Movement in the distance. Jo was blanketed by the dark, but Iylah could now make out the bright yellow shorts atop the water. She looked to be floating on her back.

The engine beneath Iylah's feet roared to life, surprising her.

"Iylah!" Mark called again. "What are you doing?"

Iylah watched her sister for a moment and then said back, "Sorry. Just making sure the ladder was up." She knelt and pulled it up out of the water and snapped it in place.

"We're all set? Everybody's downstairs?"

"Yeah," she called back. She stared coldly in her sister's direction, certain Jo could hear the engine whirring. She thought she heard Jo call something out, but she wasn't sure. It was hard to hear over the engine. Finally, she turned back to Mark and gave a thumbs up. "All good!"

Epilogue

NOW

"Wake up." The voice was faint, garbled as if it were under water. The enclosing night began to lighten. The girl in the bed struggled to open her eyes. Flashes of light sent waves of shock to the front of her head. "Ow," she mumbled.

"There you go," the voice said.

She blinked several times, trying to wash away the blur. The overhead light was off, but the sun was pouring in from a window beside her. She couldn't make out her surroundings, only that someone was standing above her. Focus had become a little clearer.

"There you are," the unfamiliar voice said. Whoever it was, kissed her lightly on the forehead and stroked her arm. "Iylah. Can you hear me?"

She stared back, confused. Her vision was still partially blurry. A hand ran over her face. "It's Erica," the voice whispered.

"Who?"

"Erica Lang," she replied. "We're friends. High school . . . ?"

"Where am I?"

"You're in the hospital. You've been out for almost two days, baby girl," Erica replied.

The girl moved her head anxiously from side to side, trying to take in the room. "I, um . . ." she paused.

"What is it?" Erica asked. She didn't reply, just kept looking around, unsure of what was happening. Finally, she sat up in a burst of energy and at once felt dizzy. She laid back down. "Whoa, whoa, whoa. Hey, you okay? You want me to call—"

She shook her head softly, taking hold of Erica's hand. She opened her eyes and scanned the ceiling as if admiring a painting, then raised her hands, surveying the tubes that protruded from her skin.

"Iylah," Erica said, running her hand soothingly over her arm. The girl in the bed took note of the exposed parts of her body, trying to piece everything together. She made another attempt to sit up but fell back with an exhale.

Erica laughed. "Need to work on those abs, baby girl. Here." She put an arm around her friend and helped her up, positioning pillows behind her. "Good?"

She nodded. "I've been here two days?" A surge of pain; it burned to talk.

"Doctor said you may have a hard time talking for a bit. Breathing tubes might've done a number in there."

She swallowed and winced at the pain, raising a hand to touch her neck. "Water?" she asked.

"Yeah, yeah," Erica said, jumping up and pulling a water bottle out of her bag. She dumped it into the thermos beside the bed and slid the straw inside, placing it near her friend's lips for her to drink. "Of course, the five minutes I go look for a snack is the time you choose to wake up." She smiled. "Slow down. Don't want to dump a bunch in there at once."

She let up and took a deep breath. "My mom and dad?"

"They're here, yeah. They're downstairs getting coffee. Everyone's been here. I get like, fifteen calls a day checking up on you. It's been mostly me and your mom though, hangin' out, waitin' on you. Your dad and her switch off at night." Erica sat back in her chair wearing a face of astonishment. "Girl, you had us all freaked out. Shit was messed up."

"What happened?" She asked.

"You died. Like, legit, dead. You must have fallen on some glass or something. You had huge shards stuck in you when we found you. Doctors don't know what did it. You didn't bleed out all that much, and you didn't sever anything major. But you were definitely dead. They were able to revive you in the ambulance." Erica peered questionably at her. "Do you remember anything from that night?"

She looked down. "Not really."

"You, uh . . ." Erica checked behind her as if someone might be listening. "You remember playing that game?"

She nodded, still looking down. "I remember that," she replied in a strained voice. "And a kid."

"Cole. Yeah. Cole and Sherry," Erica said.

She nodded again, expressionless.

"You remember some kid losing his fingers?" Erica asked.

"Kind of . . ." she replied softly.

Erica shook her head. "Iylah, what happened in that house? What I saw in there looked nothing like the game you and I played, and that was horrific enough." The girl sat still, her eyes now transfixed on the sheets. The two of them were quiet for a short moment before Erica continued: "I didn't say anything, by the way. About us; the game. Didn't know what you'd already said—if anything—and well, to be honest, no one's gonna believe it anyways, right?"

Another slow nod. "Yeah."

"I don't think the kids are talking either. They said someone tried to rob the house; used a knife on the other kid. You tried to stop them and fell onto the shattered glass," Erica said, pointing to her stomach.

She carefully looked down at her wrists and felt along her side which was heavily bandaged up.

"I told the cops you'd called me earlier to come hang out at the kid's house—just, you know, to watch a movie. And when I got there, I found you like this." She didn't reply. "We can chat about it later if you want. I'm sure this stuff is the last thing you wanna talk about—"

"Oh my God!" Another voice called out from the door. The girl's heart leapt as she turned to look. The cup of coffee that was in her mother's hand fell to the floor as she reached to cover her mouth in shock. "You're awake. Sam! She's up!"

That voice! Warmth blossomed in her stomach as she saw her mother approaching. Silvia Maddox ran over and embraced her child with loving force.

"Ooo, ow, ow," she winced.

Mrs. Maddox straightened, immediately apologizing. "Oh! I'm sorry. I'm sorry."

"My hand," she tried to speak, lifting her arm. Her voice was almost inaudible. "It's fine. It was just squished." She looked up at her mom, feeling a sudden nervous tingle over her skin. She studied every inch of her mom's face, raising her hands to touch it. "It's really you," she whispered.

"It's really me," Sylvia replied.

She immediately reached up and wrapped her arms around her mother, holding on with every bit of strength left in her. She could feel fatigue at once beginning to set in but held on. Her mother was saying something, but the sound was muffled.

She felt the bed depress. Her eyes opened to see her dad sitting beside her. "Come on, give her some room." He said, already tearing up, trying to smile.

When she saw her dad, she felt her eyes tighten with tearful joy. Sam wrapped an arm around his daughter, cradling her to his chest as she threw her arms around him too. He kissed her head, and broke down immediately, saying over and over how sorry he was for what had happened and how much he loved her.

She was in and out of consciousness much of that day. Nearly three days had gone by since the incident at Cole's house. She later discovered that paramedics had arrived at the Gibson's house shortly after Erica found her and were able to get her heart beating again on the way to the hospital. Doctors kept a close eye on her but were positive she would be okay and were hopeful for a return home within the next couple of days. Erica stayed at the hospital with the parents, sleeping on a makeshift pallet atop a group of chairs.

When she awoke again, the room had darkened, except for a soft glow from the lamp by her bed. She felt a breath against her neck and turned her head to see her mother lying against her. She lay still, staring at her for a long while before Silvia's eyes peeked opened. "Hey sweetheart," Silvia whispered with an affectionate smile. "How you feeling?"

She nodded. "Okay." Silvia ran a hand down the side of her face, already becoming misty eyed again.

"What's wrong?" she asked, softly.

"I thought you were gone." Silvia's eyes closed, pushing the tears down her cheek. "I thought we lost you too."

She reached up to take her mom's hand and held it tight against her face. "Mama, it's okay. I'm here."

Silvia nodded and sniffed. "I know. I was just so scared." She kissed her daughter on the head and pulled her close. She could feel herself beginning to drift into sleep when her mom's phone chirped. Silvia shifted and reached for her phone. "It's your dad."

"What time is it?" She whispered.

Silvia sat up, putting on her reading glasses. "Almost mid-night."

"Where is he?"

"He's at home," she replied, typing out a text. "He's got a job interview at Murray middle school in the morning. He'll be here right after. Erica's sacked out over there."

She maneuvered her arms and struggled to sit up but was unable. Her mom helped her, situating the pillows to rest against. "Can I have some water?" Her throat was still ablaze. Silvia re-filled the thermos beside her bed and held it for her to drink. "Thanks," she whispered, leaning back with an exhale. When she opened her eyes, she caught a glimpse of herself in the mirror across the room, hanging over the sink. She stared at the dimly illuminated reflection, scanning her features.

"How ya doin'?"

"Tired," she replied. She noticed the stack of bright pink and white envelopes on the chair beside her bed.

Silvia caught her curiosity. "You've had a lot of visitors," she said, pointing to the assortment of balloons tied to the foot of her bed. "Do you want to look at some?"

"Sure."

Silvia took a seat, scooting a chair closer to the bed, and situated the stack of cards on her lap. Before she started reading, she took hold of her daughter's hand once more, gripping it as if it would dart away from her. She leaned forward, rubbing it on her cheek, and then touched it to her lips. Both of them smiled. "Alright then," Silvia said, wiping her eyes. "Let's see here. How 'bout I open them, and then you can read them."

She teared up in seconds of seeing the signature. *Iylah*, it began. *We'll be on our way by the time you read this, but your grand-father and I love you so much and are praying for your quick recovery.*

We love you and will see you soon. XOXO. Mee-Maw and Papa. The next one was from her uncle. Then one from her favorite cousin. Then one from her old youth minister and his wife that included a large stack of cut-out comics from different newspapers. *For when you get bored,* he wrote. By the fifth card, she was having a tough time breathing from all the tears.

"Okay," Silvia said, removing her glasses and standing up. She moved the cards from her daughter's lap and sat beside her, wiping her face with a tissue. "Maybe we should take a break." Her daughter's head nuzzled onto her shoulder. "Not everyone brought a card, but you've had so many stop by. I wrote them all down in my phone."

She nodded.

"You want me to get you something to eat? You hungry?" Silvia asked.

A gentle headshake before she asked, "When can I go home?"

"As soon as you're ready," Silvia replied. "Doctors wanted to keep you until you have the strength to stand on your own and are feeling better. They said you've been doing great. Might be good to see if you can get some food down. They said that could be an issue."

Her eyes shifted up toward the chair on the other end of the room. There was a tall gift bag sitting on top of it. "What is that?"

"It's nothing," Silvia replied, passively. "Don't worry about it."

A period of time must have passed because she felt herself wake up when her mom began talking. "Renee's son and his friends mentioned a robbery in the house. The police have been here several times to try and speak with you—which they understand may take a while. But Cole mentioned something about a game." Her daughter's eyes opened. "Did you all play a game while you were there?"

"I think so . . ." she replied.

"What did you play?"

She sat quietly for a beat and then said, "I don't remember. Just something he had at the house."

"Well." Silvia paused. "I don't know if it's a good time to ask, and if it's too much, just tell me, okay? But he described something that sort of reminded me of . . . well . . . a game your sister made."

"What do you mean?" She asked.

"I'm not entirely sure. Renee told your father and me that she found something at her house—a board game. Described it as a black box with a hole in the top and marbles that you move toward the center. Cole told her it was something you'd brought over. I asked if she could bring it to me, but she said that Cole had thrown it away in the trash pickup. It reminded me of that game Jo made for school when you both were little. *Zombie Run* or *Escape Zombies*—something like that." Silvia got up and crossed to retrieve the gift bag, placing it on the bed.

Her daughter promptly reached forward which resulted in a searing wave of pain across her side. "Iylah, be careful," Silvia said. Not to be deterred, her daughter shoved down the pain and reached in as excitedly as her body would allow. Her hand fumbled around with something only for an instant before she stopped and took in a breath. Delicately, she removed four black, wooden panels and a tall, oblong, three-dimensional black box.

"You know, when we moved, your father and I, *we* didn't pack up her things." Silvia exhaled, appearing as if this bit of news had been weighing hard on her. "Our friends came in and boxed up her stuff for us. We never even looked through it." She wiped at her eyes. "We tried. Neither one of us had stepped into her room since that day. And I told him we could just have movers do it, but your father, God bless him. He didn't want strangers having to do what he couldn't. He was determined to be the one to go through and organize her things." She tried to veil her anguish with a short laugh. "He took one step in her room and began sobbing like a child. We just couldn't do it. So, we had Ivan and Maddie pack up her things for us." She took her daughter's hand, squeezing. "When Renee told us about the game she found . . . well, we couldn't sleep as it was, so, last night, your father and I, we opened up those boxes. Spent the whole night going through what they'd packed up: putting things into piles, crying, telling stories, laughing about the two of you and how you used to get after one another. That was in a box with several of her notebooks. It was covered with sticky notes of drawings and ideas. She must've been working on it." Silvia paused, studying it with a troubled heart. "*That* day. Before you all left."

"Wow . . ." she whispered.

"You remember playing this with her?"

She nodded.

"You didn't bring anything like this over, did you?"

She shook her head softly. "No."

"Yeah," Silvia said. "My imagination probably just got the best of me. Thought maybe Jo made another one." Silvia examined the structure. "She always talked about wanting to sell her games."

She couldn't contain the elation. She picked up one of the four panels, moved it to the base of the tower, and clicked it into place with ease.

"It took us about ten minutes to figure that out." Silvia smiled warmly. Her daughter hastily connected the other three panels to the bottom, completing the game's board: a tower in the middle of a cross pad.

She motioned for the bag. "There should be a little sack with the pieces—yup, that's it." Her mother held up a small pouch with a drawstring. The girl dumped the contents into her hand: a die and four marbles. Her mother asked if she remembered how to play, and she said she did. She attempted to explain the original game and how it worked, then asked her mom if she wanted to play.

Silvia laughed and said it was too late for her to keep focus on something like that. "Maybe tomorrow you could teach me. You should probably get some sleep." Silvia took a seat on the bed and ran a hand through her daughter's hair, down her face.

She held the game on her lap, admiring it as if it were a collectible antique, before finally, carefully, detaching the panels from the base, and placing them back in the bag. As she lifted the tower to return it, she noticed the bottom and brought it closer to her.

"What is it?" Silvia asked.

Without pause, she slid out a thin wooden piece—a false bottom to the tower—and held it in her hand. She put it under the light.

"Well, look at that. How'd you remember that was there?" Silvia smirked.

Scribbled in blue on the unfinished wood were the words:

> For Lala,
> My favorite co-op partner.
> I love you. 'oghta jo'Sevln.

Something blossomed in her stomach as she read those lines over again.

Silvia leaned in closer to read it. She ran a finger over the foreign script. "What is that?"

"It's *By Josephine* in Klingon. It's how . . ." She paused a moment. "It's how *she* would sign her name on the games she made."

"Oh. Your father and I saw that on a couple of the ones we pulled out. Didn't know what it was." Silvia stood back. "She really did look up to you, Iylah. She loved you so much."

The sensation she was now feeling was not one of affection but of dread. Hatred almost. She handed the wooden square to her mother for further inspection then leaned back against her pillows, staring over toward where Erica was.

Silvia scooped up the tower to try and wedge the piece back onto the bottom. "How'd you get this in here? Just slide it in—"

"Throw it away," the girl whispered coldly. She winced at the razor-sharp pain at the back of her mouth and stroked at her throat.

"What? Why?"

She faced her mother. "I don't want it." Her hand inched up toward her mouth, her index finger resting on her lips.

"Iylah . . ." Silvia sat still as her daughter looked away. "I'm not gonna throw this away. You both loved playing this. It was one of the first full games she did."

She continued staring toward the window, fingers curled together in front of her mouth. She could feel herself starting to fidget nervously. "I don't want it. Please. Just throw it away."

"Well," Silvia clicked her tongue, "I'm definitely not going to throw it away." She placed the game and extra pieces back in the bag. "I'm sure you're just tired right now."

"Mom." She turned to her mother. She was trying to be as sincere as possible. "I don't want it. Please."

"Okay, okay," Silvia replied calmly, standing up. "We'll figure it out later." She stood and walked the bag over to the chair.

She watched her mother re-cover Erica and adjust the pillows around her. "It's been nice having her here with me," Silvia whispered. "Really helped to keep me calm." She watched her walk back over to the counter and check her cell phone. "I'm gonna use the restroom. You need anything?"

She removed her hand from her mouth and gave a brief, soft smile. "I'm okay." Another wince from the clawing pain in her throat.

"Aw, sweetie. I'll see if I can find you some tea and honey once I'm done. I'm sure they've got some. You want the remote?"

"Sure," she answered. The TV illuminated the room in a silvery, blue radiance sending an aching sensation through her head as her eyes adjusted. It faded soon after. She stared at the screen as if in a trance, no longer tired—just weak. Her eyes drifted over to the bag with the game. She wanted to get up and throw it away herself. She knew her mother would keep it, maybe even set it out for show. Perhaps it would find a home on top of the bookshelf under the TV. Or on the side table beside the couch where her parents liked to read. It would sit for her and everyone to admire. Except, to her, it was nothing more than a troubling, constant reminder of everything that had happened.

"Iylah," a voice said.

A memory of a strained relationship.

"Iylah," it said again, quietly.

A memory of what her sister had done to her.

". . . *Josephine*." The girl jumped with a startle, drawing in a breath, and jerking her hand away from her face.

"What?"

Silvia was standing beside the bed, looking at her with unease. Silvia cocked her head to the side. "I said *you must miss Josephine.*" There was no reply. "Are you okay?"

"Yeah," she replied. "Just zoned out, I guess." Silvia eyed her curiously. "What?"

"You sure?" Silvia asked.

"Yeah. Just tired."

"I've seen you tired, but I've never known you to do *that?*" Silvia pointed briefly at the bed, or at something on it. "When did that start up?"

She glanced down toward her arm and lifted it, thinking maybe something was underneath. "Start what up?"

Silvia grabbed hold of her hand as it was in the air and tenderly turned it over for her daughter to see. "*That.* You've never done that before." Silvia chuckled to herself, letting go of her hand. "You *must* be out of it. I can still hear you griping about her doing that. It used to make you so mad."

She stared down at the back of her hand. The stiletto tips on two of her fingers had been torn off and the nails underneath were chewed down. The other daphne blue tips remained intact. "Hunh," she muttered. "Just picked it up, I guess. Must be stress."

"We'll have to buy you some of that sour nail polish," her mother said, coming back to take a seat.

She was too busy looking at the mirror across from her bed to respond. Her reflection stared back at her. She ran a hand through her hair, staring expressionless at herself. She raised the corners of her mouth, grinning. She relaxed for a second and did it again. Then, she stretched back her cheeks—a tighter smile—and showed her teeth in a very fake, over-the-top expression. Her mother mumbled something. Once more, her mouth went slack before finally, with her pinky fingers, she forced back the corners of her mouth. Her expression was almost clown-like.

Her mother leaned over, watching her in the mirror. She chuckled. "I hate that Jo never liked her smile. And that you constantly ragged on her over it. I always thought it was so jubilant."

She let go of her mouth and relaxed her face, staring blankly back at the reflection. "I miss it, now." Her mother was giving her a cozy smile. At the sight of it, pressure in her face began building. She tried to return a smile of her own but became so overwhelmed with joy that she broke into another sob.

"Oh, sweetie," Silvia said, taking a seat beside her.

She rested her head against her mom for a moment before wiping her eyes with the sheet. Her reflection in the mirror came into view once again. She found herself happily fixated on the scene in front of her: the two of them sitting peacefully on the bed; she in her mother's arms. She gazed at it in wonderment, and a trembling sigh blew from her mouth.

Silvia stroked her daughter's hair. "What are you thinking?"

The girl smiled and took hold of her mother's hand. "I'm thinking about how much I love you," she whispered. "And how happy I am to be alive."

THE · END

Acknowledgements

The most important "thank you" goes to my outstanding wife, Gina. Thank you. You were always willing to read sections, chapters, and even the whole story if necessary. Your notes improved this story in so many ways, as did your insight into the female mind. I literally couldn't have written this without you. You're right: you are a catch, and I am incredibly lucky to have you by my side.

Rachel Kuldell, thank you for having me over to your back yard (on so many occasions) to talk through this story. And for suggesting I make it longer than 50 pages.

Hannah England, thank you for another excellent cover and for being such a joy to work with. You're patient with all my texts, emails, conversations, and random ideas, and you somehow manage to take all of that jumbled nonsense and craft something extraordinary—even better than I imagined. Your talent as an artist is incredible.

To Jaye Manus, thank you once again for turning a Word file into something professional and sleek.

Jeannie Katzenmiller and Ashley Daviau, you both did me a huge favor and I can't thank you enough for taking the time to help.

Eve Hall, thank you for your edits, ideas, and overall encouragement as I put this story together. It's not easy to find someone who can tear apart your work and build you up at the same time. This story took on a whole new life with your assistance. Thanks for choosing to work on it with me.

And to you, the reader, thanks for making it this far. There are so many great stories out there, it means the world to me that you picked up this one—whether you bought it, checked it out, or stole it—and spent 5–8 hours to finish it. Thank you. I hope you enjoyed it.

Before you go, could I trouble you for a favor? Would you mind leaving a review? Anything is fine, even a simple star rating. Reader responses are like gold to indie authors.

Clayton Tune is the author of *The Burgers Brothers' Family Funeral Home* and *What Lies Between the Lakes. Josephine's Game* is his third novel. He is a licensed massage therapist, a sports enthusiast, and a '90s nerd. Currently he resides outside Washington DC with his wife Gina, their two children, and a dog named Sausage Ball. He also makes a decent Old Fashioned.

Made in the USA
Monee, IL
29 November 2022

18959175R00184